Ru~~sh Creek~~

Terry Seigler

TO Karen)
Thank you and I
hope you enjoy this

Terry Seigler

1

Rush Creek
Copyright © 2014 by Terry Seigler

ISBN-13: 978-1497386297
Printed by Createspace

Dedication

This book is dedicated to and inspired by so many of my friends from church. It is one of a series of books I have written with them playing the roles of heroes and villains. They are a group of Christ-loving friends who love me in spite of myself. We canoe together, worship together, laugh and cry together. Because of the love and friendship they have shown to me, I have written this and other stories to hopefully show them in some way what they mean to me.

Preface

The Buffalo River is an incredible place. It flows from West to East with headwaters south of Boxley Valley. It meanders its way through the Ozark Mountains of Arkansas for almost one hundred and fifty miles before joining the White River. Arkansas history can be seen and felt as you paddle along with the crystal clear water; passing old homesteads, towering rock bluffs and magnificent trees leaning over the water.

When we float the Buffalo River, we end our journey at Rush Landing because to continue would commit us to a twenty-five mile stretch of river with no take out points until reaching the White River.

The drive back to the highway takes us through the ghost town of Rush where a few old buildings still remain along the road. Signage along an interpretive trail display old photographs that show what the town looked like when it was thriving. Wilderness trails in Rush lead to some of the old zinc mines now blocked by iron bars for safety reasons.

Walking these trails and seeing the old buildings of Rush gave me the inspiration for this story. I could clearly imagine the characters and images of a town full of people. I hope you enjoy reading this as much as I enjoyed writing it.

Terry Seigler

Acknowledgments

I'd like to thank Lynnette Struble for her editing expertise. Lynnette exhibited patience with me throughout the editing process. I appreciate her time and experience.

I would also like to thank those who read my early manuscript and suggested changes for accuracy and spotted numerous mistakes. Emeritus Professor Max Sutton, I appreciate your time and words of wisdom. I also appreciate the early editing work of Larry Pike. Larry is no longer with us but is in the presence of the Lord.

Most of all, I would like to thank my wife for her critical eye. Lovingly she made me aware that some of my long sentences could be shortened and modified to both sound better and make me look like I know what I'm doing. Early on, she told me that she really liked the story but there were still a few places that could use a little help, much like the loving comments she makes about me personally. I love you very much too, honey, and like my writing…consider me a work in progress.

Terry Seigler

Chapter 1

Mike Gilbert stared at the ceiling from his bed as the sun painted the eastern horizon pink. He had been awake for quite some time, peering into the darkness from under the covers with the coolness of mid April around him. On a normal day he would have been up, working alongside the crowing rooster and his brothers, but not today. Today was not a normal day.

He closed his eyes and thought back two weeks earlier, when he had told his family he was leaving. He knew there would be sadness, but he hadn't anticipated his father's anger. Rather than face his father at the breakfast table, Mike had decided to stay in bed. He knew, however, he would have to tell him goodbye, and that was something he was not looking forward to.

As he opened his eyes again, he could hear his mother in the kitchen, putting away the breakfast dishes. It was a sound he rarely heard and, though he probably wouldn't hear it again, it was comforting. There was a chill in the air, so he pulled the handmade quilt tight around his neck. With the sun almost up and more light filtering through the yellowed curtains into his bedroom, he was able to trace the pattern of the hand stitching on the quilt. It brought back memories of watching his mother sew by firelight when he was young.

Now he was twenty, and for some time he felt something tugging at him to leave the farm where he had been raised. It was the only life he had ever known but a place he could not stay for the rest of his life. It was something he couldn't fully understand, much less explain to his parents, but he knew it to be right. He also knew that he could not put off the inevitable. It was time to leave.

As Mike buttoned his shirt, he looked out the window at the familiar landscape. The pastures were already green, and steam rose from the ground as the final frost of the season evaporated with the touch of the sun. The bright yellow daffodils were in full bloom around the barn and along the walkway to the lane. In the distance he saw the hillsides dotted with brilliant white from the blooms of the dogwood trees.

A thousand memories flooded his mind as he thought of what his life had been like growing up on this farm just outside the community of Kingston, Arkansas. He smiled as his thoughts held hands with not only the hard work but the fun of playing in the creeks and streams, wrestling with his brothers, and hunting with his father.

After dressing, Mike stepped around the corner of a doorway to see his mother, Rachel, kneading dough on the kitchen counter. He watched as she pushed into the dough with the heels of her hands then folded it over onto itself to repeat the process. Her graying brown hair was tied back to keep it out of her way as she worked, except for one thin tendril which had fallen loose at the side of her face. It swung back and forth as she moved. As he continued to stand in the doorway, he watched her hands work with a rhythmic precision. Mike gently cleared his throat.

"I don't have eyes in the back of my head, but I know you're there."

She turned her head to look at him briefly without interrupting her rhythm. She wasn't smiling, and he began to feel his heart pounding a little harder. He knew that the moment he had been both anticipating and dreading had finally come.

"Mornin', Ma."

Rachel stopped her work and stood straight, pushing the tendril of hair out of her face and behind her ear with the back of her hand.

"There's some bacon for you in the stove and biscuits in that basket over there with the towel over it. Coffee's cold but it's easy enough to warm … if you want a cup."

Crisp and cold at first, her words softened as she got to the part about the coffee. Mike was aching inside because he knew he was the reason for her sorrow. She was trying to be strong, but he could tell she was being devoured inside. He hadn't given it much thought earlier on, and, even though he knew this day would eventually come, he had never stopped to think about how it was going to sadden her. He had never stopped to think about how it was going to sadden him to see her grieve.

Plopping the dough into a glass bowl and covering it with a damp towel, she placed it into the warm oven and began to clean the flour from the countertop. But she stopped and turned to face Mike instead, pausing as she looked up into his eyes. Mike felt uneasy because he always had a difficult time with decisions that disappointed his parents, especially his mother. In that moment he saw a tear escape from her watery eyes and roll down her cheek. Then she spoke in soft words which were barely audible, "Are you sure this is what you want to do?"

Mike took a deep breath as he disconnected from her gaze to look around the room. In only a few seconds all of the memories he had made in that very kitchen flashed through his mind. He thought of the meals around the old wooden table he had helped his father make from a big oak tree that had fallen after the King's River had flooded one spring. He remembered all the times his mother had made him and his brothers go back outside to take off their boots because they were tracking in thick red mud. He recalled the good times and heard the laughter of years past. He couldn't believe this day had finally arrived.

"Yes, Ma—you know I have to go," he answered, looking back into her tearful gaze.

She closed her eyes and lowered her head. Mike reached out to put his arms around her and draw her to him. Resisting at first, she finally leaned into him with her arms at her sides. He felt her begin to sob against him.

"It's not forever," Mike said as he tenderly placed his chin on top of her head.

Rachel pulled away and began wiping her cheeks, forgetting about the flour on her fingers. She turned around and walked to the sink, pumped a little water to wash her hands, and dried them on her apron.

"I'm not frettin' about forever; I just don't think you should go."

"You mean you don't want to see me go," Mike said, instantly realizing that his reply sounded sassy.

Rachel placed her hands on her hips, "Mike, you're leaving what you've known all your life. You were born here, you've grown up here. Its hard work but it's made a fine man out of you."

Rachel looked down at the floor, "You know ... this is killing your father."

"My father just cares about having an extra hand to work the farm."

Rachel looked back into his eyes, warning him of his tone.

"This farm is great and I wouldn't trade what I've had here for the past twenty years for anything. But I'm not a farmer. You know it and Pa knows it. Mark and Luke love to farm and that's fine for them, but I'm tired of feeding cows, mending fences, cutting and stacking hay. Is there something wrong with not wanting to be a farmer?"

Rachel turned back around to the white porcelain sink and looked out the window. She gripped the front edge and gazed at the rolling hillsides where the cows were feeding on the early spring grass.

"We all feel restless at times, and I hoped you would change your mind after you told me last year you were thinking of leaving."

"Ma, I'm just not a farmer."

Rachel released a sigh of surrender. "I guess I've known that for a long time," she said, still gazing out the window. "Something inside of me told me that this day would come, but I didn't want to think about it. From the time you were a little boy, you always dreamed about what was out there in the rest of the world." She lowered her head and looked into the sink. "And you are right ... I don't want to see you go."

She turned to face him and clasped her hands in front of her. "I guess there comes a time when a mother has to let go. I just always thought that time would come when you got married and built a house somewhere on this place. Never thought I would be lettin' you go and you goin' to God only knows where."

There was a pause as her eyes watered again.

"I'll only be a few counties over and ..."

Mike knew it wouldn't comfort her to say, *and I'll come back from time to time*, so he didn't finish his sentence.

"Your father is mending the fence down the road. I expect he'll want to see you before you leave.

Mike was already dreading that moment. "I reckon he will."

Rachel reached out, pulled Mike to her, and this time, she held him tight. They stood in the kitchen with the early morning rays of sun streaming into the room, showing the glow of the tiny dust particles in the air hovering and meandering in the light as if not knowing where to go.

"You take good care of yourself, Michael." She pulled away and gazed into his eyes with the smile he was used to seeing. "It's a big world out there."

"I will, Ma," he said as he smiled back at her.

"I've packed food for you that should last a few days. It's sittin' over there on the counter." With her eyes glistening, she hugged him one last time, gave him a kiss, and left the kitchen.

That wasn't quite as bad as I thought it was going to be. He took one last look around the kitchen, "I'll be back. Don't you worry," he said to all the inanimate objects in the kitchen, "I'll see you again."

***

William Gilbert strained against the twelve-inch-long, rough piece of wood in his hands. As he twisted it, the brace wire between two heavy fence posts slowly tightened, causing the barbed wire to become taut.

Two more sections of fence needed repair by noon if he was to get the run along the road finished by supper. As he twisted, he thought about how much faster the job would go if Mike were helping. He was better at building fences than his brothers, and William always felt good knowing that Mike was doing the fence work. His anger grew as he thought about his son surprising him with his decision to leave the farm ... to go off and do whatever it was he thought he wanted to do. William continued to twist the wire but lost track of how many turns he had made. *How in the world is everything going to get done around this place now?* Suddenly the twist wire broke, allowing the brace posts to loosen and the barbed wire to go slack. He shouted at the stick in his hands as if it were its fault the wire broke. "I don't need this!"

Reaching for his wire cutters he saw a horse and rider coming toward him from the farmhouse. He watched for a moment and then returned to his work.

Mike drew near on his horse, and William continued working with his back to the road. As he untwisted the wire from the stick, he heard Mike stop his horse next to him. He didn't look around at his son, and he didn't say a word.

"Can I give you a hand?"

"I can manage."

There was an uncomfortable pause as William continued to work without turning toward Mike.

"I wanted to tell you goodbye before I left," Mike said, breaking the awkward silence.

William stopped his work and finally turned toward him, removing his leather gloves. "You just figure you'll ride out of here and make your way in the big world, do you now?"

11

Mike squinted with the morning sun in his eyes. "Pa, you know I'm not a farmer. I can do it as good as anybody, but I don't much like it."

"This farm needs you, son. We were finally building it into what we want it to be and ..."

"You mean what *you* want it to be."

William clinched his teeth and took a step toward Mike at the interruption.

"Don't get fresh with me, boy. I can still pull you off that horse and teach you how to show respect."

Mike pulled on the reins and his horse took a couple of steps back.

"Pa, from the time I was big enough to carry a shovel, I've been working as hard as you and Mark and Luke. I've worked from before daylight until dark. This has been a great dream for you, and I respect that, but it's not my dream. Can't you see that?"

"What I see is my son throwing away everything I've worked for. I built all of this for you and your brothers. This was going to be yours someday."

"Pa, I don't want it. I don't know what I want yet, but I don't want this. I love you and Ma and my brothers, and I know you are all happy here, but I'm not. Not anymore."

Remaining silent and twisting his jaw sideways, William digested what Mike had just said. Twenty years of his perfect world had come crashing down around him in an instant. He had been completely surprised when Mike had told him and Rachel two weeks earlier that he was leaving, but it was only now genuinely soaking in. It had him twisted up inside with a deep gripping pain he had never felt before.

William turned around and slowly put his gloves back on. He picked up the wire cutters and began removing the broken wire on the posts.

Mike looked back toward the farmhouse and out across the pasture, "Guess I'll be going now."

The next words he heard from his father practically ripped his heart out of his chest, and pulled the cool morning air from his lungs. "If your bed is empty tonight, don't bother coming back." William clipped a wire and slung the broken piece into the pasture.

Mike watched the piece of wire fly through the morning air and come to a rest in the greening grass. At that moment, he didn't notice the warmth of the sun shining on his face, just the cold coming from the father whom he dearly loved.

"Bye, Pa."

He pulled his collar tight around his neck to cut out some of the crispness of the morning then nudged his horse down the lane toward the main road.

***

Mark and Luke Gilbert had been busy all morning prying large, exposed stones from the ground of the east pasture. They would cut hay from this section come summer, and the protruding rocks would make it more difficult. They were already working on their second load of the day, and Mark was hoisting a stone the size of a watermelon. When he saw Mike riding toward them in the lane, he placed the rock on the wagon and backhanded Luke, who was struggling with his own rock. Irritated by the smack, Luke turned his head around and saw Mike on the other side of the fence.

"I hear lifting rocks is hard work," Mike said with a grin.

Luke released the rock he was working with, and both brothers made their way to Mike at the fence.

Mark leaned against a rotting fence post. "Did you talk to Pa?"

"Wasn't much of a conversation."

"He'll come around," Mark said, "he's just hurt."

"Not easy for me, neither," Mike quickly replied.

"You're the one leavin'," Luke said as he removed his hat and wiped the perspiration from his forehead with the back of his arm.

There was silence between them because none of the three wanted this moment to become sentimental.

"You're gonna let us know when you get settled, ain't ya?" Mark asked.

"I'm sure they have mail service where I'm going." Mike forced a grin. "This is the twentieth century."

"Well, just because it's 1900 now don't mean everything has changed into a magical world of wonder."

"Mark, I'll be sure and send you all a letter when I get there. I'm headed toward Marion County. I hear there's a little mining town there where a fella can make some good money if he works hard."

"Well, you never were one who was shy about workin' hard, that's for sure, big brother," Luke said affectionately as he lowered his head and spit onto the ground.

"I'll miss you too, Luke. Take care of Ma."

Raising his hand toward his brothers, and without saying another word, Mike urged his horse to move forward once again. They returned his wave with sad smiles, knowing that the world as they had always known it was forevermore changed.

Chapter 2

Mike turned his horse south when he reached the main road. He traveled for half a mile along his father's fence row gazing across the rolling pasture. The sun was higher in the light blue sky now and felt warm on the left side of his face. It gave him comfort as he rode toward town.

Through backbreaking work and smart decisions, his father had become very successful. Even though farming hadn't made him a rich man, William Gilbert's holdings of land and livestock were among the largest in Madison County. Mike was full of pride when it came to his family heritage, and he deeply respected what had made his father such a great man. He had always looked up to him for his strength and guidance. It was breaking his heart to leave the only life he had known, but mostly to leave behind those he loved.

As he passed the corner post marking the southeast edge of their property, Mike remembered him and his brothers replacing the old post with the new one of bois d'arc two years earlier. He smiled as he remembered how the three of them had struggled, because of how tough the wood is, to cut the tree and shape it into the post. He almost laughed out loud as he remembered Mark wanting to be the first one to drive an axe into the tree, only to have it bounce out and barely miss his leg.

Mike stopped his horse and looked back. He had come far enough that he could no longer see the house or barn, only a few cows grazing in a pasture of green. He thought about what his brothers would be doing for the next few days, and even a year from now. He thought about how many pies his mother would bake in the next week, and how much room Mark would have in the bedroom for the first time in his life. . . Mike's dreams of leaving had finally become a reality, and, though he wouldn't admit it to anyone else, he was scared.

A robin caught his attention, chattering at him from a tree nearby, defending her nest. "It's alright girl, I'll be moving on soon." He took one last glance over his shoulder and then urged his horse on again.

Only fifteen minutes from town, Mike hoped he wasn't too early for the bank in Kingston to be open for business. He knew bankers' hours were different than farmers' hours. His wallet contained seventy-five dollars he had saved without his family knowing. Work he had done on the Parker farm next door had afforded him the luxury of putting some of his earnings away in a mason jar under his bed. He was amazed that he had been able to keep the jar a secret from his brothers. A few years earlier his father had also started giving him and his brothers a small amount of money for work they did on the farm. This was something most didn't do, but Mike's father was a fair man and knew that boys needed some spending money jingling in their pockets. He had always taught them that with money comes the responsibility of saving and, most importantly, putting some of their earnings into the offering plate at church.

"Good morning, Mike."

"Good morning, Mr. Parker," Mike replied as he rode by his neighbor, who was cutting a tree next to his fence. "Getting a head start on the firewood for next year?"

Everett Parker removed his hat and wiped sweat from his forehead with the back of his shirtsleeve. "I'm gettin' dad-blame tired of fixin' my fence because of limbs fallin' off this blasted tree ... that's what I'm gettin'."

Mike stopped his horse. "It's a shame to cut down such a big old oak tree, though."

"I got a thousand more in the holler if I need to look at one," Everett said with an annoyed grin.

"Give Mrs. Parker my best." Mike touched the brim of his hat and directed his horse back down the road. Within

16

a few seconds, he heard Everett Parker's axe striking the oak tree once again in a steady rhythm.

As he neared town, Mike reached into his inside jacket pocket and pulled out a folded piece of newspaper. He had gotten a copy of the Mountain Echo newspaper, published in Yellville, Arkansas, when he was in Kingston the previous summer. It was dated June 7th, 1899. Most of the paper he had thrown away after reading it. It had contained the usual: "Mrs. Jenkins is visiting relatives and will be back in town next month." "Mr. Capps was kicked by his mule and is recovering nicely." It was the usual local filler in the paper, and the writing style of the editor was good for a chuckle or two.

One short article had captured his attention. Even though the article itself had not sparked his desire to one day leave the farm, the name of the article caused him to read the story with interest and offered him clarity about the direction of his life.

He held the yellowed scrap of paper in his hand and read the title again, "The Rush to Rush, Arkansas." He remembered reading the article several times when he was alone over the past several months. He had also found other articles about the town of Rush, and what had been interest became a strong desire to go and see what the excitement was all about.

The community of Rush was in Marion county, a couple of counties east of Madison county. He had read about how zinc had been discovered a few years earlier and that the deposits were so rich an ore mill had been built. The article in his hands talked about the Morning Star Mine and how the town was growing quickly. . . Even though he didn't know the first thing about mining, the thought of being part of a bustling town excited him. There was something inside him that caused him to believe he could build a good life in Rush. He refolded the paper and placed it back into his pocket as he neared Kingston. The sadness of leaving was beginning to wane as he looked forward to his adventure.

Though he was apprehensive, he didn't believe there was anything that could ruin his day.

***

Clifford Davis unlocked the front door of the Kingston Bank and turned around the "Open for Business" sign. He had already spent an hour cleaning the counter at the teller window, sweeping the floor, taking care of the rubbish, and unlocking the safe. His only employee was a young, single lady named Maude Larkin, who usually took care of such things in the mornings. On this day, however, she was at home, ill with something called la grippe. Clifford was in his fifties and knew everyone in the area. . He had been the banker in the little town of Kingston for the past ten years. Though he had gotten close to marriage a couple of times, for reasons that he didn't understand, it had eluded him. He had become comfortable living by himself with two cats just a few doors away from the bank.

Everyone liked Clifford and he was highly regarded by those who knew him. He was even-tempered and easy to get along with. As far as anyone could remember he had never been heard to so much as raise his voice. He was usually asked to be the Master of Ceremonies at gatherings, and had even called a few square dances. He wouldn't be fondly remembered for calling dances, however, since he sometimes confused his *Allemande lefts* with his *Do-Sa-Dos*. In the middle of a rip roarin' square dance, that could cause all sorts of confusion.

Clifford made his way to the teller window to assume Maud's duties. "I'll have to tend to my mountain of paperwork after we close at four o'clock," he mumbled. Pulling double duty was a slight irritation to him but nothing insurmountable. In a small town like Kingston, there was usually nothing much to get all worked up over, and he noted to himself that it would feel good for a turn to exchange greetings with the dozen or so customers who would likely wander in. Deciding to remove his suit coat for a change while he sat behind the decorative iron bars at the teller window, Cliff also tugged at his bow tie to loosen its grip on his neck. With a deep sigh, he was ready for business.

He was busy counting the fifty-cent pieces when the door opened. Looking up, he was greeted by the smile of Mike Gilbert.

"Well, what are you doing behind the bars today, Mr. Davis?" Mike removed his hat. "Where's Maude?"

"I'm afraid she has a severe case of la grippe. Came down with it just yesterday and is in fairly poor shape from what I understand."

"Well, I hope she recovers soon." Mike walked to the teller window in front of Cliff.

"What brings you in so early of a morning? Running errands for your Pa, I guess?"

"Well ..." Mike began but remained silent for a moment as he looked around the room.

"Everything all right?"

"I need to withdraw my savings, Mr. Davis."

Cliff was surprised at the request. He didn't have a problem with withdrawals, but for Mike to abruptly enter the bank and request his money caused Cliff to be a little bit concerned.

"May I ask why you need to withdraw your savings?"

As far as Mike was concerned, it wasn't any of Cliff's business why he wanted his money and the query made him angry. He looked down at his feet to regain his composure and calmly responded. "Mr. Davis—I'm leaving town. I need my money for travel, and to get settled in where I'm headed."

Cliff's brow furrowed as he cocked his puckered lips sideways at the news. "I'm afraid I won't be able to do that, Mike, at least not until your Pa comes in and approves the transaction."

"Approves? Mr. Davis, I have over two hundred dollars in your bank. It rightly belongs to me, and I want to withdraw it."

"Son, I know that the money belongs to you. I've watched you come in and make deposits for quite some time

19

now. In fact, I've felt proud to see you be so frugal with your money."

"Then what does my father have to do with me withdrawing it?"

"The account is in your father's name," Cliff said in his most tender voice. "I can't legally take money out of his account unless he approves by being here or signs the withdrawal slip. Surely you understand my position."

Mike's anger grew, knowing that the money in his pocket would not get him very far and that the rest of his money was just on the other side of that window. He had been planning for months and needed his savings.

"Mr. Davis, I need that money. It's mine. I worked long and hard for it, and now you're telling me I can't have it?"

"Son, you need to settle down. I'm sure we can work this out. Just have your father come in and ..."

Mike rarely lost control of his emotions, but this was something he hadn't expected and it caught him off guard. In an instant, the thought flashed through his mind that his exodus was already over before he had even gotten out of town. In a burst of anger, Mike raked a stack of papers and the ink pen off the marble counter and sent them crashing against the wall. The ink from the ink bottle became an indigo stream cascading down the papered wall as the container bounced onto the floor.

Cliff took a step back from the window in anticipation of what might come next. The expression on his face was surprise mixed with a slight amount of fear. This was something he had surely never expected from Mike Gilbert.

"I want my money," Mike said, in an angry yell. "I need my money!"

"Mike, I can't give it to you ... I'm sorry," Cliff apologized, taking still another step away from the window.

Mike stood for what seemed like minutes with his eyes locked onto Cliff, his jaw muscles pulsing from the clenching of his teeth. He looked at the mess on the wall and the floor. As he looked back at Cliff, the front door to the bank opened, breaking the tension. Mike turned his head to see the intruder. He immediately placed his hat back on his head, turned, and almost knocked Frank Vallines over as he stormed past him, bumping into him with his shoulder.

"Mike?" Frank exclaimed as he watched Mike storm out of the bank and into the dusty street.

The day didn't seem as nice and pleasant to Mike anymore as he straddled his horse and left town in a hurry. He continued his journey east, away from his home, his town, and his money.

Chapter 3

Now that the chill of the morning had been replaced by a warm southerly wind, Jeeter Morse unbuttoned his overcoat and placed it into his saddle bag. His camp was a few miles east of Fayetteville by the White River. He had been through this area before in his travels, and the spot he had chosen was a secluded place between the river and a rock embankment on a small gravel bar. He was traveling the back roads as much as possible because he hadn't exactly made many friends the last time he had passed this way. In fact, if a certain Washington County constable found him, he knew that a cold jail cell would become his home.

For the most part, Jeeter was a small-time thief and bank robber, but he had never been very successful at either. At twenty years of age, he and two of his friends attempted to rob his first bank in Harrison, Arkansas; he was lucky to make it out of the debacle alive. Both his friends had been killed and his getaway had been clumsy, but because of his mask, he had not been identified. For the next couple of years, he drifted between Missouri and Arkansas, pilfering here and there from farms he passed along his way. Jeeter was smart and could have easily made a living in his father's accounting firm, but living on the edge seemed to suit him.

He cinched the buckle on the saddlebag and patted his horse on the side of her neck. "Gracie, you ready to make the trip over to Kingston?"

Pausing as if waiting for an answer, Jeeter was met with only a blank stare from her dark eyes. "There's a little bank there that I need to do some business with." He grinned as he patted her a few more times. Looking around to make sure he had left no sign of their presence, he mounted his horse, took the reins and guided her up a dirt bank.

He headed Gracie east toward Madison County. Jeeter planned to be in Kingston on the eastern edge of the county by the next morning. He'd heard that the bank there was small and unprotected. He knew there probably wouldn't be a lot of money in it, but it might be enough to get him to his final destination, where he could lay low for a while. He wasn't thinking about settling down to a real job, but he had a feeling he could make some good money where he was going. Hoping there would be a lot of people willing to part with their money in a growing and thriving mining town, he smiled as he began planning what he had in store for Rush, Arkansas.

***

Clifford Davis wiped the sweat from his forehead as he sat down behind the teller window again.

"What was the Gilbert boy all muddled over?" Frank asked as he walked up to the counter. He saw the ink splattered on the wall and the floor.

"He was more than muddled," Cliff replied. "He was downright angry."

"I can see that now." Frank knelt down to pick up the ink blotter and the bottle that was mostly empty.

"What set him off, Cliff?"

Clifford made his way around the counter and knelt down to help Frank with the cleanup. He picked up some of the ink-splattered paper and looked around the floor for the pen. Frank was about to ask his question again when Cliff finally spoke. "I couldn't give him his money from William's account." He let out a grunt when he bent over to see if the pen had rolled under a nearby table.

"Why didn't he just have Bill come in and get it fer him?" Frank stood and looked at the ink stains all over his hands. He appeared helpless as he tried to figure out where he could set the ink-covered objects.

"I have some rags in the back room," Cliff said as he saw Frank looking at his hands. "Hold on a second and I'll get us a couple." Cliff disappeared through a doorway and soon returned with two white rags. Frank handed him the ink

23

bottle along with the stained paper and began wiping his hands.

"I don't think William knows Mike wanted the money," Cliff said as he wrapped the inky bottle up in a rag. "Seems Mike is on his way out of town. I suppose William would have come in and gotten the money himself if he was okay with Mike leavin'. I know William Gilbert well enough to know that I should err on the side of caution. Besides, I don't think Mike would have gotten angry unless he didn't want to go back to see his father about the money."

Frank furrowed his brow. "Wonder why Mike is leavin' town?"

Kneeling to the floor and wiping at the remaining ink as best he could, Clifford responded, "I haven't a clue, but I know Bill's not gonna be happy when I tell him that someone's gonna have to pay for fixin' up this mess." He shook his head from both the sight of the stains and the distress he still felt from his encounter with Mike.

Clifford took the rags from Frank and walked through the half door, latching it behind him. He dropped the stained cloth and the ruined papers in a waste bucket.

Cliff chuckled, "Frank, how are we gonna get this ink off our hands?" He anticipated a reply but only heard the opening of the front door. He turned to see Frank's backside as the door closed behind him. *Won't take long for that word to spread around town.*

For the rest of his day, Clifford was twice as busy as usual. Not with banking business but with people coming in to stare at the inky mess then ask questions to which he didn't have the answers. He was careful not to plant any more seeds in their minds by speculating about why Mike had erupted. He also decided to pay William Gilbert a little visit in a day or two after banking hours. First, he had a mountain of paperwork to complete and file.

***

The nine-mile trip to Boxley Valley gave Mike time to calm down. Since he and his brothers had traveled to a

24

farm near Boxley three years earlier to purchase an Angus bull and heifer from Pearl Evans, this part of the trip was familiar to him. His father had talked to other farmers about the Angus breed and how they wintered better and weighed more when it came time for slaughter. Heavier weight meant more money. But the Angus breed had not been in the country from Ireland for long, so a good breeding pair had been difficult to come by and very expensive. He remembered how his father had thought long and hard about the cost of the pair versus the payoff in the future before making the investment. He figured if nothing else he could at least breed the bull with his other cows and hopefully strengthen his stock with the Angus bloodline. Mike remembered how he and his brothers had taken a short tour of Pearl's farm where they purchased the Angus pair. Her husband had died a few months earlier, so she needed to sell everything on the farm as quickly as possible to pay off all of her debts. She wanted to move a few counties east to Flippin, where her widowed sister lived. Pearl had tried to sell them not only the cattle but every piece of equipment and every tool on the place. He smiled as he thought about his brother Mark giving the old lady fifty cents for her hound dog and the look on his father's face when they dragged the bonus creature home. It took days to remove the ticks from the old hound, and his mother almost shot the mutt once when it dug through her bed of marigolds and lilies.

Mike's thoughts drifted back to his current situation. He had only seventy-five dollars in his pocket and some food his mother had insisted on him taking. Because there were no straight roads in the Ozarks between Kingston and Rush, he figured it would take three days to make his trip, providing he could keep up his current pace. He decided to camp a little north of Boxley, beside the upper end of the Buffalo River. He could cross the river there the next morning and, with luck, make it past Jasper and get as close to Yellville as he could before nightfall. He would then be only a few miles away from Rush.

From what he knew, Rush was next to the water on the lower end of the Buffalo River, twenty-five miles or so upriver from where it joined with the White River. He was looking forward to seeing what the Buffalo River looked like at that end. He hoped it was as clean and clear as it was on the upper part.

He had spent the last couple of months looking at a map of Arkansas, purchased when he had traveled a few miles west to Huntsville on an errand for his father. On it, he had plotted his path to Rush; much of the roadway was rural and rugged. He hoped he wouldn't encounter any difficulty along the way. Arkansas was beginning to join the rest of the country in becoming civilized, but he knew that some of the rural folk didn't take kindly to strangers getting too close to their land or, more particularly, to their stills. He had heard that "shoot first and ask questions later" was the rule. The counties in that area were dry counties and working stills were commonplace. Moonshiners kept the constables very busy trying to find them. Sometimes the constables went so far into the hills searching for a still that they were never heard from again; at least, that's what Mark had told him. He didn't know if he put much stock in what his brother said, but he'd be on the lookout just in case and stay on the main roads.

Mike came to a junction in the road. To the right was Boxley, so he turned his horse left onto the road that would take him down to the Buffalo River. Because the road into the river valley dropped in elevation, the air became cooler as Mike rode. Even though it was late afternoon and there were still a couple of hours left in the day, the sun had begun to set behind the hills. The valley was shadowed and still. To his right was an open pasture leading down to the water, and he watched as a small herd of deer grazed on the new grass. He wished he had a nickel for every deer he had hunted during his lifetime on the farm.

He had tried to keep the thoughts of home out of his head and focus on his journey, but now, in the cool dampness of the Buffalo River valley, he allowed himself to think about his mother and brothers having their first supper together without him. He couldn't help but dwell on the last words he heard from his father. Now that he was actually on his way and leaving familiar territory, his eyes began to water as he realized what he was doing. He was leaving home to be on his own, away from everything he had known and into a world he had only read about. He closed the top of his jacket tight around his neck, not only to cut out the coolness, but to try and relax the lump beginning to grow in his throat. *This is really happening, isn't it?* He knew it would be quite some time before he saw his family again.

Watching a meadowlark atop a fencepost and listening to it throw a familiar tune into the still air, Mike neared the river crossing. So far this spring the rains had been light, and, though he would get a little wet, crossing the river would be easy. *I should probably make camp before crossing, so I don't get my clothes damp before nightfall.*

To be away from the road, Mike worked his way several yards down the riverbank and made camp, then led his horse to the river's edge to allow him a good long drink and to nibble on some grass. Although he didn't have anything to cook, he gathered dried sticks and driftwood along the gravel bar and built a fire—. It would comfort him to have its glowing warmth.

The increasing darkness of the valley melted into night. Mike tethered his horse to a piece of bleached and weathered wood protruding from the gravel bar and spread his bedroll out beside the fire. Since it didn't look like rain, he didn't bother to set up the cloth shelter. He simply lay down beside the fire, staring at the millions of stars above him, and dreamed of a future he had only imagined. he traced shapes from star to star, but it wasn't long before the crackling of the fire faded away, and the gurgling of the water over the rocks and the songs of frogs kept him company until he fell asleep.

***

27

Early the next morning William Gilbert awoke before daylight as he always did. Having slept for an hour at best, he was already tired as he sat on the edge of the bed—and his day had not even begun. His heart ached from the events of the previous day, and he had thought about nothing else. Although he knew that each of his sons would someday grow to be their own man and follow their own dreams, it had never crossed his mind that the dream would take one of his sons away from him. He wished he could erase what he had said to Mike moments before he rode away, but he couldn't. He hadn't even told his wife because she would scold him more than he had already done to himself.

Hanging his troubled head, William closed his eyes and remembered the hurt on Rachel's face when they were around the supper table the previous evening. Of course, she was sad, too, because Mike had left the nest, but she was also hurt because of the tension between her husband and son. She hadn't spoken a word to him all evening, not out of anger but from sadness. No one knew what to say, but nothing needed saying. William knew they all felt the same loss.

Regardless of his heartbreak, William knew the cows and chickens still needed to be fed. The stumps and rocks in the new pasture wouldn't remove themselves, so he got up to dress. It was then that he noticed Rachel still in bed. Usually she was up before him to prepare breakfast and begin her day. She had her back toward him, but he could tell that she was awake. He started to question her about her routine but decided to let it go. He was sure there was some ham and biscuits left over from the previous evening. He could get the coffee boiling himself, so he decided to let her be.

Mark was already in the kitchen when William walked through the doorway. The burden of regret showed on William's face as he crossed the floor to the wood stove.

28

"It's not the end of the world," Mark said, his tone flippant.

"No, son—it's not, but it gives me a little taste of what the end of the world might feel like."

"Sorry, Pa; I was just tryin' to lighten the mood a little."

"Your mother is not feeling herself this morning, so we'll have to fend for ourselves. I'll get some coffee boiling. Go make sure your brother is up and around. You'll both need a full day to get the rest of those rocks out of the ground if we intend to plant soon."

Without another word, Mark left the kitchen to roust his brother. William leaned over and placed several small pieces of wood into the stove, onto the glowing embers left from the night before. He closed the tender door and opened the damper to make more air available. Before long the fire heated the top of the stove, and water began to boil for the coffee. He knew that he not only had some fence mending around the new pasture, but he also had some mending to do with his wife and, especially, Mike.

***

Mike awoke as the first rays of sunlight turned the sky pink behind the tower of trees on the other side of the river. Even though his blanket was damp with morning dew, he was warm underneath the covers. He had used his saddle as a pillow and had put the saddle blanket beneath his bedroll to give some extra padding between him and the small river rocks. Because he had been so tired, he hadn't moved much during the night. When the rock under his left hip dug into him, he winced a little and tried shifting positions so he could lie there a little longer. But he was now awake and the day was upon him. His adventure was calling to him, and he had reconciled himself to the fact that he had only the money in his pocket and the belief that, as his mother always quoted from the Bible, "God will provide."

Wiping the slumber from his eyes, Mike felt the dampness of the morning all around him. The air was heavy and cool. He had slept in his clothes because he was traveling light and didn't have much room for extra clothing in his travel bags. He had one change with him and had planned on buying what he needed after he reached Rush, but now he would have to make do. He knew he would figure something out—he always did. *Here goes.* Taking a deep breath, Mike pushed the damp blankets off him.

He stood and stretched, working out the kinks from his body. Without putting on his boots, Mike untied his horse, Rusty, and took him to the water's edge. He looked out across the shallow river and along the banks. The river was waking up also, and the sounds of the frogs were already being replaced by the chirping and calling of the cardinal and thrush. A river willow beside him held between two branches the delicate work of a spider, —the symmetrical web pattern adorned with tiny globes of moisture hanging along every strand.

A school of minnows was visible just under the surface of the water's edge. They gathered around Rusty's muzzle as he drank, waiting for tiny bits of food and debris to drift from his mouth. In the early morning light, Mike noticed a couple of turtles in the water, already looking for a suitable rock or tree trunk to climb up on-to, so they could be warmed by the sun.

Before gathering his things, Mike ate a biscuit with ham and finished it off with an apple. Instead of building a fire to make coffee, He washed down breakfast with a cool drink from the river.

With Rusty saddled and seeing there were no embers remaining from the fire of the previous night, Mike placed his hat on his head and mounted. "Come on Rusty, we've got a long day ahead of us."

The splashing water got his pants wet up to the knees, and even though it made him shiver, it was refreshing at the same time. He knew he would have to keep a steady pace if he was going to make it close to Yellville for the night. Since he had to conserve his cash, he would use it only for food along the way and be content to sleep under the stars again. He was satisfied for this to be part of his grand adventure.

Chapter 4

Jeeter Morse was up with the dawn and only a few miles from Kingston. He had never been to the community so he didn't know what to expect. He had done a bit of homework and knew that the sheriff of Madison County was in Huntsville, several miles west. As he cinched the saddle, he hoped the good sheriff was currently in Huntsville—as his homework had indicated—or, better yet, at the other end of the county.

Before getting onto his horse, he took a few steps to fill his canteen from the King's River where he had camped. As it filled, he became apprehensive with what he was about to do.

I'll get in and out faster without a partner tagging along; since it's a small town and bank, what could go wrong? Besides, I'll be long gone before the sheriff gets on my trail. With the canteen filled, Jeeter mounted and turned his horse toward the road leading south into Kingston.

***

The sun was finally beginning to peek over the horizon as Morse came to the Gilbert farm. He watched as the cattle grazed in the pasture. It reminded him of working his uncle's ranch in Kansas when he was younger. He remembered getting up before daylight day after day. *Smelly animals.* He thought about how much he had hated constantly mending fences and chasing strays in that dry, flat land.

As he continued on in the dim morning light, he saw two men working in a field. They were lifting rocks and putting them on a wagon. He watched them struggle together as they hoisted a large rock, only to have it slip from their grasp and crash to the ground. He watched as they both bent over and placed their hands onto their knees to catch their breath. *Hard way to make a livin'.*

The Gilbert boys hadn't noticed him as he passed, and, as they bent down in unison to try again at the rock, Jeeter turned his eyes back onto the road in front of him.

He rounded a small bend in the road and spotted a large oak tree lying on top of a tangled mess of barbed-wire fence. He could see that someone had deliberately chopped the monster down, but it had fallen in the wrong direction. *Bonehead hillbillies.*

It wasn't long before the road widened and he passed a few small houses. From an open window, he caught the drifting scent of ham frying in a skillet. The aroma caused him to feel the hunger in his belly. It had been a while since he had eaten a decent meal, and the jerky he had an hour earlier was not keeping his stomach from growling. He rode on, trying to get the thought of a succulent breakfast out of his mind.

A group of buildings emerged in front of him along the road. Some of them were whitewashed, and some of them were built with brick and stone. When he reached them, the road took a curve to the left. He looked around and spotted the bank nestled along with other businesses on the north side of the street.

Not much to this place fer sure. This is gonna be the easiest money I ever made.

He rode through the square and stopped his horse at the edge of town, surveying the bank from the tree line. *Not many people stirrin' around.* Easing out of the saddle and back into the shadows, he tied Gracie to a tree off the road in case someone came by. He wanted to make sure no one took notice of him.

***

Clifford finished his morning routine of coffee and toast. His druthers would be biscuits, but he had never gotten the hang of making good biscuits. He had tried to make them like his sister had shown him many times before, but they always turned out dense and hard.

Since sliced bread was easy enough to toast on the stove, it was his usual fare.

He placed his cup on the counter beside the sink and pulled the watch out of his vest pocket, pushing the crown with his thumb to flip open the case. "Time for work," he said out loud as if he were about to say goodbye to someone else in the room. He replaced the timepiece and grabbed his hat as he walked out the door, feeling the warming glory of the springtime sun.

He walked to the bank, which was only a few buildings from his house. He tried to soak up as much of the morning as he could before he had to tackle the dual task of being both teller and accountant. *I wish Maude would hurry up and get better. I would rather be back at my desk. I'm getting tired of making pleasant talk with people who want to prattle on about the weather, or crops, or whose cow had to be put down. And if I have to explain to one more person about the ink-stained wall…*

Clifford locked the door behind him as he entered the bank, and within thirty minutes he was ready for the day. He removed his jacket, unlocked the door, and sat on the stool behind the barred window. It wasn't long before the door opened.

"Why, Clifford Davis," he heard a high-pitched voice exclaim. He looked up to see Meryl Atkins glide across the floor toward him. "I heard that Maude was a little under the weather. I had to come into town for some baking needs and thought I'd say hello."

I wish you hadn't. "Morning, Mrs. Atkins."

Cliff always felt sorry for Meryl because her husband had died three years earlier after contracting blood poisoning. However, he never felt sorry enough to consol her with courting. She was the kind of woman who would rattle off several sentences without even taking a breath. Then after she was finished, he often had no idea what she was trying to say.

"Isn't it a wonderful day?"

"Yes indeed. Very nice."

"I just love this time of the year because everything seems so crisp and new. The redbud trees are in bloom; all the leaves are so fresh and bright green. Makes a person feel young and full of life, don't you agree, Mr. Davis?"

Clifford smiled from behind his barred window because he knew she could not reach out and touch him. She often did that as she talked to people. She couldn't converse without touching, and it irritated him whenever she would catch him outside of the bank.

"Oh, yes ma'am. Fresh air is good for the soul. Is there something I can do for you today, Mrs. Atkins?" He tried to turn the encounter into a more businesslike affair.

Meryl noticed the change of subject, but, before she had the opportunity to respond, the front door opened behind her. A man wielding a gun and wearing a white hood with two eye holes in it rushed in. She tried to scream as the man grasped her arm and pointed the pistol at Cliff on the other side of the counter.

"Don't make a sound," Jeeter snapped at Meryl. "You," motioning the gun at Clifford, "put the cash from the drawer into a bag and toss it to me."

Clifford remained calm as he saw the horror on Meryl's face.

"Do it now," Jeeter ordered as he jerked Meryl's arm. She let out a squeak of pain as he shook the gun at Cliff.

With the cash drawer opened, Clifford spotted his pistol resting on a shelf below it. He thought of reaching for it, but since Meryl was being used as a shield, he couldn't risk letting her get hurt. He sighed. *I'll just give him the money and get him out of here.*

"Hurry up, mister, or I swear I'll put a bullet in her."

Clifford calmly reached for a leather bank bag and filled it with the tender. He then slid the bag under the bars toward the man.

Jeeter shoved Meryl toward the end of the counter, causing her to fall to the floor. He grabbed the bank bag and turned for the door. Clifford seized the moment and grabbed his gun. As Jeeter flew out the door, Clifford quickly lifted the countertop door separating the bank lobby from the teller. Seeing that Meryl was only stunned, he exited the bank in time to see Jeeter mount his horse. He pointed his pistol and fired a round at Jeeter, missing him completely. Jeeter's horse reared at the shot, and as soon as he could turn, fired back, sending wood splinters into the air not far from Clifford's head. Clifford took a quick side step and pulled the trigger again as Jeeter kicked his horse into high gear toward the edge of town. This time the bullet struck Jeeter in the leg, and Clifford knew he hit his target because the rider lurched and grabbed his left thigh.

By now Jeeter was too far away for another shot, and several people were in the street. To shoot again would be too dangerous to the onlookers. Clifford watched helplessly as Jeeter galloped out of town, followed by a cloud of dust.

***

It had been three hard days sitting in the saddle, but Mike was finally within a few miles of Rush. Along the way he had soaked in the beauty of the Ozark hills and mountains. At times the narrow roads and trails took him into cool, shaded valleys where the trees crowded him on both sides, creating a canopy of green leaves and grape vines. At other times he found himself traversing the hilltops, looking down upon the endless valleys and pasturelands. It still looked like home to him and reminded him of what he had left behind. However, he was committed to this adventure and his new life, and he hoped and prayed that he had made the right decision.

Riding into the little town of Yellville, just north of Rush, Mike decided to get something to eat. All the food he had brought with him was gone; although he didn't want to start digging into his seventy-five dollars, he couldn't ignore the hunger in his belly.

He knew Yellville was the county seat of Marion County. It was nice looking and quaint, complete with a well-kept town square. He hadn't known what to expect, but the town was bigger than his small community of Kingston. From Yellville his route would turn south and, within a few miles, he would reach his destination.

Spotting the White River Café, Mike tied Rusty to the rail and entered. Inside, he noticed a couple who had already been served. He sat down at a table on the other side of the room from them. As Mike removed his hat, a rather plump lady appeared. She was somewhere around forty and wore a white apron, complete with sauce stains. Her red hair was twisted into a single braid that hung quite a ways down her back. He was surprised to hear a high, squeaky voice when she spoke.

"Where are you from?" she began. Her smile showed enough of a gap between her two front teeth that it looked as if a tooth was actually missing.

Mike took the slate she offered him—the café's offerings poorly written on it—and concentrated on it to avoid staring at her gap as she continued to smile.

"I'm from Kingston," he said, glancing up at her from the corner of his eyes.

"Never heard of it; been traveling long?"

I really don't want to be rude. I just want to eat and go.

"Three days."

"Long time to be in the saddle."

Mike just smiled.

"I'll start with some water."

"Water's in that pitcher beside you, hon."

37

"Sorry, I see it now."

"If you want ice, it will be a nickel extra."

"I'll just have it plain, thanks."

Again he turned his attention to the slate. *This would be easier if she wasn't standing next to me.* Finally he decided. "I'll have meatloaf, beets, and green beans."

She showed her gap again as she took the slate from him. "By the way, I'm Bertha. I'll be right back with your order." At that, she turned and walked back through a swinging door, into the kitchen, and out of sight.

I hope she doesn't stand here while I eat, too, or—worse yet—invite herself to sit with me since business is slow.

After he poured some water into his glass, Mike looked at his surroundings. The room was nothing special, but it was nice enough. Faded curtains added to the atmosphere. Unlike some other eating establishments he had seen, everything seemed very clean. He glanced at the couple across the room. They seemed to be enjoying their meal, but as he continued watching, he noticed they weren't speaking to or even looking at each other. The only sounds in the room were those of their utensils against their plates and the ticking of a mantle clock on the shelf close to the black pot-bellied stove in one corner of the room.

As he lifted his glass to take a drink, he saw his food heading in his direction. *That was fast.*

"Here you go, hon," Bertha said as her thick hands sat the food in front of him.

"Thank you, ma'am." Closing his eyes, Mike inhaled; the aroma instantly made him desire to dig in as fast as he could.

"If you need anything else, just let me know."

To his relief, she walked back into the kitchen, allowing him to enjoy his meal in private. Before devouring his food, he bowed his head and thanked the

38

Lord for safe travels and for the great-smelling food he was about to devour …and devour he did.

Thirty minutes later, Mike finished the last bite of the rhubarb pie he had treated himself to and paid for his meal. *Thirty-five cents wasn't bad, especially for a meal that tasted as good as that one did. I gotta be careful though. Money has to last until I find a job.* He left a nickel on the table for Bertha, placed his hat on his head, and walked back out into the afternoon sunshine. After checking the straps on his saddle and seeing everything was in good shape, he walked Rusty to the water trough so he could have a good, long drink.

While his horse was quenching his thirst, Mike spotted a couple of old gentlemen playing checkers across the street under the cover of a porch at what seemed like a dry-goods store. He walked over to the men and waited until they acknowledged his presence.

"Afternoon," Mike said politely.

"Afternoon, young fella."

"I'm on my way to Rush. Can you tell me how close I am?"

The two old men looked at each other and grinned.

"You and about half the state of Arkansas is on their way to Rush seems like these days," one of them replied.

"I'm Mike Gilbert." Mike extended a hand.

"I'm Darrel and he's Cleon." Darrel pointed to the other man seated across from him. "Where ya from, boy?"

"I'm from Kingston. I've been on the road for a few days."

"Wasn't yore aunt from Kingston?" Darrel asked, turning to Cleon.

"That weren't my aunt, that was my cousin," Cleon replied. "And she weren't from Kingston, she was from Kingsville."

"Kingsville, where is Kingsville?"

39

"Kingsville is way on t'other side of Harrison in Missouri," Cleon said as he gestured. "She lived there fer about ..."

"Excuse me," Mike interrupted. "About how long did you say it was to Rush from here?"

Both of the men stopped their conversation about Cleon's cousin and looked back at Mike.

"Don't recollect sayin'," Darrel said, scratching his head, "but you should be there before dark."

Mike turned to get his horse. "Thank ya kindly."

As he walked away, he heard the two men continue their conversation about where Kingsville was located.

Rusty was finished with his drink, so Mike saddled up and urged him back onto the road. As he turned south, he crossed Crooked Creek. Looking up the creek, he saw some children playing at the water's edge, and it reminded him of when he used to play in the King's River as a young boy. He thought about all the times he and his brothers fished in the river and brought home fresh catfish or bass for his mother to fry in her big, cast-iron skillet. Thinking about home made him a little sad, but his sadness was mixed with the excitement of his goal. In only a few hours, he would finally be in Rush.

Chapter 5

Rachel Gilbert pumped cold water into a pitcher of tea she had steeped earlier in the day. The cold water diluted the concentrated tea to perfection. Carrying the pitcher and a glass through the kitchen door, she made her way to the barn—only a few steps away. William was working in the barn on their best plow, which needed the tip replaced. She figured he needed a break and could use a nice, cold drink. She also needed to speak with him, and since the boys were putting the finishing touches to the east fence, it would be a good opportunity to have him to herself.

She entered the barn and crossed the hay-strewn floor. She knew William was aware of her presence, but he continued working with his back toward her.

Rachel set his glass onto an old milking stool next to him. "Thought you could use a nice, cold glass of tea."

William stood from his crouched position and arched his back to stretch out the stiffness. He smiled at his wife as she stood there, but he could tell she was there for more than just to bring him tea. In all the years they had been married, he had no problem knowing when she had words to say.

Rachel remained silent as William picked up the sweaty glass and drank the contents.

He finished the last gulp with a smile. "Ahhh, that's just what the doctor ordered."

She took the glass from him and refilled it.

"Thank you, darling," he said as he took the newly filled glass. He looked into her eyes and decided to get the jump on the conversation. You have something you want to say to me, don't you?"

Rachel tried to smile, but her expression became troubled. "I've been thinking about what Clifford said yesterday when he came by and ..."

"Rachel," William interrupted, "You know Mike wouldn't do anything like rob a bank, no matter how upset he was. Clifford was just overreacting to a coincidence. Mike did cause some damage I'll have to pay for, but in no way do I believe Mike hung around for a day to rob that bank." There was a pause. "That being said, why do you think Mike didn't come back and ask me to help him get his money?"

Rachel hesitated for a moment. "Why do you think, William? You didn't exactly give him a fatherly send off. You were so angry about his leaving that he probably didn't want to come back to you."

"Well, why would I be happy about his leavin'? He had a good life here, and it's like he betrayed me … us." William set his glass down on the milking stool and crouched back down to continue his work on the plow. Rachel stood watching for a few moments.

"William," she began, "do you remember how difficult it was for us when you left your parents' home and started this farm?"

William continued to work with his back toward her.

"That was different," he finally replied.

"Why? Your father was so angry with you that the two of you didn't speak to each other for a whole year and we had moved only a few miles away. Is that how you want things to be between you and your son?"

There was silence as William continued to work.

"I didn't stop being a farmer, I just needed my own farm. We had different ideas about how to build a place, and I needed to show him I could do it on my own—without his help."

Rachel walked to William and gently placed her hand on his shoulder. At that, he stopped his work and stood again. He turned to look at her, and she could see that his eyes were red and misty.

"I think that's what Mike is doing. He wants to show you that he is a man on his own terms, not on yours. He's different, William. He always has been. He doesn't want to be a farmer, but he wants you to be proud of him nonetheless."

William looked down at the tools in his hands, and neither of them spoke as she gently rubbed him on his shoulder

"He's going to be okay," Rachel said, regaining William's attention. "He has so much of you in him."

She picked up the pitcher and walked out of the barn, closing the creaky wooden door behind her and leaving William alone to his thoughts.

William knew his wife was right, as she usually was, but this time there was more to it.

The nail of regret had been pounded into his soul after Clifford's visit. William believed that Mike's angry outburst was his fault because of how he had treated him from the first time Mike had announced that he was leaving. And the fact that his banker friend would imply that Mike could have done something out of desperation had upset him even more.

It was then that William decided to go into Kingston the next day and pay Cliff a visit, to pay for the damages and speak to him again. He hoped they could discuss the problem and get it all straightened out before rumors drifted in the sheriff's direction.

As William looked around the barn, years of memories invaded his thoughts. He had carefully planned all of their lives around the farm but had not taken into account that his sons would someday grow up and possibly start their own farms, as he had done. He wished he could take back what he had said to Mike before he left. Maybe if he hadn't been so cold to him, his son would have returned instead of making a scene at the bank. Then there wouldn't even be a question about his involvement in the bank robbery. William dropped his tools and picked up his glass of tea. He took a long drink and headed toward the house.

***

Realizing there was not much daylight left, Mike urged Rusty into a trot. A man he had passed on the road earlier told him that Rush was fifteen miles from Yellville. Eleven miles on the main road, and another four miles on the side road leading to Rush. He had hoped to get into town before dark so that it would be easier to find a place to stay. He was about to conclude he would be spending yet another night along the road when he spotted the weather-worn sign pointing the way to Rush.

He turned his horse east and began following the four-mile-long road. It was in good shape, considering how rural it was. Darkness began settling into the valley, and, as he continued to ride, the darkening trees seemed to close in on him. The spring peepers began signaling the oncoming night, and through the treetops he could see the first star in the indigo sky. He could barely see the road in front of him as he advanced, but his determination became stronger than his desire to stop and spend the night in the woods.

Over the sound of his horse's hooves, he thought he heard the faint sound of music. He pulled Rusty to a halt to sit and listen. It was there. Off in the distance in front of him, he could hear violin music and the sound of people clapping rhythm to the tune. The sound was sweet to his ears; he had finally made it.

Once again he urged his horse forward, and within minutes he could see lantern light through the trees. The lights were on both sides of the lane, but there didn't seem to be any buildings. As he neared one group close to the road, the lights illuminated nothing more than a canvas pitch over a wooden platform. A wash tub sat at the front of the platform and rocks were used as steps up into what was a shanty. There were no wooden walls, just canvas nailed onto vertical wooden supports. A campfire, surrounded by rocks to contain it, was crackling on the ground in front, sending up sparks into the calm night air. A teepee of metal rods held a large pot over the fire.

As he slowly rode by, he saw a glowing ember brighten beside a tree next to the road in front of him. Two men were smoking and nodded as Mike passed them.

44

"Evenin'," one of them said.

"Evenin'," Mike replied.

As his eyes became accustomed to the darkness, he noticed canvas dwellings on either side of the road and in the woods around him. It wasn't what he had expected, and he hoped this wasn't the future that awaited him here.

As he rounded a bend in the road, he was relieved to see the town finally appear in front of him. It was more of what he had expected—and yet it was night—so he could hardly wait to see his surroundings in the full light of day.

Mike stopped in front of a dry goods and food store but it was closed. He noticed a trough full of water, so he tethered his horse next to the trough but was distracted again by the music, which seemed to be coming from a building down the street.

Leaving his horse, Mike walked down the dusty street toward the music. The double doors to the building were wide open, and several men stood outside. As he neared, he could hear the tune of "Soldier's Joy" being played by a fiddle, guitars, and even a banjo at a rather brisk pace, with people clapping and yelping. From in front of the building, he could see about a hundred people inside, dancing and enjoying themselves. Although he wanted to join in the fun, he knew he needed to find a place for the night. He walked toward a group of young men standing close by.

"Evenin'," Mike said as he approached.

"Evenin'," one of them said.

"I wonder if you could direct me to the nearest hotel."

"Fresh meat," someone said out loud, followed by laughter from the others.

Mike awkwardly stood there as the laughter died.

"And you are?" one of them asked.

"I'm Mike Gilbert, from Kingston over in Madison County."

"Mike Gilbert from Madison County. You just ride into town?"

Mike shifted his weight from one leg to the other. "Just minutes ago."

"That buildin' across the street over yonder is Morning Star Hotel. Someone can help you there," the oldest man in the group said.

"Thank you kindly." Mike nodded his head. He continued to stand there for a few seconds, looking into the building.

"Looks like big doin's goin' on," Mike said, trying to make friendly small talk.

"It's a birthday gatherin' for friends and family of the Morning Star Mining Company. Mr. Harrison's daughter turned eighteen today."

"Eighteen," Mike said, raising his eyebrows.

"And Pam is the prettiest girl in Rush."

Mike continued to look into the building and grinned to think that he might soon get to be part of this kind of enjoyment.

"Well, maybe someday I'll have the pleasure of meeting her," he replied.

One of the boys in the group stepped toward Mike. "What makes you think she would want to meet a hick like you, farm boy?"

"Who are you?" Mike asked.

The boy now facing him was about his own age. Even in the dim lantern light Mike recognized the challenging expression on his face. The boy lowered his head and spit tobacco onto the ground, some of it landing on Mike's left foot. There was a little shuffling from the others standing there as Mike looked down at his foot and back up at the spitter. Being new in town, he decided to calmly smile at the event. He raised his left foot and wiped the juice off onto the back of his right pant leg. There was a little more rustling from the group.

"I'm Jay Finch," the young man replied as he took another step forward.

46

"Well, it was nice to meet you all and especially you, Jay. Thanks for the warm and juicy welcome. Goodnight."

Mike turned from the group and walked back up the street to his horse.

Finch stared at Mike as he disappeared into the darkness. For some reason, he automatically didn't like Mike. While his other friends returned to their business and continued their conversations, he fixed his glare into the darkness toward the newcomer. Finch had his heart set on courting Pamela Harrison, and no newcomer was going to threaten his desires. Though it was only a comment, Jay would make sure Mike kept his distance from the girl.

After making his way to the Morning Star Hotel, Mike tied his horse out front and walked inside to find an abandoned counter. He walked to it and rang the bell for service. Within seconds a tall, skinny fellow entered from a doorway. The older gentleman's hair was dark and parted in the middle, gleaming from hair wax. His round ears stuck straight out from the side of his head, causing Mike to think that the man would have a difficult time in a wind storm. He wore wire-rimmed glasses, and, though he showed no expression in his brown eyes, he sported a wide grin as he welcomed the potential guest.

"May I help you, young man?" he asked, exposing rather large, yellowed front teeth.

"I just need a room for the night. What's it gonna cost me?"

"Are you an employee of the Morning Star?"

"No, I just now rode into town."

"Then it will be one dollar and fifty cents." He said, pushing the guest book toward Mike.

"A dollar fifty?" Mike exclaimed out loud before he could catch himself.

The man looked at him with raised eyebrows, which made his forehead furrow.

"Is that the cheapest room you have?"

"Young man, this is not a cheap hotel. It is brand new by only a few months, and you are lucky. We are usually completely full, and you have asked for the last room we have available."

Mike thought for a moment about spending almost two dollars just to sleep for one night.

"The room does include a nice hot bath," the clerk said, trying to persuade Mike to make his decision.

"Are there any other rooms around town?" Mike finally asked, knowing he would probably offend the clerk.

"This is the only hotel in Rush," he responded with a smirk. "Any other room available will rent by the week or month, not by the day. And besides, it's late. I wouldn't advise going around town banging on doors to find a room at this time of night."

I guess I don't have much of a choice unless I want to sleep on the ground again. A nice hot bath would do me some good, though, especially since I'm going to look for a job tomorrow. I have to get a place soon. My money's not going to go very far at this rate.

Mike reached into his pocket and placed two silver dollars onto the counter. The clerk picked them up and threw another jolly smile in Mike's direction as he handed him four bits in change. "Thank you, sir, and I hope you have a wonderful night. Do you have any baggage to be taken to your room?"

"What I have is on my horse, and I'll get it myself, thanks. Oh, by the way, where is the livery? I need to bed my horse for the night."

"Sir, we can take care of that too."

"How much will that be?" Mike asked, afraid of the answer.

"We won't charge you a penny more," the clerk replied, handing Mike a key to his room. "Our stalls are right out back, and I'll have Samson take care of your horse."

Mike was about to ask who Samson was when the clerk began banging on the counter bell. Within seconds, a rather large man walked in through a doorway behind the counter, having to bend his neck a little to avoid banging his head on the door frame.

"Samson, take Mr. umm … I'm afraid I haven't gotten your name."

"Mike Gilbert."

"Take Mr. Gilbert's horse around back and bed him down for the night."

"Yes sir," Samson said in a deep voice and heavy southern accent.

Mike watched as Samson plodded through the front door and into the night.

"I can see why you call him Samson," Mike said with a grin.

"Oh, we don't call him that because he's big and tall; his momma named him that when he was born."

"Now that's quite a coincidence," Mike said, picking up the pen to sign the register.

"His momma was the daughter of a plantation owner in Kentucky, and his father was a big Frenchman from Canada, from what I understand. He's not too bright but he works hard. He walked into town 'bout three years ago and he's worked for Mr. Harrison at the Morning Star ever since."

Mike returned the pen to its holder and looked at the clerk. "Is Mr. Harrison the owner?"

"Oh no; he is the manager though … been with the company for years. I guess he's been here almost as long as the Morning Star Mine has been in operation."

"So I reckon he's the one throwing the dance down the street for his daughter?"

"You'd be right. Pam has pretty much grown up here in Rush. She's turned out to be a beautiful young lady … a mighty grand catch for some lucky fellow." The clerk blotted Mike's signature and closed the book.

"It's not too late in the evening; can I have someone get that bath ready for you before you turn in? You said you just arrived, so I imagine you would really enjoy a good, long soak."

"How long will it take?"

"The bathing room is just down the hallway here, and the tub will be hot and waiting for you in about thirty minutes. I will knock on your door when it is ready. My name is Sidney, and if there is anything you need, just ring the bell."

Mike took the key from Sidney and walked up the stairs to his room. As he opened the door, he remembered he hadn't retrieved his things from his horse. He was about to turn around and go back downstairs when he spotted his bags sitting in the middle of his bed.

Even though the hotel was new, the rooms were small; but it beat sleeping on the cold, hard ground. He had slept on the ground plenty in his lifetime, but as he got older, a mattress beat out the hard earth any day of the week.

He noticed that a pitcher of water and a bowl were waiting on the sideboard next to the bed. Although he was going to be bathing in a short while, he decided to take the opportunity and shave.

After Mike finished, he wiped his face, and by lamplight, inspected his neck in the mirror. There were no cuts this time. He was getting better; that or his face was becoming used to the razor. Either way, he was satisfied with his shave and plopped onto the bed.

It wasn't long before there was a knock on his door. "Mr. Gilbert, your tub is ready."

"Thank you, Sidney."

Mike found the bathing room and closed the door behind him. The room was barely big enough for the tub and the space to turn around in, but that's all the room he needed. He eagerly peeled off his dirty clothes and slid into the white porcelain tub. He leaned back and sunk into the water until it touched his chin.

"Wait until I tell everyone back home that I paid close to two dollars for a bed and bath," he muttered. The warm bath felt so good that after he had lathered and scrubbed all over, he leaned back in the tub again and the next thing he knew, he was being awakened by a knock at the door.

"Mr. Gilbert … are you okay in there?"

Mike awoke with a start and realized that he had been asleep for quite some time because the water in the tub was already cool. He sat up so fast that he splashed water onto the floor.

"I'm fine … I'll be right out."

He stepped out of the tub, dried off, and dressed. Mike noticed Sidney looking over the top of his glasses at him as he walked past the front desk and headed toward the stairs.

"You're not the first one to do that," Sidney said with a chuckle.

Even though it was a strange place, it didn't take Mike long to fall back to sleep within minutes of snuggling under the covers. He was bathed, he was shorn, and he couldn't wait to see Rush in its full glory under the Ozark sun. He fell asleep thinking of home.

Chapter 6

As William rode his horse down the lane toward the main road, the morning sun was still behind the trees, but the air was already warm, as spring appeared to be rushing toward summer. *The year seems to be warming a little earlier than usual. I'd sure like to get an extra cutting of hay for the winter; we can always use that.* He surveyed the pasture where the boys had removed the exposed stones. With the rocks gone and the fence in good repair, the field looked like it was in good shape.

Riding along, William couldn't help but think about his last conversation with Mike. *I shouldn't have said what I did to Mike. Now he's gone ... I have to fix things with him somehow. Shouldn't take long to iron things out with Clifford ... he knows Mike didn't rob his bank ... should be somethin' to point to who did it.*

Reaching the main road, William turned his horse south toward town, glad to get the sun out of his eyes. He hadn't ridden far before he saw Ed Parker working on a tangled mess of tree and barbed wire just past his own property line.

"Can I give you a hand?"

"I didn't even hear you ride up." Ed straightened his back and wiped the sweat from his forehead.

"I didn't mean to startle you, but it looks like you could use some help."

"I got dad-blame tired of limbs breaking on this old tree and messin' up my fence so I decided to cut 'er down. I don't know how, but it fell the wrong direction, and you can see the mess I'm in."

William couldn't help but chuckle as he examined the tangle of barbed wire lying underneath the oak tree.

"I need to run my cattle in this field, but I have to get this mess cleaned up first. It's gonna take me a while with my back the way it is." Ed bent down to cut some more wire and let out a little moan as he did so. William saw Ed looking at him from the corner of his eye.

It didn't take an education to see that Ed was fishing for some sympathy, so William replaced his grin with a solemn look. He decided to be a little mischievous and have some fun with his neighbor. "I'm so sorry your back is out of sorts, Ed. That will make cuttin' this tree much more difficult."

Not expecting that reply, Ed employed a different tactic. "This gettin' old is for the birds." He placed his hands on the lower part of his back and slowly straightened again, closing his eyes as if in intense pain. "Even my hands can't squeeze these wire cutters like they used to."

William watched Ed flex his fingers as if they were rusty and needed oil. "Rachel has some mighty good liniment that she puts on me whenever I have an ache or pain. I'll see if she can get some over to your wife this afternoon sometime. I'm on my way into town now so it's gonna be a while."

He turned and walked back to his horse. Glancing back, William noticed that Ed looked disappointed to see him go. Although he had to tend to business in town and didn't have time to play with Ed any longer, William was never one to leave someone stranded who needed help, whether they were a neighbor or anyone else.

"Say, Ed," William called out as he settled into the saddle, "I'll have the boys come over first thing in the morning after their chores, and they'll have this all taken care of for you by noon I'm sure. You may have to feed them afterward, though. They get a powerful appetite after cutting wood." He smiled and waved to his neighbor.

Ed's bewilderment turned to a full grin. He returned the wave and dropped his pliers into his wooden tool carrier. He glanced back up again and just shook his head as William continued toward town.

***

After he tied his horse in front of the Kingston bank, William entered the tiny lobby. The bell on the door caused Clifford to turn around on his stool. He was relieved to see someone other than another well-meaning widow woman.

"Morning, William." Clifford leaned close to the barred teller window.

"Clifford."

William couldn't help but notice the ink stains on the wall and floor. *That's quite a mess.* "I'm here to take care of the damages my son caused."

"Well, it's not that bad," Clifford said. "It shouldn't cost too much to fix. A little sandpaper to the floor and some varnish on it, and it'll be good as new I think. I have some leftover wallpaper in the back. Ink's not expensive.

"How much, Cliff?"

"I figure about ten dollars ought to cover everything. I'll have Abraham take care of it. He's pretty handy with such things."

William looked back at the floor and tried to imagine the scene. He reached into his pocket for his wallet, pulled out a ten-dollar bill, and handed it to Cliff.

"If it ends up costing more, let me know, and I'll take care of it."

Clifford took the note from him. "William ... I'm sorry."

"Don't fret yourself. I'm sorry you had to deal with all of this."

"Thank you, William."

So he wouldn't have to continue looking at his friend through the ornate bars, William walked over to the half doorway at the side of the room. "Do you have time to talk about the robbery?"

Clifford left his stool and met William beside the teller window. "There's not much more of anything to say about it. The sheriff came by late yesterday afternoon, and I told him everything I told you. A hooded man came in first thing, grabbed Meryl, and demanded money. I followed him out of the bank and shot twice, hitting him in the leg. That's all there was to it, and it happened just that fast."

"Did you happen to say anything about Mike causing a ruckus in here the day before?"

Clifford raised a hand and scratched behind his ear.

"You didn't tell him that you thought it could be my son, did you, Cliff?"

"Oh, no … no, I didn't at all." Clifford put his hands up and gestured with them. "Eh …" Clifford paused, knowing that what he was about to say next would probably upset William.

"What is it, Cliff?"

"Well, and I don't know why he did this, he noticed the ink mess and asked me about it."

"Well, what did you tell him?"

"Now wait a minute." Clifford began nervously gesturing with his hands again. "All I told him was that I'd had a little problem with a customer the day before but it had been taken care of."

William lowered his head and closed his eyes at the news. He then released a deep sigh and shook his head.

"I wasn't gonna lie, and I tried like the dickens to be evasive, but he kept asking questions."

William looked back up at Clifford, who was quite pale. A trickle of sweat ran down the right side of his face.

"Like what questions?" William furrowed his brow.

Clifford paused again.

"Tell me, Cliff, I need to know."

"He … he asked me what the trouble was about and who'd caused it."

To avoid looking at Clifford, William turned his head sideways. He pursed his lips and sighed again.

Clifford stepped out into the lobby with William. "I told him it was just a misunderstanding, and that in no way did I think your son had anything to do with it. I told him Mike was a good kid and always had been."

William stood there for what seemed like minutes, struggling to contain his emotions. The only sound was the ticking of the grandfather clock.

William finally made the first move by placing his hat onto his head. "Clifford, I need to withdraw my son's money, if you please," William said in a calm and emotionless voice.

Seeing no movement, William looked into Clifford's eyes. He saw there the stun of sadness on his face and knew he was also saddened by the whole affair. "I need it now if you don't mind. I need to get back to the farm."

Swallowing hard, Clifford hesitated for a moment then turned and made his way back to the teller window, where he filled out the withdrawal slip and slid it under the iron bars. As William was signing his name, Clifford counted the $247.00 twice, making sure it was correct, and handed it to William.

"Thanks, Clifford, I'll make sure that he gets this."

With that, William turned and made his way to the door. Pausing in the doorway, he turned back. "If I owe you any more on the repairs just let me know. I'm sure I'll be into town again in the next few days."

Cliff raised his hand and gestured goodbye to his friend.

***

"Good morning, Mr. Gilbert," came a voice from behind William as he untied his horse. When he looked over his shoulder, he saw Meryl walking up to him on the wooden sidewalk.

"Morning, Mrs. Atkins." *I don't have time to talk.*

"It's another perfect morning for being out and about, wouldn't you say? By the way, I haven't seen Rachel in town for a while. How is she doing? We missed her at the quilting two nights ago at Bea's. She's so good with her stitching, and Bea's stitch lines weave all over the place, I'm afraid."

William halfway smiled as she talked, waiting for the breath which would allow him to excuse himself.

"I guess you heard about the robbery the other day. I was so scared and thought I'd seen my last day on earth. I was praying to the good Lord above that if it was my day to go to make it quick …"

There was the pause he had been waiting for. "I'm so glad you weren't hurt, Mrs. Atkins. This community just wouldn't be the same without you around. I'll tell Rachel you said hello and that she's been missed."

Mounting his horse and clicking his tongue, William headed back toward his farm. He turned his head in time to see Meryl disappear into the bank with a basket of cinnamon rolls in her hand. *Just not your day is it, Cliff?* He turned his attention back to the road ahead.

***

The sunlight was sifting through lacy white curtains, sending beams of hazy light into Mike's hotel room. It took him a few seconds after he opened his eyes to remember where he was. He blinked hard a couple of times then wiped the crusty dreams out of his eyes. After a few minutes, he sat up and swung his feet onto the floor. Walking to the sunlit window, Mike pulled back the curtains and smiled as he looked out at what he could see of Rush. There was already activity on the streets.

He dressed as quickly as he could and bounded down the stairs.

"Good morning, Mr. Gilbert. Did you sleep well?"

Although Mike was almost through the front door, he turned to see Sidney at his post. "As soon as my eyes closed, it was time to get up."

"Oh, by the way, your checkout time is noon."

"Thank you, Sidney."

Excitedly, Mike walked through the front door and out onto the porch. He stood there for a few moments soaking up the sunshine and breathing in the fresh morning air. Another spring day was fully awake in Rush.

Supply wagons rolled down the dirt road before him. From not too far away, he heard the hiss of steam and the pounding, grinding noise of heavy machinery. Closer was the sound of a heavy hammer striking an iron anvil. The local blacksmith was already earning his wages.

He stepped down from the porch and into the street. Although the buildings didn't seem to stretch very far in either direction, looking back at the hotel, Mike could see other buildings around and behind it.

He had been so enthusiastic to get started with his day that, at first, he hadn't noticed his belly grumbling. *I need to eat something soon. Surely that little store is open.*

Instead of going to the livery, Mike turned and walked up the street to the store where he had watered Rusty the night before. On the way, he had to step to the side to let a wagon pass with its load of crushed zinc ore. The side of the wagon had the name *Morning Star* burned into it. *Just looks like plain rock to me, but what do I know?* After it passed, he spotted the general and dry goods store across the street, so he crossed and walked up the steps onto the front porch.

Before entering, he took some time to examine the town from where he stood. Looking out, he could see the area around the hotel a little more clearly. A short, white picket fence ran quite a ways on either side of the hotel then turned and made its way to the back. Because of the trees and vines blocking the view, he couldn't see where the fence stopped. It looked like there were several buildings located inside the perimeter of the fence, as if it were some sort of compound. Even though it had weeds sprouting in it, the fence made a nice little border. Mike wondered how far back the fence went and what businesses were inside.

The porch he stood on ran the width of the storefront, its support columns covered by leafy vines tangling up to the fascia. The building was constructed of wood, with some rock at the bottom of the supports. Mike noticed an old dish at one end of the porch. *Must be a dog around here somewhere.* Looking around, he didn't see one, so he entered the store.

Inside was a fairly large room, stocked with hardware and tools of all sorts. He didn't even recognize some of the implements, so he assumed they were mining tools. In front of him, but at the other end of the room, stood a big black woodstove with metal piping going up and through the ceiling. A small table in front of the stove supported a checkerboard game. Chairs on opposite sides of it, scooted back a little, invited someone to come and play. He noticed a counter off to one side and next to it a doorway that seemed to lead into the dry goods and grocery area.

Mike walked slowly around the dimly lit room and examined the tools hanging on and leaning against the walls. Some of the boards under his feet creaked as he walked, reminding him of the post office floor back in Kingston. *Seems I can't do much of anything without being reminded of home.*

"Could I help you with something, young man?" A woman's voice called out from behind him.

Mike turned to see the question coming from a tall, plump lady standing in the doorway that led into the grocery side. "Morning, ma'am."

"Morning, yerself. Haven't seen you before; you must have just gotten into town."

"Late last night." Mike took a few steps toward her.

The lady grinned at the news. "So what do you think?"

"Think of what?"

"Of our little town here, full of hustle and bustle."

"Oh—well I haven't seen much so far." Mike removed his hat.

"Have ya eaten?"

Mike placed a hand onto his stomach. "Actually I haven't, and I'm feelin' starved."

"I got a table in here if you want some eggs and bacon."

"I'm so hungry I could eat anything you put in front of me."

"I'll throw in some coffee. The whole thing will cost you only two bits."

Mike followed her through the doorway and into the grocery section of the store, amazed at how many canned goods and packaged items there were. He was tempted to grab a pickle out of the barrel on his way back to the food counter but decided against it when he caught a whiff of frying bacon.

"Have a sit down and I'll be right back with your food. Oh, by the way, I'm Rosie, but some folks call me Rose. Either one will work."

"I'm Mike Gilbert from Kingston over in …"

Rosie interrupted. "I know where Kingston is. I've been through there several times. Not much of a town, though. More like a community than anything else. Am I right?"

She was right, but Mike was a little offended—it sounded like Rosie was belittling his hometown. "It may be small, but I like it."

As she made her way back to the iron skillets on the wood cook stove, Rosie turned her head. "Didn't mean anything by that darlin', just makin' an observation."

Mike looked around the room while Rosie checked the bacon and retrieved some eggs from a wire basket. His back to Mike, a lone man wearing suit pants and a matching vest, seated at the only other table, read a copy of the *Mountain Echo* newspaper. .

"I'll be right there with your coffee," Rosie said.

At the same time, Mike heard the front door open and, from his vantage point, saw a couple of men enter.

"Beth, I need you at the stove," Rosie shouted. She left the stove to attend the two men. A second lady, obviously Beth, appeared from a doorway next to the stove and kept an eye on the bacon. Seeing it was about ready, she reached for the eggs.

"Are these eggs for you?" Beth asked Mike.

"Yes, and the bacon, too."

"You want your eggs scrambled or fried?"

"What do you fry them in?" His mother always fried eggs in bacon grease and, without bacon grease, he just preferred them scrambled.

"Bacon grease, of course." "I'll take four fried, then, and leave the middles a little runny."

Without saying another word, Beth went to work on the eggs. The smell of bacon and eggs was making Mike's belly growl something fierce. He could hardly wait.

"Can I have a biscuit or two for the eggs?" Mike hoped there were some in a basket somewhere behind the counter.

Beth set the food down in front of Mike. "Coffee, four eggs, bacon, and biscuits. You've got quite an appetite this morning."

"It was a long trip gettin' here."

"Beth take care of you, boy?" Rosie walked back into the room. Mike had his mouth already stuffed with a large bite of egg and a good-sized chunk of biscuit. He tried to respond but couldn't, so he quickly raised his coffee to his mouth to wash the food down. When he burned his lips, Rosie laughed.

"Could I have a glass of water, please?" He mumbled through his food-filled mouth.

Still chuckling, Rosie set the glass of water on the table, and, although it was too late, Mike drank enough to clear his mouth and temporarily soothe his pain.

"Guess I should slow down." The other patron folded his paper and left thirty-five cents on his table. Without a word, he walked out of the room and through the front door.

"He's a friendly fella." Mike and Rosie watched the front door close.

"He never says much. He's been in town for about a week. I think he's from up north and down here checking up on the Morning Star."

Mike took another drink of water and finished his breakfast.

"I think we're done with breakfasts for the day, Beth," Rosie said. "You can start cleanin' up now."

Beth began carrying the skillets and utensils through the narrow doorway and into a room out of sight.

Rosie seated herself in the other chair at Mike's table. "If you don't mind me askin', what's a nice looking kid like you doing here by his self all the way from Kingston?"

Usually, Mike didn't like personal intrusions, but there was something about Rosie that made him feel comfortable. He was beginning to like her, so he swallowed the bacon he was chewing and replied. "My parents have a big farm north of Kingston, and I've been workin' it all of my life. I realized I wanted to do something else besides farm, so I left and came here."

Rosie cocked her head sideways and looked at Mike for a few seconds while he sipped on his cooling coffee. "But what made you come to Rush, son?"

With his last bite of biscuit, Mike sopped the runny yolk off his plate and popped the piece into his mouth. "I read an article in a paper."

"You came all the way over here after simply readin' a story in a paper?"

"I figured this would be a great place to find a job and a little excitement."

"Honey, this place is about as excitin' as a turtle fight in the winter. Nothin' much ever happens around here. The county's dry, and, without liquor around, you won't find very much excitement." Rosie chuckled again.

Mike removed the cloth napkin from the neck of his shirt, where he had stuffed it, and dropped it onto the table. "I figured I'd get a mining job to start with."

"What do you know about minin', farm boy?" Rosie began to laugh again. Mike frowned.

"Nothin' yet, but I can learn and I'm a hard worker. I could outwork my brothers any day of the week."

62

"Well, that'll get you about twenty-five cents an hour, and, if you don't kill yerself in the mines or plumb wear yerself out, you might just get to spend it."

Mike hadn't even thought about the danger of mining, but he wasn't going to let Rosie know that she was getting under his skin. "First I have to find a place to live; then I'll look for work. Know of any place to rent around here?"

"That paper must not have said anything about living quarters in these parts. Most of the miners have to live in makeshift hovels or shanties. They use whatever materials they can find or afford because there ain't many houses or rooms around here to let. Sorry to burst your bubble, farm boy."

Even though he liked Rosie, he'd had about enough of being called farm boy this morning. He dug into his pocket, pulled out a quarter, and laid it on the table.

"Bein' this is your first day here, breakfast is on the house. Rosie displayed an infectious smile on her face. "Keep your quarter. I have a feeling yer gonna need it."

That comment didn't make Mike feel very good. He was beginning to get the feeling that things might not go as smoothly as he had hoped, but he was determined not to let Rosie dash his spirit.

"I've got a room I let, back behind the store, but it's occupied now. I live upstairs. I've been thinkin about adding a couple more rooms, but since my husband died two years ago, I haven't gotten around to it."

"I'm sorry for your loss."

"Yeah, well, I loved the man, but we didn't get along too good. Been kind of nice not to hear all the yellin' I got from him. I do miss him sometimes, I suppose ... the rest of the time I'm awake." Rosie let out a whoop, followed by deep laughter, at her own joke. Mike felt uncomfortable but allowed himself to laugh along with her.

As Rosie was winding down from her belly laugh, he stood. "Thanks for the breakfast."

"I sure hope you find a decent place and some good work. I like you, Mike, and I hope I see you around here often."

Rosie stood along with Mike. Just then, a loud steam whistle blew from a distance and pierced the air. Immediately, Rosie stopped laughing and became deadly serious, turning her head toward the east window. Mike noticed the sudden change in her demeanor and could tell that the blowing of the whistle wasn't good.

He followed Rosie into the hardware side of the store, and, before he could even ask the question, she said, "Oh good Lord above, there's been an accident."

Chapter 7

The Morning Star Zinc Mill was in total chaos. The rock crusher had been stopped and a large boiler was releasing a massive amount of steam into the air. Curious about the disaster that had just occurred, a crowd of workers gathered around the machinery.

A call came from the middle of the crowd. "Someone get Doc Lipscomb." Two men on the outside of the group immediately left to fetch the doctor, who was hopefully in his office directly behind the Morning Star Hotel.

"Give me a little room here." Another voice came from outside the crowd. The group of men parted as Jacob Harrison, manager of the Morning Star Mill, made his way into the center of the group.

Harrison looked down at Leon, who was attending a severely injured man on the floor. "What happened?"

"He got his arm caught in one of the belts."

Harrison knelt down to survey the arm, which was severed at the elbow. Although Leon applied pressure to the arm, by the look of things, the injured worker had already lost a considerable amount of blood, and he had lost consciousness.

"You men go back to what you were doing." The manager waved away the onlookers. "You can't help and the doc will be here shortly."

Aware that it would probably be too late by the time the doctor arrived, Harrison looked back at the man on the brick floor. In an attempt to help with the blood loss, he removed his leather belt and made a tourniquet on the man's arm just below his shoulder.

Pulling it tight, he looked up at Leon, who had done his best to help. They both realized there was nothing more either of them could do. Leon's face was pale from the experience, and Harrison could see the pain in his eyes because of the co-worker on the floor.

"Doc's on his way!"

The proclamation caused Harrison to turn in anticipation. He kept an eye on the doorway for a few seconds then turned his attention back to the injured worker. He continued to hold pressure with his belt. It was about that time he realized the man was no longer breathing. He leaned his head to the man's chest and checked for a pulse. Slowly, he stood and looked at Leon. He didn't have to say a word because, by the look on Harrison's face, Leon knew the man was gone.

Dr. Lipscomb ran through the doorway and toward them with his medical bag. Harrison turned to greet the doctor. "Wasn't anything could be done. By the time I got here it was already too late."

Dr. Lipscomb looked down at the man and released a heavy sigh. "I'll send Samson over to fetch him. Then he looked at Leon. "Is there anyone to notify?"

"He's here alone. I don't think he has any family … least not that I hear."

He looked back over at his co-worker lying on the floor. "You mind if I take a walk, Mr. Harrison?"

"Go clear your head, but we need to get this machinery running again as soon as possible."

Leon motioned to a friend, and the pair left the mill.

***

Mike left Rosie's store and walked back to the hotel, where he paid Sidney another dollar fifty for one more night. He figured that if he couldn't find any place to live after one more day, he would do like so many of the other miners and build a shelter until he could do better. He also decided he would go to the Morning Star Mill the next day, after everything had settled down, to talk with a manager or someone who might possibly help him with a job.

Although his dream wasn't beginning as he had anticipated, he also knew it would take some time to get settled into a new place. For now, he would do a little exploring and become familiar with this area he would call home. He didn't know how long he would be exploring, so he headed back to Rosie's for some cheese, soda crackers, beef jerky, and maybe even a couple of pickles. He walked onto the porch, reaching for the door handle, just as Leon and his friend exited, almost knocking him over. After the pair passed, he went inside to find Rosie with a distressed look on her face. He hadn't known her for long, but her sadness was unmistakable.

"Rosie, are you okay?"

"Mike, twice in one day." She tried to smile.

"I was going to do some explorin' and thought I'd get some food to take with me. What's wrong?"

Rosie was silent for a few seconds. "You still lookin' for a place to stay?"

Surprised by her question, Mike answered her. "Sure. Haven't had time to look yet, but I can't afford to stay in the hotel much longer; why?"

"A place just became available, if you're interested."

"Right now I'd take anything. Where is it?"

She turned her back to him and began arranging product on the shelves. "My place behind the store, here."

"Your place? I thought it was occupied."

There was silence as Mike waited for a response from Rosie. With her back still to him, she continued to arrange a shelf, and then she stopped and turned back around. "There was an accident at the mill today." She paused. "Vernon Dobbs died while working the crusher. He was the one renting from me." She paused again and sighed. "If you want it, it's yours. He didn't have any family, so I'll just move most of his things out and store them until I can figure out what to do with 'em. Give me until tomorrow though."

Mike didn't quite know how to respond to the news. It was both tragic and a blessing for him at the same time. He stood and pondered what she had said for a few moments.

"Thank you, Rosie, and I'm … sorry to hear about Vernon. I'll need to find a job, though, if I'm going to be able to stay for long."

She tried to muster a pleasant look on her face. "The room's fifteen dollars a month. I'm sure I'll have to clean the place. Vernon wasn't the neatest man in the world, but I shore liked him—everybody did. He's gonna be missed."

"Would you like some help with the room?"

"Naww honey, you go do what you were gonna do today. I'll get it done and ready by tomorrow afternoon. There's something I need to tend to now, so Beth will have to help you with your food."

With that, Rosie walked out the front door, and Mike watched her walk in the direction of the mill. He paid Beth for his groceries and packed them into his saddlebag. Though it was at the expense of a man's life, Mike couldn't help but be excited at the turn of events that had now given him a place to live. The only thing left was finding a job. Hopefully he could find one soon somewhere in this town.

Though the day had been tainted by disaster, the sun was still shining and birds were unaware of the day's events. Mike turned Rusty toward the Buffalo River, anxious to see what the water looked like this far downstream. After that, he didn't know where he would go, but, all things considered, it seemed to be a perfect day for exploring.

As he neared the Buffalo River, he traveled along Rush Creek, which gave the town its name. It was a narrow, but beautiful, stream nestled into a rocky creek bed. Mighty oaks, maples, and tall sycamore trees leaned from the creek bank, creating an ever-present shade over the water. Wild grape vines slithered their way up the tree trunks, their tendrils hanging low in long bows below the canopy, as if being grabbed and pulled down toward the earth by some unseen hand. Filling the space under the trees, the undergrowth of various plants created thick greenery, interrupted by blossoms that the sparse spring rains had brought to life.

The day was getting hot and Mike's forehead began to sweat under his hat. As he neared the river, he detected the distinctive odor of soured mud, combined with a fish smell, reminding him of the King's River back home. Rounding a slight bend in the road, he saw the river through the trees in front of him. The road then descended to the Buffalo River. It was a beautiful sight.

Mike dismounted Rusty where Rush Creek infused itself into the Buffalo then stood in awe as he looked out across the water. The river wasn't as wide as he had expected, but it was still clear and clean. He took off his boots and stepped into Rush Creek then let out a sudden whoop. "Dang that's cold!" *Gotta be spring fed.*

As he stood in the water, covered by the shade of trees, he soaked in his view of the Buffalo. He knew that the upper part of the river was floatable only by flat-bottom boats during periods of rain, but he thought about what an adventure it would be to take on the whole river from start to finish. Maybe someday he would make the attempt. For right now, it was just a fanciful dream.

Although it would be more than brisk, the thought flew through his head to jump in for a swim. He didn't entertain the thought for long, though, and told the river that he would be back some day soon to play in her inviting water—when it warmed.

Mike decided it was time to break out the food he'd brought and get a jump on his hunger. After sitting down and putting his damp feet back into his boots, he stood and thought he caught the sound of a man's voice down the river a short distance from him. The wind was lightly blowing, rustling the leaves, but he continued to listen. There … he heard it again. He didn't know if there were any mines down this close to the water's edge, but he decided to investigate. Tethering Rusty in the shade by the creek, he made his way along a slightly used path which paralleled the riverbank. Now he was close enough to the voice to hear what was being said. As he listened, he realized it wasn't a conversation someone was having but … it sounded as if someone were giving a sermon.

Continuing to stand in silence, Mike listened to the speaker talk as if speaking to a congregation. The would-be preacher threw in Bible verses that were terribly misquoted; his voice warbled and varied in loudness and pitch as he tried to make his sermon points. Even though the speaker was just beyond some rocks out of his sight, Mike gave his presence away when he began laughing. He couldn't contain himself as he heard the man tell his invisible church that Noah led the Ishmaelites from bondage out of the Promised Land.

With that, the speaker stopped.

"Who's there?" Mike heard from the other side of the rock outcropping.

Trying to contain his rude snickering, Mike stepped around the rocks to see a young man, about his own age, wearing overalls with no shirt and standing in front of what seemed to be a mine entrance. The boy looked at Mike with surprise and frustration at the interruption.

"I'm sorry. I really didn't mean to interrupt."

"This is my place. You shouldn't be here. This is my place." The boy continued repeating his words.

Mike realized that there was something not quite right with this boy, and, in an instant, the boy seemed to become embarrassed that Mike had been listening to his sermon. Mike took a step backwards to give the boy some room and not crowd his space.

"No one comes to my place. This is my place."

The boy clutched a tattered book. *He must be pretending that's a Bible.* "I'm sorry." Mike backed away a little farther. He turned and walked around the rocks and out of the boy's view. *Looks like I found one of the town's local characters.* He smiled as he made his way back down the little path.

Returning to where he'd tethered Rusty, Mike removed some food from the saddlebag and figured he would sit in the shade to eat his lunch. He thought about his odd encounter with preacher boy as he took the first bite of his pickle. The juice squirted and ran down his chin. As he wiped his mouth with the back of his sleeve, he heard a voice from behind him.

"Did you like it?"

Mike turned to see preacher boy standing between him and the river.

"Did I like what?" He knew what the boy meant, but he thought it would give him a little more time to come up with a polite answer.

"What I was sayin' up there at that old mine." The boy talked with a slight speech impediment.

"Well, you really had me listening to what you were sayin', that's for sure."

At that, the boy smiled from ear to ear, obviously pleased with what he took as a compliment. The pair continued to stand there in silence for a few seconds then Mike spoke. "What's your name?"

"I'm Charley!"

"I'm Mike; nice to meet you Charley. Do you live down here by the river?"

"Shoot, no. I live up in town. I just come down here to clear my brain. Sometimes I just have to come down here to clear my brain because it gets so full of stuff."

Mike noticed Charley looking at the pickle in his hand. He looked down at his half-eaten pickle then back at Charley.

"Say, Charley, care to have some lunch with me?"

Charley stood there for a moment, rubbing his big toes over each other in the powdery dirt.

"I've got plenty," Mike said.

"Whatcha got?"

"A little jerky, cheese, and soda crackers. I even have another pickle if you'd like it."

"I ain't had a pickle in a spell. I had a hankerin' for one but ain't had one."

"Well, here," Mike said, as he turned to get the rest of the food out of the saddlebag. When he turned around,

Charley was practically in his face. Slightly startled, Mike took a step back and smiled.

"Here you go." Mike handed the pickle to Charley.

Without saying a word, Charley accepted the gift. He took one bite, lifted the pickle up to the sky, and began dancing around.

"I guess that means you like it." Mike began laughing. He watched Charley spin around in circles, as if the pickle was the best thing he had ever tasted in his life.

"Want any soda crackers or cheese? How 'bout some jerky?"

Charley simply ignored Mike as he continued his happy dance and got farther and farther away. Soon, he stopped twirling and began walking briskly up the road toward town. Before he was out of sight, Charley turned his head and looked at Mike with a big grin, still clutching the last bite of pickle. He disappeared over the hill and left Mike standing in the shade beside his horse in complete bewilderment.

"Well, that was interesting," he said to Rusty, who had no idea what he was talking about.

Mike finished his lunch uninterrupted and threw a few rocks into the Buffalo before heading back into town. It was mid afternoon, but he wanted to do some exploring in town, since he hadn't seen the whole place in the daylight.

***

As Mike reached the hotel, the afternoon was beginning to cool. Reaching a narrow lane between the hotel and the livery stable, Mike turned Rusty into it and made his way up the hill. He had just passed the livery when he noticed a tall square structure looming in front of him in the lane. From his vantage point it looked like an oversized chimney, standing rigid as a sentinel guarding its prisoner. The lane bypassed the structure to the left, and Mike took his time to inspect the rock and mortar creation as he rode past. It had several openings on the lower part, but he was confused as to what this lonely structure could be. He would certainly have to satisfy his curiosity by asking a local.

He could see several buildings ahead of him as he continued along the white picket fence that surrounded the hotel and other structures. Finally, he could see the end of the fence, where it cut back to the left. In the distance he noticed billows of steam above the treetops and a mechanical sound which grew louder as he neared. Immediately across the street to his left was a building with a sign on it that identified it as the Morning Star Store. It now dawned on Mike that he was in the middle of the Morning Star holdings in Rush. Since the Morning Star Hotel was within the enclosure, he figured that the buildings within the white fence probably belonged to the Morning Star Mine also.

Before following the little road to the left, he looked to his right and could now clearly see the Morning Star Mill and a few of the mines on the bare hillside. Columns of steam were exiting the building from two tall pipes on the main building, and the mechanical sound was much louder from where he sat.

A woman with two small children exited from the Morning Star Store and caught his attention. The lady was struggling both with her bundle and two young children who seemed to have desires to chase butterflies rather than stay close to her. Seeing her difficulty, Mike rode over to the three—the lady scolding the young boy, who seemed to be doing a great job ignoring her.

"Afternoon, ma'am." Mike caught the lady off guard.

"Howdy, mister!" The young boy exclaimed.

"Can I help carry your groceries for you? Looks like you could use a hand."

"I could use three hands." The reply was accompanied by a tired smile.

Mike reached down, and she handed him her cloth bag of meager supplies, which allowed her to hold onto the hands of her young ones.

"I'm much obliged to you, mister." The three walked briskly to keep up with Mike on his horse.

Mike thought that the woman was about thirty, yet she seemed tired and walked as if she carried a heavy burden on her shoulders.

"You can just call me Mike."

"I'm Esther, this is Laura, and ..."

She was interrupted by her uninhibited son.

"I'm Chase," the little blond-headed boy piped up as he began skipping while still holding onto his mother's hand.

"Chase, don't be rude."

Chase pretended not to hear her as he continued to skip.

"It's not far, now, just around the corner and to the right."

Within a couple of minutes they reached the place Esther called home, one of the canvas and wood shacks Mike had seen on his way into town. It was tidy but minimal and had just enough covering and walls to keep out the rain and allow for some privacy.

Desiring to be proper, Mike remained on Rusty, and as soon as Esther let go of the little hands, he handed the sack to her. He tipped his hat to her and turned his horse. "Much obliged," she said again as he rode back into town.

With the shadows growing longer, Mike went back by Rosie's with a mind to purchase a few more items to eat in his room for supper. He also wanted to buy some writing supplies to let everyone back home know where he was, and that he was doing fine.

Rosie's store was busy when he walked inside. Looking around for her but not spotting her, Mike browsed until he found a small pad of paper and a pencil. He figured a pencil would be better than messing with ink; it was also cheaper.

On the grocery side Mike picked up a can of beans and had Beth cut him a wedge of cured ham. He still had some soda crackers left from lunch, so with that, he figured he would be just fine for the night.

"Where's Rosie?"

"She's been gone all afternoon." Beth wiped her forehead with her sleeve. "Ain't no tellin' where she is."

"Would you tell her I'll be back tomorrow, sometime in the afternoon?"

Beth smiled. "I will if I can remember." She handed Mike his purchase and made her way to the next waiting customer.

He pocketed the change and headed back to the front door. Before leaving the store, he looked around for Rosie one last time but didn't see her, so he left and walked Rusty back to the livery before returning to his room.

When Mike entered his hotel room, the first thing he did was light the oil lamp. As the flame flickered to life, he lowered the glass globe into place and raised the wick a little to give a brighter light to the room. He carried the lamp over to the writing desk and set it down, leaving barely enough room for his tablet. Since the desk was in front of the window, he pulled back the curtains and opened it. Taking a deep breath, Mike let the cool evening breeze fill his lungs, and he inhaled the sweetness of honeysuckle now filling his room. The tree frogs and crickets played a familiar melody as he pulled the chair out and sat at the desk. Once again he thought about home and about what his family would be doing at this time of day.

He stared at the blank paper on the desk and picked up the pencil to write, but, for some reason, he had trouble putting together the words that he had thought would come easily. He wanted to tell his family that he was alright, and that he had made it to his destination, but he desired it to be more than about him arriving. There was so much he wanted to say, but he knew that if he wrote all that was on his mind it might get jumbled up; he wanted his first letter to be perfect. He still didn't know what to think about Rush, but it felt right to be in this strange place.

Thinking about what he would write, Mike supported his head with his left hand while his elbow rested on the table. With his right hand, he played with the pencil. He closed his eyes and replayed the last few days in his head, trying to unscramble his thoughts and make sense of what he wanted to say.

Chapter 8

Mike awoke with faint sunlight streaming onto his face. He lifted his head from the desk and realized that he had slept all night with his head on crossed arms, and they were asleep. He pulled his arms off the desktop and let them hang at his sides. Leaning back in the chair, he blinked a few times and noticed that the lamp was still burning but had little oil left in the reservoir. He also looked at his writing tablet rereading the words he had penned before nodding off. It was what he wanted to say.

Finally, his arms were awake enough to move them. He blew out the lamp, folded the paper, placed it in an envelope, and tucked it into his shirt pocket then walked over to the bowl and pitcher sitting on the sideboard beside his bed to freshen up.

It was still early, but Mike decided that, after eating, his first order of business for the day would be to buy some more clothing and get the ones he was wearing laundered. He had never washed his own clothes before and didn't want to start now, so he hoped he could find a launderer. Since he had fallen asleep after writing the previous night, he remembered he still had food that he hadn't eaten, so at least he had breakfast taken care of.

Downstairs, Mike exchanged salutations with Sidney at the desk then walked out into the early morning. The town was bathed in a thin fog, which gave it a ghostly appearance. In the near distance he heard the hiss of steam as the Morning Star Mill began its day.

He rubbed his face, and, though he could feel his whiskers growing, they were still fine and light enough that he felt presentable. Deciding to pay Mr. Harrison a visit at the mill and hopefully find work, Mike walked to the livery to get Rusty. Although he hadn't asked, Mike hoped he could find another stable for his horse, one which would not be too expensive. Rather then mount up, he walked Rusty down the narrow lane past the big rock structure—which he still was curious about—then turned right at the end of the white fence, leading him to the mill.

The mill was full of activity when he entered through a doorway that had a sign above it saying: Office. The first thing he noticed was the loud sound of the machinery gearing up to crush the stone that was already being loaded into the hoppers.

A man walking by in overalls and with grease-stained hands noticed Mike. "What do you want?"

"I'm looking for Mr. Harrison." Mike raised his voice to be heard.

"Who wants him?" .

"Name's Mike, and I'm looking for work."

"Mr. Harrison don't hire; you want Mr. Riley." The greasy man walked away and back into the mill.

Mike mumbled, looking around the dusty room. "I wonder how I find Mr. Riley."

He was about to follow the greasy man into the mill when the door behind him opened and two men walked in.

"Who are you?" One of the men clenched a pipe in his mouth.

Mike held out a hand because he could tell from their attire that the two were more than just workers. "I'm Mike Gilbert and I'm looking for work."

Ignoring his outstretched hand, the two continued on past him.. That irritated Mike as he lowered his hand back to his side..

Before the two disappeared into the Mill, still ignoring him, Mike tried again.

"I'm looking for Mr. Riley." "I'm Riley." The one with the pipe muttered something to the other man, and, with a nod, he left Riley and disappeared into the mill.

Riley reached up and pulled the pipe from his mouth. "Ever worked in a mine or a mill, Gilbert?"

"I never have sir, but I'm a hard worker."

78

Riley looked at Mike from head to foot, crossing his arms in front of him. "I don't need anyone right now. I got all the workers I need. You might try some of the mines in the area."

When Riley turned to walk into the mill, Mike stopped him. "Mr. Riley, isn't there anything I can do?"

"I told you kid, I don't need anyone right now." With that, he left Mike standing in the room by himself with only the noise for company.

Mike left the room and drifted back out into the morning. Since he didn't know anyone here, with the exception of Rosie and the strange Charley he had met down by the river, Mike headed back toward the store to see if Rosie was in this morning and prod her for information. Surely someone could use some help in the mines. He wasn't going to let one rejection discourage him. He had just passed the Morning Star Hotel when he noticed a group of young men in a cluster over to one side of the street. As he approached, he could tell that there was trouble, and quickly made his way over to see what was going on.

As he got to the group, he could see that two were in the middle of the cluster, and one of them was Charley. He stood at the outside of the circle for a few moments trying to figure out what it was all about when he recognized the other one. *Jay Finch ... you seem to be the town trouble maker.*

"Hey, Charley, why don't you try to take it from me?" Mike heard Jay's taunt.

He noticed Jay holding a toad up in the air with his left hand, keeping it away from Charley. The look on Charley's face was one of both anger and fear as he lunged at the toad in Jay's hand.

"He's too slow. He thinks slow, too. I bet Charley's retarded."

Then Mike heard several of the boys laughing at Charley as he continued to lunge for the toad. Mike watched Jay put his hand out and push Charley away, laughing as Charley became more adamant. Finally, Charley made one huge lunge. Finch backed up and stuck his foot out, tripping

79

Charley and causing him to fall into the crowd. The others immediately pushed him back into the center of the circle.

Mike had seen enough, so he pulled two of the boys away from the outside of the group, sending them crashing to the ground in stunned silence. Charley and Jay saw the commotion at the same time, and Charley took the opportunity to grab the toad. In an instant, Mike burst into the center of the circle between Charley and his tormentor.

"Leave him alone, Jay." This time he faced Jay in the misty morning light.

Finch just smiled and looked around at the group. "Looks like we got someone here who likes retarded people."

The others began to laugh.

Mike heard a commotion from behind him, and he turned to see two boys grab Charley, causing him to drop his toad. Before Mike could say anything or react, the toad made some hops toward him. Jay took a couple of steps and placed his boot on the toad, mashing him into the street. Charley released a painful cry as the group began laughing again, still holding tightly onto him.

"Jason Finch, if I remember correctly," Mike looked into the eyes of the toad squasher with controlled anger.

"You got a good memory for a farm boy."

"Like I said, let him go and leave him alone."

Mike heard Charley moaning behind him as Finch took a step forward, his smile turning into a smirk.

"Oh … are you going to save the stupid boy?" Finch dared Mike to react.

That's all it took. Without warning, Mike made the first swing, and his blow hit its mark exactly on Jay's chin, sending him down fast into the dirt. The group erupted in excitement, releasing Charley, and some of them came at Mike. With a couple of blows, Mike had punched two others before anyone could lay a hand on him, and they went down. Someone grabbed his arms from behind, but it only allowed him to raise his feet and put both of them into the chest of an oncoming attacker. When he pushed, he and the boy behind him fell to the street, and his weight knocked the wind out of the boy. In an instant, Mike was up, and, with four boys on the ground or holding themselves in pain, he stood there daring anyone to come at him. Suddenly, he was plowed into from the side by Finch, who had gathered himself enough to lunge at him, and the pair fell to the ground. With Finch still a little dazed by the chin punch, it didn't take long for Mike to push him off and stand up, but Finch lunged again, and, as he did, Mike sidestepped and kneed him in the face, sending him backward and back onto the ground. Another boy came at Mike, but, before he had time to swing, a loud metallic clang rang out. Everyone turned to see Charley standing outside of the circle with a man who wielded two long pieces of black iron rods in his hands.

"I know how to use these if anyone wants to try me."

The group was quiet for a moment then finally began moving away, picking up their hats from the dusty street. One of them helped Finch up, as he was holding onto his bloody face. When he got to his feet, Finch looked at Mike and then at Charley.

"This ain't over."

Mike took a couple of steps and picked up his own hat out of the dirt. As he walked over to Charley and his friend, he dusted himself off.

With the crowd gone, Charley went to where his toad lay dead in the street and knelt down to examine it; he began to cry.

The other man lowered the rods and put both of them in his left hand." I'm Douglas Sprouse." He held his hand out.

"Mike Gilbert." Mike took the offered hand, wincing at the pain in his left side and at Doug's grip.

The pair looked at Charley, who was grieving over his toad.

"I'm glad you came when you did." Mike looked back at Doug.

Doug grinned. "Looked like you were holdin' your own."

"We need to have a funeral." Charley said through sniffles.

Doug walked over to Charley and put his hand on his shoulder. "Charley, we're not having a funeral, but I'll help you bury him."

Charley remained crouched, looking at his toad. "Can we do it now?"

"I'll help you do it before it gets dark. I have orders to fill at the shop. You go find a box for him and I'll help you later."

"Promise?"

"Promise." Doug turned back to Mike, who was standing in silence taking it all in.

"He's lucky he has a friend like you."

"Well, actually, I'm his brother. Charley and I live behind my blacksmith shop in a little place I built on to it. It's not much, but its home."

"You're a good brother." Mike placed his hat back onto his head. "He's not all ..." Mike didn't know how to continue.

"Charley's a little different. I have to get back to the shop, but why don't you come by for dinner tonight? How do beans and cornbread sound?"

Mike couldn't pass up an invitation like that. "I'll be there."

With that, Doug turned and headed back in the direction of the blacksmith shop. After a few steps he turned back. "Come on, Charley."

Charley scooped up the squashed toad and carried him in both hands to where Doug stood. The two of them hurried up the road and into the shop.

Things just get better all the time. Mike headed in the direction of Rosie's store. As he walked, he began thinking about his work situation again, but smiled knowing he at least had a place to live. He knew something would turn up.

He had been raised in a Christian home, where he had been taught to have faith in God and faith that God would take care of him. Though he had learned it, it was difficult to live it. He decided to do his best to not worry. After all, God had taken care of him so far.

Chapter 9

When Mike walked into her store, Rosie was talking to three miners. She glanced at him and winked to let him know she noticed his presence. While she was chatting and taking money for the new lanterns they were purchasing, Mike browsed the shelves and came across a kitchen gadget that he recognized as an apple peeler.

Immediately, it reminded him of late summer days of picking apples from their trees and the many hours his mother worked in the kitchen cutting the fruit and preserving it. Some of the apples she would slice and dry into fruit leather. Some she would core; cut into rings; and cook with cinnamon, sugar, and red food coloring. Then she'd preserve them in jars with the cinnamon syrup. But his favorite was when she would preserve apple pie filling in quart-sized Mason jars for her famous apple pies, which she made in the dead of winter. He closed his eyes and remembered the sweet cinnamon aroma as it had danced throughout the house.

The door jingled, and Mike turned to see Rosie standing behind the counter, placing money into the till drawer. She looked up and Mike smiled.

"Ready to see your room, hon?"

"You mean it's ready? I didn't come expecting it until this afternoon. I just thought I'd see if you knew of any work available. I figured if anyone knew of work you would."

"Well, now … I don't know how to take that, Mr. Gilbert, but I'll give you the benefit of the doubt and believe that you aren't accusing me of being a nosy busybody." Rosie walked toward the front of the store, motioning with her arm. "Come on."

Laughing, he followed her through the door and onto the wooden porch. The front porch the side of the building going all the way to the back, where there was another doorway and a set of wooden steps leading down off the porch. Rosie opened the door, which looked like a back door to the store, and ushered Mike inside. What he saw was minimal living quarters, but decent indeed. The room was about fifteen feet square. To his left was a bed with an iron headboard and footboard. It was already dressed and ready to sleep in. To his right was a potbellied wood stove with a small stack of split wood beside it. A small table with two chairs sat under a window next to the doorway, and on the opposite wall, between the bed and the woodstove, was a small countertop with a sink and, of all things, a pump for water. When he noticed the pump and realized he wouldn't have to carry water from outside, Mike smiled at Rosie.

"It's a nice room, kid. Most people here don't have indoor water."

"This will be dandy."

"I thought you'd like it. You'll have to gather and split your own wood and keep the sheets washed yourself. I'm not a laundry service."

"I can manage just fine."

"You'll be wantin' a few things I'm sure, so whatever you get from the store I'll let you pay out, since you're just gettin your feet under ya. This is your place now, so you can come and go as you please."

Mike wanted to hug her for providing such a nice place, but, instead, he held back and shook hands with her to seal the deal.

"The rent's due on the first day of every month, and if you're late, I'll throw you out on your back side." She winked, but Mike knew she was probably serious about tardiness of rent money. They left the room and walked back into the store.

"By the way, you were askin' for work around here, weren't ya?"

"Yeah, I already stopped by the Morning Star and Mr. Riley said they weren't hiring right now."

Rosie rolled her eyes. "Oh poo, boy. They always need help of some kind. He just didn't want to mess with it right now. He must have been busy. Try it again; I'm sure they'll have something."

Mike didn't want to be a pest, but if that's what it was going to take, then he'd just keep badgering Mr. Riley until he got a job ... any job. He desperately needed to earn money.

"They said that Mr. Harrison didn't do any hiring himself."

"Is that so?" Rosie closed her eyes to a narrow slit. "Mr. Harrison fires, so he's just as capable of hiring. You get yourself back over to the Morning Star and tell Harrison that Rosie said to give you a job. He owes me a favor or two."

Mike was about to question Rosie about her advice when the front door of the store opened, and in walked the prettiest girl Mike had ever seen. As she walked toward them, he felt like his heart was going to beat out of his chest.

"Well, good morning, Miss Pamela. We was just talkin' about your daddy this very minute." Rosie held out her arms for a hug. The two embraced as if they were long lost friends reuniting after years of separation.

Mike stood silent as the pair separated; then Pam looked over at Mike and smiled.

"Pam, we have a new boy in town. This here is Mike Gilbert from Kingston over in Madison County."

"Pleased to meet you." Pam held out a hand.

Mike took her hand into his. Her hand was soft but her grip was firm. He liked that.

Pam was dressed in denim overalls with a white, long-sleeved shirt underneath. Her hair was pulled back into a single braid down to the middle of her back.

"Yore daddy wasn't around when you got dressed today, I see." Rosie chuckled.

Their hands parted, but Pam continued to look at Mike.

"Daddy wants me to dress like a lady and wear a dress at all times, but it's hard to explore the woods or ride my horse through the creek clothed like that."

"Pam's a bit of a tomboy," Rosie said.

Mike grinned. *If she looks this good in overalls, I can't imagine how good she looks in a dress.*

Pam turned back to Rosie. "I came by to see if my new saddle had arrived from Chicago. I guess I'm getting anxious."

"No child, you're not bothering me one bit. I'm always glad to see you bounce into my store; seems to make the whole place light up a little." The two laughed.

"Oh, Rosie." Sensing girl talk coming, Mike was about to excuse himself when Pam looked back at him.

"So, tell me about yourself, Mike from Kingston. When did you get into town?"

"Well ..."

Rosie interrupted as she shooed them toward the door. "Why don't you two go out on the porch and get acquainted. I'll bring you a couple of glasses of tea."

"That would be grand." The pair reached the door. "Do you have time, Michael?"

Michael? No one had ever called him Michael before. He started to protest and tell her it was just plain Mike, but he let it go. "Sure, I have a little time." For some reason "Michael" sounded agreeable coming from Pam, and now that he thought about it, he kind of liked it.

"Say, Rosie, will you mail this for me?" Pulling an envelope out of his pocket, Mike handed Rosie his letter to home.

"I'll take care of it, darlin'."

Mike and Pam walked through the door and sat in a couple of rocking chairs facing the street. Mike felt nervous again after a few moments of silence.

"So ... tell me something about yourself." Pam asked him again, as if he were supposed to have already started.

After a few minutes, Rosie interrupted their private party with two glasses of tea. Mike swallowed his first gulp; the sweet tea tasted incredible. As Rosie walked back into the store, they said their thanks.

"Well, I hope your folks don't miss you too terribly much, but it's nice that you're here." Pam took a sip of her drink. "Rush is a pleasant town."

Mike smiled. "I like it better every day too. Now, why don't you tell me about yourself and about Rush?"

Pam began telling Mike about coming to Rush after her father was hired by the Morning Star several years earlier, and how her mother was away visiting relatives in Boston and would be gone for another few weeks. They continued to chatter, and Mike mostly just listened as the words flowed across Pam's lips about herself and the town. For the next hour Mike and Pam talked and laughed and emptied a few glasses of tea; somewhere during that hour, both of their hearts fell in love.

***

Jay Finch pulled the reins slightly to the right so that his supply wagon would join the main road leading out of Rush. He had a delivery and a pickup in Yellville, not a drive he looked forward to. Because the road was rough and steep in places, the trip would take most of the day.. Usually, when he knew that a wagon trip to Yellville was needed, he would try and make himself scarce so that someone else would be chosen to make the haul. This day, however, since he was nursing bruises from his fight with Mike, he had gotten to the mill later than usual. As soon as he walked through the door, he was told to make the run. He couldn't avoid it, and the bruises would make the trip even more painful than usual.

As Jay rode down the dirt street, past the Morning Star Hotel, the bruise on his chin ached, causing him to think about his run-in with Mike. The anger swelled in him and he began plotting his revenge.

Approaching Rosie's store, he saw Mike and Pamela together on the porch. *You gotta be kiddin' me.* He pulled at the reins and stopped his wagon directly in front of the store.

"Mornin', Miss Pamela." Jay reached up to touch the brim of his hat.

"Good morning, Jay." The pair turned their attention to the voice from the street, and though Pam had addressed Jay, Mike didn't follow suit.

"I'm takin' a load to Yellville, and it is a nice surprise to see you. I would surely appreciate some company; it looks like a great day for a ride." He had never been so bold as to ask her to ride along with him on a haul, but seeing Mike sitting with her caused him to feel possessive and do his best to get her away from him.

"Thank you kindly, but I believe I'll pass on the offer. By the way, have you met Mike Gilbert? He's new in town by a couple of days."

Reluctantly, Jay turned his gaze toward Mike. He paused for a moment before replying. "We've met."

"Yes, we have," Mike said.

The three were silent for a few moments to the point of becoming awkward. To Jay, Mike was an intruder who didn't belong here.

"Sure you won't take the ride with me? I'll be glad to get a cushion for ya, to make the ride more pleasant."

"Thank you, no … I don't think there's anything that can make the ride to Yellville and back pleasant."

Jay tried to hide his frustration and realized he had to get moving if he was going to make it back by dark. He was getting a late start as it was. *I'll take care of you later farm boy.* He smiled and touched the brim of his hat once again then flipped the leather straps in his hands and headed out of town.

"He seems to be sweet on you." Mike tilted his glass for the last swallow of tea.

"Who, Jay? He works for my father and was just being friendly that's all."

Mike stood. *Of course.* "Well, I have some things I need to tend to today, so I best be getting to 'em."

Pam sensed tension between Mike and Jay but thought it best to leave it alone. It was no concern of hers, and she had other things on her mind, like getting to know Mike Gilbert a little better. She stood with him and offered to take his glass into the store so that he could be on his way. Anyway, she wanted to chat a little more with Rosie.

"I enjoyed our time together, Pam." Mike handed her his glass.

"I enjoyed it also, Mike. Maybe we can find time again."

Mike smiled and placed his hat on his head. "Count on it." He walked down the steps into the street, where he had tied Rusty by the water trough. After mounting, he took one last glance at the porch to see Pam wiggle her fingers goodbye to him while sporting a smile that made him tingle inside. She watched him as he rode back in the direction of the hotel to get his things.

***

Charley sat in the corner of the blacksmith shop while Doug pounded on some iron to repair one of the ore carts from the White Eagle mine. Because of all the mining activity, the smithy shop was continually in motion. The forging of equipment parts and building material was demanding and difficult. The coolness of the springtime air was greatly appreciated this time of the year in the forge; however, this year was an exception, and the days were already almost as hot as the summer days in July.

"Eleventeen ... thirteen ... sixteen ... seventeen ... twelve...." These were some of the few numbers Charley knew past ten. He counted as best as he could each time he would drop a forged nail into a pail. At sometime during the day, Doug would ask Charley to count the nails for him, partly to give Charley something to do, and partly to make Charley feel needed, as if he were doing something important. In fact, it had become such a ritual that Charley felt he had to count nails before he could sleep at night.

"How many do we have in the bucket today?" Doug slammed the hammer down onto the white hot piece of iron.

"One hundred." The answer was the same every day. It was the biggest number Charley knew and, to him, was the biggest number in the world.

Charley's mood was different today than on most days. Usually, he was bright and cheery, but today he counted the nails with less enthusiasm. When he set the bucket down, he slumped and looked at the ground.

Although Doug was busy with his repair, he watched Charley and could see that something was troubling him. He had taken care of his brother for a couple of years on his own, and rarely did his mood seem clouded. When he had finished pounding out the metal, he scored it. While it was still red, he folded it onto itself and placed it back into the coals to reheat. He motioned for his helper to pump the bellows, blowing air into the coals, causing them to become white hot. He then walked to where Charley sat.

"Are you still upset about your toad?" Doug assumed this was the reason for Charley's sadness.

There was a pause as Charley chewed on his lower lip and looked around the shop.

"It's going to be okay, Charley. I'll look under every rock until I find you another toad. Will that make you happy again? I hate for you to be unhappy."

Charley continued to sit without saying a word.

"I'm going to get back to my work. Why don't you go see what's going on down by the creek."

Doug stood to return to his anvil when Charley spoke. "What does retarded mean?"

The question caused Doug to freeze in his tracks. He closed his eyes and processed the question for the explanation he had hoped to never have to make. Charley knew he had some challenges and was unable to care for himself, but for some reason that hadn't mattered until now.

91

Doug slowly turned and sat back down beside Charley. With the roar of the forge hanging thick in the air, Doug first tried to evade Charley's question. "It's just a name some people call another person when they're trying to be ugly." Usually, being evasive worked well with Charley, but for some reason today was not one of those times.

"It means I'm stupid and dumb, don't it?" Charley stammered as he looked down at the ground and swiped the dirt floor from side to side with his toes.

"Charley, you're not stupid."

Charley slowly looked up at Doug.

"There's nothing stupid about you."

"Maybe I'm retarded 'cause I'm different than other folk."

Doug hesitated in making his reply, thinking about how to handle this since being evasive hadn't worked. It was then that he decided to handle this head on. He quickly said a prayer for an answer and heavenly help with this dilemma. "You are different. You are different from everyone else here in town."

Charley looked at his brother with a sad look on his face, but before he had a chance to comment, Doug continued. "I'm different from everyone else in town. Joseph over there on the bellows is different from everyone else in town."

Charley's demeanor seemed to change and his countenance became inquisitive.

"God made us all different from each other, Charley. Each one of us is special in his own way. Some of us have brown hair and some of us have red hair. Some people are big and some are small. Do you understand what I'm trying to say?"

"Not 'zactly,"

Doug shifted his position, took a deep breath and continued. "God made each one of us special in some way, and gave us all a special purpose in life."

"Even me?"

92

"Especially you."

Charley lowered his head again and thought for a moment. Doug continued to watch his brother, wondering what he should say next or if he had said enough.

"Do you know what your special purpose is?" Charley looked back up at Doug.

"It's ready." Joseph stopped pumping the bellows. The coals glowed white hot and threw glowing embers into the air.

"Start shaping the rod, and I'll be there in a minute." Doug turned his attention back to Charley.

"Charley, I love you with all my heart, and you need a little help to live in this world, don't you?"

"I reckon."

"I think my purpose right now is to take care of you, and help you get along in life, and be the best big brother I can be."

Charley digested what Doug said and thought again for a moment. "How do I know what God made me for? What special purpose do I have?"

Doug paused, and then grinned. "You make people happy all over town, Charley. You always have a bright smile, wherever you go. That's an ability not too many people have. Everyone likes you."

"Not everyone."

"Little brother, we all have someone in our lives we have to ignore and forget at times ... even me. There are a couple of guys at the mill who cause me problems, and I just have to deal with it, and think about all the other people who do like me."

Charley remained silent.

"And besides ... how would I know how many nails I have if you didn't count them every day?"

"That ain't very important." Charley still tried to figure out what his brother was telling him.

Doug smiled and looked at his brother. He tenderly placed his hand on Charley's back. "Sometimes it's easy to know what our purpose is, and sometimes it's hard to know.

93

Sometimes we don't know why God put us here on earth, but it's our job to ask him to show us. Although you may never know exactly what your special purpose is here on earth, God has everyone here for a reason, and you are here for an important reason too, Charley."

Charley thought for a moment then his face transformed into a smile. "I think I know what my special purpose is!"

"Really, Charley … what is that?"

"I like to preach, and someday I'm gonna help a lot of people know about God."

"Wow, Charley, that's some purpose."

Charley stood so fast that he knocked over the bucket of nails he had been counting. Without saying another word, he left the shop and almost ran down the street.

Doug raced to the door. "Be back here before dark. We're having company, remember?"

Without turning around, Charley continued his brisk pace and raised a hand acknowledging that he had heard his brother. Doug stood in the doorway for a moment shaking his head then turned back into the shop to take the iron rod and hammer from Joseph.

"Charley okay?" Joseph asked.

Doug began pounding the metal rod. "He's just fine…I think."

Chapter 10

It was mid afternoon when Mike entered the Morning Star Mill. The sound was deafening as the ore-bearing rock was crushed and separated. He watched wood being loaded into the fire chamber under the steam boilers that supplied the power. A man in the rafters was applying heavy grease onto the bearings around the rotating shafts being turned by the steam motors. Wide canvas and leather belts turned around the spinning shafts leading in several directions, operating various machines. It was an incredible marvel of mechanics, he thought, as he continued to watch in awe. He had seen a smaller version of this once at a furniture maker's shop, but the shaft was driven by a belt connected to a steam tractor. It was the same idea, only on a much smaller scale than this. Mike scanned the room for Mr. Riley, but he was nowhere to be seen. Neither he nor Mr. Harrison were anywhere in sight.

A woodman walked by, pushing a cart of split oak. "Excuse me," Mike said. The man looked at him but continued on his way to one of the boilers.

Another man walked close, so Mike got his attention. "Excuse me, can you tell me where I can find Mr. Riley or Mr. Harrison?" Mike was nearly yelling because of the noise.

"Mr. Harrison is at Buffalo City, where we load our ore onto barges at the White River. He won't be back until tomorrow. I don't know where Riley is … sorry." The man continued on his way and left Mike standing in the noisy room.

He was about to leave when he heard a voice from behind him. "Hey kid."

Mike turned to see a man dressed in overalls and no shirt. He was dirty and sweaty.

"Do you work here?"

"No, I'm here to ask about work, but I can't find Riley."

"We need more wood cut for the boiler. Can you swing an axe?"

"Better than anyone." Mike shouted above the noise.

"Go around to the side at the wood pile and start splitting. I'll talk to Riley about you. We need another man on the wood pile."

Confused about what he should do, Mike stood there for a moment.

"Get going, man. We have to keep the boilers going strong."

"Yes sir." Mike smiled and walked back out into the day. Around to the side, he found the huge mound of wood, and two men already splitting it as fast as they could. Because he'd had no idea he would be splitting wood, he wasn't dressed for this kind of work, but he made the best of it. Looking around, he spotted an axe leaning against a section of oak. Although he didn't have gloves, rather than request a pair, he picked up the axe and began splitting as fast as he knew how.

Despite the fact that the other two men were at a distance from him, they noticed his enthusiasm as he split the short, cut logs into four even sections. With a quick and hard swing, the wood easily popped. Mike loved splitting newly cut oak sections. They separated much easier than wood that had been cured for a while. As he swung, he hoped the man would talk to Mr. Riley, and that this would be the beginning of his employment. He continued to split and toss the sections into another pile, ready for others to load it and haul it to the boilers.

Since the early May days this year were already as hot as the middle of summer, Mike worked up quite a sweat maintaining his steady rhythm. Of all the chores from the farm, splitting wood was the thing he enjoyed the most. He really loved the feeling he got when the axe split the wood with only a single blow.

For the next hour or so, he split wood, and his pile grew faster than it could be carried away. He had lost track of time, and the shadows were beginning to blend together and turn late afternoon into evening.

"Day's about over, boy," one of the other choppers said across the woodpile. "There's water over by that rock wall."

Mike leaned his axe against the next piece of standing wood he was ready to split and walked over to the water. He lifted the lid from the container and lowered the dipper into the cool liquid. It tasted sweet and refreshing as he swallowed. He dipped another drink full then replaced the lid.

"We've got enough wood split to get us going in the morning. Go take a load inside to the boiler. Someone will show you where to unload it."

"I'm Mike Gilbert. I just started working here, I think." Mike spoke to the man who was obviously in charge of the wood.

"I'm Jim Smith. Get that load in and call it a day. They're about to shut down the boilers."

Mike grabbed the wheeled cart and loaded it with the sweet-smelling oak sections. He followed another man hauling a load and, once inside, they dumped the wood and stacked it onto the pile.

"Let's shut 'er down," a man said, and that was the end of the day. ¶Although Mike looked for the man who had put him onto the wood detail, to ask him to make sure and talk to Mr. Riley, he was nowhere to be found. So he wheeled the cart back out to the wood pile and placed his axe under it for the night.

Mike looked for Jim, who had just finished his last split for the day. "What time am I supposed to be here in the morning?"

"They get the boilers goin' around six o'clock. Be here shortly after."

"I'll be here."

"And don't be late. Mr. Riley don't take to tardiness, ya hear?"

"You don't have to worry about me." Mike dusted off his pants.

"You might think about wearin some more suitable work clothes, too. You look like yer dressed fer church."

I hope Rosie is still open. I do need work clothes, and if I come back like this tomorrow, I'll never hear the end of it. "I'll be ready."

Mike walked from the mill, followed the white picket fence to the main road, turned the corner, and within a few more steps arrived at Rosie's. He was relieved to see her "Open" sign still turned, so he bounded up the steps and through the door.

"Well, where have you been all afternoon?" Rosie, seated at a small table with a strange man, called out from the back of the room. . They had a checker board between them with a game already in progress.

"I don't want to interrupt your game, Rosie, but I need some work overalls, another shirt, and a pair of gloves."

"Now don't tell me you already landed a job."

"I've been splitting wood at the Morning Star for the last couple of hours—seems they were a man short."

"Gotta keep those boilers chuggin' away," Rosie moved a checker. "Just find what you need and let Beth know what you got. You can take care of it after you get paid."

"Much obliged." Mike began rummaging through the denim overalls.

"Oh, and by the way, a certain young lady took a fancy to you today. I think you made quite an impression." Rosie chuckled as she contemplated her next move on the checkerboard.

Mike blushed and didn't know what to say, especially with a stranger around. "She's nice."

Rosie just rolled her eyes but didn't say another word until she jumped three of her opponent's checkers and let out a deep belly laugh in delight.

"Doggone you, Rosie, you did it again." Clyde exploded as he leaned back in his chair and surveyed the damage on the board.

As he took his purchases around the corner and spotted Beth, Mike smiled. "Hi, Beth. I need to get these, and Rosie said I could wait till my first pay to take care of it."

"I'll start you a bill, Mike." Beth pulled out a pad and wrote down his items.

"Obliged, Beth."

"I guess we won't be seein' you as much now that you're a workin' man." Rosie hollered at Mike as he walked toward the door.

"'Night, Rosie," he said. After he had cleaned up, he changed into his new work clothes. He grabbed the oil lamp and walked out into the evening. Seeing Rusty tethered by the steps, he realized he would have to figure out the best place to keep him.

"I'll bring you some oats tomorrow. Mike patted Rusty on the neck. "We'll find you a better place to stay soon."

It was a short distance around the corner and up the hill to the blacksmith shop. As he neared it, he could hear the roar of the furnace, still being heated with air from the bellows. The door was open, so Mike walked in and saw Doug still working. Charley was on the bellows, pumping air into the coals, which would get bright orange with every whoosh of the pump.

"Hey, Gilbert, come on in."

As Mike walked up to the pair, Doug looked back at his work and Charley smiled."Sorry I'm runnin' late, but I have a couple of rods to bend and shape for supports at the mill. Ol' man Harrison is always expandin' and makin' improvements, and when parts can't be ordered fast enough I have to make 'em if I can."

"It's okay. I haven't been around a forge in a while. For some reason I really like the smell of coke and charcoal." Mike leaned against one of the heavy wall beams.

"Work around it all day every day and see what you think about it then. Seems I can never get the smell out of my clothes."

"Speaking of clothes, what's the best way to get your clothes washed around here?"

"You mean besides doin' it yourself?" Doug chuckled.

"Do you do your own washing?"

"Of course. Every Sunday afternoon Charley and I get out the tub. We scrub and wring and get 'em done. By Monday morning they're dry, and we're ready for another week."

"Isn't there anyone around here you can take 'em to?"

Doug and Charley looked at each other at the same time then began to laugh.

"Where do you think you are, Gilbert? This isn't the big city."

Mike felt a little embarrassed at their teasing.

Doug pulled a rod out of the charcoal with his tongs and began bending it with his hammer around the round end of the anvil. Small sparks flew from the iron as he continued to work and bend the rod into the desired shape. He lifted it for inspection and compared it to the master pattern he had. Content with the shape, he dropped it into the tub of water to quench and harden it.

"I've heard there are some ladies around who do laundry for a little extra money. I'm sure if you ask around you can find one. In the meantime you can use our washtub and wringer if you like."

The thought of doing his own laundry didn't excite Mike, but if it would get him by until he could find someone to do it, then that's the way it was going to have to be.

"I'm hungry 'nuff to eat a whole horse," Charley piped in, "and I'm tired of pumpin'. Can we be done?"

"I've got one more rod to bend, but if you're tired, maybe you could talk Mike into pumpin' air for me. Why don't you go check on the beans and see if they need some more seasoning?"

Charley relinquished the bellows and left the shop. Mike walked to the rope and awaited Doug's orders.

"Okay, just gently pull the rope, and it will pump the bellows. Not too much, because I don't need this to get very hot."

Mike took the rope and pulled it down. There was more resistance then he thought there would be, so it took a few pulls to get the rhythm he needed.

"That's perfect. Doug stirred the coals around the iron bar now heating up. "What do you think so far about Rush?"

"It's nothin' like Kingston, but I like it. Kingston moves a little slower than things do around here. Always seems to be somethin' going on."

"Yeah, but nothin' very exciting ever happens. We just all do our work day in and day out."

"But I like it. There's so much more going on here. I like the people, the town, and the Buffalo River. There's just somethin' about a clear river that makes me feel good."

"Me and Charley go fishin' every chance we get. We have a little flat bottom tied up down by the river, and it's there every time we need it. You're welcome to it as long as you tie it back up. Don't want the river washin' it away if it rises too high after a rain."

"Maybe I'll have to go with you and Charley next time you go."

"I think Charley would like that."

There was a pause as Doug pulled the rod out to check the color of the glow. "Almost ready." He plunged the rod back into the embers.

"Say, Doug, do you know much about Mr. Harrison at the mill?"

"What do you want to know?"

"Well, how he is to work for, and what he pays, and where he lives, and that kind of stuff."

Doug smiled and looked back at the coals. "You mean you want to know about his daughter."

Mike blushed.

"I had to run an errand this morning and saw you two sittin' on Rosie's porch together."

"Is this one of those towns where everyone knows everything?"

"I'm afraid so. Isn't every small town the same way?"

Mike paused for a moment and stared at the glowing embers. "So does Pam have a steady or anyone right now?"

"Why are you asking me?"

"Thought you might know since you seem to see everything around town."

Doug laughed and pulled the rod out of the coals. It was ready, so he instructed Mike to stop pumping. He shaped the rod into the exact replica of the one he had quenched only minutes earlier, then dropped the iron into the tub; it sent a cloud of steam into the air as it sizzled.

"I imagine the beans are ready. I hope Charley hasn't already dug into 'em. He does that sometimes when he's really hungry and is tired of waitin' on me."

Doug dropped his gloves onto the anvil and untied his body-length, leather apron, hanging it on a nail by the door. Mike blew out his lantern and the pair rounded the building and into Doug's house.

***

A horse and rider turned off the main road from Yellville and headed down the dark, narrow road leading to Rush. From sheer exhaustion, the rider slumped in the saddle as his horse slowly plodded down the dark passage, following the wagon ruts. Night had completely engulfed the forest, and the dim light of the stars occasionally peeked from between the gathering clouds. Normally, the rider would have stopped for the night, but he was driven by hunger and knew that Rush was only a short distance away. Not too far away into the woods, an owl began hooting and continued his haunting melody for some time while the spring peepers and crickets joined in harmony to the tune he was all too familiar with. He hated living outdoors, but it had become his life for the last year. Reaching into his inside jacket pocket, he pulled out a small, flat bottle of bourbon. He had drained most of the bitter liquid, which he had been carefully nursing for a couple of days. Tilting the bottle up to the sky, he took the last swallow. Some of the liquid dripped down his chin as he removed the bottle from his lips then carelessly tossed it into the woods. He wiped his chin with the back of his sleeve and slumped again.

He continued to ride, listening to the forest sounds and the heavy steps of his horse, the saddle leather creaking and squeaking with every step. The damp evening and the coolness of the night air was probably the only thing keeping him awake in his saddle.

He was becoming angry with the total darkness when he spotted a light through the trees in the near distance. It was faint but grew brighter as he rode closer, placing his hand on the gun that was tucked inside of his belt under the front of his coat. Though he had no idea what or who was at the light, he had learned that, in his life, he could never take chances.

Just as he rounded a bend in the road, the yellow glow disappeared for a brief moment then came into full view. He could now hear the faint music of a violin. He listened as the notes drifted through the trees, and he recognized the tune from the hymn book his mother used to make him sing from when he was a boy.

As he drew near, the light from the campfire illuminated what looked like a canvas shack of some sort. When he finally reached the fire, he saw two men seated around it; one played a fiddle and the other sat on a stump, smoking a pipe. Holding a small child in her lap, a woman

103

sat in a rocking chair on the wooden platform, gently rocking in the dim light.

He stopped his horse in the road as the two men noticed his presence. Looking at the weary traveler, the fiddler lowered his bow

The rider nodded his head. "Evenin', folks."

"Evenin', mister." The fiddle player looked first at the stranger then at the other man beside him.

The rider turned his attention to a cast iron pot hanging above the embers. "Would you fine Christian folks happen to have some food you could spare for a starving stranger?"

"We'd be happy to share what we have with you, such as it is, mister." The man smoking the pipe stood.

After dismounting, the rider walked his horse close to the fire, where he tethered it to a small tree. "Much obliged," he said. He sat on a cut piece of wood, using it as a chair. "Keep on playing; I like fiddle music. You don't have to stop on my account."

The fiddle player placed the instrument under his chin and played a different melody than the previous one.

"That smells mighty good." The rider leaned over the simmering in the pot.

"It ain't much. I hope you like rabbit stew," the lady said.

"I cut my teeth on rabbit stew, but it never smelled nearly as good as what you got brewin' in that pot, that's fer sure."

"Noah, fetch him a bowl of that stew before he passes out."

Noah placed his pipe between his teeth, scooped a couple of ladles of the stew into a metal bowl and handed it to the stranger, who didn't even wait to be handed a utensil but just turned the bowl up and began pouring it into his mouth. The three watched as he devoured the offering in only moments. He lowered the bowl and looked at the black pot again.

"Help yourself, mister, thar's plenty … always happy to help someone in need."

The bowl was filled and emptied two more times before the rider was finally satisfied.

"Where ya from?" Noah said.

"Oh … here and there. Thought I'd come and see what all the talk was about. This is Rush, ain't it?"

"It's just down this road a piece."

The rider gazed at the makeshift camp and saw the jumbled condition of their living quarters. Canvas stretched over wooden pole supports nailed to a wooden floor, and it looked as if it was built from scrap lumber. There was a partition between two beds, and there was a small cradle next to one of them. Wooden crates were used as shelving, which held a meager supply of canned goods.

"You wouldn't happen to have any tobacco you could spare would you?"

Noah pulled out a tin can from his pocket and handed it to the stranger. He took the tin of tobacco and, with his other hand, retrieved some paper from a pocket. Within seconds his rough hands had rolled a cigarette and placed it between his lips. He handed the can back to Noah and pulled a box of matches from his shirt pocket then struck the match with his thumbnail and placed it at the end of the cigarette. The match flame illuminated the features of the rider. It exposed the face of Jeeter Morse.

Chapter 11

"Best beans and cornbread I've had in a long time." Mike placed his spoon on the table and wiped his mouth with his towel.

Doug and Mike looked at Charley as he leaned back from the table, protruded his stomach and patted it. "I'm so full I'm gonna pop."

Mike lifted his hand as if to shield his face. "If you explode, turn the other way, please."

Doug laughed at the thought. "Charley, go get those dried plums from the cupboard."

The jar of dried plums was retrieved and placed on the table. Doug removed the lid to reveal the dried, wrinkled fruit, which had been sprinkled with sugar and cinnamon. "Dig in."

A second invitation was not needed. Mike took one of the plums and popped it into his mouth. The plum immediately began to melt and release the most wonderful, sweet cinnamon flavor he had ever tasted. It reminded him of the apple pies his mother made in the late summer when the ripe apples were plentiful on the trees. He would have to remember this treat and tell his mother of yet another way to preserve a fruit with cinnamon and sugar.

"Mighty tasty." Mike reached for another piece. "Did you make these things?"

"Charley and I get to the folks' every now and then, and Ma always sends back a few jars. We hang on to 'em for special occasions." Doug reached for another himself. "I have to keep an eye on Charley when we get them out or he would finish off the whole jar."

"Once I ate a whole jar of 'em and got a belly ache," Charley boasted as he reached for his fourth piece of fruit.

"That's probably enough." Doug replaced the lid.

Charley pouted as the lid was screwed on tight, realizing there would have to be another special occasion before he could enjoy some more.

The three sat there in the flicker of the oil lamp and savored the last bites of their sweet treat. The crickets and tree frogs were singing in unison outside, and the occasional owl could be heard in the distance.

Doug broke the silence. "Looks like you made a nice enemy today."

"You mean Jay? He's just a bully. I usually don't worry much about folk like him. I'm more leery about them that call you friend and then getcha when you're not looking."

"There's truth to that," Doug replied.

"It was really nice meeting Pam today."

Doug and Charley looked at each other with their eyebrows raised. Mike couldn't help but notice, and realized there was something they were thinking but not saying.

"Something wrong with that?" Mike shifted his gaze between the pair.

"She's Mr. Harrison's daughter—the manager of the Morning Star."

"I know. And what's that supposed to mean?"

"Mr. Harrison finds out and you'll be looking for another job."

Mike leaned back in his chair and eyed Doug for a moment. "Sounds like Mr. Harrison is overprotective."

"Not overprotective. Mr. Harrison has money and wants his daughter's suitors to be wealthy likewise."

"Anyone else around have money?"

"No, that's why he's going to send her away to finishing school next year … so she can find a proper rich man," Doug said.

A grin spread across Mike's face. He leaned back in his chair placing his hands behind his head and clasping his fingers together. "I may just have to help Mr. Harrison change his mind."

At that, Doug and Charley began laughing at their new friend.

"You don't know Mr. Harrison," Doug said.

"You don't know me," Mike replied.

***

The early evening air was cool and smelled of cedar trees as Finch directed the company wagon deep into the woods on a narrow trail. He had completed his run from Yellville and before he drove the wagon back to the Morning Star Mill had a personal matter to attend. He could see lamplight ahead and knew it was his destination. The trail was familiar to him and he knew every turn. When he was close enough to the light, he stopped. He placed his hands up to his mouth and whistled in a tune which poorly mocked the song of a whippoorwill. He did this twice and listened in the darkness. Within seconds he received a similar reply. He prodded his team forward.

A small campfire was burning, sending glowing sparks into the air with the occasional pop of moisture being released from the burning wood. Three men sat around the fire, two of them holding rifles. Jay stopped his team and tethered them to a tree. "Where's Raif?"

"He's out behind a tree, he'll be here directly."

Jay looked around the camp and spotted two clay jugs with cork stoppers. There were also several small glass bottles standing beside them reflecting the firelight.

"How'd the new batch come out?" Jay eyed the bottles.

"Better than the last one."

"Good. Some of my customers weren't too happy with it."

"Jay Finch...yer a sight for sore eyes." From out of the darkness, a voice interrupted.

Jay looked up in time to see Raif Talbot come into the glow of the firelight buttoning his britches. "Likewise, Raif."

"How many do you want this time?" Raif got right down to business.

Raif was a man of few words and wasn't much into lollygagging when it came to money. He had been into many business ventures in his lifetime, all of which were illegal. Since Marion County was dry, it didn't take long after he had arrived in Rush to decide that bootlegging would produce good money for him and hopefully become very lucrative.

"I have a few more customers this week; I'm not sure you have enough." Jay gestured toward the bottles.

Raif chuckled as he sat down in an old wooden chair next to the fire. "I've got more stashed out in the woods, my friend. Don't worry about the supply."

"I've been thinkin' about movin' some of this upriver to Gilbert. I'm not sure if there is anyone cookin' up there."

"You know folks upriver?"

"I make supply runs from time to time for Harrison … I've gotten to know a few. I ran a load for him today up to Yellville; might be a few up there to sell to."

There was a pause as Raif leaned forward to stir the little fire with a stick. The glow of the flames revealed the deep wrinkles which many years of hard living had created.

"Don't get too rambunctious." As he stared into the fire, Raif cautioned Jay in a deadly serious tone. "I don't want any attention around here."

Jay knew what he meant by that. Raif probably wouldn't hesitate to get rid of anyone he thought might become a liability and pose a threat to his little operation .

"Don't fret, Raif … you just keep supplyin' and I'll keep sellin'."

"Don't get cocky, son. You ain't invincible and you make me nervous when you talk like that. You just be mighty careful. Now pay me fer what yer takin', and you best be on your way."

The coolness in Raif's tone was evident to Jay, so rather than sit around jawing like he usually did, tonight he simply paid Raif, filled his burlap sacks with the bottles, and made his way back down the dark trail and eventually to his small shack outside of Rush.

Jay's place was a small log cabin which had been built in the mid 1800's by fur trappers. When the war broke out, it had been abandoned and unused until Rush was established. It had become the property of the Morning Star Mining Company, and luckily had become available when Jay came to Rush a year earlier. Since it was out of the way and at the edge of town, it was a perfect place for him to hide his stash of bootleg whisky. Over the past few months, Jay had been able to build himself a nice little business selling the stuff, and now that he was running some wagons for Harrison, he was planning to grow his operation into neighboring regions. He made more money selling bootleg than he did working for Harrison, but working at the Morning Star gave him a good cover, and using the delivery wagons to increase his business was an added bonus.

As he sat on the edge of his bed, however, he couldn't keep his mind from drifting back to earlier in the day when he had seen the girl he wanted sitting on the porch with Mike Gilbert. As he thought about seeing them enjoying each other's company, the anger welled up inside him again. Although Pam had never shown interest in him, Jay had vowed to someday have her, and no one was going to stand in his way. He had to somehow get rid of Mike Gilbert. He didn't know how just yet, but he would.

***

Faint starlight filtered into the bedroom as Rachel lay awake. It had been several days since Mike had left home and they had not heard a word from him. Only moments earlier she had finished her prayers, and they were most intense as she prayed for God to protect her son. She sensed that William was also awake next to her, and, even though they hadn't said much to each other about it, she knew that his thoughts were also on Mike.

"He's going to be all right, isn't he, William?" Her words sounded as if tears were waiting behind them.

110

There was a long pause, and then she felt his hand reach across under the covers and gently clasp her hand in his.

"He's gonna be just fine, Momma. You told me so the other day in the barn, remember? I'm sure he's gonna be just fine."

Words from her husband didn't give much comfort to her, and a tear trickled from her eye and down her cheek.

"I miss him, William."

"I miss him too, Rachel."

***

The next morning Mike was up as the roosters began crowing. He had become so accustomed to getting up before sunrise that his body was ready for the day earlier than most folk. He dressed, wolfed down some cheese and sourdough, grabbed his hat, and was out the door. He hoped the manager had put in a good word with Mr. Harrison so his woodcutting job would be permanent. He checked on Rusty and made sure he had water for the day, and then he made his way down the street.

The sun was beginning to throw some light into the sky, and the day felt crisp and wonderful. It didn't take long to make his way to the Morning Star and to the woodpile behind it. Mike placed his hands into his gloves and looked for his splitting maul and axe. They weren't where he had left them the afternoon before, and he was hoping they had not been stolen. Frantically he began to look all around the woodpile and the building, but still could not locate the tools.

"You're here awful early."

Mike turned to see Jim Smith putting on his gloves and walking toward him.

"I can't seem to find my axe or the splittin' hammer and wedges."

"We put 'em up every evenin'," Jim said. "Don't want stuff walkin' away."

"Well, I'm ready to get started."

"I admire your excitement, but payroll don't start for another hour."

111

"You mean I can't start when I'm ready?"

"Look kid, we work when we're supposed to start, and stop when we're supposed to stop. Most get paid by the hour and Harrison won't pay for overtime."

"Overtime?"

"Yeah, you don't get paid for more than ten hours a day. I'm sure Mr. Harrison wouldn't mind you workin' extra hours for free, but you ain't getting paid fer it. You might as well wait till everyone else starts."

Mike hadn't thought about working set hours since all of his life he simply got up and worked until the work was finished.

"Then why are you here so early?"

"I'm management, kid … they pay me by the week so I have to make sure everything gets done no matter how many hours it takes. I get here early of a mornin' to sharpen the tools and get things ready."

"Need some help?"

Jim chuckled at Mike's unusual eagerness. "Well, since yer already here, it would be nice to have company for a change. How good are you at sharpening?"

"Give me an axe and I'll show you," Mike said with a smile.

"Come on, kid," Jim said, "yer gonna do just fine here."

***

It was the middle of the morning when Jim called for a break. Mike made a final swing with his axe and then drove it into his splitting stump, leaving it poised and ready for his return. The wood splitters all gathered around the water barrel and took their turn with the refreshing liquid. After Mike had finished his drink, he walked to the end of the mill. He was beginning to get used to the noise of the crusher, and wondered what it would be like to work inside or even in one of the mines. For some reason he was curious about mine work. Even though he had been told that it was dangerous, he looked forward to some day getting a look inside, and especially seeing the raw zinc ore and how it was separated from the host rock. As he stood and watched the town, a wagon pulled up from around the building and cut across his line of sight. The driver stopped the wagon directly in front of him.

"Did you get a job here, farm boy?"

Mike looked into the face of Jay Finch and didn't reply.

Jay spit tobacco on the ground at Mike's feet. "I'm surprised they hired you, but you can handle cuttin' wood, I reckon."

"You got a problem with me, Jay?" Mike placed his leather gloves back onto his hands.

A crooked smile formed on Jay's face with the tobacco bulge showing in his right cheek. "No, farm boy ... I ain't got a problem with you, but if you want to keep your job, stay away from Pam."

"Threats don't bother me."

"Not a threat—just givin' you a friendly piece of advice."

"Break's over, back to work!" Jim yelled in Mike's direction.

Mike turned his head toward Jim to acknowledge hearing the command then looked back at Jay.

"I'll see who I want to."

Jay chuckled and spit once again, then flipped the reins to direct his load out of town. "Stupid farm boy," he muttered as he rode away.

Mike watched for a moment then made his way back to the stump and his axe. *First Doug warns me about Mr. Harrison if I try to court his daughter, and now Finch threatens me.* Mike smiled to himself at the challenge that lay before him. He would show Doug that he was wrong, and, as for Jay, he allowed himself to imagine the next piece of wood as Jay's head. The wood split with a "pop" when Mike picked up his axe and swung it with an accurate blow.

***

It was nearly midday when Jim loaded a wheelbarrow full of split wood then made his way into the mill. Before he reached the wood pile beside the boiler, he was met by Jacob Harrison.

"Morning, Mr. Harrison." Jim stopped rolling the wheelbarrow and let go of the handles.

"Morning, Jim. Who's the new kid you have out on the wood pile with you?"

"Name's Mike Gilbert. He just got into town a few days ago from over in Madison County. He's a hard workin' kid and doesn't do any lollygagging, that's for sure.

"Riley hire him?"

"No, actually we needed help at the end of the day yesterday. He jumped right in and helped us get caught up on the wood pile."

"Well if he wasn't hired, why is he back today splitting wood?"

"We told him we'd put in a word for him and hopefully get him on." Jim now felt uneasy with the conversation.

"So he's splitting with all the other workers out there and not even on the payroll?"

"Yes sir ... kinda crazy, ain't it? He was even here early with me this mornin' and helped me sharpen the tools."

Harrison thought for a moment. "Put him on at two bits an hour and make sure he's paid for yesterday."

"Yes, sir, Mr. Harrison. I'll give him the good news."

"And keep me informed on how he does. I might be able to use a hard workin' kid like that somewhere else."

Harrison turned and walked toward the office, leaving Jim hoping that he wasn't going to lose his best wood splitter soon. He emptied his load and pushed his wheelbarrow back out into the sunlight to give Mike the good news.

***

The door closed behind Mike as he fell back onto his bed exhausted. He had finished his first full day of work and,

114

finally, things were beginning to go the way he wanted. He still felt like an outsider, but hoped that with his job he would be accepted soon.

Since the next day was Sunday, he decided he would take Doug up on his offer and borrow his washtub to wash clothes. He didn't know how he was going to do it, but he would do his best to figure it out.

There was still a little daylight left before the night chased it away, so he decided to bed Rusty while he could still see, then fix a bite to eat and go to bed early. He had learned that even though there was a little church in town, the parson only came by every other Sunday. It wasn't something he was used to, and he began to feel a little guilty of the thoughts he was having, but he decided to get a little extra sleep in the morning if he could before doing his laundry at Doug's.

The sun was beginning to shove its way into the shoulder of the nighttime sky as Mike lay awake in his bed. He intended to get a little extra sleep since he wasn't going to church, but, like all other mornings, he was wide awake. He could see the faintness of light through the window over the sink, but closed his eyes to try and force himself to lose consciousness again; it was no use.

He decided to get up and build a little fire in the stove so that he could make some coffee—his first coffee. His feet hit the floor, and he sat there for a few minutes wondering what would ease the growling in his belly. When he had decided to leave home, he hadn't even thought about all the other things that go along with being on your own. His ma had always taken care of the washing and food and all sorts of things he had never done. Now he had to remember to buy food, prepare it, wash up, and even do his own laundry. He had to do everything himself, and he was beginning to feel overwhelmed. He yawned, scratched his head then decided to boil some water to make mush from a bag of cornmeal he had purchased from Rosie's store. *That shouldn't be too hard.* Mike walked to the stove to start the fire.

After opening the cast iron door and placing some tinder inside, he then lit it with a match, placed some larger pieces of wood on it, and closed the door. He opened the damper all the way so that the small flame would grow and devour the larger wood, creating the heat needed to boil water. He pumped some water into the porcelain-coated metal coffee pot that the former occupant had left behind. Pouring water into a small pan, he set them on top of the metal plates over the fire. He knew it would take some time to heat, so Mike took the opportunity for a trip to the outhouse.

Upon returning, Mike noticed that the stove was heating and the water was beginning to warm, so he measured out the coffee grounds and placed them in the coffee pot. It wasn't long before the fire was roaring in the stove, and the heat began boiling the water for the coffee. The smell of the coffee brought back twenty years worth of mornings on the farm. Coffee had always been the first thing he had smelled upon awakening, and the friendly scent wrapped around him, comforting him like his mother's arms when he was a young boy.

He measured out some cornmeal and poured it into the boiling water in the pan. He had never made the hot cereal before. It wasn't long before Mike realized he had put too much into the water, because the cornmeal swelled and turned into a thick paste too thick to even stir. He tried to thin the concoction with more water, but that only made the problem worse. Before he knew what was happening, the mixture swelled to overflowing and began spilling over onto the hot stove, producing smoke and an irritating smell of burnt corn that soon filled his room. He grabbed the pan handle in a panic, but he had forgotten to grab it with a towel. He immediately dropped the pan onto his floor, sending the hot, sticky cereal bolting out of the pot and splattering across the room, just missing his bare legs.

Trying to usher out the smoke which was still being born from the top of the hot stove, Mike opened the door and the window over the sink. He grabbed a towel and picked up the pot to take the remains of his experimental breakfast outside to be thrown into the woods, but just as he made it to the door, another sound gripped his heart. Turning, he was just in time to see his coffee boiling over onto the stovetop, sending up another aromatic plume of smoke to thicken the air to mingle with the burnt-corn scent.

With his other free hand, he grabbed the only other towel he had, picked up the coffee pot and set it down in the sink. As he quickly turned to head once again for the door, he stepped into a pile of the slick cornmeal mush on the floor, and, faster than a lightning strike, he found himself flat on the floor with the remainder of the cornmeal mush splattered across the rest of the room, which had at first been untouched by the calamity.

Mike sat there for a moment in the smoky room and didn't know whether to be angry or to laugh. He decided instead to feel sorry for himself and pout, but as he carefully got up, he realized that pouting with no one around to see it was of no benefit, and the only thing left he could do was clean up the mess ... so he did. He figured he could at least hopefully have a little coffee from the pot if he hadn't ruined it, too, by scorching it.

By seven o'clock the disaster had been cleaned and the smoky air had cleared. The only thing remaining was the memory. He had been able to salvage a couple cups of coffee, which didn't taste half bad, and he had stopped the rumbling in his tummy by eating some hardtack with jelly he had purchased. It wasn't exactly a breakfast his ma would approve of, but it would get him by.

After dressing, Mike walked out onto the porch and plopped onto the top step. He sat there feeling sorry for himself as he watched Rusty grazing nearby. He had made a disaster out of breakfast, and he could hardly wait to see how he was going to mess up the laundering of his clothes later in the day.

As he looked out across the dirt road from where he sat, he could hear sounds of the town waking up. From somewhere not too far away, he smelled bacon as it sizzled in a skillet. He closed his eyes and remembered the heaping plate of bacon his ma would place in the middle of the breakfast table to give them strength for the work day. He took a deep breath, and, as he exhaled, he was startled out of his memory by the sound of soft footsteps coming toward him on the wooden porch.

"I was hopin' you wasn't burning down the place."

Mike turned to see Rosie a few feet away from him, wearing a housecoat and standing in her bare feet.

"Boy, you made one awful smell this mornin'. Were you burnin' corn on the stove?"

Mike's face turned redder than it had ever been, and for a moment he was so embarrassed that he became angry. He just sat there without knowing what to say.

"Oh, cut it out kid; I'm just funnin' ya. It takes a while to learn how to cook. The first time I tried to make coffee I scorched the fool out of it."

She cocked her head and waited for a response, but Mike only sat there feeling the heat of embarrassment radiating from his neck.

"Come on in, sweetie. I have some bacon, coffee, and cornmeal mush on the stove. I made extra cause I figured your breakfast weren't fit to eat."

With that, she leaned back and began laughing, and it was such an infections laugh that Mike couldn't help but crack a smile; however, he did his best to not join in with her laughter.

Rosie turned and walked back toward the front of the store still chuckling. Mike, though he still felt like an idiot, got up and followed her into the store where he sat and enjoyed a wonderful breakfast, which he hoped someday he would master.

They talked about the last couple of days and his new job. As he leaned back away from his empty plate, he swallowed one last time, taking his pride along with it. "Rosie, how do you make cornmeal mush?"

Chapter 12

Sunday came and went with Mike learning a thing or two about how not to wash clothes. He was embarrassed when Charley had to show him the proper way to wring then hang his clothes on the line. But with laundry day finally behind him, his new job awaited him. Although he had hopes of moving from the wood pile, he was happy and content to at least have a job, and he had high hopes that he could move into something more satisfying soon.

Mike arrived ten minutes early and helped Jim with the tools as they waited on the other workers. He could already hear the roar of the fire in the belly of the steam boiler, soon to begin yet another day of supplying power to the belts and pulleys which moved the jaws of the rock crusher. He worked the gloves onto his hands and grabbed the axe, but before he began his work, he tilted his face up to the sky, closed his eyes, and spoke aloud. "Thank you, Lord, for this job you gave me."

***

Jacob Harrison hurried to his office. It was still early morning but he had a wagon full of boiler parts that needed to be delivered up the river to the town of Gilbert. He had recently made a deal with the logging manager, Leon Pike, to pick up and ship parts to him from Buffalo City and anything else he might need on a regular basis.

A flustered mood was evident on Harrison's face as he entered through the doorway and saw Larkin Riley speaking with another worker about modifications to the zinc separating bins.

"Riley, have you seen Finch this morning?"

The two men turned and immediately gave Harrison their full attention.

Larkin pulled his cigar from his mouth. "I saw him up above the belts greasin' the joints about fifteen minutes ago."

Without so much as a reply or gesture, Jacob turned and headed back in the direction of the steam boiler. As he neared it, he began looking up into the rafters among the turning axles and gears that always needed grease. Jacob slowed to a stop under the machinery above him but saw no sign of Finch.

"What are you lookin' at, Mr. Harrison?" A worker loaded wood into the fire of the boiler.

"Have you seen Finch up there?"

"I seen him head out toward the woodpile just a minute ago."

When Harrison exited the building into the sunlight, he spotted Jay Finch leaning against the building, taking a long drink from the water barrel as he glared at Mike.

"Finch!" Harrison yelled, startling Finch and causing him to spill the remainder of water in his ladle.

"Finch, I've got a wagon full of parts that needs to get up to Gilbert. It needs to be delivered to the loggers."

Jay wanted to protest because he wasn't in the mood for another wagon ride. He was about to ask if someone else could take the load when Harrison interrupted him.

"Get yer tail over to the wagon, boy. The team is all hitched up and waiting. Find Leon Pike when you get to Gilbert. He'll have it unloaded, and then you give him this bill. He owes for this load and two others from last week. Don't leave until he pays you. If he tries to put you off, tell him that he doesn't get another load until he pays. You got that?"

Jacob handed Jay a yellowed envelope with the bill folded inside. Jay took the envelope and stuffed it into his back pocket.

"Get a move on, son … we don't have all day."

Mike caught the whole episode from the corner of his eye, and even though some of the other splitters had stopped to watch the exchange, he continued to swing his axe.

Harrison stood in the damp morning air and noticed Mike's pile of split wood. "Wish everyone worked like that boy," he mumbled.

Jay flipped the reins against the rumps of the horse team and began his trek to the community of Gilbert. As the crow flies, it wasn't far, but the sorry roads he had to take would cause it to be a long, bumpy ride. He hadn't planned to make his move just yet, but, as he rode, he decided that this would be as good a time as any to find out if anyone was making 'shine at Gilbert.

Since he was making a pretty good profit around Rush, he had formulated his plan a few weeks earlier to muscle his way into the Gilbert area. Gilbert was growing too, and since it was also in a dry county, whisky was in big demand. Loggers as well as miners had a strong desire for the distilled fire water.

As he continued up the steep and winding, narrow road out of Rush, Jay knew that his first step would be to ask around and find out from one of the local drinkers where the still was located. He hoped luck would be on his side, because once he found the still, step two would be to put pressure on the moonshiner and force him out of business, leaving the territory wide open for him. He knew he couldn't do it by himself but figured he could take a couple of Raif's men to help him with the gentle persuasion. He smirked when he thought about all of the money he would be able to make selling his liquor as he expanded his territory, and having lots of money held a lot of weight with ol' man Harrison. His smirk grew even larger when he thought of his chances with Pam expanding along with his liquor route.

***

Pam Harrison held the handles of a cloth sack in the bend of her elbow as she walked up the creaky wooden steps of Rosie's store. Earl, Rosie's gray cat, was standing on the railing next to the steps watching Pam with curious interest.

"Good morning, Earl." Pam stopped to rub her hand down his back for a few strokes. Earl slightly raised his hind end each time Pam's hand got close to his tail, and he began to purr as he spoke to her with a couple of meow's.

Earl didn't lack for attention, but he seemed disappointed when Pam stopped petting him and continued on to the door. He made one last meow, but it was ignored as she entered the store.

"Good morning, Sunshine."

Pam looked in the direction of the voice and saw Rosie stacking work boots onto one of the shelves. "Hello Rosie."

Rosie turned from her work and noticed the bag in Pam's arms. "Looks like someone's gonna do some shoppin'."

"I just need a few things, Rosie. I'm running errands for my father and this is one of my stops."

Rosie noticed Pam's attire , and she wasn't wearing her usual overalls or men's dungarees. She was wearing a dress, complete with a cameo pin and even earrings.

"Lordy, girl." Rosie crossed her arms across her big bosoms. "Why are you all gussied up today? Church ain't for another week."

Pam blushed as she avoided Rosie's direct eye contact.

"Oh, I just felt like dressin up today. Can't a girl put on a dress if she has a mind to?"

"Pumpkin, you never have a mind to put on a dress unless yer daddy is practically standin' over you."

Then Rosie stopped because she could see the red in Pam's cheeks. Immediately she realized what the occasion was. Being subtle, she changed the conversation.

"You headin' over to your daddy's office?" Rosie said with a sparkle in her eyes.

"I figured I'd take him some lunch today. Since Momma's been gone he forgets most days to take his lunch along with him even though Aunt May Bess sits it out for him. I just thought I'd do something nice and take it to him for a change."

"May Bess been showin' you how to cook since your ma's been gone?"

"She's been tryin'. I'm afraid I'm not a very good student."

Rosie chuckled at Pam's remark and the two began walking toward the grocery side of the store.

"You're not the only one who needs cookin' lessons around here," Rosie said.

Pam shot Rosie a puzzled look as the two stopped in front of the counter.

"Mike just about caught the place on fire yesterday. He's rentin' my room behind the store and thought he'd whip himself up a lovely breakfast."

Pam began to chuckle as Rosie told her about the whole episode, not because she was laughing at Mike, but because she thought it was cute and saw him as vulnerable, in need of someone to mother him.

"Now don't you go tellin' him I told you that when you see him in a little while."

"In a little while?"

"You know what I mean, Sugar …I 'm not blind."

Pam was at a loss for something to say. She didn't know whether to change the subject or start pulling canned goods from the shelves, but, since her plot had been discovered, she decided to spill the beans to the jolly storekeeper and friend.

"Do you think he'll notice me?"

"If he doesn't, he's the one who's blind. He'll notice you all right. Just make sure that, when you walk by, he's taking a water break and not swinging an axe. You wouldn't want him to cut off a toe, now would you?"

The pair laughed at such a notion, and, as they continued to chuckle, Pam completed her shopping and headed back to her house to prepare her father's lunch. All the way, she thought about what Rosie had said and hoped she was right, because she certainly wanted Mike to notice her. She might even say hello.

***

With his wagon unloaded and money in his pocket from Pike, Jay began his search for the still's location, assuming there was one. He saw a group of men beside the Gilbert store and decided to park his wagon and begin with them.

He walked up to the group, who were discussing new areas to log and how difficult those areas would be to access. As he made it to their circle, they stopped their conversation and turned their attention to the stranger.

"Afternoon, boys," Jay said. A couple of them returned his greeting. "I'm Jason Finch over from Rush. I just made a delivery and was wonderin' if any of you fellas knew where a guy could get something warm to drink around here."

Not knowing what to say, the men rolled their eyes back and forth at each other. Area marshals were frequently trying to find the locations of stills by inquiring about how to get a bottle.

"My supply has dried up at Rush and us boys over there sure could use something to settle us down at night." Finch tried to encourage someone to help.

"You say you're from Rush?"

"Yeah, that's my wagon over there from the Morning Star." Jay pointed toward his parked team. The group turned their heads in the direction of the wagon and saw *Morning Star* burned into one of the side rails.

Jay turned back to the group. They looked back and forth at each other again, and one of the men finally stepped away from the huddle and motioned Finch to follow him. *That was easier than I thought it would be.*

The pair walked up the road in silence until they were away from the store and others who were milling about. Finally the man spoke.

"You say your supply dried up in Rush?"

"Yup, dry as a bone." Jay sounded like a boy who had lost his puppy.

"I'll take you to Deacon up the road a piece. He's the one we buy from. We don't go to the 'shiner hisself."

"Why not?"

"Too risky; don't want the law to find out where the still is; then we'd be all dried up too."

They continued to walk as Jay tried to figure out how to get the guy to spill the beans about the location of the still.

"You know, to be perfectly honest with you, I was thinkin' of buying directly from the moonshiner hisself and take a load back to Rush. If I buy from this Deacon fella, I can't make as much profit."

The other man suddenly stopped in the middle of the road. Jay took a couple more steps then stopped also and turned around to him.

"I can't take you to the still. I could get into a heap of trouble. Talk to Deacon; mebbe you two could work somethin' out." The man's face showed hesitancy.

Finch walked back to the man, who seemed to have his mind made up like that of a mule with his feet planted firmly onto the ground, reluctant to move. Jay thought for a moment then reached his hand into his pocket and pulled out a twenty-dollar gold piece. As Jay held it out to him, the man eyed the large, shiny coin.

"This is yours if you take me to the still, my friend. And I'll remember you in the future when I make my runs back again." He held the coin up in front of the man's eyes, and he could tell that the old logger was certainly being enticed and sorely tempted.

"Come on, I want to buy several bottles and take them back to Rush. The guy will probably thank you 'cause you'll be helpin' him expand his territory so that he can make more money. Don't you imagine he'll thank you for that?"

The man raised his hand up to his mouth and rubbed it across his three-day-old stubble, the motion sounding like crumbling dry leaves. Jay could tell he was getting to the man. He took the man's other hand and placed the coin in it, closing his fingers around it, allowing him to feel the cool metal. That cinched the deal, and the man slowly placed the coin into his pocket.

"That was a smart decision." Jay gave the man a toothy smile as he placed his hand on one of the man's shoulders. "Now, let's go do some business."

***

By the end of the day, Mike was exhausted from splitting and stacking wood next to the mill. The hunger of the large steam boiler was nonstop, not to mention that of all of the other, smaller boilers which ran other machinery throughout the mill. Split wood was in constant need, and any slack in supply would definitely hamper the operation.

He finished his final swing then slung the axe onto his shoulder as he walked to the tool shed to store his implement for the next day. He handed his axe to Jim, and, after it had been placed inside the shed, the two shook hands for another successful day and said their goodbyes.

As Mike walked in the direction of his place, he could still hear the pounding of metal at Doug's shop, so he decided to make a detour and see what was going on with his blacksmith friend. Along the way, he began thinking about seeing Pam during the day, and how beautiful she had looked with the midday sun reflecting from her earrings. His heart began beating faster as he remembered her smile when she had waved to him, and to him her wave wasn't just a friendly gesture. No, it was one of those "Hello, sweetie" waves he had seen some of the girls back home in Kingston give to their fellas. He was sure that was the wave. In the same instant he remembered the warnings he had gotten about staying away from Pam if he intended to keep his job. But he never was one to back away from a challenge, and he wasn't about to start now. He had his heart set on Pam, and it would have to be her telling him to stay away, not her father.

Mike rounded the corner of the picket fence and could see through the open doorway that Doug was heating a rather large piece of iron. As he neared, he saw Doug pull the glowing metal from the forge and begin pounding it, sending out huge showers of sparks with every blow of the hammer. Doug was so engrossed in his work that he didn't notice Mike step through the doorway. About to speak, Mike heard Doug begin humming a tune, keeping rhythm with his hammer. He listened for a few seconds but didn't recognize the melody. The hammering stopped along with the tune, and, as the metal was placed back into the glowing embers, Doug noticed Mike watching him.

"So how long you been standin' there watchin' me?" Doug wiped the perspiration from his forehead with his sleeve. He sported a tired smile as he reached for the bellows handle and began pumping air into the coals to increase the temperature of the metal being reheated.

"Well, I heard you hummin' some tune as you were workin' if that's what you're wonderin'."

Mike would have seen Doug's cheeks turn red if they weren't already crimson from the heat and strenuous work over the forge. Mike looked around the room as Doug continued pumping the air.

"Where's Charley?" Mike picked up a horseshoe straddling a metal rack to inspect it, but as quickly as he picked it up he felt searing hot pain in his fingertips. Within a split second, the hot horseshoe was on the dirt floor and Mike plunged his hand into the bucket of water used for quenching hot iron. It had happened so fast that Doug had not had time to tell Mike the horseshoes on the rack had been quenched but were still hot to the touch. He just looked at Mike with a huge smile that was holding back a laugh he didn't know if he should let go of. Mike looked up from the bucket and into the eyes of his friend, who was doing his best to keep from laughing. In the awkward moment, Mike just said the first thing that came to his mind.

"Don't take me long to look at a horseshoe."

With that, Doug could contain it no longer and laughed so hard that he temporarily stopped pumping the bellows.

127

Mike smiled a little as his friend got entertainment at his expense and was glad that the horseshoe had not been hotter than it was. Within a few moments, the laughter subsided and Doug was pumping the bellows once more, sending glowing embers up into the air with each breath of the big leather lung. The embers were drawn into the chimney chute that hung above the forge to pull them and some of the hot air out of the room as it radiated from the glowing coals.

Mike pulled his hand out of the water to inspect his fingers, which had not been burned enough to cause blisters but would certainly be a little tender for the next few days.

"Well?"

"Well, what?" Mike placed his fingers back into the bucket of water just because it felt good.

"What did you think of the song I was humming?"

"Oh, that. I didn't recognize it but it sounded good. What's it called?"

Doug began pumping the bellows again and after a few strokes replied. "It's actually a song I wrote myself to sing to Sandy."

"Who's Sandy?"

"Why she's the purtiest, most sweetest girl in all of the Ozark hills, that's who. Her father manages the Morning Star Company Store just down the street."

"Why'd you write her a song?" Mike sat down on a wooden barrel.

A wide grin appeared on Doug's face as he stopped pumping the air and pulled the glowing metal from the embers with his tongs.

"Because I'm gonna sing it to her when I ask her to marry me Saturday night at the dance."

Mike was stunned for words at the sudden announcement. He hadn't known Doug for long, and he hadn't even met his girl, so he didn't really know what to say except "Congratulations."

128

Doug began pounding once again on the white hot iron. "I haven't told anyone yet."

"Well then, I feel honored," Mike said as he made a slight bowing gesture.

"By the way, are you going to the dance Saturday night?" Doug asked between hammer blows.

"Didn't know there was a dance."

"It's the annual spring dance that the Morning Star puts on. It's for the whole town so it's a big event." Doug sounded a little winded from his pounding of the iron against his anvil. He turned the piece over and inspected it then, while it was still red hot, hammered it over the edge of the anvil top, making a right angle. After a moment of tweaking it to get it just the way he wanted it, he plunged it into the water bucket, releasing a plume of steam into the air.

At the same moment Charley bounded through the door with something cradled in his hands. As he walked up to the pair, they could see that it was a bird's nest which had three blue, speckled eggs inside. Doug could see that two of the eggs were cracked.

"Hey, Charley," Mike said as Charley walked by, only to be ignored.

"Can you help me put this back into the tree?" Charley held the nest up to Doug.

"Charley, I don't think it will do any good. You can't put a nest...."

"But the momma's looking all over for it, and it has her babies in it."

Doug looked past his brother at Mike who had his lips pressed together tightly and his eyebrows lifted causing his forehead to furrow.

"Charley, I understand your feelings, but I can't stop work right now. Why don't you set the nest over there out of the way, and I'll see if I have time later to help you."

Charley didn't like the answer he got from his brother, but he knew it was the best he was going to get. So, with a dejected look on his face, he walked over to his usual place and gently set the nest on top of a wooden crate.

Keeping a watchful eye on his nest, he sat down beside it and began counting nails, talking to the nest occasionally as if the baby birds inside of the eggs could hear his words of comfort.

Doug spoke, almost in a whisper as he leaned over so only Mike could hear him, "By the way, I haven't told Charley about me asking Sandy, so don't let on anything."

"Mum's the word."

Doug took advantage of the moment and slumped onto a tall stool next to his forge. Mike could see that it had been a long day for him also. The tired blacksmith picked up a mason jar of water and drank most of it before stopping to take a breath.

"So, are there any words to it?"

Doug took one last swallow of the quenching liquid. His expression was blank for a second, trying to figure out what Mike meant.

"Your song…does it have any words?"

Doug smiled as he lowered his hand and rested the empty jar on top of his leg.

"As a matter of fact it does. Would you like to hear it?"

"Sure," Mike said. He was curious as to the singing ability of his blacksmith friend.

"I have a friend in Chicago who could publish it if he thinks it's good enough. I plan on sending it to him when I complete it." Doug sported a proud grin. "I'm not sure if all the words are right, and I'll keep working on it, but here goes."

With Charley continuing to count nails and Mike sitting in anticipation of the performance, Doug stood beside his forge; as the coals quietly crackled, he cleared his throat and began to sing:

Let me call you sweetheart, because I love you …
Let me hear you tell me that you love me too …
Keep the love-light glowing in your eyes so blue …

Let me call you sweetheart; I'm in love with you.

"Bravo. Bravo! Not only is that a good song, but you have a great voice."

He continued clapping as Doug placed his right arm across his stomach and took a deep bow.

"Thank you … thank you."

"I hope he wasn't singing that song to you." A sweet voice came from behind Mike. In an instant Mike whirled around on his perch to see Pamela Harrison standing in the doorway, grinning from ear to ear. Mike stood so fast that he knocked over the barrel he was sitting on. Doug's face showed redness again, only this time from embarrassment.

"He wasn't singin' to me." Mike stood the barrel upright.

"Oh, I know that, you silly man." Pam handed an order form to Doug. "But I was beginning to wonder if this was a blacksmith shop or if Doug was practicing to be in a barbershop quartet."

Mike didn't know what a barbershop quartet was, but didn't ask, fearing he would show his ignorance. Pam turned her attention back to Doug, who had relaxed somewhat and was studying the new order in his hands.

"Daddy needs those things by the end of the week. He knows you already have other work orders to complete, but he said those have to be ready on Friday come hell or high water … to use his vernacular. Daddy does have a flair for the dramatic."

Doug just gave a polite smile to Pam as she turned to walk toward the door, and then something happened which had never happened before. Charley stopped counting his nails before he was finished, and, gently picking up the bird nest, walked over to Pam.

"Hello, Charley."

"Miss Pamela, would you help me put this back up in the tree? I sure do imagine the momma is unhappy that it fell on the ground. I found it just a bit ago."

131

Pam looked at the nest which Charley carefully cradled in his hands then looked at Doug, who was sporting a sideways grin. Pam looked back at the nest and could see the tenderness in Charley's desire to put it back into the tree—even though she felt it would remain unattended.

"Charley, I was wondering what I was going to do for the next few minutes, so I'll be glad to help you."

Charley's face lit up like the sunrise after a long night of hard rain. The two of them walked to the door, and, as they exited, Pam turned around and focused on Mike's eyes. She hesitated for a moment then sent Mike a smile that melted his heart like a candle on a hot stove.

"Come on," Charley called.

With that, she left the doorway.

Mike stood motionless, staring at the opening as if at any moment, Pam would return for a repeat performance. Doug continued looking at the order that Pam had given him, knowing that it was going to be a long and difficult week ahead of him.

Breaking the silence, Mike finally spoke. "I reckon I'll be goin' to that dance Saturday night."

"I reckon you'd be a fool if you didn't. But you know you are playing with fire, don't you? Just be a little more careful than you are with hot horseshoes." There was a pause as Doug grinned at his own joke.

"You're a funny man ... a real funny man." Mike placed his fingers back into the bucket of water.

Chapter 13

Night came, leaving the air damp and thick. The waxing half moon was serenaded by the crickets and tree frogs, happy that the sun had finally gone to sleep behind the hills.

Jay Finch directed his horse down a narrow pathway, crowded by trees and the tangle of vines mixed with underbrush on either side. His mind was torn in many directions as he rode; his love of money, his desire for Pam Harrison, and his hatred for the new boy in town. He tried to concentrate on his mission as he rode through the heavy darkness. He was sure that Raif would be glad to hear the news about the location of the still in Gilbert, thirty miles up the river.

He had his plan worked out in his head. He would take a couple of Raif's men with him in a few days and make a little visit to Joshua Cain. This time, however, instead of buying his brew, they would strongly suggest that he leave the area and set up his business far away. This would expand Jay's territory and probably more than double his profit. In fact, he was thinking that he might, one day, even get into the distillation business himself. As he continued to ride, his mind thought of the endless possibilities. The area was so rural that it would be easy to carry on a bootleg business without the interference of the law.

He rounded a bend in the little-used trail and saw the light of Raif's campfire through the trees. As he drew closer, he was greeted by one of Raif's men, wielding a shotgun.

"Evenin', Able," Jay said in a low tone as he passed. Able didn't say a word, just lowered his shotgun and stepped back behind a tree to let Jay pass.

Jay stopped his horse at the edge of the firelight and walked to the crackling flames where three men were seated on logs close to Raif.

"Evenin', Jay," Raif said, not looking up from the roasted chicken leg he was nibbling on.

Jay looked at the other three men who were sitting on logs with the firelight illuminating their faces. Jay knew two of the men and saw them almost every time he came to Raif's camp, but the third was someone Jay had never seen before.

"Raif, I got some news you'll be interested in." Jay eyed the stranger.

Raif tossed the cleaned chicken bone into the fire and picked his teeth with the long dirty fingernail of his pinky finger as he looked up at Jay.

"Do tell." He sucked his teeth with an annoying sound.

Jay hesitated as he gazed at the stranger.

"Go ahead, Jay, what'd you come here to spout about?"

Jay looked back at Raif and continued.

"I made a visit to Gilbert today and found out where the still is. Figured I could take someone with me and run ol' Joshua Cain out of the county. I'll probably be makin' regular runs to Gilbert, and we could sell more 'shine there with him gone."

Raif stared into the fire, digesting what Jay had said. Jay shifted his weight from one leg to the other then crossed his arms, uncomfortable with the silence.

"You figure you can just waltz over there and scare Cain away, do ya now?" Raif finally turned his gaze to Jay.

Not how I thought you would react Raif.

"Shouldn't be much of a problem." Jay manufactured a confident tone. "He's an old man. Weren't anyone else around when I went there."

Raif looked up at the stars for a moment, as if stretching his neck, and then back into the flames. He let out a deep breath through his pursed lips.

"I didn't know Cain was still in these parts." Raif picked up a small stick from the ground at his feet. "He used to be a friend of mine."

This caught Jay by surprise, because now he could imagine Raif defending his old friend and not allowing Jay to shut Cain's operation down. He felt his business expansion slipping away like dry leaves being washed down the river.

"You may not can tell just by lookin' at him boy, but Cain don't scare easy." Raif tossed the stick into the fire.

Jay stood for a moment, believing that the matter was closed and it would be business as usual.

"Well, I guess I best be getting back to town then."

"Why don't you sit yerself down," Raif said in a low but demanding tone. "I didn't say we was finished."

Jay seated himself on a log, and watched as Raif leaned back on his perch to sit up straight.

Raif began. "Cain used to be my friend. We had a fallin' out a few years back and we most killed each other before we was pulled apart. We went our separate ways, and I figured he went back east where he was from; never figured he'd stay in these parts."

As Raif talked, Jay's composure returned. He felt his plan might have been resurrected. Raif paused as he looked at the unfamiliar man in the group then back at Jay. Jay released the breath he had been holding and noticed the cool dampness in his lungs as he began breathing again.

"You just might have a purty good idea, Jay," Raif continued, "but like I said, Cain won't be easy to scare. You're gonna need someone with you and I got just the man."

Jay looked at the two familiar souls seated beside Raif. They didn't look too intimidating; however, Jay knew that either of them would be support at least. In his mind Jay could see roughing up the old man and battering his still into a useless heap of metal if that's what it would take.

"Jay, this here is the man I'll be sendin' with you."

Jay was puzzled as Raif looked past the two and directly at the stranger who had been silently sitting in the fire's glow.

"Whadda ya mean, Raif? Who's this fella? I've never seen him before." Jay protested at the idea of taking a stranger with him on his mission.

The stranger leaned back onto his log, sporting a half-evil grin at Jay's tone, which was aimed at him.

"You might have a good idea, Jay, but I don't want you wanderin' over to Gilbert half cocked and reckless. You think you can just muscle your way up to Cain and say 'boo,' waving a stick around, and he'll run away with his tail tucked between his legs?"

"Look, Raif," Jay began, but was interrupted.

"No, … you look, boy. You're gonna do what I say and you're gonna do this my way, you hear?"

Jay clenched his teeth tightly and the muscles bulged in his jaws. He was holding back his anger, knowing better than to let it get out of control with Raif. He continued to sit in silence, with the acrid smell of wood smoke invading his head, glaring through the fire at the interloper.

"You got a problem with me, boy?" The stranger sported a cocky grin aimed at Jay.

Jay's eyes flashed back to Raif, who was glaring at him, expecting him to answer the question.

Jay looked back at the stranger and was reluctant to answer. "Naw … I guess not. But I don't even know your name. I've never seen you in these parts before. How do I know I can trust you?"

"You don't worry about that, Jay," Raif snapped. "You just do what I tell you and there won't be a problem."

Jay felt the anger welling up inside of him even stronger at being pushed around like he was only a boy who didn't know what he was doing. The addition of a stranger being in league with Raif made matters even worse.

"Tell me your name!" Jay looked across the fire, at his new travel companion.

"I'm Jeeter Morse," the stranger said. His tone held no expression. "And don't worry my friend ... we'll take care of things and have Cain out of the area in no time, and our problem with him will just float away."

With that remark, Raif looked at Jeeter then back at Jay. There was another pause in the conversation, and the air was thick with dampness, wood smoke, and tension. Jay felt like he was about to explode. Every fiber of his body seemed like a coiled spring ready to burst out of him. He didn't expect this action from Raif, and he didn't need this Morse fella taking charge of his plan.

"You come back tomorrow night, Jay, and we'll discuss the details."

"Details?" Jay said in an angry tone as he stood. "What details?"

"Watch your mouth, boy." Raif cocked his head sideways and narrowed his eyes at Jay.

"I don't need Morse comin' with me." Jay realized he was letting his emotions get out of control. "Just send Ed over there with me. We can handle it."

"You'll do as I say." Raif stood to match Jay's offensive stance.

Figuring he would push the limits too far if he said much more at the moment, Jay bit his tongue. His heart pounded in his chest, and, in the pause, he noticed that he was shaking with anger.

Raif took a few steps and stopped in front of Finch. As their eyes remained locked, Jay held his position. Without warning Raif quickly hit Jay across the right side of his face with the back of his strong right hand. Jay was a stout boy, but, being caught off guard, he lost his footing and took a step sideways as his head was snapped to the left. He turned back around to face Raif and could taste blood in his mouth. He slowly raised his arm and wiped the red trickle from his chin.

"Now, do we have this little matter settled?"

Jay remained silent and looked down at the ground sideways as he moved his tongue around the inside of his cheek, in search of the origin of the blood.

Raif turned to walk back to his wooden throne. "Good. Morse and I have become what you might call ... business partners. I think he's just what we need around here to expand this little operation ... and don't think I don't appreciate you finding that still, Jay. I'll make sure you get something extra for that."

Jay spit blood onto the ground and placed his hat back onto his head. This wasn't going at all as he had planned, but, for the moment, he didn't know what to do about it. His best play was to go along until he could figure something out. No one was going to take this away from him, not Raif and certainly not this Morse fellow.

"Go home, Jay," Raif said. "Come back tomorrow night after you have calmed yourself down. I'll have it all figured out. You'll see ... everything will be all right. There'll be enough business here for everyone."

Jay detected sarcasm in Raif's tone but, instead of saying anything, he turned and made his way back to his horse.

"Tomorrow night, Jay."

Jay mounted his horse, shot one last look over his shoulder at Morse, and then nudged his ride back down the dark pathway. Now he had another problem on his hands. To get the money he was after, he would have to somehow get rid of Jeeter Morse. He didn't know how he would accomplish it, but surely he could figure out a way. He wasn't used to being pushed around and wasn't going to let it start now.

Urging his horse to quicken its pace, Jay muttered to himself. "Things are getting out of control." As he plodded back toward his cabin, he could feel his cheek throbbing, and he vowed to give Morse what was coming to him one way or another.

***

A low rumble of thunder, and rain spattering against Mike's windowpane, woke him earlier than usual. He pulled the covers tight around his face. He didn't know whether it was dark outside because of the rain-producing clouds, or if it was just early. Either way he decided to listen to the rain for a while and not get out of bed yet.

He listened to the thunder coming from some distance away as the thunderstorm approached. He didn't exactly know why, but the sound of thunder and rain was something very calming. He remembered lying in his bed back on the farm, listening to a spring thunderstorm, and how it would wake him up suddenly, but then almost as quickly lull him back to sleep.

Thunderstorms usually came from the west, and it made him wonder if this storm had passed over his family in Kingston before making it to Rush. He wondered if his mother or father were awakened by it when it passed, and if it made them think of him. There was another rumble, this time a little louder. How he missed his family, and a small part of him wished he were back at home, under one of his mother's quilts in his familiar bed. He had only been in Rush for a few days and it was still a strange place to him.

A bright flash of lightning, accompanied in the same instant by loud thunder, made him flinch. The spring storm was on top of Rush, and rain fell in torrents being pushed by strong winds. Mike listened to the storm as it raged outside and, even though it was not severe, he would be glad when it had passed. Gentle thunder and rain was soothing. Storms were another matter.

Before long the lightning became less violent and the thunder began to fade away in the distance again. The hard rain was replaced by the sounds of a gentle shower. Now Mike could begin to see a little brightening of the sky through the window, and that signaled it was time to get out of bed and begin his day.

He lit the oil lamp on the table, got dressed, and looked through his bag for his rain gear. He knew he would have to split wood today whether it was rainy or dry. There was enough split wood for a day, but that was it. He found his rain slicker and decided to put it on and go check on his horse.

The rain continued to fall gently as Mike made his way to the Morning Star. The air was much cooler than it had been, and Mike shivered in the dampness. He got to the wood pile as Jim Smith was removing the tools from the shed to sharpen any that needed it.

"Let me give you a hand with those." Mike took two axes from Jim's grasp.

"It's gonna be a messy one all day, I'm afraid." They began making their way to the sharpening wheel.

"This heavy coat isn't going to make splitting very easy, either," Mike replied.

Jim sat at the rock wheel and began sharpening one of the axes. "We had a tin roof to work under until a wind ripped it off the building last month. Harrison hasn't had it replaced yet … says he'll get to it soon."

"His intentions don't help us today, do they?" Mike chuckled and noticed that his breath was steaming. He shuddered again in the dampness. "I guess splitting wood will warm us up."

"Yeah, but keep your raincoat on … wouldn't want you getting sick on me. Being cold is one thing … being wet is another … but being wet and cold could kill a body."

"Jim, you sound like my mother."

Jim smiled.

"But she's prettier than you."

The two had a laugh, and, after they had finished inspecting the tools, they met the other two choppers, grumpy about the weather, and began splitting wood. The knee-length coat kept Mike reasonably dry but was cumbersome when it came to swinging an axe. He had never had to split wood out in inclement weather before, because they had always been able to split wood in the barn back home if need be.

After a couple of hours, the rain lessened to a drizzle, and, since Mike had been fighting the slicker all morning, he decided to take it off and work without it. He was relieved to shed the heavy outerwear and was warm enough as long as he kept up the pace.

By the end of the day, Mike was wet from the steady, cold drizzle but had split his usual pile of oak sections. His overalls were heavy from the water they had absorbed, but that hadn't bothered him as much as the long, bulky raincoat had. Now that he had stopped splitting, he felt the cold again, only much more than earlier now that he was wet. He sought the refuge of the discarded raincoat for extra warmth, and, after donning it, buttoned it tight, in an attempt to hold in his body heat, what little there was of it.

Mike placed his axe into the tool shed and hurried back to his place, where he planned on making a fire in the stove to help him warm up. As soon as the door closed behind him he shed his wet clothes and put on dry ones. Although he felt better, he was still shivering. Before long, a fire was burning in the cook stove. He piled as much wood into it as he dared so it would begin radiating its warmth as soon as possible.

It didn't take long for him to feel the heat radiating from the wood stove, and he slowly turned in front of it as if he were a pig on a spit, being rotated over a fire for even cooking. If anyone else had been there with him he might have placed an apple in his mouth and made the image complete. Thinking about the apple made him realize he was hungry, so when he was warm enough to stop shivering, he checked his supply of food only to realize that he needed to buy some more.

He cringed at the thought of buying more food because he hadn't begun to receive a weekly pay, and he had to be careful with what little money he had left. If he had only been able to get his money from the bank he would have no worries … but. He stopped thinking about what he couldn't change and walked around the porch to Rosie's. He hoped she had a fire burning in her wood stove next to the checkerboard. He might back up to it and stay for a while to warm up with her wood since his was a more limited supply.

Mike was disappointed to find that Rosie was not in her store, so he made small talk with Beth about the cold, rainy weather and, after making a few purchases, said goodbye to her and walked back to his place. He set his supplies onto his little table and slumped onto the edge of his bed. He hadn't noticed it before, but his head was beginning to hurt a little. Hoping his headache would go away, Mike decided to disregard his hunger pangs and lie back on his bed. Since he wasn't prone to headaches, he figured a little rest under the warm covers would help. It didn't take long after warming up for Mike to doze off to the sound of the wood crackling and popping in the wood stove. It was still early evening but Mike was fast asleep.

***

The rain had stopped, but the sky was still clouded, making the night even darker than usual. Jay rode away from Raif's camp angrier than the night before, but he had not let his anger get the better of him this time. Although he still felt the bruise on his right jaw, he was able to calmly discuss the plan Raif had put together.

Jay was scheduled to make another run to Gilbert on Saturday to deliver more parts, so he would ride out of town and pick up Jeeter Morse on the road. The two of them would get to Gilbert and make a trip to Cain's place. Hopefully he would be alone again, which would make it easy to persuade him to leave the area. Jay was still frustrated that Raif was sending Jeeter along with him, and he was still in the dark about this "business arrangement" Jeeter had with Raif. There was nothing he could do about it at this point but accept it for what it was and bide his time until he could sort things out.

At least he would have help getting rid of Cain, and then, after that was done, he could figure out what to do about Morse. Raif had suggested strongly that he wanted to get rid of Cain without trashing his still. That would make the persuasion a little more difficult, but Jay understood now that Raif needed that equipment to be able to handle the extra liquor production, something he had not thought about.

If all went well, Jay's plan was to get back to Rush in time to make the dance in the evening. Thoughts of dancing with Pamela caused him to smile. He dreamed of the day when his pockets would be filled with enough cash to make old man Harrison sit up and take note of him as being an eligible suitor. Hopefully, if his crafty new plan panned out, his lucrative endeavor would reach that point very soon.

***

Mike awoke on Wednesday morning feeling achy in other places besides his head, and his dull headache was still present. Even though he had adequate covers, he felt chilled. Mike noticed that the room was much brighter than it usually was when he got ready for work. He stood too quickly, and for a moment the room spun around him. He steadied himself against the chair at the table and, when the spinning stopped, grabbed his pocket watch and flipped the case open.

Immediately he panicked because he was fifteen minutes late for work. He could feel his heart pound in his chest at the realization of being late. He dressed as fast as he could, splashed some cool water onto his face and bolted out the door, putting on his light jacket as he went. The morning was cool and crisp but the sunlight felt warm on his face as he ran toward the Morning Star.

When he arrived, Jim and the others were already splitting, and he broke out in a cold sweat from his embarrassment.

"About time you showed up, lazy bones," Jim said in a playful tone.

"I'm sorry, Jim." Mike rushed past him to the tool shed to grab an axe.

Jim stopped his work for a moment as he looked at Mike. "You're as white as a glass of milk. You feel okay, kid?"

Mike headed back toward his wood pile. "Got a bit of a headache, but I'm okay."

Mike placed his first piece of wood section onto the chopping block.

"You don't look too good to me."

"I said I was fine," Mike snapped.

"Okay." Jim returned to his work.

Mike split wood at an accelerated pace to make up for the time he had lost getting to work late. He had just made his first swing on his fifth piece of wood when he became dizzy again, only this time it didn't go away. With the axe raised for another blow, he lost his balance and staggered. He momentarily regained his balance and lowered the axe.

"Jim, I don't feel so good." With that, Mike dropped to one knee.

Jim released his axe and rushed to Mike's side. At that point the only thing holding Mike up was the tool he was leaning on. Jim took Mike by the arm and, as he lifted him, the axe fell to the ground. As Jim placed Mike's arm around his neck, Mike's knees buckled. Jim motioned for the closest man to take Mike's other arm and help get him into the building.

Inside Harrison's office, they placed him into an armed chair and leaned his head against the high, padded back.

Jim felt of Mike's forehead. "You're burning up with fever."

"I'm okay, Jim. Just let me rest here for a minute and I'll be okay."

"You're not okay, boy. I told you not to take your coat off yesterday, but you wouldn't listen."

Mike mumbled again with his eyes closed, noticing that every joint in his body was aching. "Quit squawkin' at me, Jim."

"What's goin on in here?"

Jim turned to see Harrison standing in the doorway surveying the three workers inside his office rather than out splitting wood.

"The dang fool is sick from getting wet yesterday," Jim said.

Harrison looked annoyed at the intrusion into his office. "Does he need two nursemaids?"

There was silence.

"One of you go find Doc Lipscomb and the other get back to work. That wood won't split itself, you know."

"Leon, go find Doc, and I'll get back outside." Jim whispered, "I'll swear there isn't a caring bone in Harrison's body."

Leon smiled and left to find Doc as Harrison's glare followed him out the door.

"Just rest kid, Doc Lip will be right here." Jim turned to make his way out of the office and back to the wood pile.

Wiping his face with his hand, Jacob Harrison looked at Mike slumped into one of his chairs. He could see that Mike was truly ill, but his mind turned to productivity on the wood pile. He had a thought, so he turned and made his way back into the mill. Within moments he found Jay filling the grease can, preparing to climb and lubricate the pivots and joints above the main boiler.

"Finch!" Harrison hollered over the noise of the machinery.

Jay looked up to see Harrison headed in his direction.

"Finch, I need you on the wood pile."

"Wood pile?" Jay began to protest. "I was about to …"

"Never mind what you were about to do; Jim needs you to split some wood. We're a man short today."

Jay hesitated for a moment too long.

"Now, Finch!" Harrison barked. "I can find someone else to be the grease monkey."

In his frustration, Jay set the grease can down a little too hard, and some of the thick goo spattered out of the can and onto his neck. He acted as if he didn't notice it and stormed off toward the door, waiting until he was out of Harrison's sight before wiping off the greasy glob.

Making his way back to his office, Harrison found yet another surprise.

Pam was crouched next to Mike, who was asleep in the chair and breathing with a heaviness that was causing her concern.

"What in the world are you doing here, Pamela?"

Pam turned to see her father glaring at her over his round spectacles.

"I came to bring you your lunch, which you forgot again this morning."

Jacob tried to make his voice sound more endearing. "Sorry, sweetheart, but the boy's sick, and you shouldn't get too close."

"Yes, Mike does look and sound like he's in pretty bad shape."

"You know this boy?"

"Yes; I met him just the other day. We had a nice long chat on Rosie's front porch."

"What have I told you about the boys around here?"

"Relax, Father, he's just a nice boy. No harm in being polite to him, is there?"

"Politeness coming from a pretty girl is usually taken in a different way with boys." Just then Doc Lipscomb opened the office door and entered with his black bag in hand.

Lipscomb sported a smile. "Nice day for a house call, wouldn't you say?" He was a short, round, jolly fellow who always had a good word to say. His years of seeing sickness and sometimes death had not rusted his fixed enthusiasm for life.

"There's your patient, Doc." Harrison pointed to Mike in the chair. From where he was standing, Lipscomb could hear the clatter in Mike's chest as he breathed. Pam backed away a few steps and allowed the doctor plenty of room to check Mike out thoroughly.

"I think with a little medicine and some rest he'll be in good shape in a day or two."

146

"Couple of days?" Harrison moaned.

"If we don't take care of this, it could turn into influenza or pneumonia. Don't want that, do you? I know you want him back to work, Jacob, but the kid has to rest."

"Can you take him back to your place to keep him medicated?"

"'Fraid my two beds are in use right now."

"He could come to our place," Pam said.

"You know better than that, Pamela."

"Please, Father. You said you want him back to work as soon as possible, and he needs someone to medicate him so he can."

"Sorry ... out of the question." "He could stay in the guest room. It's not improper. You know May Bess is always there and ..."

"She has a point, Jacob. Besides ... I have a feeling that he wouldn't be in this shape if you had replaced that tin shelter that blew away." The doc looked over at Pam, letting her know she had an ally, then back at Harrison. Jacob Harrison was at a loss for words, which rarely happened.

"I'll put him in my wagon and take him around the corner to your house. I'll see that he is tucked into bed and give the instructions along with the medication to May Bess."

Being outnumbered by his sweet daughter and the good doctor, Jacob lifted his arms out to his sides then back down again in surrender.

Jacob looked directly into Pam's eyes. "Just remember, as soon as he can get up and on his feet, he's out of the house."

"Oh, Father, you make it sound like a wounded stray you're getting rid of."

"Good. I see you get my point." At that, Jacob turned and made his way back into the mill.

"I'll go tell May Bess to get things ready," Pam said.

She left the room before Doc had time to ask for help loading Mike into the buggy. He looked at Mike, who was still asleep and shrugged his shoulders.

"Come on, boy." He patted Mike's face with his hand. "I'm gonna need your help."

***

Several hours passed before Mike awoke. At first, with haziness still roaming around in his head, he thought he was back at the farm in his own bed. As he became more aware, he opened his eyes and knew he wasn't on the farm but still couldn't identify his surroundings.

He coughed thick mucus from his chest into his throat. His head was pounding. Though Mike didn't know where he was, the soft bed beckoned him to remain under the covers. Because of the way he felt, he complied and closed his eyes once again. He became aware of his other senses and could hear the ticking of a mantle clock somewhere in the room. He also caught the faint aroma of something that smelled like chicken being cooked. In his mouth he had a bitter taste that reminded him of laudanum, a medicine he had used several times in his life and hated with a passion.

He coughed again, and, as he laid his head back onto the feather pillow, he heard light footsteps coming toward his room from the hallway. The footsteps stopped at his door, and it opened with a soft creak. He turned his head toward the doorway and parted his eyelids.

"It's about time you woke up, because you need to take some more medicine."

Mike opened his eyes wider and saw Pam leaning against the door frame with her arms folded in front of her.

"What are you doing here?"

"I live here."

Mike closed his eyes tight and winced at the pain in his head.

"You passed out at the mill and Doc Lipscomb sent you here because he had no room at his office."

"It feels like I've been run over by a delivery wagon then drug behind it."

Pam laughed.

"How long have I been here?"

148

"Since about eight o'clock this morning. You've been asleep for five hours."

"Five hours? I need to be at work."

Pam walked closer to his bedside. "You need to be right where you are for at least a day, maybe more, according to the doctor."

Mike didn't mind where he was, because the presence of Pam was sure to be more medicinal than the bitter fluid he'd probably have to ingest, but he knew that he was needed at the woodpile and didn't want to let Jim down.

"Your dad ..." Mike began.

"Don't worry about him; he didn't have much of a chance between me and the doc, and besides, May Bess is here and she's the one lookin' after you. I'm just enjoying the company."

Mike couldn't hold back the slight smile that formed on his face.

"Who's May Bess?"

"She's my father's sister. She stays with us and helps with the housework. Mother is gone seems half of the time, and May Bess is like a second mother to me. In fact, I think she likes me more than my own mother does."

Mike closed his eyes again. "Oh, I'm sure that's not so. Do you think I could have some water? I'm really thirsty."

"Yes, and you need to stay awake for a while. May Bess made some chicken with dumplings, and the doc says you need to eat a little something with your medicine or you will get sick to your stomach."

"Okay ... I'll try to stay awake." Mike opened his eyes again.

Pam tilted her head as if to get a look at Mike from a different angle and remained silent as she smiled.

"What?"

"Oh, nothing. I'll go see if May Bess has your food ready."

Though it smelled good, food didn't seem that interesting to Mike. He wanted to go back to sleep, but he

149

persuaded himself to stay awake. It wasn't long before May Bess came to his room with a tray. On the tray was a bowl of steaming soup, and beside it were a glass of water and a brown bottle of medication.

"Mike, this is May Bess," Pam said.

Mike managed a smile as May Bess helped him sit up and propped pillows behind him. She then placed the tray across his lap.

"Thanks." Mike looked into the bowl of mostly chicken broth.

"Make sure you eat as much of the chicken stock as you can before you take your medicine."

Mike looked at the spoon, desiring more sleep. With a sideways grin, he looked back up at the pair standing next to his bedside. "You … gonna watch me eat?"

The two women rolled their eyes and began walking back toward the doorway.

"I'll be back in a little while to take the tray away," Pam said. "And take two spoonfuls of medication when you are finished eating. Then you can drift back off into dreamland. Oh, and I'll know if you took your medicine."

The pair walked out of the room, where Mike was once again left with only the sound of the ticking clock. He stared at the bowl for a few minutes, and then he picked up the spoon, slurping the liquid from it. The warm, salty flavor was soothing in his mouth, and the moisture felt good in his throat. He swallowed the first spoonful and before he knew it, the bowl was empty.

He dreaded taking the medicine and wished he would have had the forethought to save some of the soup to wash the bitter taste from his mouth. "Here goes," he said out loud. Mike forced himself to swallow the medicine then pushed the cork stopper back into the bottle. His lips twisted in agony at the bitter taste, and he was glad no one was around to see it. He lifted the tray from across his lap and set it beside him on the bed. Snuggling back down under the

150

covers, he closed his eyes, and within moments, sank back into a deep sleep.

Before collecting the tray, Pam stood in the doorway and watched him. She could hear his breathing, which was beginning to sound better than it had a few hours earlier. She crept into his room and picked up the tray. Before leaving she leaned over and kissed him on the cheek. He didn't stir as she stood, lingered for a moment, and then exited the room.

Back in the kitchen, Pam handed May Bess the food tray. "He seems to be a nice boy," May Bess said.

Pam stood beside the sink and smiled. "Yes, he does. He certainly does indeed."

Chapter 14

It didn't take long for Mike to recover from his illness, and by Thursday morning he was feeling fit as a fiddle. His fever had broken sometime during the night, and, though he felt a little weak, he believed he could swing an axe again. Although it was still dark outside, as he dressed he noticed a fresh bowl of water and a clean towel on the dresser. After washing up, he made the bed and crept down the hall toward what he hoped was the front door. He carried his boots in his hands so that he would make less noise walking. The sky was now beginning to show the morning light outside, and he hoped no one was awake.

Making his way into the front room, he spotted the front door. He was halfway across the room when a low, deep voice stopped him in his tracks.

"Work doesn't start for another few hours, Gilbert."

Mike turned to see Jacob Harrison, through the darkness of the room, seated in a padded high-backed chair next to a small table with a Holy Bible on it. Harrison was still in his house coat and brown leather slippers, and it appeared he had just sat down before Mike had entered the room.

"Sorry if I woke you up, sir." "Where are you off to at this hour?"

Mike paused for a moment before he answered. "Just figured I'd go back to my place and put on some clean clothes before headin' in to work. I've got some catchin' up to do."

"Son, I appreciate your enthusiasm, but don't you think you should take another day to rest? Jim has it covered until you return."

"Oh no, sir … I feel just fine. Just need to get some solid food in me and I'll be...."

"Well," Jacob interrupted as he stood. He lit the oil lamp next to him and placed the extinguished match into an ash tray. "Why don't you stay here and have a little breakfast first? I think we're having cured ham with biscuits and gravy this morning. May Bess should be in the kitchen any time now."

Mike stood in the dim morning light with his boots in his hands and didn't know how to respond. He was surprised that the manager of the Morning Star was inviting him to stay for breakfast. He remembered Harrison protesting his coming the day before.

"Sir, I should probably be going. I appreciate the kind offer, and I'm sure the biscuits are wonderful, but if I'm going to get to the wood pile on time I need to get back home."

"Well ... suit yourself Gilbert, but I'd strongly suggest you take the day and rest. I wouldn't want you driving an axe into your foot."

Mike cringed at the thought, but knew he would be fine.

"Mr. Harrison, I appreciate your hospitality lettin' me stay here overnight. May Bess took care of me like my own momma would have." He looked around the room. "And you have a very nice home here."

"Thank you, Michael, and I'll pass the compliment on to my sister."

There was another pause, and then Mike smiled and made his way to the door. As his hand reached the doorknob, Pam entered from the hallway.

"Leaving so early?"

"I've got work to do." Although he replied with a smile, he quickly removed it from his face when he saw Mr. Harrison studying him.

"Goodbye, Mr. Harrison ... goodbye, Pam. I guess I'll see you around."

Mike opened the door and let in the fresh morning air. The day was going to be a sunny one, and it already felt warm, unlike two days earlier. As he was closing the door behind him, he glanced one last time at Pam, still standing on the other side of the room. He mentally kicked himself from turning down the breakfast invitation. He was tempted to change his mind but closed the door instead. He sat down on the top step of the wooden porch and put on his boots.

After checking on his horse, Mike quickened his pace and entered his room, where he changed into a fresh set of overalls and a clean shirt. He decided to spend a few cents and see what Rosie had for breakfast. Anything would taste good to him. After being up for a while, his appetite was coming back, and he knew he would need the energy.

"Morning, darlin'." Rosie smiled as Mike entered and walked up to the counter. He noticed the two small round tables were in use, but there was a tall stool at the counter, so he hopped upon it and smiled.

"What's got you grinnin' from ear to ear today?" Rosie poured him a cup of coffee, which she knew he would request. "By the way, I heard you got sick. Feelin' better?"

"News travels fast in this town, don't it?" Mike picked up the hot cup of coffee.

"I'll be back with you in a minute." Rosie left the counter and walked to one of the tables, which had four suited men around it.

"Mornin, Beth." Mike greeted her when he saw her elbow poking out from behind the doorway. Beth leaned back where just her head and left shoulder were visible to see who was sending her the salutation.

"Good mornin', Mike. I thought that was you." She returned out of view to her chore.

After a few minutes Rosie returned to her place behind the counter and without even asking Mike what he wanted, began preparing him three eggs, some ham, and toast.

"Three eggs, Rosie?" "Eggs'll give you energy after you've been sick. And I don't know which is worse, bein' sick or drinkin' that quack juice the doctor always makes a body take. These ham and eggs will perk you right up and

154

give you back your get-up-and-go that the medicine took out of ya." She turned the eggs over and flipped the ham in the skillet. "I swear … no matter what's wrong with you, that doctor will give you the same medicine for everything. You'd think it was some kind of miracle cure he got from some peddler drivin' a wagon through town."

"Well, whatever it was, I sure do feel better now."

"Oh, piddle. Yer just feelin' better because you had you some good ol' fashioned attention over at Harrison's house."

"Does everybody tell you everything around here?"

Rosie chuckled. "Not everything, just the important stuff."

She plated the food for Mike, and as she handed it to him he leaned over and asked, "Who are the fancy pants over at that table?"

Rosie shifted her gaze in their direction then back at Mike. "They're here to see if there are any investments they can take advantage of."

Mike shoved the first fork-full loaded with eggs into his mouth. "What kind of investments?"

"Oh I dunno … prosperous mines, cheap property to build on, maybe even put in a bank."

"A bank would be nice," Mike said. "Could I have some milk?"

Rosie poured milk from a nearby pitcher and set the glass in front of Mike.

"Maybe they would like to buy your place, Rosie."

"Humph, nobody in their right mind would buy this place."

Mike laughed as he chewed on a piece of ham that made his right cheek bulge. Finishing his meal, he left two bits on the counter and said goodbye to Rosie. When he arrived at the mill he found Jim sharpening the tools.

"Hey, Jim."

"Mornin', Mike. Nice to see you back."

"Feels good to be back."

"Boss wanted me to tell you to take it easy today and don't get into too big of a hurry; said he didn't want you to get yourself hurt."

"I'll be just fine, Jim. Don't worry about me."

Mid-morning, Mike took a break and made his way to the water bucket. While he was drinking his second ladle full, he saw Pamela walk from around the corner of the building with something in her hand.

"Thought you could sneak out and leave this behind did you?" She handed him the bottle of medicine the doc had left for him.

"Doctor Lipscomb said you had to take the complete bottle no matter how you felt." She sounded as if she were scolding him.

Mike looked at the other workers, who were watching the couple with interest.

"Uh…thanks, Pam." Mike took the bottle from her and slipped it into his pocket.

"Can I trust you to take it on your own?"

"I don't know … this stuff tastes pretty darn bad, and I feel just great."

"Oh, don't be such a baby."

"I'll take it."

"Just make sure that you do. Wouldn't want your fever to return and you get sick all over. But then again …" She smiled. "Well, I best get back to the house." Goodbye."

Mike watched until she disappeared around the corner of the building.

"Goodbye." Jim and the other two wood cutters all spoke in unison, using an affected high voice as if it had been rehearsed. Mike's face turned as red as a beet. He didn't turn to face the trio but walked back to his axe and began splitting oak sections once more. For the rest of the day, he could think of nothing other than Pam. He didn't understand what she had done to him, but in only a few short days she had already gotten a tight grip on his heart … and he liked it.

156

By the end of the day on Friday, Mike had regained his strength and was back to his normal self. When the time came to quit for the day, he had produced his usual pile of wood and then some. Since he had missed a couple days of work, he decided to work for at least half a day on Saturday to make up for it. He didn't want to work all day, however, because he needed time to clean up for the dance. He hadn't seen Pam since she brought his medicine bottle to him the day before. He was anxious to ask her for a spin or two around the floor, or however many dances she would grace him with.

After washing his dinner dishes, he decided to do a little reading before sleep. He lit the oil lamp and opened his Bible, something which he hadn't done since leaving home. He began reading in the book of John, and felt the comfort he always received when he read the Holy Scriptures about his Savior.

Within thirty minutes his eyelids began to get heavy. He placed a ribbon at the page where he had stopped reading. As he started closing the book, the pages fell together leaving the cover still open in his hand. He looked at the inside page of the cover and read what he had read many times before in his life:

This Bible Is Presented To: Michael Gilbert
On: July 12, 1892
 By: William and Rachel Gilbert.
Occasion: Baptism in the King's River by Rev. M.B. Russell

He placed his fingers on the handwriting as if trying to touch his parents in some way. Although he was beginning to settle into his new life, his mind was constantly on them and how much he missed seeing them. He hoped he would be able to go home sometime during the summer or fall and see them all again.

He closed the cover and blew out the lamp. As he shut his eyes after settling under his covers, he said a prayer of protection for his family and for comfort to them as they were still certainly mourning his leaving. Within minutes after closing his prayer, he drifted off to sleep listening to the crickets and spring peepers singing to him in the night air.

***

Work on Saturday mornings started just the same as any other morning on the Gilbert farm. The daylight was beginning to brighten the sky earlier each day as the springtime reached for summer. The last frost of the season had evaporated two weeks earlier, and the days were quickly becoming almost hot overnight. Some of the seeds which had been planted were already sprouting and poking their crooked necks out of the warming soil.

It was seven o'clock in the morning, and William Gilbert had already completed two hours of work. He was in the barn repairing a stall door when his blue tick hound began baying, signaling the approach of a visitor. William had learned the different barks and bays of his dog, and could tell the difference between a treed raccoon and an approaching horse. Placing his hammer on a nearby bale of hay, he picked up a rag to wipe his hands as he exited into the early morning sunlight.

He stopped and shielded his eyes with his forearm to try and see who was riding toward him. The rider noticed William and stopped in front of him.

"Mornin, William."

"Hey, Jimmy. What brings you out this way so early in the morning? You're not even open for business yet, are ya?"

Jimmy Barnes's feet hit the ground and he walked to William.

"No, the store doesn't open for an hour yet, but I thought I'd bring this over to you. It came yesterday. I didn't know when you would be in town to check your box, and I knew you would want it as soon as it arrived."

158

William looked puzzled as Jimmy reached into the pocket of his jacket. "What's so important that you had to get out so early?" Jimmy handed him a white envelope. William turned it over and noticed that the envelope was addressed to the Gilbert family. William's countenance brightened as he saw that the sender was Mike Gilbert.

"I thought you might want it as soon as possible," Jimmy said again.

William looked up at him with a grin as wide as his barn door. "Thanks, Jimmy ... thank you kindly." William began moving toward the house.

"I hope it's good news!" Jimmy shouted.

William didn't even ponder the rudeness of leaving Jimmy standing in the lane holding the reins to his horse. His only thought was opening the letter and reading it to Rachel. It had been almost two weeks since Mike had left, and they were finally hearing from him. He leapt over two wooden steps and landed on the small porch outside the kitchen door. He flung open the door with such force that it rolled the cat, who had chosen that very spot for a nap, across the wooden floor, wailing as it crashed into the table legs. At the same instant, Rachel dropped her stirring spoon into her pot and gasped as if the walls were collapsing around her.

"William Gilbert, why in Heaven's name are you bursting into my kitchen? You just about scared the life out of me and darn near killed the cat. Did you even stop to wipe your feet?" She placed her hand up to her chest as if gasping to catch her breath.

William walked over to her and held up the envelope for her to see. "We got a letter from Michael."

Since it was calving season, Mark and Luke were out checking on the herd. As soon as calves were dropped, they were easy prey for coyotes and stray dogs. It was their job to count the calves which had been born overnight, and help in the delivery if they saw a cow in distress giving birth. William knew that it would be at least a couple of hours before they were finished with that task and came back to the house. He couldn't wait that long to read Mike's letter to everyone, so he and Rachel sat at the kitchen table as he eagerly opened the envelope. He placed his reading glasses onto his nose, pulled out the single page of paper, and began digesting every word as he read aloud.

Dear Ma and Pa,

First of all I want to tell you that I am doing just fine. My trip was uneventful and Ma's food took me most of the way. I had to stop in a town for one meal just before I got to where I was headed.

I'm in Rush, Arkansas, just a few counties over east. It is a Zinc mining town and it is next to the Buffalo River. I read about it in the Mountain Echo *paper last year and it sounded like a place where a fella could make a good living for himself. I haven't met many people yet but I have gotten to know a lady who runs a store here. Her name is Rosie and she is real nice. I am in a hotel tonight but hope to find living quarters and a job soon. There is a lot of activity here with all of the miners and a job should not be hard to find.*

The Buffalo River is as pretty here as it is at the other end. It reminds me of home. Seems everything here reminds me of home and even though I miss all of you I feel like I am in the right spot. I will write you all again soon when I have my own place to live and have more news. I hope you are all doing fine and tell Mark that I hope he is enjoying the extra room. Will you also give my apologies to Mr. Davis at the bank for my behavior? I'm sure he has told you what happened. He was just doing his job and I will repay him for the damages the next time I am that direction. I will write again as soon as I can.

Love
Mike

P.S. Ma I sure do miss your cooking

William removed his glasses and stared at the letter in his hands, thinking about the boy who was so far away.

"Where exactly is Rush?" Rachel said, breaking the silence.

"Never heard of the place. But I'm sure gonna find out where it is."

He folded the piece of paper and placed it back in the envelope. Handing it to Rachel, he stood from the table, seeming a little saddened by the letter.

Rachel looked up at him as he started to the door.

"Did you expect him to say he was homesick and was coming home?"

"I'm not sure what I expected." William placed his hat onto his head. "For some reason I had the idea that he was at least going somewhere with a grander plan than to become a miner."

"I'm sure he has bigger plans than that." Rachel rose to her feet. "After all, you have to start somewhere. Even a mighty river begins with a single drop of rain."

The harsh words William had said to Mike on the day he left were on his mind. Now that he knew where Mike was, his thoughts were on making peace. He loved his son and wanted him to somehow know. He couldn't send a letter back, because he had no return address. For now he would just wait and try to figure out how to settle things between them. He walked back out into the morning sunlight, where he was met by the smell of spring flowers mingled with the sharp fragrance of cow manure. "There's no place like home," William said out loud to himself as he walked toward the barn.

Chapter 15

Charley counted the nails for his brother earlier than usual, and, after proclaiming he had a hundred, wandered over to Rosie's as he so often did. As usual he was wearing denim overalls without a shirt. The early morning springtime air felt cool and refreshing as it touched his bare skin.

He walked through the door and over to the grocery side, looking for his jolly female friend.

"Mornin', Charley boy." Rosie stood up from behind the counter.

Charley walked to the counter where Rosie was preparing a bill for a customer.

"Is there somethin' I can do for ya this morning?" Charley's hands were in his pockets, pushing them down as deep as they would go.

"Can't think of a thing right now, hon." She finished with her customer. "What's that brother of yers up to today?"

"Just fixin' horses like he always does on the day before church day."

"Is tomorrow church day?"

"Church day, and the parson's gonna be here."

"I plumb forgot, Charley. I'm so glad you reminded me."

Charley got a look of pride on his face for reminding Rosie, even though she had never set foot in the community church since she had been in Rush.

She stepped out from behind the counter to face Charley. "You know, come to think of it, I do need something delivered to ol' man Jenkins over at the livery. You could save me a few steps if you would take it to him for me."

Charlie's face brightened with that news. He loved running errands for folks and every day made the rounds to as many people as he could. No one seemed to be pestered by Charley, and most everyone was fond of him.

"Why don't you sit yerself down and have a biscuit or two before you go. I'll get Beth to bring them right out."

Charley sat down at a little table close to the counter, in a wooden chair that had one leg shorter than the other three. He slid down into the chair enough so that his head could lie on the top of the back rest. While he waited for his biscuits, he placed his hands into his overall pockets again and rocked the chair back and forth from side to side, causing the chair to make an annoying rhythmic clunk on the wooden floor with each lean.

Two men seated next to him at the other table stopped their conversation after a few moments and glared at him for continuing the monotonous sound. Charley looked at them and smiled, not knowing why they were scowling at him. He pulled a hand out of a pocket while he continued to rock and gave them a slight wave.

"Mornin'." Charley replaced his hand into his pocket.

"Do you mind?" one of the men said.

"I mind all the time," Charley said. He gave the man a big grin, proud that he was not a trouble causer.

The man motioned with his eyes toward the chair legs. "I'm talking about the chair. Please quit making that annoying racket."

Charley stopped rocking the chair and his cheeks turned red, as if he had been scolded by the preacher.

The two men turned back to each other and continued their conversation. Charley had seen men like them come and go, always concerned about how productive the mines were but didn't care at all about acting polite to the local town folk.

Charley tried to be still, but every once in a while he could not resist the temptation to clack the chair legs back and forth a few times. It was difficult for him to not wiggle, but he didn't want to cause any problems.

It wasn't long before Beth appeared and set down a plate with a couple of biscuits on it. In the middle of the biscuits she had placed thick cut slabs of sizzling bacon, allowing the bread to soak up the wonderful bacon grease.

"Here ya go, Charley." She set a glass of milk down with the plate.

The plate barely had time to hit the table before one of the biscuits was already up to his mouth. Beth smiled and walked back behind the counter to wipe it down with a rag.

Charley lifted the glass to his lips, and, as he washed the first mouthful of bacon biscuit down, he overheard part of the conversation from the table next to him.

"Just last week … I read it in the paper. Seems the gunman had a hostage and got away with several hundred dollars," one man said.

"Kingston isn't too far away from here. That robber could be anywhere in these parts," the other man replied.

"Well, from what I understand, the banker took a couple of shots and hit the scoundrel in the leg as he rode out of town."

The other man shook his head as he gazed out the window. "You'd think we were back in the wooly west. If you ask me, when they catch that man, they aught to hang him like they did in the good ol' days, and maybe that would stop that sort of thing. We're living in the twentieth century now, for Heaven's sake."

"Charley, you about done?" She walked up to him from the doorway of the hardware side of the store.

"Yes 'm." He stood, holding the remaining couple of bites of biscuit in his hand. He stood so fast that his legs pushed the chair back then over onto the floor with a loud bang. The two gentlemen turned around, startled at the sudden noise against the wooden floor.

"Sorry, fellas," Rosie said. Charley righted the chair then walked into the other room to receive instructions for his delivery. The two men shook their heads and finished their meal.

***

Jay pulled away from the mill with a load full of boiler parts. As he rounded the building, he noticed Mike at the wood pile. The two of them glared at each other, but Finch didn't even bother to smirk. He allowed himself to imagine running over Mike with the wagon and dragging him down the road. He then turned his head back toward the road in front of him and flipped the reins.

Finch's wagon full of Iron parts slowed as the team strained to pull the weight of the load up the grade out of Rush. Jay continued flipping the reins, trying to encourage the horses onward. Slowly they made their way to the crest of the hill then were able to resume their steady pace.

Jay watched with interest as a bobcat walked across the road in front of him. It stopped in the bushes to take a look at him and the team, and after observing for a few moments, darted into the underbrush. Jay turned in his seat to see if he could catch a glimpse of it as it darted through the trees. Suddenly, the team stopped, and Jay whirled around to see Jeeter standing in front of the horses.

"You were supposed to meet me at the junction up ahead. We're too close to town, and someone could see you."

Jeeter walked around the wagon and climbed into the right side of the seat. The rusty springs creaked as the seat lowered with the extra weight.

"Didn't want to go that far when I could catch a ride from here." Jeeter spoke with a solemn frankness.

Jay continued his glare, and for a moment thought about shoving Jeeter off the wagon with his foot and dealing with Raif at a later time about the reckless actions of his new "business partner."

"Well, hadn't we better continue?" Jeeter said sarcastically, "Wouldn't want someone to see me ridin' with you, would we?"

For now Jay would bide his time and get the day over with, then figure out how to handle Jeeter. He needed the extra muscle with him when he dealt with Cain in Gilbert. Through the next couple of hours there was not a word said

165

between Finch and Morse as they rode. They each had their own thoughts and kept them to themselves.

Rounding a bend in the road, they approached Gilbert. The first order of business was to deliver the parts and receive payment; then they would head to the still.

Jay stopped the wagon at the edge of town and turned to Morse.

"Why are we stopping here?"

"This is where you get off," Finch said. "We don't want anyone seeing you with me."

Jeeter looked around and then hopped off the wagon. "I think I'll walk into town and get me a soda water."

"Hang yourself for all I care, just meet me back here by that oak tree yonder in an hour. That's about how long it will take to unload and get paid up at the office."

"Oh, don't you worry." Jeeter smiled. "I wouldn't want to miss this for the world."

Jay didn't like the sound of his comment but didn't reply. He flipped the reins and left Jeeter standing by the side of the road.

"Maybe someone will shoot you before I get back," Jay mumbled.

With the wagon unloaded and payment received, Jay drove his team to the edge of town where he hoped Jeeter would not be present. But as he neared, he spotted Jeeter resting under the oak tree with his hat pulled down over his eyes. Though he didn't want to stop, Jay pulled back on the reins and sat there waiting for Jeeter to acknowledge his presence.

"We don't have all day." Jay tried not to let his nervousness show.

Jeeter lifted the brim of his hat and looked up at Jay. He raised his hand to shield his eyes from the sun, which was directly over Jay's shoulder. "Sounds like you're afraid you won't make it back in time for the dance tonight."

Jay remained silent. Sure he wanted to get back for the dance, but without even wanting to admit it to himself, he was becoming a little nervous with what they were about to do. Not only that, but he still was apprehensive about bringing a stranger along with him. *I sure hope Raif knows what he's doing.*

Jeeter lowered his hand and stood. He took his time walking around the team and clambering up into the wooden bench seat.

"Before we get too close to Cain's place, you'll need to get back into the wagon and cover yourself with that tarp. I don't want Cain to get spooked if he sees me already bringin' a stranger along with me."

Jeeter finished brushing pieces of grass and leaves from his sleeves and pants. "Yer joshin' me, right? I'm not gettin' back there and hidin' from nobody."

"Yes, you will, or I'll turn this wagon around."

Jeeter smiled as he peered off into the woods. "I don't think Raif would take too kindly to that."

"You let me worry about Raif. If we're doin this deal, you'll do what I say."

"Yer gettin' kinda' uppity ... and I don't like it."

"Well I don't think Raif would like you spookin' Cain so we could never get within a mile of him again."

Jeeter's eyes narrowed and his jaw muscles pulsed. He was silent for a moment. "Alright ... boss man, tell me when to duck for cover." He spit out the piece of straw he'd been chewing on and produced a crooked smile as he glared at Jay. "I'll follow your lead." He looked into the forest and mumbled, "For now anyways."

Jay struggled to remember each twist and turn in the maze of narrow trails leading to Cain's place. It was tucked away about a mile up a narrow stream which eventually tumbled its way into the Buffalo River. Cain's still was situated next to a tall bluff of dark gray rock, and partially hidden from the front by another outcropping of rock jutting abruptly up from the ground. The stream wound its way between the two monolith structures, making the location of the still virtually un-findable unless you were right up on it.

"Time for you to get back in the wagon."

As Jeeter complied, Jay began to feel his nerves jittering. He hoped that Cain would be by himself like before, because it would make this event much easier to handle. He had worked out plans for any scenario … at least he thought he had … hoped he had.

He spotted the last bend in the double-rutted path, which seemed barely used because grass and small trees were growing in it. A faint wisp of smoke could now be seen rising through the trees from Cain's fire underneath the boiler.

Suddenly, Cain stepped out from behind a large sycamore tree wielding a double-barreled shotgun. He stood like a solemn sentinel in front of the team, with both barrels pointed directly at Jay. Calmly, Jay pulled back on the leather straps in his hands.

"Now hold on, Cain, don't you remember me? I was here just a few days back." Jay wondered how fast he could get to the pistol he had tucked into his pants if he needed it.

"I 'member ya." Cain maintained his bead on Jay.

Jeeter peered out from under the tarp to see Cain with his shotgun aimed at Jay. He pulled his pistol from his pants and placed his thumb on the hammer ready to cock it.

"I just came round for some more of your 'shine." Jay tried to hide a quiver in his voice.

"What makes you think you can just prance out here anytime you wants ta?" Cain began lowering his shotgun.

Jay felt a little relieved as Cain lowered the barrels. "I got some fellas back in Rush who could sure use your brew …didn't figure you'd mind sellin' as much as you could make."

Cain studied Jay and his Morning Star wagon for a moment, and then completely lowered his shotgun, pointing it toward the ground.

"Come on." I got four jars right now and will have more in a couple of days. This stuff will only cook so fast, ya know."

168

Jay jumped down from the wagon and followed Cain to his still, where the smell of wood smoke mingled with the aroma of the corn alcohol. He looked back over his shoulder, sure that Jeeter would be following along secretly, but Jay didn't see him.

Four quart-sized Mason jars were lined up next to the rock bluff, beside about two dozen or so empty bottles and jars ready to be filled with the harsh liquid.

"You need to make this stuff a little faster, ol' man." Jay joked with Cain.

"I'd need to make me another still." Cain had an irritated look on his face. "But another boiler would make more smoke and might draw attention."

"Way out here?"

"Never can be too careful." Cain leaned his shotgun against a boulder and picked up a burlap sack for the jars. Jay's hands became clammy as he reached for his pistol. His plan was to begin with a threat then trash the still as a last resort, with Jeeter holding Cain at gunpoint. Jay looked around again for Jeeter but still didn't see him anywhere. He couldn't do this on his own and hoped Jeeter hadn't jumped out of the wagon and left him alone, in which case he would probably just have to purchase the whisky and leave.

Suddenly he heard the jars land on the ground with a loud clank. He turned his head back around to see Cain standing frozen, looking at something which Jay couldn't see because his view was blocked by the rock outcropping.

"I should've figured." Cain hurled curses at someone in front of him then turned back to look at Jay.

Just then Jeeter stepped into view with his pistol pointed at Cain. The shotgun was too far away for the old man to reach, so he stood there waiting for someone to break the silence.

Jay relaxed, and his hand retreated from his gun handle. He walked up to Cain, whose face was red with rage.

"Ol' man, we're here to politely ask you to leave this area and set up business somewhere else." Jay walked to the shotgun.

169

The words had no more left Jay's mouth when a shot rang out and a puff of blue smoke flew from Jeeter's pistol. Cain's face twisted in pain as he gripped his midsection with his hands. He took a couple of steps backward, and then stood motionless for a brief moment as blood began flowing from between his fingers. He looked at Jay, who was too stunned to move and even looked as surprised as Cain did.

Then Cain staggered and lost his balance. He fell against the cold rock bluff, which momentarily held him upright. He closed his eyes, his knees buckled under him, and he slumped to the ground. A slight groan was heard as he stretched out one of his legs, and then he became motionless. His arms relaxed until they came to rest on the leaf-scattered ground.

"What did you do that for?" Jay screamed as he looked back around at Jeeter in a panic. "I can't believe you just shot a man in cold blood."

Jay rushed over to Cain and could tell that he was dead. He looked up from his crouched position as scared and angry as he had ever been in his life. He watched Jeeter place the gun back into his waistband with a smirk.

"He weren't gonna leave with your polite words; besides, I had my orders."

"Had your orders … had your orders? What do you mean you had your orders?"

Jeeter walked down to where Jay was still crouched beside Cain.

"Raif wasn't in a mood to play around with this Cain, said he wouldn't scare off, so this was the only way."

Jay couldn't contain the anger bottled up inside of him any longer. From his crouched position he lunged at Jeeter, catching him off guard. Jeeter fell back hard against one of the rough boulders, which caused him to wince in agony. Though he was in pain, he held on to Jay with his arms and was able to sling him off and onto the ground. Jay regained his composure and turned to lunge at Jeeter again but was suddenly halted by the clicking of a revolver hammer. For the second time in the day, Jay was looking into the barrel of a gun. He stood frozen, awaiting the shot that was sure to come.

Jeeter stood, still cringing from the pain in his back, with his gun drawn on Finch. There was silence for a few seconds until Jay realized the shot wasn't coming, at least not yet. He slowly stood, shaking with anger.

"You want the same as ol' Cain got?"

"You didn't have to shoot him."

"You gonna come at me again?" Jeeter lowered his pistol. "If you do, I'll shoot next time. I'm sure Raif will understand if I tell him it was self defense."

Jay didn't answer but reached down and picked up his hat. He dusted it off as he walked back over to Cain's lifeless body.

"Now what do we do?" Jay looked at the crimson flow, soaking into the soil.

Jeeter stuck his pistol in his waist band and walked over to Jay.

"You're gonna help me get rid of the body, that's what."

Jay began to protest, but realized his reluctance would only cause a further problem. Besides, he didn't know how much time they had until someone else came along. Since he was trying as hard as he could not to panic, he knew that they needed to take care of this in a hurry.

With reluctance, Jay grabbed Cain's feet. The pair loaded him into the back of the wagon and covered him with the tarp.

"What do we do with his body?"

Jeeter grabbed the reins for their return trip. "Oh, I reckon we can toss him in the river somewheres."

"Wouldn't it be better to just dig a hole and drop him in it?"

"I don't want to dig a hole ... do you? Besides, I plumb forgot to bring a shovel." Jeeter began to cackle at his poor attempt of a joke.

Jay felt like pulling his pistol and taking care of Jeeter, but he knew that was something he couldn't bring himself to do, so he continued to ride in silence and did his best to calm down.

"You know of a place where the river is deep and we can pull down to it without no one bein' there?"

Jay didn't answer which only made Jeeter angry.

"Listen boy, we got to get rid of this body, and no one can see us. So far we ain't seen a soul, and I want to keep it that way, so you best be thinkin' of a place where we can dump him and think of it fast, ya hear?"

Jay released a deep breath as he thought. "There's a small pathway that leads to the river in another mile or so. It heads to a swimming hole with a rope tied to a sycamore tree leaning out over the water. Since the river's still too cold to swim in, there won't be anyone there."

"Thank ya, Jay. I knew we could work this out just fine."

They continued along the road until they came to the barely visible turnoff that ran through the thick undergrowth. The river was not far from the road, but the path was rough for the large wagon and team. They managed to get the wagon far enough into the trees to hide it from the road then stopped. They hopped out into the underbrush and struggled back to the wagon to retrieve Cain's body. After a few awkward moments they had Cain out and were dragging him toward the embankment. The trail terminated at the top of a bluff that was about ten feet above the water.

Jeeter surveyed the river. "This'll be just dandy. We're lucky the water is up a little and still muddy from that rain the other day. He'll be down the river in no time."

Jay didn't wish to waste any more on this morbid ceremony, so he reached down and rolled Cain into the river by himself. He stood, and Jeeter smiled at him out of surprise.

"Goodbye, turtle food." Jeeter chuckled and turned back to the river to watch Cain's body sink below the current.

At that moment, Jay became nauseous. He turned, bent over, and vomited.

"Would it make you feel any better to know that this is my first one?" Jeeter patted Jay on his back. "It does make you queasy at first, don't it? But you'll get used to it. Jeeter looked back out onto the river. I already have."

Jay was still bent over, leaning against a tree, when he heard Jeeter walk back toward the wagon. "Come on. We need to get back to town."

Jay's face was pale and his lips were trembling as he turned his head to see the back of Jeeter walking away. *Now what do I do? What have I gotten myself into?*

Chapter 16

It was mid-afternoon when Mike finished splitting wood for the day. He was tired, but the thought of the dance later that evening reinvigorated him. He placed his axe in the shed and, without even saying goodbye to Jim, walked as fast as he could back to his place. He had just enough time to pull the oval shaped, galvanized wash tub out from under his porch for a bath. He crouched down and slid it out into the open. As soon as he turned it over, he let go of the handle and backed away. A copperhead snake cocked his copper-colored head in a defensive posture. They stared at each other for a second, and, as Mike looked around for a wooden weapon, the snake slithered away into the cluttered leaves and debris of the forest floor.

Rattlesnakes, copperheads, and cottonmouths were common where he had grown up, but they never ceased to startle him. He had developed a healthy respect for these scaly creatures and hated the thought that there was a poisonous snake living nearby, but there were other things to think about now rather than hunting it down.

Mike carefully picked up the tub, making sure there wasn't a mate still hanging around in the leaf debris, and wiped out the cobwebs. After dragging it inside, he built a fire in the wood stove.

It would be a while before the water was hot for his bath, so he pulled out paper and pencil to write another letter to his family. This time he could include a return address.

As he folded his letter and placed it into the envelope, he heard the sound of his water boiling. He poured the bubbling, hot water into the tub and swished it around with his hand. The water was sufficiently warm enough, so he stripped down and treated himself to a soak. Even though he had to keep his knees up out of the water because of the size of the tub, it was enough room to wash and shave in.

Soon the water cooled, so he dried and re-dressed. He dragged the tub full of soapy water out through the door and onto the edge of the porch. He was about to tip it sideways and empty it when he noticed Rosie walking toward him on the wooden walkway from the front of the store.

"'Bout time you used that tub," she said in her usual boisterous tone.

"Evenin', Rosie," Mike stood to greet her. "It's not the first time I've used it."

He noticed Rosie clutching in her hand a small glass bottle that was half full of an amber-colored liquid. When she reached Mike she held it out to him.

Mike looked at the offering. "What's this?"

"Thought you might be able to use this tonight, Romeo." She handed the bottle to Mike. "You may look purty, but it wouldn't hurt to smell purty too."

Mike looked at the label on the bottle: "Eau de Toilette." He glanced back at Rosie with an *I'm-not-wearin'-this-stuff* look on his face.

"Ah, come on kid; it was my husband's. We ordered it straight from France. Whenever he splashed a little of that on after bathing it was all I could do to keep my hands off him."

Mike rolled his eyes at Rosie, hoping she didn't continue telling him about her womanly desires. He opened the bottle and smelled the fragrance. He had to admit, it did smell clean and manly.

"They call the fragrance *Sandalwood*, even though I haven't the faintest idea what sandalwood smells like."

"I guess like this." Mike chuckled as he replaced the stopper.

"Have fun tonight, kid." Rosie turned and walked back toward the front of her store.

"Thanks, Rosie." She didn't reply as she turned the corner and out of sight.

He emptied the water from the tub and placed it upside down under the porch, then retreated into his room for a final inspection. He looked at the toilet water and decided to splash a little on. He had never used such stuff, so he poured out a handful and patted it on his face. In an instant his shaved area began to sting, and, no matter how much he tried to rub with a towel, it still took a few minutes for the stinging to go away.

"That was refreshing," Mike said out loud. *I wonder if it's supposed to do that.* He thought the potion might be spoiled. Beginning to feel a little nauseous from the strong scent, he headed to Doug's to let his face air out, hoping the strong smell would fade with the outside breeze.

Charley answered Mike's knock and opened the door. Immediately he put his hand to his nose and pinched it closed.

"*P U*, you stink." He backed away.

"Hi, Charley." Mike decided not to enter.

Charley continued to back away. "What did you get into?"

Walking through the a doorway, Doug noticed the scene but had not yet caught the strong smell coming from Mike.

"You can come in." Doug looked into a mirror to make sure his bow tie was straight.

"I'd better not."

It was then that Doug inhaled the strong odor and realized what was going on. "Maybe you better try to wash some of that stuff off. Charley, toss him a wet cloth."

Charley wet a small hand towel and threw it to Mike in the doorway. "Don't think it's gonna help." Mike wiped his face and hoped to remove most or all of the strange scent. "I wish I hadn't used this stuff."

Doug tried not to laugh at his friend. "As long as the flowers don't wither along the way to the dance, I'm sure it'll be just fine."

176

Mike tossed the cloth back to Charley, who plopped it into the sink and doused it with more water. Seeing that everything was straight, properly tied, and buttoned, the trio headed in the direction of the Morning Star Hotel.

***

The hotel had a large room, attached to the back, that faced a type of courtyard. Harrison usually reserved the accommodations for his special guests and events, but annually opened up the area for this occasion. It was something he thought was a good thing to do for the community. He had wanted to use the area for Pam's birthday party two weeks earlier, but she had preferred the building across the street for some reason, so the hotel had not been used for a party since Christmas.

Along the way, Doug noticed Charley lagging behind as he usually did, taking notice of the interesting world around him. Doug took the opportunity to reach into his pocket and pull out a narrow wedding band with a small diamond set in the middle.

"You're serious about this, aren't you?" Mike's voice was a little too loud.

"Serious 'bout what?" Charley piped in from behind.

"Nothing, Charley," Doug said, frowning a warning at Mike.

Charley didn't respond and continued his slow gait.

"Sorry, Doug. I forgot you were gonna propose tonight."

Doug slipped the ring back into his pocket and patted it as if to make sure it was still there.

"Sometime during the evening, I'll have you get the guitar from Leon and bring it to me. He already knows I want to borrow it, but he doesn't know why."

"Alright, I'll keep an eye out for you but I may be a little sidetracked."

"Oh, I'll find you. I'll just follow the smell."

They both had a laugh, but Mike didn't think it was as funny as Doug did.

Although faint daylight still sifted through the trees, the oil torches were already burning around the dance area, and the inside was filled with oil lamps and candles. On a wooden platform built as an extension to the back porch, the musicians were already tuning their instruments.

Mike looked around but didn't see Pam. He knew they were a little early but had hoped she would already be present. As usual, Charley had wondered off to play with the young boys. Doug began introducing his friend to those already gathered. Mike did his best to remember the names as he was led from one group to another.

Now the slight spring breeze finally tired from its day's work, leaving the early evening air still and humid. The violet clouds overhead brightened as the sun sank below the horizon, throwing a pink hue on everything the light touched. The colors and shadows mingled with the guests and flickering torch lights.

For some reason, Mike was acutely aware of the atmosphere, and did not ignore it like those around him. They were wrapped in conversation and laughter, whereas he was soaking up the colors of the sky and the mood of the warm Ozark evening air. He never tired of watching what nature had to offer, and always marveled at the signs showing God's presence.

As he continued to gaze at the ever-changing colors of the clouds, the musicians began playing. Mike turned toward the porch as they started with "Arkansas Traveler." It was a fast tune and the mood of the crowd changed, erupting into dancing intermingled with whoops of enjoyment. The party had officially begun.

Doug captured Mike's attention by backhanding him on the arm. "There she is."

He turned to see Doug already making his way across a growing crowd toward a young lady casting her gaze in his direction. Mike watched as Doug was greeted with a smile, which even Mike could tell had *love* written all over it. Doug took her by the hand and led her back to Mike.

"This is Sandy I've told you so much about."

Mike looked puzzled and acted as if Sandy was a total surprise. "You never told me about her."

Sandy smiled and turned to Doug. "What you told me about him is right. He'll fit in around here just fine."

They all laughed for a moment, and, with another song beginning, Doug invited Sandy to dance.

As Doug moved her toward the crowd, Sandy spoke over her shoulder. "Nice to finally meet you."

Mike smiled at her comment then watched the couple as they danced.

The stars were becoming visible as the torches flickered, illuminating the community of people gathered for the festivities. One song after another kept couples on their feet, while most of those who were not dancing, tapped rhythm with a foot on the grass.

Continuing to scan the crowd for Pam, Mike made his way to a punch bowl set up on a table close to the back porch of the hotel. He waited his turn and as a cup was handed to him, he noticed the familiar face of the hostess.

"Hello, Mr. Gilbert, so nice to see you again."

"Hi, Esther, it's nice to see you again too. How are those two young-uns of yours doing— Laura and Chance?

Esther laughed. "Laura and Chase."

"Oh, I'm sorry." Mike looked a little embarrassed. "I was close anyway. They around here somewhere tonight?" He looked around the crowd, still expecting a sighting of Pamela.

"You know how kids are at things like these." She turned her attention to another customer desiring the sweet drink.

"Make sure no one pours anything strong into the bowl tonight," Mike said, turning to walk away.

"That's one reason I'm here." Esther handed a cup to an elderly lady.

After eavesdropping on their conversation, the elderly lady chimed in. "It certainly wouldn't bother me one bit if that did happen. This punch is about as exciting as creek water." Mike and Esther both laughed.

"Nice to see you again, Esther."

"Have fun tonight, Mike."

Sure do plan on it anyway. Mike turned to see if he could spot Doug and Sandy. He didn't know when his friend would ask him to get the guitar, but he had to keep himself available for the task. He assumed it would be when the group took a break from playing, but he had no idea when that would be. He made his way to one of the torches where Doug could spot him when the moment arose.

He had only been standing there for a few minutes enjoying the evening when he heard a voice from behind him.

"You know you get more bugs in your drink if you stand next to the light."

Mike recognized the voice and turned to see Pamela walking toward him. His smile turned into a look of amazement as he gazed upon the most beautiful girl he figured God had ever created. He was at a loss for words, and later he wanted to kick himself for what finally came out of his mouth.

"Pamela, you look.... Uh ... what I mean is..."

"I'll take that as a compliment." "You look beautiful tonight ... I mean you always look...."

Pam remained quiet, still smiling, wondering how he was going to finish his stammering sentence.

"Can I just start over?" Mike said with a red face. "You look lovely."

"Thank you, Mike."

"I've been looking for you all evening. Can I get you some punch?"

"I'd love some."

"Great, I'll be right back."

"I'll come with you," Pam said. "I might lose you in this crowd."

Mike grinned and led her to the punch bowl where Esther was still serving the ever-growing number of guests.

**

Later than he had intended to be, Jay made his way down the lane toward the music. The events of the day played constantly in his head, and anger festered inside him like a wooden splinter begging to be extracted. His emotions over Pam seemed out of control, and now he was even a party to murder, something which he had not ever imagined possible.

As he walked, he thought about his desire for Pam, who was slipping further away from him because of the arrival of the farm boy. Not only was his soul tormented by his deeds, but his desire to have Pam was causing him to think in ways he had never thought before. His need to get rid of Mike was becoming stronger than his desire for Pam.

As he rounded the bend in the road, Jay's face was solemn and he clinched his teeth. He could see the crowd of people inside the picket fence behind the hotel.

A voice came from out of the darkness. "Where you goin' in such a hurry?"

Jay turned to see the face of Jeeter in the dim glow from the distant torch light.

"Go crawl back under your rock, Morse." Jay continued to walk.

"Hold on a minute, Finch." Jeeter caught up to Jay. "You headin' over to that fancy dance?"

"What business is it of yours?"

"Raif has some deliveries for us tonight."

"Not tonight. I'm busy."

Jay thought about the girl he desired to find and dance with if possible. He wanted to forget the events of the day, even if it was only for a few hours, and simply enjoy himself. But now he felt his chances with Pam melting away like the last of the winter snow in the spring rain.

181

Chapter 17

Charley was frantic as he searched for a good hiding place. Ten-year-old Joseph knelt at an old tree stump with his face buried in the crook of his arm, counting to twenty-five. Several children, including their large friend Charley, were in the dirt streets surrounding the party playing hide and seek. It was something they often played on long summer evenings.

He knew he didn't have much time, so he ran to one of his favorite spots. The other children knew of Charley's favorite hiding place but would sometimes walk past it on purpose, knowing he was hidden there. The hiding place was a large piece of corrugated sheet metal that was partially wrapped around a tree. Charley was large but could crouch down in the bend of the metal between it and the tree. It was a good hiding spot, one he used every time they played and sometimes several times during a game. The light from the torches illuminated one side of the sheet metal. It seemed to make the shadow he was folded into darker than usual. It was quite a ways away from Joseph and the others, so he hoped he would not be found.

Joseph finished his counting and stood up proclaiming, "Ready or not, here I come."

Charley peeked around the edge of the metal and saw Joseph walking in the opposite direction from his location. Watching his friend continue to search, Charley whispered, "He'll never find me here."

After a while, Charley figured that someone had surely been found and it was probably time to hide once again. He was about to leave his hiding place and rejoin the game when he heard the voices of two men talking not too far from him, and they were coming toward him. He decided not to stand when he recognized one of the voices as Jay

Finch's. He continued to remain silent as the pair stopped only inches away from his position.

"I don't care what Raif says," Finch said in a low tone, "I'm not makin' any deliveries tonight. I got other things on my mind. Tell Raif if he don't like it he can find someone else to run for him."

Jay tried to take a step but Jeeter grabbed him by the arm to hold him in his place.

"Get yer hand offa me." Jay tried to keep his tone down.

Charley shivered when he heard the other man's voice. His heart began to race, and he felt tears filling his eyes.

"Now you listen to me, my friend. We got us a little gold mine here, and nothin's gonna mess it up, not you, not nobody." Jeeter pulled Jay closer to him. "You understand me, boy?"

There was a pause, and Charley was sure they could hear his heart beating. He remained as still as possible.

Jay jerked his arm, causing Jeeter to lose his grip.

"You gonna shoot me like you did ol' man Cain today?"

Jeeter smirked. "I just might have to, to protect my interest ... if it comes to that."

Now Charley shuddered. He couldn't believe someone had been shot and that he knew who had done it. It was all he could do to remain silent and hidden. He didn't know what would happen to him if he were discovered, but he didn't feel like he could stay there much longer. He wished they would go away. He closed his eyes and called in his mind for his brother to come and find him.

"I've been wonderin, Morse, how does someone like you come up with money to become partners with Raif? Been stealin' from little old ladies?"

Jeeter grinned. "It's shore none of your business, but let's just say I had a little banking business to take care of over in Kingston before I got here. The folks there are real generous with their money."

Charley remembered the conversation between the two men in Rosie's store, and even though he didn't know the man Jay was talking to, he knew that he was going to have to tell somebody. However, he was now even more scared than he had been. He began to cry and it came upon him so fast that he couldn't contain his whimper, even with both hands over his mouth.

"Did you hear that?" Jeeter said, cocking his head in different directions.

When Charley let another whimper slip, a hand grabbed the tin sheet and pulled it back, exposing Charley. Jay reached down and grabbed Charley by the collar and pulled him up to them. While looking around, the pair pulled Charley out of the faint light and into the dark shadows behind the Morning Star Company Store.

***

The musicians took a break after finishing a waltz. The crowd showed their appreciation with applause, and the guitar player informed the group that the food would be ready momentarily.

"But before we eat, we have a special treat in store for you," the fiddle player proclaimed from the stage.

Doug looked at Mike and nodded slightly, which was the signal for Mike to get the guitar. The crowd murmured as Mike walked the instrument to Doug, handing it to him. Sandy looked around in surprise, because now every eye was on the pair. Doug shouldered the guitar and faced Sandy. Without even addressing the crowd, Doug began strumming and everyone became silent. Sandy's cheeks flushed as Doug began to sing.

"Let me call you sweetheart because I love you ..."

At that, the ladies in the crowd swooned and, almost in unison, said, "Awww."

"Let me hear you tell me that you love me too ...
Keep the love-light glowing in your eyes so blue ...
Let me call you sweetheart I'm in love with you."

The crowd broke into a cheer, thinking that was the extent of Doug's proclamation to his girl, but as the voices continued, he handed the guitar to Mike then dropped to one knee. That action silenced the crowd once more; this time everyone knew what was coming next. Even Sandy knew what to expect and her eyes began to water.

Doug pulled the ring out of his pocket and held it up to Sandy. "Sandy, I may be clever most of the time, and I never have a problem running my mouth ..."

"He's right about that," some gentleman in the crowd blurted out. Everyone broke into laughter and Doug's cheeks flushed as he smiled, looking around to see who had made the comment.

He turned back to Sandy as the laughter abated, and then finished his sentence. "... but right now my tongue is tied for words, so I just simply want to ask you to be my wife."

The only sounds were the tree frogs continuing the serenade in the trees around them.

Sandy reached toward the ring and slipped it onto her finger. Her hands were shaking and she could scarcely see the ring because of the mist in her eyes. She began nodding her head as she returned her gaze to Doug. "Yes."

The crowd exploded into cheers and laughter, and the couple embraced while everyone applauded. With a huge smile on his face, Mike turned to look at Pam, who had tears running down her cheeks.

"Well now, why are you cryin'?" Mike reached for a handkerchief.

"Because that was the sweetest thing I ever did see."

Mike handed the guitar back to the player on the porch, and the group decided to play one last song to cap the event before the food was served.

"Congratulations." Mike shook the hand of his friend.

Pam and Sandy hugged and the crowd now gravitated toward the food that was about to be served.

"This is the happiest day of my life," Sandy said, turning to Doug.

"Mine too," he said, with the song concluding in the background. "I just hope Charley feels the same way."

"Where is he, by the way?"

"Oh, he's out playin' somewhere like he always does. He'll come around when he finds out the food is being served. I'm sure he's having a good time." Doug looked over the crowd.

"Well, let's go grab a plate. I don't know about you all, but I'm starved." Mike led the group toward the food.

***

Charley was thrown face first against the back wall of the building, and he began crying out of sheer terror. Jeeter grabbed his shoulder and spun him around, then slammed him against the building again. Charley raised his hands in front of his face in a defensive posture.

"Now what are we going to do?"

"Only one thing we can do." Jeeter held onto Charley's shirt and looked at Jay.

"Yer not gonna shoot him."

"He heard everything," Jeeter replied. "We don't have much of a choice."

At that, Charley cried out louder, and Jeeter immediately threw a fist into his stomach, hoping to silence him. Charley doubled over in pain and immediately threw up.

"We can't shoot him."

"Like I said, we have no choice." Jeeter looked back at Charley, who was still bent over in pain and leaning against the wall.

Jay's mind was racing and spinning in all directions. He didn't want another killing on his hands, but he didn't want Charley talking either. He quickly formulated a plan that he hoped Jeeter would agree to.

"You stay there, Charley, and don't you move." Jay took Jeeter by the arm and stepped away. "He's just the town

186

moron." Jay motioned toward Charley. "He won't say anything if we scare him enough."

"Are you out of your mind?"

"We don't need another killin' on our hands, 'specially him."

"And just why not?"

"That old man today ain't gonna be missed at all, but if Charley goes missin', this whole area's gonna be crawlin' with the law. Everyone in the town will be lookin' for him and they'll be creepin' into every nook and cranny of these woods. You want the law to find that still you've invested in?"

While his mind chewed on Jay's words, Jeeter looked at Charley still leaned over with his hands on his knees for support. "How do you know he won't talk?" Jeeter looked back at Jay in the starlight.

Jay was relieved. It looked like his plan was going to work. He didn't care a lick for Charley, but killing Charley would surely collapse what was left of his world around him. "I can guarantee it. Just leave it to me."

The pair walked back over to Charley, who was standing now.

Jay faced Charley. "You gonna tell anyone what you heard tonight?"

"I ain't gonna tell ... I ain't gonna tell." Charley shook all over.

Out of nowhere, Charley felt a blow from a fist to the side of his face. Still standing, he rolled along the side of the building. A hand turned him around, and he received another blow to the face, this time sending him down to the ground in pain. He tasted blood in his mouth and rolled into a ball, trying to protect himself.

"Are you gonna tell anyone, Charley?" Jeeter kicked Charley in the ribs.

Charley could barely breathe from the pain and having the wind kicked out of him.

"You sure you ain't tellin' nobody?" Jay bent over and served several fist blows to the side of Charley's face again.

"Noooooooooooo" was all Charley could manage to painfully cry through his hands, which now had blood on them. Another blow came from Jeeter to Charley's midsection. He picked up a rotting piece of lumber from the ground and was about to hit Charley across the back with it when Jay reached his hand up in front of him. "That's enough."

The pair stood for a moment looking at Charley, still curled into a tight ball on the ground.

Jay crouched down in the darkness beside Charley, who was quietly crying from terror and pain. He placed his hand onto Charley's shoulder. "Charley, yer not gonna tell anyone about what you heard tonight, are you?"

Charley continued sobbing into his hands and didn't answer.

"Charley, I need to hear you say you won't mutter a word, or somethin' worse is gonna happen."

Charley slowly lowered his hands and looked through his fingers at the face of Jeeter then cut his eyes to Jay.

"Charley?" Jay addressed him again, only in a sterner manner.

Charley shook his head sideways in short jerks with his eyes locked onto Jay's.

"Charley, if you tell anyone about what you heard tonight, we'll have to hurt your little playmates out there, and then we'll have to kill you, do you understand?"

Slowly Charley nodded his head. Thick strands of saliva mingled with blood dangled from his lips as he spoke. "I ... promise I won't say."

Jay looked up at Jeeter, hoping Jeeter was satisfied.

"I sure hope you know what you are doin'," Jeeter said slowly through tightened lips.

Jay patted Charley on the shoulder. "He won't tell anyone." Jay stood, returning his gaze to Charley.

"Now you go get washed up and tell folks that you tripped in the woods playin' a game and hit your head against a rock, ya hear me?"

Charley remained silent, still in shock over the sudden events. Jay stepped out of the shadows and into the faint glow of the distant torches.

"I don't feel like goin' to no party right now," Jay said. Jeeter stepped into the light with him.

Jay loosened his bow tie and unbuttoned the top button of his shirt then let his hands fall to his sides. He stared into the distant group of his neighbors enjoying a wonderful evening. He knew Pam was somewhere in the throng and would bet his best horse that she was with Mike. Hate boiled like a cauldron inside him as he watched the festivities. He would never admit it, but the person he hated more than anyone else was himself.

The pair turned and walked back down the road in the direction of their horses and, under the watchful eyes of the stars, made their way deep into the woods where Raif was waiting.

Chapter 18

After finishing their meals, Mike and Pam left the gathering and took a walk. They exited through a side gate of the fence enclosure and turned south toward the main street. Everyone was still finishing their meals, so they had the streets to themselves.

Mike placed a hand on his stomach as they continued to walk in the shadows of the faint torch lights. "I don't know about you, but I'm as full as a tick." "So you had a good time tonight?" Pam took him by the arm.

Mike looked at her in surprise and felt his heart race at her touch.

"I'm sure you wouldn't want me to fall out here."

Mike knew it was an excuse but didn't mind at all. "Of course not."

After a few moments walking in silence, Mike spoke. "All of my life has been spent in one little town. I miss home … and I miss my family, but I am enjoying this." He paused as they took a few more steps, and then finished his thought. "I'm also glad that I met you."

He could barely see her smile in the faint light but felt her squeeze his arm tighter, letting him know that she felt the same way. He didn't want to walk her too far away from the gathering because he thought at night it would be improper, so the couple turned the corner and continued to walk along the enclosure.

As they passed the tall rock structure that Mike had wondered about after he had arrived at Rush, he stopped beside it. "Since the first day I got here I've been wondering what this thing is, and I've never remembered to ask anyone about it." He placed a hand on the cold chunks of rock held together by mortar.

Pam released his arm and touched the square tower of rocks along with him as if to feel the past in some way before she spoke. "This is where zinc was first discovered in Rush," she said. "Actually, from what I understand, two prospectors thought they had discovered silver in these hills and built this smelter to melt the ore out of the crushed rock. When they fired up the smelter, no silver melted into the molds. They realized that the colored fumes above the smelter were from the mineral they were burning, which was zinc."

"I bet they were disappointed," Mike said with a chuckle.

"They were disappointed, but soon people began to stake claims in this whole area and started mining the zinc, which is very plentiful from what I understand."

"You seem to know a lot about zinc mining."

"I only know what I have heard from my father. He doesn't allow me to enter the mines and rarely into the mill. He says it's too dangerous for a girl."

At that moment the musicians began playing a slow melody. It was a waltz, and one Mike had heard played quite frequently back home at festivities. *A Farmer's Wife I'll Be.*

"Care to dance?" Mike held out a hand.

With a smile Pam took his hands and they danced in the faint torch light beside the old rock smelter.

"I like dancing out here instead of with the rest of the folks."

Pam replied with a chuckle, "And why is that— because you have more room?"

"No. It's because I have you all to myself."

Pam smiled again, but this time it was different than before. She looked deep into his eyes; before either of them realized it, they had stopped dancing, even though the music was still playing. Their eyes were locked in a gaze that neither of them had ever experienced. Mike gently placed his hands on her sides, and, before he knew what he was doing, he began leaning toward Pam, who had already tilted her head back and closed her eyes to receive his kiss.

Suddenly the music stopped, and people inside the picket fence enclosure began gasping; ladies' voices were heard ordering someone to get wet towels. The magical moment was interrupted as the couple turned to see a crowd gathering around someone. In an instant, Mike and Pam both could make out the person who was being tended to. It was Charley. Even from their distance, they could tell he was bleeding.

"Come on." Mike took her hand, and the couple made their way to the commotion.

"I was playing hide and seek … and I was hidin' in the woods … and I musta tripped and fell. I hit my dang head on a rock or sumpin'."

"Charley, come over to the light so I can see better." Doug led his brother to one of the torch lights.

"Owww!" A wet towel was swiped across his temple and cheek bone, wiping away enough blood to be able to see the extent of the damage. He struggled to pull away not only because of the pain from his head, but because his ribs were bruised and extremely painful, even though he told no one about that injury.

"What happened?" Mike asked as he and Pam arrived.

"Charley said he fell." Sandy had taken charge of the wet towel. She gently continued to swab the injuries, making Charley wince.

From Doug, Mike received a look that showed doubt about Charley's story but for now left it alone. He would have time later to try and get the true story. They cleaned him up as best they could and saw that the wounds were not deep and that they had already stopped bleeding.

The crowd settled down and the musicians began playing once again. Even though the party would continue for some time into the evening, Doug decided to take Charley home and get him into bed.

By this time Charley had been led to a wooden bench where he was recovering, hoping that everyone would pay no more attention to him.

Doc Lipscomb walked over to the group of friends and handed Doug some white pills and a small, round silver tin.

"You better get that boy home and into bed. Give him these two tablets tonight, and if his head still hurts in the morning come to my office and get some more. He doesn't need to be sewed up, but keep the wound clean of scab or he'll have a nasty scar. Put a generous amount of salve from that tin onto his wound after you clean it each time."

Mike spoke as the doctor left. "I'll go with you."

"Thanks, but I think I can handle it," Doug said. "You stay here and enjoy the rest of the evening. Come on, Charley boy." Doug placed one of Charley's arms over his shoulder. The action caused Charley to moan in pain. As Doug attempted to lift Charley from his seat, Charley's legs became weak and he had a difficult time standing. Doug lowered Charley back onto the bench.

"Maybe you better take the other arm, Mike. Charley's weaker than I thought."

Mike turned toward Pam, who looked concerned about Charley.

"Go ahead, Mike; I was about to return home anyway. I had a wonderful evening." Her eyes twinkled.

"Goodnight then." Mike resisted showing any sign of affection toward Pam.

Doug and Sandy said their goodbyes as well, and the two men lifted Charley and helped him stumble back to Doug's place. They had a time getting Charley to swallow the two pills, but after the struggle ended and the pills were in his belly, Doug was able to get him slipped into bed where he soon fell asleep.

"You might want to stay up most of the night if you can and keep an eye on him." I have a feeling he didn't just fall onto a rock like he said he did, and, if he has a bad head injury inside, you may have to go get the doc."

193

"I was already thinking that very thing." Doug looked down at his battered brother.

Mike headed back to his place behind Rosie's store and all the way replayed the evening. He smiled as he remembered Doug's proposal, and the smile grew in his heart as he thought about his time with Pam.

He knew he had been warned about showing any attention to Pam for fear of losing his job, but at this point he couldn't help himself. Like a fish on the end of a pole, he was hooked and there was nothing he could do about it. He didn't know where things would go from here, but he was already looking forward to tomorrow, or the next day, or whenever his next time with Pam would be. As for her father, he would have to take his chances with him, but was sure that he could figure out some way to win his approval.

Reaching his steps, he thought he heard voices coming from inside the store. As he listened, he could hear Rosie for sure, but he couldn't make out the other voice that belonged to a man. The two were in a heated argument, and it sounded as if a fight could break out at any moment. He decided to eavesdrop so he quietly walked along the porch until he made it to the front corner. From there he could hear the voices clearly.

"Rosie, stop acting like a stubborn mule." The man's voice boomed.

"Why don't you stop being such a jackass? I told you I wasn't going to sell to you and that's final," she replied frankly.

The man lowered his voice, but Mike could still hear his words. "Rosie, you're gonna lose your store because of your stubbornness. Most of the town buys from the company store already. You have a high-producing zinc mine down by the river that would get you out of debt, and you could retire in style. Sell it to me and your worries will be over."

"My husband wouldn't sell you the mine before he died, and I'm not sellin' now. I'll go down with the ship before I'll let you get your hands on my mine."

"If you don't sell me that mine, you most certainly will go down with the ship." "Is that a threat, Mr. Harrison?" Rosie sounded as if she were standing her ground against an entire army.

"Mr. Harrison?" Mike thought to himself. "This is not good." He was about to walk into the store and interrupt for Rosie's sake when the front door exploded open, and Harrison stormed out onto the porch, down the steps, and toward the hotel.

Mike stood still, stunned by what he had heard. He walked to the front of the porch and watched as Harrison faded into the darkness. He was about to head to his room when he heard Rosie speak from behind him.

"Heard all of that, did ya?"

Mike turned to see his friend standing in the doorway, silhouetted by the lamplight from one of the counters behind her.

"Sorry, Rosie." Mike felt a little embarrassed that he'd been caught. "Most of it I guess."

She walked out onto the porch and stood beside him.

"Rosie…"

"Save it, kid. I know you mean well, but I couldn't live with myself if I sold the mine my husband worked so hard in, to that man. I wouldn't give you a wooden nickel for ol' man Harrison. The Morning Star may own this town, but it ain't gonna own me, I'll tell you that much for sure."

Without even so much as a pause, she changed the subject. "How are you makin' out with Pam? That girl must have gotten all of her sweetness from her father, because he doesn't have one single drop left in his entire body."

Mike could do nothing but laugh at his boisterous friend.

"I think I'm making headway."

Though she was still flustered, Rosie forced a smile. "That's real good, kid. Come inside; I've got somethin' I want to discuss with you."

Surprised, Mike followed his friend into her store, where she located freshly baked sugar cookies and made hot tea with water in a kettle she had been warming before Harrison arrived. The pair settled at the counter across from each other, and, just as Mike was about to place the cookie into his mouth, Rosie said something that caught him off guard almost as much as his near kiss with Pam earlier in the evening.

"Kid ... how would you like to be the owner of a very high-producing zinc mine?

Chapter 19

Unable to sleep, with his fingers clasped together behind his head, Mike stared into the darkness above his bed. He could hear crickets and tree frogs outside his window, and, somewhere in the distance, a whippoorwill began singing its endless song.

He could almost imagine lying in his old bed back home on the farm. So much around him felt and sounded familiar, and yet everything was different. His world had changed and it was rushing toward him at enormous speed. As soon as he adjusted to one aspect of his new life, another surprise grabbed him around the ankles.

The biggest surprise of all not only entangled his ankles on this evening, but wrapped around every part of his soul, and caused his senses to feel numb. He didn't know why Rosie made the offer of her zinc mine to him, but because of it he felt overwhelmed, as if a giant weight had been placed onto his shoulders.

"I don't know one blasted thing about zinc mining," he said into the darkness as he closed his eyes. "I'm a wood splitter; I'm a farm boy; but I'm not a miner."

As he tried to think about his moments with Pam earlier in the evening, his mind kept returning to the offer Rosie had made to him. The mine was his if he gave her twenty percent of everything he took out of it.

His thoughts were interrupted by a tree limb tapping on his tin roof from a slight breeze blowing through the valley. He tried to get more comfortable on the mattress by rolling over, but he had a feeling it was going to be difficult to sleep on this night. He was already looking forward to daylight.

Then he had a thought, so he slung his feet onto the floor and dressed. *I might as well see if Doug is still awake watching Charley. Maybe I can pick his brain and he can help me figure this thing out.* If there was anything he needed right now, it was some words of wisdom from a friend.

Mike walked down the steps and into the rutted dirt street. A gentle, southerly breeze blew warm and humid air around him. The sound of the breeze through the leaves on the trees was a soft, comforting rustle. He turned the corner and made his way up the hill to Doug's small house behind the blacksmith shop. He was relieved to see a faint light glowing through a curtain-covered window, and thankful that his friend was still awake.

Mike knocked gently on the door, hopeful it was loud enough for Doug to hear. Within a few seconds the door opened and Mike was bathed in the light from a single candle.

"What are you doin' out at this time of the night?" Doug whispered.

Mike walked inside. "I couldn't sleep." Doug closed the door behind Mike and invited him to sit.

"How's Charley?"

"He seems to be fine," Doug said. "Want some coffee? Since I'm staying up, I figured I better brew a pot."

"You might need something stronger after I tell you what I'm about to tell you."

Doug hadn't known Mike long, but he knew him well enough to know that Mike wasn't prone to be dramatic. Instead of retrieving another cup of coffee, Doug sat back into his chair. "Go ahead, Mike, spill the beans."

"Do you know much about Rosie's personal life?"

"Not really," Doug said. "I don't go into her place much. Mostly I do business with the Morning Star Company Store."

Leaning forward, Mike placed his elbows onto the top of his knees. He looked at the floor, clasping his hands together. Doug could tell that Mike was a little anxious about something.

"Apparently," Mike began, "Rosie's husband had a very high-yielding zinc mine down the road close to the river." There was a pause.

"Well, I guess I knew that much," Doug said. "Everyone knows about that mine. It's been untouched since Matthew died. It's because of the mine that Rosie has her store."

"Yeah, well brace yourself, because tonight she offered the mine to me."

At first Doug had to process Mike's words and then was not sure if he had heard correctly. "No offense, but how can you afford to buy a mine like that? Harrison's been trying to buy that mine from her for the past couple of years."

"Well, I overheard him trying to buy it again tonight, and he wasn't being very pleasant about it." Mike leaned back into his chair.

They heard a faint groan and both looked at Charley in time to see him roll over in his bed but remain asleep. There was a pause again as Doug patiently waited for Mike to continue his story.

"Not only do I not have the money," Mike continued, "but I don't know a cotton pickin' thing about mining zinc."

"I'm a little confused," Doug said. "You don't know anything about mining ... okay. And you don't have any money ... fine. Where is the turmoil coming from that I see you struggling with?"

Mike looked back down at the floor and then up at Doug. "She offered me the mine for twenty percent of the product."

"And?" Doug asked as if waiting for the other shoe to drop.

"And nothing," Mike replied. "She said she would help me with the tools and supplies, tell me what she knew, and help in any other way she could besides actually digging. All I have to do is work my little backside off, dig the stuff out of the walls and haul it to the mill."

"Just like that?"

"Out of the clear blue sky, just like that."

The pair sat in the flicker of the candlelight, silent, while Mike waited for Doug to tell him it was a bad idea and that he should stick to splitting wood. He wanted Doug to tell him that he needed to gain much experience before getting into the mines. He wanted Doug to tell him that he didn't need the new battle of Mr. Harrison flying into a rage when he learned that Rosie had sold the mine to someone else. But the words he heard were none of those.

Instead, Doug clasped his hands in his lap and buried himself deeper into his chair. "I think you can do it."

Mike was shocked at his words. "But I don't know the first thing about mining. I don't know how to brace the ceilings, I don't know how to get zinc out of the walls ... I'll swan, Doug, I don't even know what the blasted stuff looks like."

"Believe me, Mike, it won't take long for you to learn all of that; however, Rosie was right about one thing."

"What's that?" Mike felt even more at his wits' end than he had before talking to Doug.

"You're definitely going to work your little backside off."

***

Mike stayed with Doug through the night and managed to get a little rest in the chair. When a faint glow appeared in the sky, Mike thanked Doug for the conversation they had for most of the night, and expressed his relief that Charley was awake and had no headache.

"You takin' your horse to church with you?" Doug asked as Mike was leaving.

"I think I'll just walk, it's not that far."

"Charley and I'll meet you in front of your place and walk with you."

"Think he'll feel up to it?" Mike doubted it.

"It would take a team of twenty mules to keep him away from church."

"I'll wait for you then," Mike said. He began backing away and Doug closed the door.

Mike walked back to his place with only a single star remaining in the sky. He still felt a little numb from the lack of sound sleep, but mostly from Doug's confidence in his ability to make Rosie's mine productive once again. He had been surprised at Doug's advice, but was beginning to feel a little confidence in himself as well.

Once inside his room, he lit a lamp and prepared a pot of cornmeal mush, this time with Rosie's instructions. To his surprise, the hot breakfast cereal turned out almost perfect, and it mostly tasted like his mother's, with the exception of the bacon grease she put in hers. *I gotta remember to get some bacon this week.*

With breakfast cleaned up, he had almost an hour before leaving for church. He didn't allow himself to sit back onto his bed for fear of falling asleep and missing the service. Instead, Mike crouched to his knees and took the opportunity to spend some time with God and pray for God's direction in his life—not only for direction but also for the wisdom to see it and follow it. He also thanked God for his care of him, and prayed for his family in Kingston. He didn't pray out loud for God to make things work out with Pam, but he knew that God could read his mind.

***

After waiting five minutes on the road, Mike saw his two friends round the corner and head in his direction. From a distance Charley seemed as fit as ever, but, as he approached, Mike could see the bruises on his cheeks and the cut across his temple. Although his left eye was swollen, the injuries didn't seem to slow Charley down one bit. He had his usual spring in his step as the pair reached Mike.

"Hey, Charley," Mike said, "that must have been a really big rock you tangled with. You sure it wasn't a bobcat?"

"Feels like I got in a fight with a bear."

"I guess that'll teach you not to play hide and seek in the dark." Mike grinned at Charley as the trio began walking.

Charley remained silent at that remark. Mike and Doug glanced at each other and continued down the road.

They walked in silence for a few minutes before Charley spoke. "Yer gonna like the preacher." Charley kicked a small rock, making it bounce down the road in front of them. "He preaches real good."

"I can't wait to meet him," Mike said. "By the way, Doug, I guess it's okay if I come over to your place this afternoon and do my washing?"

"Sure. The more the merrier."

"I don't consider doin' my washing very merry no matter who I'm doin' it with." Mike chuckled.

Mike wanted to talk to Doug about his proposal the night before but didn't know if Doug had mentioned it to Charley. "It was really nice to meet Sandy last night," Mike said, testing the waters.

Doug got a panicked look on his face, which let Mike know the cat was not out of the bag yet. He knew Doug would have to tell Charley soon because half the town knew. Not knowing how Charley was going to handle the news, he figured Doug would tell Charley after church.

"I think she's nice," Mike said.

"I like her too," Charley blurted as he continued to kick the same rock further down the road.

As they continued to walk, they heard a buggy coming from behind them on the road, so they moved to the edge. As it passed, Mike looked at the occupants and was surprised to see Jacob Harrison, his sister, and Pam in the buggy. Jacob pulled the horse to a slower pace at his daughter's urging.

"Morning, Mike." Pam addressed him boldly as her father looked on. "Um … you boys need a ride to church?"

The trio looked at each other, then back at Pam.

"Good morning, Mr. Harrison," Mike said.

Doug repeated Mike's greeting.

Harrison just nodded his head without a muscle moving on his face.

Mike responded to Pam's invitation. "Thanks, Pam, but we're almost there and the walk is doin' us some good this morning, wouldn't you say, Doug?"

"It's doin' me good." Doug glanced over at Charley, who was chasing his rock down from the edge of the road so that he could kick it again.

Mike and Pam had their gaze entangled, and Harrison didn't need a college degree to see there was something between them in that look.

"Are you sure?" Pam asked them again, adding some charm to her words.

"They said they don't need a ride." Harrison turned and urged the horse on at a faster pace.

As the buggy and its occupants rounded the curve and out of sight, Mike watched. Pam looked back at him over her shoulder and give a little wave; it melted his heart.

***

When the three arrived at the church a few minutes later, it looked as if the little white building would be packed. They hoped they could find a seat inside. As they drew closer, Mike could see the minister standing at the front door greeting the arriving members. He continued to watch with interest and suddenly recognized the man shaking hands.

"Pastor Russell!"

MB Russell had turned to enter the church, but he wheeled around to see Mike with an outstretched hand.

"Michael Gilbert," the pastor said in complete surprise.

The two clasped hands for a second then completed their greeting with a hug.

"I am completely flabbergasted to see you here," Russell continued.

Mike laughed. "I can tell by the look on your face. You look as if you've just seen Jesus raised from the dead yourself."

"It almost feels like that my boy. Come inside, if you can find a seat, and we'll talk after the service."

"Mornin', Pastor Russell!" Charley parked his rock and lunged at the reverend with an embrace.

"Good morning, Charley." MB patted Charley on the back and greeted him with a big smile and a chuckle . "What on earth happened to you?"

"He fell against a rock last night." Doug reached out to shake the pastor's hand.

"Good morning, Doug. Always great to see you."

"You two know each other?" Doug looked at Mike and then back at the minister.

"Yes. I used to pastor at his church in Kingston for years. Why, I practically watched Mike grow up. He comes from a wonderful family, and I miss seeing them now that I am over in this neck of the woods. Mike, you'll have to stay around after the service so we can catch up on things." Pastor Russell put his arm around Mike's shoulder and shook him. "You're a sight for sore eyes, for sure."

Mike and Doug followed the pastor inside. Charley had preceded them and had already found one of the few remaining seats. Doug spotted him and surveyed the available space.

"Its okay, Doug, I'll find another spot. There's not enough room for me, too."

Mike was finally able to squeeze into one of the back pews. The little Yoakum brothers didn't like to sit so close together, but a look from their father squelched their complaints.

Mike gazed across the congregation where several of the women were already fanning themselves, even though the windows were wide open. The little country church reminded him of his church back home in so many ways. Even though the faces were different, the sounds and smells were the same. The wooden floors creaked as folks walked on them, and the well-worn pews did a bit of creaking themselves when everyone shifted on them waiting for the service to begin. The smell of old wood pleasantly invaded his head. Mike looked around and spotted Pam and her

204

family. Pam turned her head at the same moment and spied Mike, giving him a quick smile as the organ began to play.

The church had been blessed three years earlier when a member of the community died and left money, specifying that it be used to purchase a pump organ. Unfortunately, no one in the area knew how to play the thing. It sat gathering dust for a couple of years until Pastor Russell began preaching every other Sunday. His wife, Brenda, was gifted with musical talent, so now the boisterous instrument bellowed out the chords to *At The Cross* while the congregation stood and sang along.

Charley still felt much pain from the previous evening, but he sang loud and clear, though he was even more painfully off key. Sunday was his favorite day of the week, especially every other Sunday when services were held. Those around him did their best to sing the right notes, but it was difficult because Charley was so loudly inspired.

After three songs were sung, the deacons passed the offering plate, a few announcements were made, and the congregation settled into their seats. Pastor Russell then walked to the hand-crafted pulpit. Smiling, he placed his Bible onto the stand and opened it to his bookmark. Usually Pastor Russell began his sermons by first getting the congregation to laugh a little. Of course there were a few in the crowd who believed that jokes should not be told from the pulpit. Russell's belief, however, was that if laughter was to be anywhere, it was to be in the church. He believed that God wanted people to enjoy their life inside the church, while they worshipped, as much as outside the church. This day was not unlike the way he began most of his sermons.

Noticing so many ladies fanning themselves trying to keep cool he began: "I'm amazed at how the weather is getting hot so soon this year. Why just yesterday I saw a chicken lay a hard-boiled egg."

Everyone chuckled, even though most of them had heard that joke before.

"And it's so hot," he continued, "that I even saw a couple of robins pulling worms out of the ground with pot holders."

The congregation laughed more at that joke, which even caused Russell himself to laugh along with them. After the laughter subsided, the pastor became serious and began his sermon.

Charley leaned forward in anticipation. Hardly ever did Charley remember the Bible stories correctly, but in his heart he so wanted to be a preacher and tell people about God. He paid attention to Pastor Russell's every word and even his voice inflection. He enjoyed it when the preacher became so involved in his sermon that he got red in the face from his deep sincerity for people to turn their lives over to Christ for their salvation.

Russell instructed everyone who had a Bible to turn to Matthew 5:39, and then he read the words of Jesus: *"But I say unto you, that ye not resist evil: but whosoever shall smite thee on thy right cheek, turn to him the other also."*

Then he skipped to the forty-fourth verse in order to help explain the first verse. *"But I say unto you, Love your enemies, bless them that curse you, do good to them that hate you, and pray for them which despitefully use you, and persecute you."*

Though the pastor continued to preach, further explaining how Christ taught his followers to love and do good to those who want to harm us and to pray for our enemies, Charley was fixated on the phrase "Love your enemies." He didn't understand some of the big words, but his mind kept returning to that phrase. For the rest of the sermon, he didn't hear another word. Loving your enemies troubled him, and this was something which he had never heard before. Why would Jesus want him to love anyone who hurt him? How could he love someone who made fun of him and even had beaten him? How could loving your enemies ever come to any good? Until the service was over, he pondered the words the pastor spoke about loving, being kind to, and praying for your enemies.

As one of the deacons was praying a dismissal prayer at the end of the altar call, Pastor Russell walked quietly down the aisle to stand at the opened doors. With the final *amen* of the day, folks began walking out of the building, shaking hands with the pastor as they passed him, and telling him what a marvelous sermon he had prepared. As the group shuffled out, Mike met with Doug and Charley.

"You guys go on ahead," Mike said. "I'll come over this afternoon as soon as I can."

"I'll try to keep the water warm for you." Doug placed his hand on the shoulder of his unusually quiet brother and led him out into the sunlight.

Mike watched as Pam and her family walked out, also extending their praise to the pastor. He waited until the very last to leave, so he could have some time visiting with his pastor friend from Kingston.

"Michael Gilbert, let me take a look at you," Brenda Russell exclaimed as he approached them at the doors. Continuing to look at him, and still in disbelief she was seeing him so far from home, she gave Mike a hug and kept her hands placed on his shoulders. "How long has it been … three years?"

"I think it has been about that long," Mike said. He had always liked the Russells and was sad a couple of years ago when Pastor Russell had taken a different area for the pastorate.

"What are you doing all the way over here in Rush?" Brenda still held on to him.

By this time Pastor Russell had shaken the last hand and had now turned his attention to Brenda and Mike. "I declare, Mike," MB said, "it's amazing running into you all the way out here in the middle of nowhere."

"I've only been in Rush for a couple of weeks." Mike pulled back slightly to loosen Brenda's grasp on his shoulders.

"Then we'll be seeing more of you in the Sundays to come?"

"I plan on seeing what I can make of my life here in Rush."

"My, my, you kids grow up so fast. I just figured you'd stay on the farm with your family," Brenda piped in.

"Farming wasn't for me, and I love it here."

"Well, Brenda and I just got a dinner invitation and, knowing the family, I'm sure they won't mind if we bring along an old friend.

"Oh, I couldn't," Mike began.

Brenda interrupted. "We insist. You could probably use a good home-cooked, hot meal anyway."

"Well—how can I resist your persuasion?" Mike finally relented.

"Very good," Pastor said. "We can squeeze you into our buggy if you don't mind the cramped quarters."

"I don't mind at all." They closed the church doors behind them and climbed into the coach.

On the way into town the trio talked about old times, Mike's family, and what MB and Brenda Russell were doing now in their lives. They divided their Sundays between two churches in the area, and during the week worked with orphanages in Yellville and Harrison a few miles north. As they drove past the Morning Star Hotel, the horse was directed left, and they passed the old rock smelter Pam had told Mike about the previous evening. The buggy continued until it rounded another corner and finally came to a stop.

"Well, we're here, and I'm so hungry I could eat a horse all by myself." Russell and Brenda stepped out onto the ground.

Mike remained in the buggy, staring at the house, not knowing what he wanted to do.

"Come on, Mike," Brenda urged. "You'll love the Harrisons."

"But I work for Mr. Harrison."

"Well good; then he certainly won't mind at all that you are along with us. He has a daughter about your age you know, and I'm sure you two will get along just fine."

"You really don't know how fine," he mumbled to himself.

Chapter 20

Doug removed the cast iron pot from the top of the woodstove and placed it on the table. Charley sat down at his place and immediately reached for the bread.

"Charley, you've got dirt around your fingernails. Did you wash your hands?"

Withdrawing his hand, Charley moaned because he didn't want to get back up and wash. Doug cocked his head toward the sink. After passing inspection, Charley sat back down, and Doug removed the lid from the pot. The aroma of the beef stew, which he had left simmering all morning on the wood stove while they were at church, filled the air.

After saying grace they began enjoying the meal in silence. Doug was apprehensive about telling Charley the news of his proposal to Sandy, but he knew he needed to get it out of the way.

"Say, Charley ... there's something I need to talk to you about."

Charley didn't look up; he continued loading spoonfuls of the stew into his mouth.

"Charley...you like Sandy, don't you?"

"Mmm hmm." Charley continued eating.

"And ... you like being around her, right?"

Charley got a puzzled look on his face at the sudden questions and slowed down his chewing.

"I like to be around her, and she makes me laugh." Charley still had a mouth full of food.

"Well ... I hope you like what I'm about to tell you. Charley, could you put your spoon down for a minute and stop eating? This is important."

Charley swallowed what he had in his mouth. He stuck his tongue out as far as he could and ran his tongue round his lips to clean off his mouth, much like a cow does

210

when she's eating. He then wiped his mouth off with his shirt sleeve and threw a blank look at his brother.

Rather than chide his brother about using his sleeve as a napkin, Doug continued. "Charley, last night at the dance, I … um … well, I asked Sandy to marry me."

Charley didn't say a word. He only continued looking at Doug as if nothing had been said.

"Did you hear me? Sandy and I are going to get married. Not knowing what to expect, Doug placed his spoon onto the table and slid his chair back.

"Does that mean I have to leave?"

"Oh, Charley, not at all." Doug moved back to the table and leaned toward his brother.

"Is she gonna live here?" Charley tilted his head to one side.

"She will, and then maybe we can move to a bigger place so that we can have more room."

"But I like it here."

"Charley, it will be okay. She will be part of our family soon. It will be the three of us, and she can make you laugh all of the time."

Doug didn't know that Charley was still sidetracked by Pastor Russell's sermon, and the notion of his getting married was not completely sinking in.

"I've got some thinkin' to do." Charley got up from the table.

Doug was surprised by Charley's reaction; he had expected an all-out war at the news.

"Where are you going?"

Charley made his way to the door. "I said I'm goin' thinkin'." He closed the door behind him.

Charley had only two ways of handling anything that changed his world. Sometimes he flew into an uncontrollable rage until he could be calmed, and sometimes he remained completely quiet; however, this reaction was not the one Doug had expected. He hoped that Charley's mood wouldn't change later, but for now at least the news was out and there was no rage. He decided he would look for Charley later if he hadn't come back in a reasonable amount of time.

Now that he had told his brother, Doug allowed himself to think about Sandy and how he wanted to see her as soon as he could. They had plans to make and if he knew his girl, she was already making some without him. They hadn't had time the night before to talk about a wedding date, so he hoped that later on in the evening he could call on her and they could finally talk without a throng of people around them.

When Doug had finished eating and cleaning up, he began heating water for the laundry. He hoped Charley would return soon because they always did their washing together, but, more than anything, he hoped that being married would not drive a wedge between him and his brother. He loved Charley with all his heart and would do anything in his power to make him happy.

***

Jacob Harrison was less than enthusiastic to see Mike at his door. His delight to have the pastor in his home was tainted by the fact that the boy who obviously had eyes for his daughter would be seated at his dinner table. He tried his best to keep his irritation from showing during the meal, but he made sure to keep an eye on the other end of the table.

Seated across from Pam, Mike was quiet. As he ate, he didn't allow his glances at her to linger for long. Pam was attempting to do the same, but it was a difficult thing to do when their hearts wanted to leap across the table.

"So, Pamela, have you heard from your mother lately?" Brenda Russell wanted to know. "Will she be returning soon?"

Pam turned her attention toward the other end of the table. "We received a letter from her just this week saying that she would be a few weeks longer."

"Well, I'm sure she is sorely needed by her family there for her to stay away so long."

"She's sorely needed here, too," Harrison piped in, "but we're managing fine I believe, aren't we, Pamela?"

The table was silent for a few moments until Pastor Russell began. "So, Mike, tell us what you do at the mill. We talked so much about folks back in Kingston that I didn't ask much about what you are doing here."

Mike swallowed and wiped his mouth. "I'm a wood cutter."

"A wood cutter?" Brenda joined in.

"You can't run the mill without a lot of steam, and it takes a lot of wood to keep the water boiling." Mike looked around at the group.

"Mike is one of my best wood splitters," Harrison unexpectedly complimented. "He splits almost as much as two men and gives me a full day."

Mike blushed at the compliment coming from Harrison and didn't know how to respond.

"Well, you know," Pastor Russell said, "Mike comes from a wonderful family in Kingston and was raised on hard work and godly values. He's a boy any man would be proud to call son."

"Oh, it's not hard when you enjoy what you do." Mike tried to downplay the exaggerated compliment from his pastor friend.

At that moment, May Bess stood from the table. "I will go and get the dessert. I hope you all like bread pudding."

"Bread pudding," Mike said a little too loud. The others at the table looked at him in unison. "I love bread pudding. My mother used to make it all the time, and I sure have missed it."

At that moment, Mike felt something touch his foot under the table. It startled him and he hoped no one else at the table saw his reaction. As the conversation continued at the other end of the table between Jacob Harrison and the pastor, concerning theology, Mike realized that Pam was placing her foot onto his. He rolled his eyes up to meet her gaze and noticed a slight smile on her face. He returned her smile and slid his foot closer to her under the table. For the remainder of the meal, the two held feet under the table, secretly desiring to be holding hands instead.

Their action didn't go unnoticed. As May Bess returned with the bread pudding, she saw the event under the table. Although there was a small part of her which felt it was inappropriate, the bigger part of her smiled, because, for some reason, she liked this boy. She didn't really know why, but he was different than the other boys in town, and, if it were up to her, she would give Pam her approval. She did know, however, that her brother would fly apart like a rusty boiler if he even thought for a second that there were any serious intentions being cemented between the two of them.

"I certainly don't like to eat and run," Pastor Russell exclaimed after finishing his last sip of coffee, "but we have things to attend to this evening, and I promised my wife a drive down along the creek to the Buffalo River before returning home."

Everyone at the table stood and began making their way to the front door, saying their goodbyes.

"It certainly was a pleasure sharing your table with you today." Brenda Russell leaned in to hug May Bess.

"You are welcome at my table any time, Pastor," Harrison said. "And Gilbert, I'll see you at the mill bright and early in the morning?"

"Yes, sir, you will," Mike said, walking down the front steps.

As the trio walked back to the Russell's buggy, Mike turned around for one last look at Pam. She waved from the top step of the porch, which made his heart skip a couple of beats. She then walked back into the house with May Bess.

The carriage stopped in front of Rosie's store and Mike stepped out. Brenda scooted over to give her husband a little more room on the seat. "Mike, we really enjoyed our visit with you and look forward to seeing you again."

"Yes, and maybe next time we can come a day early and do some fishing," Pastor Russell said.

Brenda turned to her husband with a chuckle. "Oh, you don't like to fish."

"I do so," he protested. "I went fishing last summer with John and Isaac on the White River. We had a great time."

Brenda chuckled again. "You didn't want to put the worm on the hook, and then you lost your pole in the water when you slipped and fell into the river." She laughed, picturing her husband falling in the current.

Mike looked at the pastor, who was turning red in the face—either from embarrassment or anger—Mike couldn't tell which.

"Who told you that?"

By this time Brenda was laughing so hard she could hardly finish what she was saying. "They said you were calling on the Lord God Almighty when they fished you out of the water. You practically baptized them again before they could get you back onto the shore."

"Sometimes Brenda likes to laugh at my expense," Pastor Russell said. "I'm going to take her to the river now. If you don't see her with me when I return, then you'll know I gave her a little push."

They said their goodbyes, and Mike could still hear Brenda laughing as he watched the buggy head down the road toward the Buffalo River. His thoughts then turned to Doug; he hoped his friend still had some hot water left for him to do his washing. He had stayed at the Harrisons' longer than he expected.

***

Mike grabbed his dirty clothes as fast as he could and carried them in a sack to Doug's. As he practically ran, he couldn't stop thinking about Pam and how he wanted to see her again. He desired to have some time alone with her, and thought about how he could see her without her father being around. He knew that if Mr. Harrison saw them together that would probably be the end of his job.

Even if he struck a deal with Rosie, he knew he would have to become familiar with the mine and how to work it before he quit working for Harrison. His mind was racing in several directions at the same time, and he felt as if he would explode. He never would have imagined his life becoming like this only two weeks earlier, and he especially never thought he could fall in love so fast.

"It's about time you showed up," Doug said, "I was about to give up on you."

"I was about to give up on me, too. Where's Charley?" Mike sat his laundry down beside the wash bucket.

"He's doin' some thinkin'," Doug said. "I told him about me and Sandy and he didn't fall apart, just said he had to do some thinkin', and he's been gone ever since. I'll go look for him if he's gone too much longer."

"That surprises me." Mike began placing his clothes into the soapy water.

"You and me both, but I don't think it's sunk into his brain yet." Doug ran his last shirt through the rollers of the wringer.

Mike began scrubbing his clothes on the washboard. "I just had dinner with the Harrisons."

"I had a feeling that's where you were headed when I saw you with the Russells. I bet Harrison choked you a couple of times in his mind."

"I'm sure he didn't want me there, but he was at least cordial to me."

"Don't go getting' a big head over it," Doug said. "You were there with the pastor"

"What's that supposed to mean?"

"You'll find out tomorrow how he really felt, since the pastor won't be around."

"Well, now you've given me something to look forward to." Mike continued to scrub.

"That's what friends are for. I'm glad I could help."

***

MB and Brenda Russell marveled at the beauty of Rush Creek while their carriage bounced along the rough dirt

216

road. As they paralleled the stream, they watched as the water trickled over the rocks in the streambed. The dense canopy of the treetops created shadows which mingled with the rays of sunlight as it filtered through and onto the road.

"I don't remember a spring that was drier than this one has been," Brenda said, noticing that the stream flow was low.

"I was told just this week that the cut trees are piling sky high at the town of Gilbert up the river, and if they don't get rain soon so they can float the logs down the Buffalo to the White River, they'll be in a big mess."

"Well, we've never dried up and blown away … still, it's unusually dry and hot for this time of the year. Oh, MB—look." Brenda directed his attention to a large rock on the side of the road.

MB turned his attention to the bird perched on the rock.

"That's an Indigo Bunting if I'm not mistaken," Brenda said as quietly as she could.

"Bunting or woodpecker; I don't know the difference between the two, but if you say it's a bunting, I believe you, dear."

The bird flew away as the couple approached, which caused them to turn their attention back to the road ahead. Within seconds the road began to descend sharply, and they inhaled the unmistakable smell of the river. The fishy smell and soured mud was not offensive but brought on a smile from them both. Their carriage rounded the last curve, and flowing from their right to left was the beautiful Buffalo River.

MB stopped the carriage and helped Brenda to the ground. They walked to the spot where Rush Creek began braiding itself into the clear water of the Buffalo, permanently infusing itself into the flow. MB crouched beside the creek, where it tumbled over the last few rocks in its bed, and placed his hand into it. "The water is still really cold."

"Rush creek is always nice and cold," Brenda said. "Remember when we dipped our feet into it in the middle of last August to cool off?"

"I remember, dear. After you walked around in it for a while, all of the little minnows began dying."

Brenda placed her fisted hands onto her hips but couldn't keep from smiling.

"You are a detestable rat sometimes, MB Russell," she said, trying to contain a laugh.

As MB looked up at Brenda from his crouched position, he spotted someone sitting on top of a boulder that looked out over the Buffalo River. Brenda saw his attention diverted and turned to see what his eyes were focused on. MB stood to get a better look at the person seated not too far from them but continuing to stare out onto the river.

"Dear, is that Charley way over there?"

"Yes, Brenda, I believe it is."

MB began walking over to Charley and, after a few steps, called out to him. "Hey, Charley boy." He raised his arm and waved.

Charley slowly turned his head in MB's direction and smiled back at the salutation.

"I'm going over there and see how Charley's doin'."

"I'll stay over here in the shade." Brenda began removing her shoes. "Cold water or not, I'm about to melt. A little wade in the creek is just what I need."

"Another fish kill." MB dropped his arms down to his sides and shook his head.

Brenda twisted her lips and made a face at her husband. He turned and walked down a pathway along the river to the boulder where Charley sat.

"How are you doin' this fine afternoon?"

Charley turned to look at his pastor friend. "I'm mighty mixed up."

"About what?" MB climbed up on the rock with Charley. Before Charley had even spoken, MB could tell that something seemed to be troubling his young friend.

218

The rock felt cool under his seat and legs as MB sat and waited for Charley's reply. While they sat, a slight breeze blew the tree limbs above them, causing spots of shadow and light to dance all around them. MB could hear the birds calling to each other up and down the river, and a kingfisher dove into the water a few feet away from them, coming up with a small fish in its beak.

Charley finally spoke. "A coupla things. I don't like feelin' this way, so I been sittin' here just thinkin' for a spell."

"What have you been thinkin' about, Charley? Sounds mighty serious." MB placed his hand onto Charley's back and patted him. "But you certainly picked a nice spot to think."

There was another period of silence, but MB didn't want to push if Charley didn't want to talk. He looked over at his wife, who was now dipping her feet into the water's edge of the creek. She was clasping her dress and holding it up to keep it from getting wet. From where he sat he couldn't hear her, but he was sure she was squealing as she eased her feet into the frigid water.

"You sure Jesus wants me to be nice to them people who aren't nice to me?" Charley finally said.

MB turned his attention back to Charley, who was drawing invisible lines onto the rock with a small twig he had picked up.

"What do you mean Charley?"

"Well ... what you was preachin' about today." Charley tossed the twig into the river. "I have to let someone hit me on the other side of the face too?"

MB could see Charley's confusion, because this sometimes was certainly a difficult teaching, but the answer to this lesson was really quite simple. "Charley, what the Lord was telling us to do as Christian people is to not repay evil with evil. When we are being tormented, we are to forgive that person and not do evil back to them."

Charley seemed more confused at that reply, and MB could tell he had more work to do, because there was obviously something at the root of the young boy's questions.

"I guess that's what I don't understand," Charley said. "Why did Jesus say I had to be nice to them that hurt me? How can I love them people that call me names and torment me?"

Charley's eyes began to water, and he turned his head away from the pastor and looked back out over the river.

"Charley," Russell began after he thought for a moment, "do you want to be like Jesus?"

"'Course I do." Charley continued to look away.

"Jesus said you are like Him when you forgive others, when you don't repay evil for evil, and especially when you do good to those people who hurt you."

"I sure want to be like Jesus." Charley said this in a soft tone as he turned his face back to the pastor. "But what good does it do to be nice to bad people?"

"Charley," MB began tenderly, "this is one of the hardest things we have to do as followers of the Lord and His ways. The Lord tells us that we are to live at peace with everyone. Don't take revenge, but leave room for God's wrath because God will take care of the evil people."

Charley looked down at his hands clasped in his lap. "He didn't help me last night."

Now MB understood what had caused the confusion in Charley, but didn't pry for fear of sticking his nose where it didn't belong. He was Charley's friend, but right now he sensed that Charley needed advice from a pastor more than anything else.

"Charley, this is difficult I know, but the important thing to God is that we obey Him. He will take care of you, and He will take care of everything else."

Charley twisted his mouth to one side as he attempted to absorb what the pastor had said and make sense out of it.

"Charley, I can't always do that."

"Do what?" Charley looked back at MB.

"I don't always do the right thing. I forget to live like the Lord wants me to at times, and I have to ask for forgiveness."

"You don't mess up, Pastor," Charley said.

"Oh, yes I do; just ask my wife."

Charley began to chuckle and MB could see that he was making some headway.

"Charley, Jesus tells us that we are to feed our enemy if he is hungry; if he is thirsty we are to give him a drink. When you repay evil with good you cause them to look at themselves and the way they behave and possibly change their ways."

"Jesus says that?"

"Jesus says that, Charley. I know it's difficult to do but Jesus said it. You never know, but it might make a change in someone if you are kind to them no matter what they do to you."

Charley's face lost expression for a moment.

"Are you thinkin' again, Charley?"

"I think I understand now," Charley said with a slight smile. "But there's just one more thing."

MB was enjoying the conversation with his friend, but he knew he needed to start back soon if they were going to make it to Yellville by nightfall.

"What's that, Charley?"

"My brother and his girl are getting hitched."

MB grabbed Charley by both of his shoulders and shook him. "That's great news, Charley! I'm happy for you and Doug."

"I don't know what to think about it, though," Charley continued. "I got some thinkin' to do about that, too."

"Well, I tell you what Charley, let's go tell Mrs. Russell to put her shoes back onto her stinky feet, and we'll talk about it on the carriage ride back to your place. Whadda ya say?"

Charley smiled a big smile at that and was helped up by MB as he stood. They both eased down from the rock and made their way toward the stream.

"Hey, Mrs. Russell, Pastor said you need to get your stinky shoes on so we can go back to town!" Charley yelled almost loud enough to be heard back in Rush.

MB lowered his head as she scolded him with her eyes, because he knew what was coming after they dropped Charley off at his place. But he would absorb her comments, knowing he had helped his friend in some way. *Thank you, Lord, for your words.*

***

"Call your brother for supper, Mark." Rachel began mashing the potatoes in a big white glass bowl. "And find your father, too."

She stopped mashing the potatoes for a moment to push her hair out of her face and place it behind one ear. She heard Mark calling for his brother through the house as she cut a few chunks of butter and mixed them into the potatoes, along with salt and pepper. As she completed creaming the mixture with a little milk, the boys and William made their way into the kitchen and sat at their places.

"Mark, I could have yelled through the house myself to find your brother," Rachel said sharply. "You know better than to cause a commotion like that."

Mark looked at his father, who agreed with Rachel by the furrowing of his brow and slight nodding of his head.

After placing the bowl of potatoes onto the table, Rachel sat down, and stared at her empty plate. The group was silent for a few seconds with all eyes on her. Finally she looked up at William. He bowed his head and gave thanks for the meal.

Upon, "Amen," hands reached for the bowls and plates of food on the table, but Rachel continued to sit. Even though the potatoes, chicken, and green beans smelled good to her, she had no desire to eat.

"You will have to excuse me." She placed her napkin onto her plate as she stood. "I'm not feeling very well tonight and I think I'll go lie down."

The boys stopped eating and William began to stand.

"Don't get up, William, just finish your dinner. I'll be okay. Put your dishes in the sink and I'll clean them later."

Rachel left the kitchen as her family continued their meal in silence. She closed the bedroom door and slipped on a house jacket after undressing. Seated at her vanity, she ran a brush through her hair. She noticed the gray beginning to show, and she inspected the wrinkles caressing her face at the corners of her eyes. Her thoughts rested on the boy who was not with them in church on that day. Even though Mike's letter had eased her pain, she couldn't help but feel the hole in her heart from his absence.

As she continued to brush her hair, she remembered how she felt when she gave birth to her twins, and how it wasn't long before she noticed something different in Mike's little soul. He was always curious about the world and asked her questions she couldn't answer.

She wouldn't dare tell anyone, not even William, but she was probably fonder of Michael than either of his brothers. She enjoyed how he would confide in her about his thoughts or troubles, something he wouldn't do with his father. She always knew deep in her heart that, for some reason, Michael would someday seek his own path. It was, however, something she never thought of much, because looking into the future seemed so far away from reality. As she put her brush down onto the table and stared back at herself in the mirror, she looked into the past and wondered where all the time had gone.

The doorknob to the bedroom turned and William walked into the room, closing the door behind him. He sat on the edge of the bed and removed his boots. "The boys are taking care of the supper dishes."

Rachel looked down at her hands folded in her lap and began picking at her fingernails. "Thank you," she said. "I didn't really feel much like going back in there tonight."

"I understand." There was a pause. "You know, there's something I've been thinking about ever since we got Mike's letter yesterday."

"What would that be?" Rachel continued looking down at her lap.

William stood and walked behind Rachel. He placed his hands onto her shoulders. After a moment of looking at her in the mirror, he pulled her hair away from her face and placed it all behind her shoulders. As he held her hair in both of his hands he bent over and kissed her on the top of her head.

"I've decided to go see Mike and take his money to him."

Rachel lifted her head and looked at the reflection of her husband standing over her. Her eyes brightened and William detected a slight smile on her face.

"You're going to Rush?"

"He needs to know that I didn't mean what I said on the day that he left."

Rachel turned on the stool and faced her husband.

"What did you say, William?"

William walked back to the bed and sat. He hung his head and looked at the floor. There was silence.

"William?"

He sighed as he looked up at Rachel. "As he was leaving … I told him there was no need to come back if his bed was empty that night."

At his words, tears pooled in Rachel's eyes, but through the mist, she noticed the same with her husband. She realized what agony he must have been dealing with for the past two weeks. She knew her husband well and now understood the cause of his sleepless nights. She sat down beside him on the bed; he looked back down at the wood floor in agony. A few tears dripped onto his socks.

"I want to leave tomorrow."

"I want to go with you."

"No, this is something I have to do alone," he said without hesitation. "I don't know anything about this town, and it might not be a place for a woman. Besides, I can travel faster alone, and there may not be boarding between here and there."

Rachel wiped her eyes and began to protest, but she knew there was no use in pushing the matter once William said no. "Then I have things to do." She stood. "I need to get you ready for your trip and send some things with you to Mike. I know he could use some more blankets and clothing. I'm sure you'll take the buggy so...."

"I'm leaving the buggy here for you and the boys, but I'll pack some things on the mule and drag her along," William interrupted.

Rachel placed her hands up to her face, and, as she removed them, exclaimed with a smile, "William, you don't know how much better I'm going to feel knowing you've seen him and that he's doing well where he is!"

"I'm sure I'll be gone all week," William said, "but you and the boys will be just fine. I'll give them their instructions for the week and plan to be back by Saturday."

Rachel wrapped her arms around her husband and sobbed with joy into his chest.

Holding his wife, William said, "It'll be good to see him again."

Chapter 21

The chatter of a noisy mockingbird brought Mike out of his dreams. *Monday morning already?* He pulled the covers over his face to muffle the birdsong and cut out the growing daylight, but it did no good. He already had a feeling in the pit of his stomach that his friend Doug might be right about Harrison, and he was not looking forward to seeing him. Mike hoped it wouldn't be as bad as imagined, but he still didn't know the man well enough to be able to figure what might happen once he got to work.

After slinging his feet onto the floor, he built a fire in the stove. While the water heated, he washed and dressed for the beginning of another work week. He sat on the edge of his bed, putting on his boots, and thought about what his week would be like. Many thoughts crowded his head all at the same time, and he was having a difficult time untangling them. Although he knew he might get a few words from Harrison, he was thinking about Rosie's mine and how he was going to tackle that overwhelming opportunity. Before he had time to ponder his situation for too long, he noticed the water beginning to boil in his coffee pot. Following Rosie's recipe, he quickly mixed together the ingredients for pancakes and placed an iron skillet onto the other grate of the wood stove to heat.

With his coffee boiling, he placed some strips of cured bacon into the hot skillet and drank in the aroma of the sizzling meat. After removing the bacon and placing it onto a plate, he then poured in the batter, making one large pancake that practically filled the bottom of the skillet. The sizzling bacon grease around the pancake made the edges crisp and darker brown, which he liked. With some luck, he was able to successfully flip the hotcake without breaking it. Feeling proud of himself he placed the cake onto his plate next to the bacon, poured his coffee, and sat at his little table. He surveyed his breakfast with a smile.

"Not bad if I do say so myself," he said out loud. And after offering thanks for his food, Mike poured some corn syrup onto his pancake and enjoyed his successful attempt.

***

"Mornin', Jim." Mike arrived at the storage shed by the Morning Star Mill.

"Well, what's got you as chipper as a canary?" Jim opened the doors revealing the tools for the day.

"Don't rightly know, just one of those mornings I guess." Mike grabbed his axe, sledge hammer, and a couple of steel wedges.

The morning was another beautiful springtime offering, complete with a cloudless robin's- egg-blue sky. Mike made his way to his area and dropped the wedges and sledge hammer to the ground out of his way. He placed the head of the axe onto the ground in front of him and leaned the handle into his legs. As he rolled up his shirt sleeves, he gazed at his surroundings and listened to the familiar sounds of the awakening town. Because of the dense humidity of the early morning air, he could hear the roar of Doug's forge being heated for the day's work. He thought of his close friendship with the blacksmith and smiled. The rumble of the boiler and the hiss of steam inside the Morning Star could be heard, alerting Mike to the beginning of another day of rock crushing and separating. He saw Finch pull away from the mill with a fully loaded wagon of crushed rock and wondered where the load was headed. Then he wondered about the world Finch lived in and what a miserable person he must be.

With his sleeves rolled, Mike pulled his leather gloves out of his hip pocket and slipped them onto his hands. He stood a piece of sectioned oak onto the chopping block and was about to make his first swing of the day when he heard a sharp voice come from behind him.

"Gilbert!"

He turned his head to see Harrison looking at him from the corner of the building. A knot formed his stomach, and this time it wasn't from the breakfast he had made.

"Yes, sir, Mr. Harrison?"

"Put your axe down and meet me in my office."

Before Mike could reply again Jacob Harrison disappeared from sight. Mike looked around at the other wood choppers; they all gazed at him. He leaned his axe against the chopping block and removed his gloves as he made his way toward the Morning Star office.

Mike opened the door to Harrison's office and saw Harrison standing with Larkin Riley. He removed his hat and fidgeted with it in his grasp.

"Gilbert, do you like splitting wood?" came an abrupt question from Harrison.

Mike looked back and forth between the two men and swallowed hard. He had a feeling he was about to be let go because of the attention he'd paid to Harrison's daughter. He had been warned and the threat was about to come to fruition.

"Yes, sir, I've always enjoyed splitting wood," came Mike's shaky reply.

"Well, I'm sorry to hear that," Harrison said, walking toward Mike with a stern face, "because I'm going to take you off wood detail and move you inside."

"Excuse me, sir?"

"Since Vernon Dobbs was killed a couple of weeks ago, we've needed someone to take his place—keep the gears greased and maintain the belts there above the steam generator."

"Not just any idiot can do it properly," Larkin piped in, lighting a cigar.

Harrison shot him a look then turned back to Mike.

"What he means is that we need someone responsible who can learn how to maintain the equipment and stay on top of things. If the bearings get dry or a belt slips off track it can cause all kinds of damage and put us out of commission for a while, and that costs money."

Mike's nervousness began to ease, and he realized he was actually being promoted...or so he thought.

"Mr. Harrison, I'll do whatever you want me to do."

Larkin rolled his eyes behind Harrison's back at the boy's devoted eagerness.

"But what about Jim and the others at the woodpile?"

"You don't worry about Jim. I can find another wood cutter, maybe not as good as you, but he'll get by."

Mike was stunned by this turn of events, especially after fretting over what this morning might bring. Instantly he remembered the scripture in the book of Matthew concerning Jesus's teachings about not worrying for tomorrow since today has enough problems of its own.

"Thank you, Mr. Harrison."

"Larkin will take you to Titus Johnson, who will teach you how to maintain the equipment properly. We'll give you another nickel an hour." Harrison stepped back to his desk.

"Thanks again, Mr. Harrison."

"You can quit thanking me and get started." Harrison picked up a stack of papers. "Those bearings won't grease themselves."

Mike placed his hat onto his head and followed as Riley made his way to the door leading into the mill.

I can't wait to tell Doug that he was wrong about Mr. Harrison.

"Oh, and Gilbert, you might want to pay more attention to your work and less attention to my daughter."

Mike, smiling, had stopped and turned to Harrison and now didn't know what to think or say. But there it was, the friendly little warning from Pam's father. The smile left his face; a look of panic replaced it.

"Come on, Gilbert, we don't have all day." Riley's voice pulled Mike out of his daze.

He disconnected his gaze from Harrison and left the doorway to follow Riley and receive his instructions from

Titus Johnson, the floor manager. As he walked toward the giant boiler, it felt to Mike as if he were walking in thick, sticky mire. His legs resisted his brain's signal to move forward. He had the feeling that Mr. Harrison didn't give second warnings, and deep inside he felt as if part of his heart had been ripped out. For now, he decided to simply follow Larkin and receive his instructions. Somehow, later, he would untangle the mess of emotions writhing inside him.

***

Thirty miles upriver from Rush, at the town of Gilbert, piles of cut timber were stacked high. Each day that passed without rain, the manager of the logging operation became more agitated.

"Stack that pile closer to the river," Leon Pike commanded. "We need to make sure they are easily rolled into the water when she comes up." He glanced at the river. "If she ever comes up," he mumbled to himself as he walked toward a couple of workers not far away.

"When do you think we'll finally get enough rain to float all these logs down the river?" One of the workers asked Pike as he made it to their group.

Pike replied in an exasperated tone, motioning with both of his arms. "How in thunder should I know? I cain't predict the blasted weather."

The two men shook their heads because they understood the pressure Pike was under. The usual spring crew was poised at Buffalo City on the White River and was ready to catch the flow of logs to be shaped into railroad ties for the ever-expanding system of tracks.

Every spring the expected rains allowed the loggers up the Buffalo to float their logs down the river until it joined with the White River. There the logs would be guided a short distance downriver, where they would be caught by a boom over the river and hauled onto shore. Most every spring the event ran like clockwork; however, this spring had been a dry one, and there had not been enough rain to raise the river level to the needed height.

"Boys, if we cain't get this wood down to Buffalo City soon, we're gonna have all sorts of problems." Pike looked out over the sea of cut logs piled and poised to be rolled into the flowing water.

"I've never prayed fer rain so hard in my life," one of the workers said.

"You ain't doin' somethin' right," the other man said, looking at his friend.

With a somber expression, Pike spoke in a warning tone. "You know that when the rain finally does come, we're gonna have to roll more of these logs into the water at a time than I like to."

"I was afraid you were gonna say that."

"Don't have much of a choice," Pike said. "You never know how long the water will stay up after rain, so we'll have to work as fast as we can."

"You know that too many logs too fast can create log jams on this river—lots of tight turns on her."

"You don't have to remind me," Pike continued. "We'll just have to put a few more men on lashed rafts to guide them downriver."

The two workers looked nervously at each other, hoping they would not be the ones told to guide the haphazard herd of logs down a fast-flowing, angry river. Each of them knew someone who had been injured or killed while untangling log jams during a normal log run.

"Let's just hope the rain doesn't wait too much longer." Pike left the group and made his way to his little office shack.

The two workers knew that the situation was already dire and that what was to come was not a pleasant thing to look forward to. Hopefully the flood rains would begin soon and allow the logs to be released in increments rather than in large groups. They shuddered to think about the chaos that could otherwise be caused along the river and with the unlucky few who would have to be on the raging water with the logs.

***

It hadn't taken long for word of Mike's whereabouts to reach the ears of Weldon Parker, the Madison County sheriff. He had already questioned Clifton Davis at the Kingston bank, but so far had no leads other than Mike Gilbert's outburst and the scene he had caused the day before the robbery.

Instead of making the trip to Rush himself, he prepared a wire to send to the local law in Marion County and get the sheriff there to bring Mike to Yellville for questioning. He would meet with the two there in a nice, comfy office and try to figure out if Mike was indeed the bank robber. As far as he was concerned, Gilbert was guilty and this was just a formality, so, in his communication, he let the Yellville sheriff know that Mike was armed and probably dangerous, and warned him to proceed with caution when apprehending him.

With the wire sent, and since the day was nice, Parker decided to run a little errand. "Don't get too many nice spring days like this," he said out loud as he walked out of the telegraph office. He pulled a previously rolled cigarette out of his shirt pocket and placed it between his lips.

"Don't expect to break the law in my county and get away with it," he said with a smirk, as if Gilbert were standing in front of him. He struck a match against the porch railing and placed the fire to the end of his smoke. He stepped out into the dusty street, mounted his horse, and headed toward a secret little place tucked away back in the woods. Parker had a desire for something to quench his thirst and knew just the man who could help him with his problem.

"Get up." He encouraged his horse to move a little faster toward his destination.

***

Sheriff Wes Smith sat in his office with a cloth swab shoved down the barrel of a shotgun when the door opened. He looked up to see a young boy with red hair and freckled cheeks bound in then toward his desk.

232

"Close that door behind ya, Jimmy; yer invitin' all the flies from Marion County to come inside and pester me." Wes released the shotgun and sat it onto his desk. "Just because you were born in a barn doesn't mean you have to act like it."

The boy turned and closed the door with a slam. Wes shut his eyes at the noise and opened one eye at first, to glare at the young man who was now standing in front of him holding a folded piece of paper in a dirty hand.

"Mornin', Sheriff. Mr. Adair wanted me to run this over to you. Said it was important and I wasn't to dilly dally."

Wes looked at the boy with both eyes now then down at the piece of white paper in Jimmy's grasp. "Well, let's just see what you got there." Wes reached his hand out toward the boy.

Jimmy handed the folded paper to Wes, who opened it and read the message to himself.

"Is it real important?" Jimmy asked as Wes continued to absorb the words.

Wes finished reading the message to himself, and then replied, "Yep, it's real important alright."

Jimmy beamed to be the bearer of something meaningful to the sheriff. Wes dug into his pocket, pulled out a penny, and handed it to the boy.

"Go buy you some candy over at the drugstore and don't be a pig with it all, ya hear? Share some with your sister."

The boy smiled, proudly revealing a missing tooth he had pulled earlier in the day.

"Go on now; I've got work to do." Wes stood and smiled at Jimmy, who was already halfway to the door with his shiny copper treasure. "And close the door quietly behind you this time." His words chased the boy out the door that was left open. He shook his head and walked around his desk to shut the door himself, but not before standing in the doorway to watch Jimmy make his way down the dusty

233

street toward the cornucopia of sweets awaiting him at the drugstore.

Wes Smith was a man who was not much taller when he stood than when he was seated; however, his lack of height was not a deterrent to his professional abilities. He was quick and strong and generally underestimated, which usually gave him an advantage when it came to dealing with lawbreakers. His easygoing nature and good looks caused him to be liked, at least by those who followed the rules. Wes was a kind man, but when a situation arose, he was as tenacious as a hound dog after a coon.

Martha Smith was busy with the task of cutting a chicken at the sink when the kitchen door opened. She turned with her usual sweet smile to see Wes walk into the room. "What brings you home in the middle of the afternoon?"

Wes removed his hat and hung it on a nail beside the door frame. He sighed as he sat at the wooden table.

Martha stopped her evisceration of the chicken, wiped her hands, and turned to face her husband. "I don't like the sound of that sigh."

"I got a wire from over in Madison County a little while ago sayin' that there was a suspected bank robber in Rush." He paused and locked his fingers together behind his head as he leaned back in the chair, balancing himself on two of the chair legs.

"Yer gonna break my chair leanin' back like that." Martha sweetly scolded her husband, indicating that she would prefer he sit with all four legs on the floor.

Wes kept his hands behind his head but complied and leaned forward to please his wife.

"So are you tellin' me that you have to make a trip down to Rush?"

"Yup, seems someone robbed the bank at Kingston around two weeks ago, and Sheriff Parker in Huntsville wants me to go bring him back here to Yellville so he can come over and question the man."

"When do you have to go?" Martha turned back to her chicken.

"Parker said he'd be here on Friday, so I figured I'd go down on Wednesday. That should give me time to find this fellow and get him back here for Parker."

"Well, you be careful."

"I always am, dear."

Martha turned back to the sink and Wes quietly leaned his chair on two legs again.

"And put the chair down before you fall over and break your neck." Martha said this as if she had eyes in the back of her head.

Wes complied and sat in silence for a moment. "When's supper?"

"When it's ready, I reckon." Martha chuckled.

"Good, then I'll be hungry." Wes stood, placed his hat onto his head and walked out into the daylight.

Martha smiled and her eyes twinkled as she looked out the window, watching the man she adored walking back toward his office.

***

Jay Finch handed the new equipment invoice to Leon Pike and climbed back onto the delivery wagon.

"Tell Harrison I need my order of Iron for the forge as soon as possible. If he's having problems getting it from Buffalo City, I'll have to find it elsewhere."

Jay half-heartedly replied to the gesture with a nod of his head. He stuffed the tender into his pocket and flipped the reins, urging the horses to get moving. He turned the team in the street and headed north back out of town. As he rounded the first curve out of Gilbert, he saw Morse lying at the foot of the big oak tree awaiting his return.

As before, Jay had taken Jeeter on as a passenger outside Rush, only this time so that the two of them could retrieve the still from the man they had shot a couple of days earlier.

Jay slowed the wagon. "Come on Morse, we don't have all day."

235

Jeeter stood and dusted off his backside. "Just hold your horses." He took his time, to give a subtle hint that he was the one in charge and not Jay. Jay stopped the team and waited for Jeeter to make his way over and climb in. As soon as Jeeter was onboard, Jay whistled and they were moving again.

"Usin' the company wagon for this makes me nervous." They began their trek toward the abandoned still.

"What does it matter to you anyway?" Jeeter stared into the woods. "You don't like that job nohow."

"It's not that." Jay looked around for anyone who might see them. "You shot a man on Saturday, and it might be easier for someone to figure things out if they see this wagon."

Jeeter interrupted. "You mean *we* shot a man on Saturday. You're in this with me, partner." Jay looked over at Jeeter, who talked as if shooting a man was no more out of the ordinary than swatting at a fly.

"Besides," Jeeter continued, "if there ain't no body, there ain't no problem."

Hatred for Jeeter boiled inside Jay. He knew that to get rid of Jeeter would only cause Jeeter to implicate him in the killing. He had been trying to think of any way he could to get out of this mess with Morse and even cut ties with Raif, but so far he had come up empty.

As the thickness of the forest closed in around them, they drove the wagon along the bumpy, narrowing pathway toward the still. From the tree limbs above, wild grapevines hung down and looped their heavy tendrils toward the ground. The forest floor was littered with the beautiful blossoms of gooseberry, May apple, and dewberries all reaching up toward the sky to grab, through the thick canopy above them, what filtered light they could. Squirrels jumped from tree to tree entertaining the bluebirds and cardinals, but Jay noticed none of this beauty since his soul was shrouded by dark clouds of guilt and hatred.

They were almost to their destination when two men brandishing guns stepped out onto the path in front of them. Jay pulled back on the leather straps, bringing the team to a halt. For a moment the only sounds were the birds around them and the creaking harnesses on the horses.

The man holding a pistol finally spoke. "Where you fellas think yer headed?"

"We was lookin' for a little liquid refreshment," Jeeter said with a playful smile.

"Turn around." The other man raised his shotgun at the pair.

Out of the corner of his eye, Jay noticed Jeeter's hand slowly making a move toward his waist, where his pistol was kept inside his jacket. *Don't do it, Jeeter.*

"You fellas sure we can't get a little shine? We bought from ol' man Cain just last week, and he was makin' extra for us to carry back to Rush. Why, I was just tellin' my friend here a little while ago…"

"I won't tell you again to turn around." The man with the shotgun repeated his order as he and his partner both cocked their weapons and pointed them at Jay and Jeeter.

Jeeter slowly relaxed his hand and let it drop to his side.

"Okay, friends, we'll turn around." Jeeter maintained his smirk and kept both his hands in plain sight. "We don't need anyone gettin' shot here."

Jeeter looked at Jay and nodded, which signaled Jay to turn the team around. There was barely enough room to pull the team into the underbrush then back onto the rough pathway. With their backs to the roadblock and heading away from the still, Jay felt his heart finally begin to slow down.

When they were out of earshot of the two men on the road, Jay jerked his head toward Jeeter and exploded. "I've had enough of lookin' down the barrel of a gun, Morse, and it ain't gonna happen again!"

"Well…look who's found a big bucket of courage. You talk pretty big for a little fella."

Jay gestured with his right hand. "When we get back I'm gonna have a nice little talk with Raif, because yer gonna get someone shot—and it ain't gonna be me."

"Simmer down, Jay ol' buddy. Raif figured there might be someone at Cain's still. We was just testin' the water, so to speak. When we get back to town, he'll just send a few of us back over to get it, now knowin' what we're facin'. Since I know how to get here, you can stay in Rush, curled up in your safe little ball while we do the hard work."

With that, Jeeter began to laugh, and he continued to laugh at Jay for quite a way down the road. For a few miles Jay considered how he could work up the courage to shoot Jeeter and push him off into the bushes. No one in Rush would miss him, but there was something inside Jay that kept him from putting his plan into action. He wasn't a coward, but he just couldn't do it. No, there had to be another way to get rid of Jeeter. He would ponder it for a while longer. The pair rode in silence for the rest of the trip back to Rush.

Chapter 22

"Let's shut 'er down," came the command of the crew chief inside the Morning Star Mill. Mike was up in the rafters applying heavy grease to the shaft bearings when the order came to stop the crusher for the day. He climbed down the makeshift ladder and placed his grease can onto the floor, where it would await him until the next day.

Mike's first day inside the mill above the steam boiler had been more difficult than he had imagined. Even though it was still early spring, the heat generated by the boiler was intense when he was above it. He figured he had sweat more on his first day inside than any two or three days splitting wood. The noise from the mechanisms and the rock crusher left his ears ringing as he left the building.

"How was your first day on the inside?"

Mike turned to see Jim Smith . "Much harder than I figured it would be."

Mike walked with Jim to the tool shed. "I can tell I'm gonna miss the fresh air."

"Well," Jim began as he put the last axe into its place and locked the doors, "cuttin' wood in the dead of winter isn't pleasant…cuttin' wood in the heat of summer is miserable, but the rest of the time I don't mind it. It'll be the same for you inside. At least you'll be out of the rain and snow."

Mike smiled. "At least there's that."

The pair stood in silence for a moment, and Jim noticed that Mike seemed a little distracted. "Sumpthin' on your mind?"

"Is it that obvious?"

"A bit. What's eatin' at ya?"

Mike leaned against the tool shed. "Jim, have you ever worked in the mines?"

239

"You've only been up in the rafters for a day and you're already looking for a job change?"

"Well..." Mike paused. "I was just wonderin' how hard it is and what you have to do to learn how to do it."

Jim smiled at Mike's question, knowing that young Mike was probably struggling with big dreams. "What do you do to learn how to ride a horse?"

Mike looked puzzled because that didn't have anything to do with working a mine. "You get in the saddle, take the reins, and say, "giddiyup." He sat down on a section of tree trunk. "But ridin' a horse is different than workin' in a mine."

"Oh, there's more to bein' a miner for sure, but that's how you get started. Just like ridin' a horse, you have to learn about what you're doin'. You'll make mistakes, but before you know it you're doin' it square."

Mike got back to his feet. "Can you make money at it?"

"Sure you can...if it's your mine and there's ore in it." Jim walked toward the street. "I'll see you tomorrow; I need me some supper."

Mike stood for a moment then began making his way to Rosie's place. The sound of the steam generator made a loud hiss as the pressure inside it was released, signaling the end of another work day.

***

Mike walked through the door of Rosie's store. "Evenin', Rosie."

Rosie sat in a chair next to the checker board at the back of the room. "I've been expectin' you, kid."

Mike walked past the stocked shelves and sat in the chair opposite Rosie. The checkerboard was set up for a new game; however, Mike knew they weren't there to play checkers. The pair sat in silence for a few seconds. Rosie was resting comfortably in her chair with her hands clasped together in her lap, and Mike was having a difficult time sitting still.

"Would ya like something to drink?" Rosie finally broke the silence. "Beth made some sun tea today, and I think she has a couple of glasses left."

"I'm okay. Thanks, Rosie."

Leaning forward, Rosie placed her arms onto the table. "Well then, what do you think about the mine? You think it's somethin' you want to tackle?"

"Rosie, I don't know a thing about mining...heck, I've never even been in one. I'm scared and excited at the same time."

"I'd be worried about you if ya weren't scared. It's not a place for the sassy. Get careless just one time and it could set you back a week's work or even kill ya. You'll come home achin' all over and you'll wake up already achin'. Flyin' rock chips will cut you on your face and arms, and your feet will be wet most of the time."

"Sounds like you're trying to talk me out of it."

Rosie smiled. "No, I just want you to know what you'll be gettin' yourself into."

"You're talkin' like I've already accepted your deal." Mike looked down at the checkers then back up at Rosie with a sideways grin.

The tone of Rosie's voice became serious. "Mike, I wouldn't have offered the mine to you if I didn't think you have what it takes to make a go of it. You're a hard worker, you have a head on your shoulders..." she paused for a moment as she looked into the fireplace then back at Mike, "and you remind me of my son."

Mike had never heard Rosie mention any other family besides her dead husband. He didn't know whether to question her about her son or let it be.

"My boy, Nathan, was a lot like you. Strong willed and wasn't afraid to respectfully tackle anything. The only thing he couldn't handle was tuberculosis."

"Rosie, I'm sorry."

"Nathan died about a year before my husband did. It's been a rough few years, but what do you do? You just have to handle it and go on with life." Rosie's eyes began to

241

water as she remembered the past. "After a while you put the pain in a box and set it on the mantle. Every so often you take the box down and look into it, get sad, then set it back on the shelf again for a spell.

The front door opened and Beth tended to the customer. The pair turned their attention from the door back to the matter around the checkers table.

"So what do you think, Gilbert? Care to be partners?"

"Rosie," Mike began then paused as if digesting the words that were actually about to fall out of his mouth, "if you have faith in me, then I'll do it." He extended his right hand over the checkers. Rosie chuckled as she placed her hand into his and the pair shook on the deal.

"I'll have a simple paper showing transfer of title for you to sign in a few days, but, as far as I'm concerned, the mine belongs to you as of right now."

The pair stood and Mike placed his hat back onto his head.

"I've got something I want to give to you." Rosie motioned for Mike to follow her. "Just a little something to get you started."

Mike followed Rosie through a doorway beside the fireplace to a small storage room. She lit an oil lamp, which illuminated a room cluttered with miscellaneous tools and clothing, then handed the lamp to Mike and reached for something on a nearby shelf. She retrieved a lantern, but it was a little different than any lantern he had seen. Rosie motioned again and the pair exited the storage room back into the main room. Mike followed her to one of the counters where she sat the lantern down.

Mike set his oil lamp on the counter so that he could better inspect the new piece of equipment.

"I just got this on Friday from a drummer who came through. We don't get too many of those guys around these parts. He said his name was Coleman and he was on his way to Oklahoma with this newfangled lantern. He also said this was his first sale. I don't know if that's good or bad, but I guess you'll find out, won't ya?" Rosie slid the lantern over to Mike, who was already marveling at some of the improvements over the commonly used lanterns. "He told me it burned gasoline, and you pump air into it to keep pressure on the gas. You light the mantle, and it's supposed to glow brighter than the light of day."

Mike placed both his hands onto the lantern. "Rosie, I don't know what to say."

"You might want to wait to thank me until after you see if this new marvel works." The front door opened again and several men walked into the store.

"Guess I better get busy." Rosie left Mike standing at the counter with his new lantern.

Mike took the lantern by the wire handle and left Rosie's store, feeling like he was about to explode. In his excitement he turned and made his way to the blacksmith shop. He could hardly wait to show Doug his new lantern, plus tell him that the mine deal had been sealed. He could hear the pounding of metal against metal when he entered but was surprised to see Doug's apprentice, Joseph, pounding the iron as sparks flew. From the corner of his eye, Mike noticed another man standing in the room. He turned to see Jay Finch, who was already glaring in Mike's direction.

"Where's Doug?"

Joseph continued to hammer. "He's over at Sandy's place. They're talkin' about weddin' particulars with her parents, I think."

Mike was deflated because he needed to tell someone his news or he felt like he would burst. He wished he could tell Pam, since she was most likely home; but he knew he couldn't get an audience with her this late in the afternoon, and her father had already made his feelings fairly clear about Mike's involvement with her.

"What you got in yer hand there, plowboy?" Jay took a few steps toward Mike.

The words grated on Mike's nerves and made his skin crawl like chalk screeching on a slate.

"It's a new lantern I just got from Rosie's store." Mike held up the lantern to boast. "It's the only one like it in the area."

Jay stopped a couple of steps shy of Mike. "Well, now, what does a plowboy like you need with a newfangled lantern like that? You figurin' on doin' a little minin', or did you get a fancy lamp like that just to go to the outhouse and do yer business?"

Joseph couldn't help but laugh as he continued sending sparks into the air.

Jay's taunting words angered Mike, and even though he felt like shoving Jay's face into the bucket of water next to the anvil, he decided to reserve that action for another time…which he knew would certainly come.

"Now that you mentioned it, I am planning on doin' some mining."

Jay was surprised at Mike's response.

"Who in their right mind would let a sodbuster like you go into one of their mines? Ol' man Harrison ain't brain dead enough to let you, that's fer sure."

"I wasn't talking about Harrison's mine," Mike replied with a smug grin. "I'm talkin' about my own mine."

"Your mine?" Jay began to laugh. "You think you can just stick a shovel in the ground around here and dig up ore? I knew plowboys was dumb, but I never seen one as dumb as you."

Mike stood stoic as Jay continued to laugh. "I bought my own mine."

Jay's laughter stopped as suddenly as a running mule stops before it hits barbed wire. "What do you mean you bought your own mine? How does a dirt-scratchin' cow milker like you get enough money to buy a mine?"

"Not that it's any of your business, Finch, but I bought the old mine down by the river."

Jay thought for a moment. "The only mine down by the river is the Red Rose Mine, and it hasn't been worked for a few years."

Mike simply smiled at Jay, who was at a loss for words. "Joseph, I guess I'll talk to Doug later." Mike turned and left the building, leaving the pair in the humid evening air stunned by the news.

"Well, everybody's gonna find out sooner or later," Mike mumbled as he walked back to his place. It had made him feel good to rub Jay's face into news like that. But now there was a voice in his heart telling him that it was wrong for him to do so, even if it was to Jay.

His stomach was giving him orders that it was hungry, so his thoughts changed to what he was going to eat for dinner. Now that his decision had fully sunk in, he was exhilarated at the thought of getting to work in his zinc mine…if only he could figure out how to do it.

***

Tuesday morning found Mike in the rafters above the steam boiler at the mill. He stood on a board that spanned two heavy beams and surveyed the pulleys, spinning shafts, and canvas belts turning and adding their clatter to the noise of the rock crusher. The marvel of mechanics intrigued Mike, and he traced the route with his gaze from the steam boiler to every gear and cog spinning and turning.

With the hiss of steam in the background, he made his way down a beam to the next set of spinning shafts, which led to the heavy belts feeding the rock crusher its power. Mike carefully crouched, cautious to stay clear of the belts. He was about to begin greasing the pivot joints when he heard a shrill voice from below him.

"Gilbert!" The shout boomed so loud and sudden that it caused him to jump and lose grip of his grease can, sending it down to the floor below. The grease can landed with a sloppy thud only ten feet in front of Jacob Harrison.

"Up here, Mr. Harrison."

"Come see me, now." Harrison turned on his heels back in the direction of his office.

Mike had known this moment would surely come, and he had not been able to sleep half the night, fearing this conversation with his boss. He descended from his perch and made his way to the company office. When he entered through the doorway, he saw Harrison looking out a window with his back to Mike. Mike pecked on the door frame with a couple of half-hearted wraps of his knuckles.

"I know you're there, Michael. Close the door behind you."

Michael? Since when had he been called Michael and especially by Harrison? He didn't like it, and he had a feeling he wasn't going to like what came next. Mike closed the door and took a couple of steps into the room where he waited for Harrison to start the conversation.

"Do you know how long I've been in Rush?" Harrison began without turning from the dirt-streaked window.

"Not exactly, sir."

There was another pause.

Harrison lowered his crossed arms and placed his hands in his pants pockets. "Almost ten years. I moved here—away from my family—for a year and watched as this town grew into life. I sweated gallons of water, and some blood, helping to build the Morning Star Mill. I swung picks and shovels and wheeled loads of heavy gray rock along rusty tracks only to turn around and get another load."

There was another pause as Harrison continued to survey the town through the dirty windowpane.

"I had big dreams just like you, boy. Just exactly like you."

Mike shifted uncomfortably to his left leg and heard the excited determination in Harrison's voice as he relived his past.

"After sending money home for a year, I was made plant manager. I moved my wife and daughter here, and it looked like my dreams were finally becoming a reality. I was able to build my house and afford nicer things. But that wasn't my whole dream, Michael. I knew the real money was in owning your own production mine, or even several. When you're in the mining business, you have to strike while the iron is hot because the ore doesn't last forever, and sooner or later it runs out."

Harrison turned slowly, with no emotion showing on his face, and sat in a wooden chair, motioning for Mike to do likewise.

Gesturing with his arms as if he were presenting himself to a dance partner, Harrison began again. "This town has grown up practically overnight, and I've been here every step of the way. I've been to weddings, funerals, and births. I've seen boys grow into manhood. I've seen the town get sick, and I've seen it overcome adversity."

Beads of sweat began forming on Mike's forehead, and he knew it wouldn't be long before they grew large enough to trickle down his face. The room was stuffy and hot, and the tension was becoming unbearable.

"With everything I've been through, Gilbert, I thought surely I had seen everything… but there's something I just don't get and it has me quite puzzled." Harrison now leaned forward with his elbows resting on the tops of his knees.

"How in the Sam Hill can a young, inexperienced farm boy like you come here and, within two weeks time, weasel your way into buying a zinc mine that I've been trying to get my hands on for over three years?" Harrison was now red in the face and sweating profusely himself.

Mike fidgeted in his chair and looked around as if trying to will someone to come into the office and break the tension or interrupt the serious fray. He remained silent, not knowing what to say, when Harrison stood, pulled his hat from his head, and threw it to the floor, causing an eruption of dust.

Mike felt like a cornered animal, knowing that the only way out might be to fight back, even though he had no desire to fight or have any friction with the father of the girl he loved.

"Mr. Harrison, I didn't weasel myself into anything."

Harrison leaned toward Mike and held up his right hand with three fingers shooting up into the air.

247

"For three years I've been bargaining, begging, pleading with Rosie to buy her mine…three years. It's one of the highest-producing zinc mines here in the valley. Her husband was becoming wealthy just before he died, and it's been sitting there ever since, flirting with every miner in the area who dreams of owning his own mine. But no matter how hard I've tried, she would not even entertain the notion of selling to me."

Harrison now began to pace as if he were in some sort of theater production and he was reciting rehearsed lines. "Have you ever swung a pick in a mine?"

"No, sir."

"Have you ever hauled a rock out of a mine?"

"No, sir."

"Have you ever cut your arms and knees along sharp rocks as you breathed in stale, damp air mingled with the smell of coal oil and rock dust?"

"No, Mr. Harrison, I haven't."

Harrison turned and placed his hands onto a small wooden desk and leaned his body close to Mike. Mike held his position and gazed into Harrison's eyes.

"Then why in God's holy name did I hear that you've bought the mine from Rosie?"

Mike had a decision to make. His first reaction was to become the little school boy and fall into the safety net of explaining things away to try and divert the attention from himself. But he suddenly reminded himself that he was on his own, a young man in a man's world. He realized that to live like a man he had to act like a man, even if it meant fighting like a man for what you believed in. To Harrison's surprise, Mike slowly stood to face him. Mike took a deep breath and realized that reasoning with Harrison would only exacerbate this struggle. Although a thousand explanations were forming to exit Mike's lips, he began calmly.

"Mr. Harrison, I have big dreams, too. I come from a family who is a little more successful than most, but I realized one day that I needed to make my own way in the world and not become a man in the way my father thought I should. I've swung axes until my hands bled. I have scars on my body from stringing barbed wire until sundown. I've gotten out of bed just as tired in the morning as when I fell asleep in my work clothes. Mr. Harrison, I know what it's like to work hard, and I won't stop until the day I die, no matter what I do. My dream was to become something other than a farmer, and I've found something in this town that excites me. My dream didn't include owning a mine I know nothing about, but if that's the direction God wants me to take, then I'll take it and learn faster than anyone ever has. I don't know why Rosie offered the mine to me, but she did and now it's mine. I won't make any excuses for that. I will need to bring my ore to you—which I'm sure your company won't mind—and as soon as I learn how to get the stinkin' rocks out of that hole, then I'll expect you to buy from me."

With a sarcastic chuckle, Harrison took a step back from Mike. "Bravo. So you know how to work hard. That's commendable, but working hard won't make you a successful miner, and you don't know what you're doing."

"I can learn."

"You can learn to get yourself killed is what you can do."

"Rosie said she would help me any way she could…"

"Rosie?" Harrison laughed again. "Rosie isn't a miner. Why…the only thing she knows about mining is what she heard from her husband."

"I tell you what, Mr. Harrison…"

"No, boy, I tell you what." Harrison took a step toward Mike and lifted his index finger. "You will stay away from my daughter. I don't want you talking to her, I don't want you looking at her, and if I ever see you with her you will wish you had never heard of Rush, Arkansas. Do I make myself clear, boy?"

Mike began to tense with anger at Harrison's words, because he knew that staying away from Pamela was something he could not do. Although he had been raised to respect authority, falling in love changed that rule, at least in his mind. He had fallen in love with Pam, and she was in love with him. Harrison's words only strengthened Mike's resolve to be with the only girl he had ever wanted.

Although Mike was never one to be antagonistic, his next words caused Harrison to boil over and fly into a final rage. "Does this mean that I'm fired?"

Mike quickly ushered himself into the morning sunlight and heard the door slam behind him. He felt both exhilarated and defeated at the same time. His friend Doug was right; fall in love with Pam, lose your job. He only wished he would not have collided with Mr. Harrison in such an abrupt manner, but now it was done.

The hard part was over, now the harder part was ahead of him. His money was dwindling, he had no job, he needed to learn quickly how to mine zinc, and the love of his life had been taken out of his reach...or so her father thought. Mike did indeed have dreams, and his latest and most heart-stopping dream was to make Pam his own...whether Jacob Harrison liked it or not.

Chapter 23

Although it was mid May, the usual mild temperatures had been replaced by a fierce heat wave, accompanied by the morbid lack of rain. As he entered Doug's shop, Mike noticed that the mid-afternoon sun was already withering the tender springtime flowers.

The heat from the forge radiated into the room, and, even though there was a slight breeze escorting some of the heat through the open doors, Mike felt as uncomfortable inside as he did walking through town. As he watched Doug pound rivets into a project, he wondered how his friend dealt with the forge heat during the swelter of summer.

Doug glanced up briefly with a smile to acknowledge his friend and, after a few more taps of the hammer, quenched the hot metal in the water bucket. He placed the metal tongs across the anvil and wiped his forehead with the back of his arm, which was as sweaty as his face. All he did with that maneuver was add dark streaks across his brow from cinder particles that daily made their residence on his arms.

Mike grinned at the new face paint on his friend but didn't fill him in on the joke.

"I've usually gotten enjoyment out of telling someone, 'I told you so,' but it doesn't make me feel good that you lost your job." Doug sat on his wooden stool and swigged water out of his mason jar.

"News travels about as fast here as it does back home." Mike sat down on an empty wooden barrel. "You'd think we had one of those telephone things I've been readin' about."

"Well, Charley was at the company store this morning, and he loves to spread news he hears there." Doug took another gulp of his water.

"I seem to have been forced into makin' money with this mine, and I don't know a blasted thing about it."

"Don't fret so much over it, Mike. Jump right in there with both feet and with fists flyin'. Dig the zinc out of the walls, fill the ore cart, and haul it to the mill."

"Simple as that, huh?"

"Simple, yes, but you're gonna work harder than you've ever worked before."

"So I've been warned."

There was a pause as Doug caught his breath and Mike looked around the room at all the tools of Doug's trade.

"Would you mind going to the mine with me and giving me your thoughts, Doug? I'd like someone to go with me who knows what they're talkin' about, and I could use all the help I can get."

"Wouldn't mind at all. I've never been in that hole, but I've been in several others around here, fitting parts I've made onto carts and equipment."

"How about this evening?"

"How about what this evening?" A soft voice came from the doorway.

Mike swiveled on his perch to see Sandy and Pamela enter the sweltering shop. A grin immediately grew on his face as he made eye contact with Pam.

"Douglas, I don't know how you stand it in here." Sandy fanned her face with a cedar shingle she had found somewhere outside.

"It's so hot that the water had practically all evaporated out of my water can before I was able to pour it onto my flowers." Pam's observation caused the foursome to laugh.

Doug glanced at Mike and indicated that he wanted Mike to answer Sandy's question, rather than spilling the beans himself about Mike's newly acquired mine.

"Uh…," Mike began, "I was just asking Doug if he could accompany me down to the river this evening and help me figure out what to do about…a project I'm working on."

"You mean you want him to look at your mine with you," Pam blurted.

"That Charley really gets around." Mike shook his head in amazement.

"No, I heard Daddy ranting to May Bess about it this morning after he stormed into the house and opened his best bottle of brandy. I didn't even have to eavesdrop to hear what he was saying, and I'm surprised the whole town couldn't hear. I was afraid some of the window panes were going to fall out from rattling."

"Well, I guess the whole town knows about it by now then," Mike replied.

"If they don't, then they must be deaf," Sandy chimed in. "By the way, we're happy for you, Mike."

Mike smiled and looked at Pam.

"I'm happy for you, too." Pam moved next to Mike. "I think it's a good thing for you."

"Pam, I thought you might be upset because…"

"Don't be silly." Pam rolled her eyes. "Daddy has enough fodder in his trough. He's gone most of the time anyway to Buffalo City, always on mill business. He left again this afternoon and won't be back for a couple of days." She smiled.

Pam's smile made Mike feel warmer than he already did, and part of the sweat around his collar was not due to the ambient temperature.

Doug finished his water from the jar. "So why are you two ladies out and about in this heat?"

"I'm out for a little sugar from the store," Sandy said. "Momma is practicing baking her wedding cookies and ran out of sugar. I saw Pam, and she said she would help me pick out material and a pattern for a dress. I need to get started on it as soon as possible."

As Sandy spoke, she made her way over to her sweaty beau and gave him a kiss on the cheek. Doug blushed and grinned.

Sandy looked around for a towel or semi-clean rag to wipe the black streaks from Doug's forehead. "You need a mirror in this place."

"It has begun." Mike and Pam began laughing at Sandy's mothering.

"By the way, Douglas, you made a promise to see my father this evening, if you recall." Sandy inspected her work on Doug's face.

Doug lifted his eyebrows and looked at Mike. "That's right, I did. I hadn't forgotten." He looked into Sandy's eyes then back at Mike.

"I'll go look at it with you," Pam said. "Daddy's taken me into a couple of the mines."

Mike looked at Pam not knowing how to gently say, "I'd love it, but no." "I can't take you down there."

Pam rolled her eyes again. "Oh, don't be such a worrywart. May Bess told me that she wanted to pick poke greens this evening before they all withered away in the heat. We've always picked them down by the river. As long as she is there, it will be just fine. She thinks Daddy is a little overprotective, and besides..." There was a pause as Pam's voice softened. "May Bess likes you."

"Pam, I've never been in that mine; it's probably dangerous, and if your daddy ever found out I had you down there, he'd either make me marry you at the end of a shotgun or put me in the ground with it."

Everyone laughed at Mike's comment, but Mike took his situation with Mr. Harrison seriously. He didn't want to be reckless with his chances with Pam, and he certainly didn't want to make the wall of tension thicker between himself and Jacob Harrison. However, he did smile on the inside at the thought of having Pam alone even if it was only for a few moments.

"When it gets cooler this evening, May Bess and I will meet you there. What can Daddy say if we happened to see you down by the river?"

Pam placed her hand onto Mike's shoulder. "I would love for you to show me your mine. I'm proud of you, and I have a feeling that everything is going to go just fine for you there."

That's all it took to overcome Mike's resolve, even though the little voice in the back of his head was telling him not to do it.

Doug stood and began pumping the bellows to heat his forge. "Well, I better get back to work."

"And we have material to order," Sandy said. "And a pattern to pick out," both of the girls said, almost in unison.

The two girls walked back into the daylight, but not before Pam turned and gave Mike a smile that melted his heart. Doug saw the smile and shook his head as he watched Mike's face blush.

"And I need to get some things from Rosie, I suppose." Mike stood. "By the way, where's Charley?"

Doug removed his work from the water bucket to inspect it. "I think he's down by the river practicing on a new sermon."

Mike walked toward the door. "Is it going to break his heart when I interrupt him in his special place?" "Special place?"

"When I met Charley he was preaching in the entrance of the mine by the river. He said it was his place."

"Oh...well, he probably has several special places around. He'll get over it, I'm sure."

"Don't want to hurt his feelings."

"You won't hurt his feelings." Doug plunged his project back into the white-hot coals. "Charley really likes you...for some reason."

Mike smiled at his grinning friend and exited the building to be bathed in the smothering heat of the bright sunlight.

***

255

The skillet-hot breeze blew dust across the dirt road as Jay Finch directed his horse east onto the narrower, tree-covered lane leading to Rush. A leather satchel containing signed and stamped deed documents from the county courthouse in Yellville hung on the saddle, destined for Harrison's office. Since being collared early in the morning to make the round trip, Finch had been in a foul mood. He pouted as he rode. The thought had occurred to Finch to keep riding and make Rush a memory, but unfinished business beckoned him back.

As he continued to ride, he wasn't the slightest bit grateful for the shade which the trees had to offer. The hot wind was even cut to near calm, but Finch hadn't noticed. He was too preoccupied with his own state of affairs to even feel the respite from the antagonizing elements he had dealt with during the day. His life in Rush had become a tangled mess and seemed to be out of control, and he hated that feeling. He had to be in control of his surroundings, but for the last two weeks everything in his world had become like a mussed ball of twine that you couldn't unravel and had to throw away. He didn't even know where to begin to get what had been his normal life back on track.

Emotions of anger and resentment were tossed back and forth inside him as if in a game of horseshoes. He harbored anger at being bullied by Raif's new partner, Jeeter, and resentment at a boy who rode into town and now, after only two weeks, was able to have what Jay had only been able to desire. Not too long ago Jay was able to hear the birds and feel the cool breeze on his face, but today he was so bitter that being able to feel anything much more than hatred was just past arm's length.

The one thing Jay knew for certain was that he was determined to do whatever it took to send the plowboy home with his tail tucked between his legs. Jeeter was another matter to deal with—later; for the moment, Gilbert was his focus. He realized that Pam was now only a dream, but he would make sure she was out of Mike's dreams also…no matter what it took.

Before making the last turn into Rush, Finch detoured to Raif's place in the woods. Although he had never been one to drink much of the wares he sold, he decided that tonight he would soothe his troubled soul and anesthetize himself as the sun went down. The dread of another day was already pressing on his shoulders.

"Afternoon, Jay," Raif said as Jay dismounted his horse. "Yer a day early for your deliveries."

"I didn't come here to pick up supplies."

"Well, what did ya come here fer?"

Jay sat on a stump next to a few old wooden crates and took a heavy breath.

"I need a bottle for myself tonight."

"Why, Jay Finch, I'm plumb surprised at you. I don't recall the last time I knowed you to want some of my shine." Raif said this in a teasing tone.

Jay maintained his somberness. "Do you have a spare?" He didn't acknowledge Raif's attempt at playfulness.

Raif's grin left his face and the loose skin fell back into position on his cheeks.

"Yeah…I got a bottle or two."

He slowly opened a potato sack and pulled out two pint jars full of clear liquid. Raif hesitated for a moment before handing them to Jay. "I'd be careful with those if I was you," Raif warned. "Yer not used to it and you have deliveries tomorrow."

Jay unscrewed the lid on one of the jars and brought the rim to his mouth. It was all he could do to swallow a small amount of the fiery poison, but he clenched his eyes shut and forced it down. When it hit his stomach, he had to use all of his strength to keep it there. Slowly he replaced the lid and tightened it.

"Thanks, Raif." Jay mounted his horse and placed the small jars into a cloth sack, tying it to the saddle horn. Without another word, he slowly rode away from Raif's camp with a thousand things on his mind, but focused on only one. Mike Gilbert would not have peace as long as he was in Rush.

***

The sun was finally behind the trees, which made movement more comfortable. Without direct sun rays, the air in the valley began to cool. Mike saddled his horse and prepared for the ride to his mine. "My mine," he said out loud to himself. Those words sounded foreign to him and probably would for quite some time. He was still numb over the fact that he was now being forced to work the mine for his living. He didn't know what to expect, but, even with his limited knowledge, he allowed his mind to dream of the myriad possibilities. He abandoned himself to the image of becoming rich and having everything he wanted. He envisioned relaxing in a big house with Pam and several children while someone else dug the ore out of the mine for him. He even saw himself returning home to be greeted by everyone in Kingston applauding his good fortune and agreeing as to how he had made the right decision to leave home and seek his fortune.

Suddenly he was snapped back into reality by the loud hissing sound of the steam being released from the Morning Star boiler, signaling the end of yet another work day. He was almost embarrassed for allowing his imagination to run away with itself like it did. He only cared that one of those dreams came true, and he was going to do what he could to ensure that it happened.

He finished tying his new lantern onto his saddle then directed his horse down the road and toward the river. As he neared he became nervous at the prospect of exploring the mine, knowing that what became of it depended upon him. It was strange, but the closer he got to the river the more weight he felt upon his shoulders. He wanted to prove himself to those around him and to himself, but most of all, even though he wouldn't say it out loud, he wanted to prove himself to his father. He wanted his father to be proud of him and his accomplishments; though his father was far away, he hoped some day he could show his father it was because of him that he had succeeded.

The air became even cooler as Mike rode parallel to Rush Creek. The cold water chilled the late afternoon in contrast to the oppressive heat of only a few hours earlier. He was always amazed at how quickly the evening would cool in the springtime regardless of how hot the day had been.

The narrow road began to descend, and Mike could smell the familiar fishy bouquet of the Buffalo River. He inhaled deeply, and it made him think about home. Within seconds, through the trees, he could see the river drifting lazily from his right to his left.

It had been several days since he had seen the Buffalo, and he was amazed at how little water was flowing. This far down from his home in Kingston, he should not be able to wade across the river, but with the lack of rain he would have no trouble. He thought back to another year when he was younger and the lack of spring rains had turned the upper Buffalo into a mere trickle.

As he allowed his horse to drink from the river's edge, he searched for signs of Pam and May Bess, but saw no carriage parked in the trees. He hoped Pam had been able to convince her aunt to agree to her plan. Pam had seemed certain all was well, but the fear of Jacob Harrison could have caused May Bess to develop cold feet, if she had even entertained the notion at all.

Mike stepped onto the gravel bank and untied his new lantern from the saddle, along with another used lantern he had purchased from Rosie. He didn't want to put all of his trust into this modern illumination without a backup. As he checked the fuel in the lanterns, Mike noticed his hands were sweaty.

"What are you so nervous about?" he said to himself out loud. He answered himself by realizing that part of it was apprehension, part of it was excitement, and part of it was the anticipation of seeing Pam.

Mike was about to make his way to the mine entrance when he heard the sound of a carriage rolling toward him. He turned in time to see Pam and May Bess coming down the rutted road. He stood with his lanterns in his hand as they stopped close to the water's edge.

Before Mike could even say hello, May Bess spoke. "Mr. Gilbert, I'm not very comfortable with this arrangement my niece has talked me into this evening, and the only reason I agreed to this is because you seem to be a trustworthy, God-fearing gentleman. I will allow Pam to venture into the mine with you under the condition that if you become aware of anything which might seem even the slightest bit dangerous you will usher her out immediately."

Pam did her best to maintain her composure, but she had the desire to laugh at her aunt's insecure guidelines for the two of them. Although they were both young adults, May Bess felt responsible for Pam's well being anytime Jacob Harrison was away.

"May Bess, I appreciate your trust in me and will certainly protect Pamela with all my resolve." Mike did his best to reply with the same fervor.

May Bess took a deep breath, feeling satisfied that she had plainly laid out the ground rules. Mike stepped to her side of the carriage and, with an outstretched hand, helped her to the gravel. Before he could make it to the other side, Pam had already jumped out and was making her way to where the two were standing.

"So this is the new lamp Rosie told me about." Pam reached for the lantern.

Mike allowed Pam to survey it. "Only one like it in Rush."

May Bess didn't seem the least bit interested and was already reaching into the back of the wagon for her baskets, which she hoped to fill with the poke greens she wanted to cook with ham the next day.

"I would like you both to meet me back here at the wagon in no more than an hour. I need to get the greens back to soak before it gets dark."

Mike made sure he had his pocket watch with him and agreed to be back promptly in an hour. May Bess looked at Pam then at Mike.

"You two have fun, but be careful, and Mike…congratulations on the mine."

Mike beamed at her words. "Thank you, May Bess."

With her baskets cradled in her arms, May Bess left the pair.

"Well, are you ready?" Pam looked up into Mike's smile.

"I'm as ready as I'll ever be," he said as the two turned toward the pathway which led along the river and to the opening of the Red Rose Mine.

***

By the time Jay reached the mill, half of the liquor was gone from one jar. Larkin Riley had been waiting impatiently for Jay to return so that he could secure the paperwork in the safe and go home for the evening.

"'Bout time you showed up." Riley showed his irritation in his voice.

"It's been a long, hot day." Finch dismounted with a bobble.

"Yeah, and I can see you've had a go at coolin' off your parched gullet." Riley noticed Jay having difficulty standing.

Jay stared blankly at his manager and handed him the pouch containing the paperwork. Riley untied the leather string to survey the contents then secured the closure again.

"Mind if I have a swallow before I head home?" Riley asked with anticipation.

"Swallow of what?"

"You smell like a still; I hope you have some whisky on ya."

Jay shrugged his shoulders and reached for the jar in the cloth bag on his saddle. Riley unscrewed the lid and took a whiff, which sent a burning sensation up his nose. He winced in pain then, after it had subsided, took a deep sip and forced it down his throat.

"That's good," he said after he was able to catch his breath.

"One more." Riley tipped the jar and took a larger mouth full.

Immediately Jay reached for the jar and removed it from Riley's grip. "Get yer own." Jay sported a slight smile.

"I would if I knew where to get it."

Jay didn't know why the idea even invaded his head—because the thought had never crossed his mind—but, without even thinking about what he was contemplating, he said, "I'll get you your own full jar if you will do me one little favor."

Riley's eyes widened and sparkled at the notion of having a jar of shine all to himself. Living in a dry county made it difficult to get one's hands on distilled spirits…especially the good stuff. "What's your price, Jay? Just name it."

"Well," Jay began slowly, "I was thinkin' of doin' a little fishin' this week, and I don't have a pole or any hooks. I wonder if you could get me a couple of sticks of fish bait from that locked room of yours in the mill."

For a moment Riley was puzzled at the request, and then he realized what Jay was requesting. "I don't know if I can do that," Riley replied nervously.

"Well, suit yerself." Jay turned to place the jar back into its holder on the saddle. As Jay stepped into the stirrup, Riley stopped him from mounting.

"I reckon I could probably get a couple of sticks out for you." Riley hesitated. "Can I ask what you really want to do with them?"

Finch grinned from ear to ear. "Like I said, Mr. Larkin…is fishin'. Ain't no better way to get fish for dinner than to throw a couple of those sticks into the water."

Riley looked at Finch, doubting that he was getting the truth, but he had such a strong desire for more corn whisky that he decided not to push further.

"I tell you what," Jay said, "you get me a couple of sticks with some fuse now, and I'll give you what I have left in this jar plus another jar tomorrow evening. Is it a deal?"

Riley was salivating at the prospect, so he told Jay to wait where he was, and within moments returned with two sticks of dynamite and a coil of fuse.

Jay's eyes brightened when he saw the explosives. He quickly pulled the jar from the bag and, after handing the jar to Riley, placed the two sticks and fuse into the bag.

"Be careful with that," Riley cautioned. "Bump it too hard and it could go off even without a lit fuse."

"I know what I'm doin'."

"We don't want you blowin' your arm off." Riley unscrewed the jar and began enjoying his whisky.

Jay clutched his prize as he mounted his horse. Before Riley could say another word, Jay had nudged his horse into the lane. Within moments he turned the corner and headed in the direction of the Red Rose Mine.

Chapter 24

Mike's new lantern worked perfectly, illuminating the interior of the mine shaft. Though it sputtered and hissed from the flow of pressurized fuel, the glowing mantle shed the brightest light Mike had ever seen from a lantern. The crisp brilliance revealed the passageway with complete clarity as Mike and Pam slowly entered the musty tunnel.

The presence of cobwebs along the walls and across the corridor waned as the couple cautiously probed deeper into the solitary shaft. Cave crickets could be seen crawling on the damp rocks along the way. The rusty cart tracks that ran along the cavern floor looked as solid as the day they were laid. The coolness felt invigorating to Mike as he surveyed the alien surroundings.

"Up ahead," Pam said with excitement, "along that wall. Can you see it?"

Mike held the lantern higher out of instinct, but the brilliance of the lantern light caused him to quickly lower it until the metal shield on the top protected their eyes from the almost blinding light. It took a moment for his vision to adjust once again.

"I see bright spots before my eyes." He massaged his orbs through closed eyelids.

Pam just chuckled. "Come on; we're almost there."

Mike opened his eyes again and followed Pam, who was walking toward a far wall where the tunnel made a right turn.

"What are we looking at?" Mike kept pace with her.

"See that yellow color in the rock about halfway up that wall?" Pam pointed.

Mike still saw faint white spots but was almost back to normal. The pair stopped next to the wall where Pam had pointed out the yellow color imbedded in the gray rock.

The rock wall was bathed in the bright light of the lantern, and Mike could now see what Pam was talking about.

"What is that? It looks like some sort of yellow crystal."

"That's *Turkey Fat*." Pam reached up and ran her fingers over the yellow mineral.

Mike turned his head toward Pam. "Turkey Fat?"

"That's what the miners call it. When it's dug out of the rock it looks like a big glob of yellow turkey fat."

"Why would you dig that out of the wall?"

"Turkey Fat is full of zinc." Pam looked at Mike and back at the band of yellow mineral.

Mike seemed even more confused. "I thought we were looking for shiny white metal in the rock."

"The zinc is in this material. It has to be refined out of it at a smelter." Pam felt like a teacher to a new pupil.

"Okay, so let me get this straight," Mike began. "I have to look for this yellow rock, dig it out and haul it to the mill?"

Pam chuckled again. "Not quite; Turkey Fat is not very common. Actually, most of the zinc is found in what Daddy said is *Amber Jack*. It's a brown-colored mineral. When you find a vein of it, you get it out with a pick, or blow it out with dynamite then haul the ore-bearing rock to the mill. The machines at the mill crush the rocks into smaller pieces. Then it goes to a separator, and that's where the men separate the Amber Jack from the useless rock. The rock is discarded and the Amber Jack and Turkey Fat are hauled on to the smelter. That's as much as I know. I don't know anything about how they get the zinc out of the Amber Jack."

"Sounds like you know quite a lot," Mike admitted, "a heck of a lot more than I do."

Pam smiled as she looked up at Mike and into his eyes. "It won't take you long before you know everything all the other miners know. Come on; let's see if we can find some Amber Jack."

Pam took Mike by the hand and urged him deeper into the mineshaft. Mike instantly felt a chill, but he knew that it wasn't from the cool dampness of the cavern. He peered cautiously ahead into the faint light, constantly watching for anything looking the slightest bit dangerous.

They hadn't walked far when Mike spotted a dark coloring of the wall to their left. Rather than a vein or wide streak of amber-colored mineral, the wall contained pockets of color. It seemed to be everywhere along the wall, and even in parts of the ceiling and the floor at their feet where the tracks still ran.

"This must be Amber Jack!" Mike walked closer to inspect the mineral.

"There certainly seems to be a lot of it…everywhere," Pam replied with wide eyes.

Mike handed the lantern to Pam and retrieved a jackknife from his pocket. He opened a sturdy blade, began digging at the brown material, and, within a few seconds, dislodged a piece as big as a persimmon. He held it close to the light so the pair could inspect it.

"I don't even know how much this stuff is worth," Mike finally said, "but by the looks of this wall, I think I may be in business."

Pam smiled with pride at the childlike wonder coming from Mike. She could hear excitement in his voice, and emotion began swelling inside her. She set the lantern onto the ground and placed her hands in Mike's, and they both stood in the warm glow of the lantern, holding on to what would surely become the first of Mike's fortune. Mike beamed as he gazed at the mineral, but his attention soon turned to Pam. Their eyes found each other's souls in the lantern-lit cavern, and instead of feeling the damp chill, they sensed only the warmth being shared between them.

Without further hesitation, Mike leaned toward Pam and they shared their first sweet kiss. Bathed in flickering

266

light they continued their first intimate moment together. It was a moment which would be forever etched into Mike's heart.

***

Jay Finch crested the hill in the road and instantly saw the buggy and a horse in the fading early-evening light. He pulled his horse to a stop and immediately turned back as he looked around for anyone who might have seen him. Jay spotted someone off in the distance bending over next to the road and soon realized through his drunken haze that it was May Bess picking greens. Satisfied he had not been spotted by her, he made his way to a rarely used footpath leading into the woods. Carefully, through the trees, he made his way to the Red Rose Mine, all the while keeping an eye out for anyone else who might have accompanied May Bess to help her with her task.

While fishing along the Buffalo River during the heat of summer, several times in the past, Jay had explored the first few feet of the mine, to rest in the coolness there. He was completely familiar with the area, so in no time he was able to make his way to the mine from the back side.

With the entrance still several yards away, he tethered his horse to a tree and gently removed the dynamite from the saddle. With faint light still sifting through the forest canopy, he removed the explosives from the bag and clutched them in his shaky hand. He paused for a moment, contemplating what he was about to do. A small voice from somewhere tucked away in the darkness of his heart pleaded with him not to proceed, but he swallowed hard and forced the urging deeper into the debris of his hatred.

He looked at the length of coiled fuse and decided to use the full length with the explosives to give him as much time as possible to retreat. With a short length of string, he carefully tied the two sticks together then cut the coil of fuse in half and inserted both lengths into the sticks. He twisted the two fuses together and, surveying his handiwork, decided he was ready.

Looking up from his creation, he began coldly walking toward the mine. He could hear his heart pounding so loudly that it almost drowned out his footsteps through the tangle of the underbrush. Within a few moments he was standing next to the entrance of the Red Rose.

He peered cautiously around the stone outcropping, hoping not to see a soul who would interrupt his plans. Seeing no one, he crept closer to the opening. Every part of his body was quivering as he peered into the dark cavern. Still seeing no one, he made his way into the mine as far as he could and still be able to see what he was doing. The anger inside him swelled as he thought about the interloper who seemed to have everything going his way. Not only had Mike gained the heart of the girl Jay longed for but would now never have, the farm boy had procured one of the most productive zinc mines in the area. Jay knew that even though the debris he was about to create could certainly be removed, he wanted to send the message that Mike was not wanted and should leave.

Jay placed the explosives on the floor of the cavern next to a wall and backed away, straightening the length of fuse. When it was in place, he pulled several matches from his shirt pocket. He crouched to the end of the fuse and, without remorseful hesitation, struck one of the matches on the cavern wall. The match broke in two. He tossed the pieces and more carefully struck another match on a rock. The head of the match flamed, and as soon as the wood began burning, he placed it to the end of the fuse.

Sparks flew as the blue flame raced toward the two sticks. Immediately, Jay stood and stumbled along the rock wall and back into the woods. Though he still inebriated, he ran as fast as he could to where his horse was tied.

***

May Bess was working her way back to her carriage, plucking the top few leaves from the new stalks of poke plants she found dotted along the edge of the road. She hoped that Mike and Pam would already be waiting for her at the carriage or would be along soon. Darkness was quickly approaching, and she wanted to get back to the house while there was still some light.

Only a few feet into the edge of the woods, she was bending over, picking, when she heard a loud noise through the trees. She lifted her head just in time to catch a brief glimpse of a horse and rider before they disappeared into the thickness of trees and underbrush.

"Someone else seems to be in a hurry to get home before dark." May Bess leaned down to pick from one last stalk.

Suddenly she heard a noise which was instantly recognizable. It was the unmistakable sound of an explosion, and it came from the direction of the Red Rose. Residing in a mining community forced her to live with that dreadful sound. She was immediately startled into dropping her basket of greens as she turned toward the deeply muffled event. The ground shook at the sound, but what followed next was an even deeper rumble that shook the ground with more intensity.

Summoning all her strength she ran to the road then toward the mine. Her mind could not process what had occurred, but she broke into a cold sweat out of pure fear. As she made her way along the path leading to the mine, through the faint light she saw billows of dust rolling from the bluff outcropping ahead of her and tumbling down toward the river. Her heart was pounding when she finally reached the Red Rose Mine, but then it almost stopped when she gazed upon what used to be the opening. As she stood in the damp, dusty, heavy evening air, panic gripped her and wrapped around her like a choking vine. She felt numb for a moment and could only stare at the tumble of rock and debris, not believing what she was seeing.

Finally, May Bess gathered her emotions and repeatedly screamed Pam's name, hoping to hear the sound of survival from within the cavern—but with each attempt she heard no reply. She frantically tugged and pulled at the smaller rocks out of sheer frustration but soon realized her actions were futile. Through tears she called again, but again heard no reply and realized she needed to get help quickly.

Forcing herself to leave, she frantically made her way back to the buggy, and, with a quick flip of the reins, encouraged her horse to travel as fast as the rough road would allow. Her heart was gripped with fear; she raced toward town. Her only thought was on securing help, and, since her brother was out of town, her mind rested on one person: Rosie Kirk. She knew that Rosie could rally the help needed.

May Bess prayed more fervently than she ever had in her life; she petitioned God to comfort the two, and prayed for his hand of protection upon them as they awaited their rescue. As she neared town, she couldn't shake the thoughts of their possibly being hurt and suffering, but she didn't allow herself to imagine that they might be dead.

Chapter 25

A lone horse and rider slowly plodded into Rush as the damp evening air grew thick and dark. Lanterns could be seen glowing behind lace curtains and through open windows as the last remnant of sunlight faded from above the trees. Nearing the heart of town, the rider saw a plump woman seated in a rocking chair on the front porch of what obviously was a mercantile.

When he saw a water trough and pump in front, he halted his horse and dismounted.

"Evenin', ma'am." He tipped his hat toward the lady, who had stopped rocking.

"Evenin', mister." The woman remained seated.

The sounds of tree frogs serenaded as the rider pumped water into the trough to allow his horse to drink. A green katydid suddenly landed on the rider's hand, momentarily startling him. Out of instinct he shook his hand to cause the winged insect to fly away.

The lady on the porch chuckled. "It wasn't gonna eat too much.".

"No, I don't suppose it was." He looked at his hand and back at the lady. "I guess I don't know where my manners are." He walked up the few creaky wooden steps and onto the porch, removing his hat as he approached her.

"I'm Rosie." She unfolded her hands and stretched one toward the stranger. "I run this store. I've closed it for the night, but if yer just gettin' into town I could fetch anything you need. Way out here, I'm sure you've been travelin' a while."

"Thank you kindly, ma'am...my name is Gilbert, William Gilbert. I've come from..."

"I know where you come from." Rosie interrupted with a smile growing across her face. You come from

271

Kingston over in Madison County. Lord sakes, I bet yer Michael's pa, aren't you?"

"Matter of fact, I am," he replied with a grin of his own. "You wouldn't happen to know where I could find my boy, would you?"

Standing from her chair, Rosie released a grunting chuckle. "You done somethin' right, Mr. Gilbert; yer boy is about my favorite person in the world. Matter of fact, I think of him more as a man than a boy."

William toyed with his hat, feeling an embarrassing pride at her comment. "I'm a little fond of him myself."

"Just so happens he rents a little place from me back behind the store." Rosie gestured toward the corner of the porch. "I don't think he's there right now, though…seems as if I saw him ride down the road toward the river 'bout an hour or so ago."

William turned his head and looked toward the dark road leading from town. "You think I could wait on your porch here until he returns?"

Rosie laughed, making her whole body shake. "Mister, you just sit yerself down right here, and I'll go inside and bring you out a glass of tea. I know we have some left, and, if I can find a piece of pie around the place, I'll grab that too."

"Oh, don't trouble yerself, ma'am…" William began.

"Don't you fret one bit. I'm sure yer tongue is parched worse than a snakeskin on a rock in the summer, and you could probably use some grub, too."

William was about to politely object again when the sound of hoofs and wagon wheels sped up the nearly pitch-dark road toward them. They were bathed in a dust cloud as May Bess pulled the horse to a sudden stop.

"Well, what's got yer feathers all ruffled up, May Bess…you'd think that…"

May Bess interrupted with panic on her face. "Rosie, there's been an accident down at the Red Rose Mine!"

"Red Rose?" Rosie echoed somberly.

"I was pickin' poke with Pamela down by the river when Mike took her into the mine to show her around. I thought nothin' of it until I heard an explosion and found the entrance blocked."

"My Mike?" William looked at Rosie.

"Your Mike, Mr. Gilbert." Rosie glanced at him quickly then walked down the steps toward May Bess.

"May Bess, you go to Jim Smith's and tell him to round up everyone he can and get here on the double. I'll open the store and gather up tools and lanterns fer them that don't have any. Now get on…we don't have any time to waste."

May Bess flipped the reins and disappeared into the darkness.

"William, I guess tea will have to wait. Come inside with me and I'll get you some gloves and a pick. When everyone gets here they'll take you down to the mine."

"I've got to get to my boy now," William said as if about to leave.

"You can't do nothin' by yourself. Rosie spoke sternly. "Dealin' with a cave-in is dangerous enough even if you know what yer doin'."

"I can try!"

"I can see where your boy gets his hard head, but if you want him to have the best chance, you'll need to wait. Besides, there's a girl in there with him, and I don't want you muckin' up her chances neither. Now come in here and help me drag out a block and tackle while we wait on everyone. They'll be here directly."

William's heart sank at the news of his son being trapped in a mine. He didn't enjoy being talked to like Rosie just had, but for now he decided to defer to her judgment. He was somber and speechless as he followed Rosie into the store to help her gather equipment.

***

Mike slowly opened his eyes and immediately felt the throbbing of his head. He blinked his eyelids trying to clear his eyes of the fine dust and grit in them. It took a few moments for him to realize where he was. His ears were ringing loudly, and he felt the cold clamminess coming from the ground beneath him where he was lying. Finally, he was able to gather his wits enough to sit up with the aid of his left elbow. There was still a thick dust in the air, which caused him to cough.

Suddenly everything flooded back into his mind, and he remembered being in his mine with Pamela.

"Pamela!" Mike called into the total darkness and listened for a reply or even the sound of movement, but was answered only by complete silence. He was still unable to gather his strength to stand, so he began feeling around the cavern floor for the lantern which had been extinguished with the blast.

"Pamela!" He called again but, again, got no reply.

Unable to find the lantern, he remembered the box of matches in his shirt pocket. Mike lifted a weak hand and retrieved the box. He remembered that there were only a few matches left, so he hoped that he could find the lantern and relight it. He removed a match and, with shaky hands, struck it on a nearby rock. The match refused to shed its light and, after the third attempt, it broke in two. Becoming frustrated, he removed another match and this time struck it with his thumbnail, realizing the rock was probably damp.

The match came to life and immediately revealed the limp body of Pamela leaning against the rock wall close to him. As quickly as he could, he crawled to her and was relieved to see that she was breathing. He had just begun surveying her for injuries when he felt an intense heat on his fingers. He shook his hand, which extinguished the match and returned them to the thick darkness.

With his match supply dwindling, Mike struck another and searched for the lantern. He finally found it only a couple of feet from him but, upon inspection, saw that the cloth mantle had crumbled, so there was no hope of relighting it. Dismayed, he turned back to Pam, who was now beginning to awaken. Carefully he placed his hand onto her shoulder to comfort her with his presence.

He moved his fingers as far away from the flame of the match as possible to extract as much of the light from it as he could, but eventually he had to drop it onto the damp cavern floor. Rather than ignite another, he decided to save his precious commodity in case he needed them at a later time.

"Pamela," Mike said as he heard her moan slightly, "Pamela, wake up."

"Michael, is that you?" Mike's eyes watered at the sound of her voice, although it was weak, and he was relieved to hear her speak.

"Pamela, do you hurt anywhere?"

There was a pause, and then she replied, "The only thing that doesn't hurt is the big toe on my left foot."

Mike smiled in the darkness and thanked God that they both were at least alive.

"What happened?"

"I'm not quite sure; all I remember is a loud sound and everything going black."

"What about the lantern?" Pam coughed from the dust hanging thick in the air.

"Busted. Think you can get up?" "I'll try."

Mike placed his hands under Pam's back and slowly tried to lift her but stopped immediately when she cried out in pain. "What's wrong?"

"My left hand hurt when you tried to lift me," Pam said.

Mike retrieved another match, and, when it came to life, he saw that Pam's hand was lodged between a large boulder and the cavern wall.

"Looks bad, doesn't it?" Pam gazed at her left hand.

"It doesn't look good," Mike said.

Before the match burned out, Mike surveyed the rock then, once again in total darkness, tried to move the boulder away from the wall to free Pam's hand. From his position on his knees, he couldn't get the boulder to budge, so, making his way to his feet, he lit another match to see if he could get a better grip. He placed the wooden end of the glowing match into a crack on the wall and, with what little strength hc could muster, pulled at the rock until he finally felt it move slightly.

Pam screamed at the rock's movement and again Mike stopped. She began to cry softly at the pain shooting up her arm.

"Pam, I know this hurts, but I have to get the rock off your hand. I'm going to tug again, and, if you can manage at all, you need to pull your hand away."

"It hurts too much," Pam replied through tears.

Mike crouched down beside her and placed his left hand onto her right cheek. Just as the match on the wall burned out, she could see his smile of encouragement and felt empowered by his strength.

In total darkness once again, Pam took his hand with her right hand and held it tightly against her face. He didn't want to let go, but he knew her hand had to be freed so that it could be tended to as quickly as possible.

"Pamela, I'm going to light another match, and when I've counted to three I'm going to tug on the rock. I need you to pull with all your might to get your hand out of the way, because I won't be able to hold it for long."

"We're going to get out of this, aren't we?" Pam still held on to his hand.

"Of course we are," Mike said with resolve. "But first we need to tend to you."

There was a pause in the darkness as Mike continued to feel his hand pressed against her wet cheek.

"Michael?"

"What is it, Pam?"

"I love you." Her voice quivered.

Mike slowly leaned down and kissed her on her forehead. "We need to do this now. Are you ready?"

"Yes, I'm ready."

Mike pulled his hand from her grasp and struck another match. Immediately he placed it into the crack in the rock wall.

"One…two…three." With one foot placed on the shaft wall for leverage, he pulled on the rock. With every ounce of strength he had, Mike pulled against the reluctant boulder until it finally moved, but only inches from the wall. At the same instant he heard Pam scream as she pulled on her hand.

"It's free!" Excruciating pain shot through her body.

Mike released the rock, hearing a dull thud as it fell back onto the cavern wall. He quickly knelt down beside Pam to examine her injury. In the dwindling match light, he could see that her swollen index finger was broken and quickly turning blue. He knew her hand needed to be bandaged, but, with only a couple of remaining matches, he wouldn't have enough light to tend to her. His mind raced for a solution to their dilemma as he helped Pam hold her arm up in an attempt to keep the swelling from worsening. Once again the faint light from the match became extinct and the pair was engulfed in total darkness.

As the couple sat in the damp darkness of the cavern, a solution to part of their problem formed in Mike's head. He remembered almost tripping over a galvanized can just a short distance from where they were. He remembered the can being a fuel can, and it had seemed to be heavy with what he hoped was coal oil.

"Pamela, I have an idea, and I need to leave you for a moment."

"Mike, please don't leave me." She pleaded, clenching her jaw from the pain in her hand. "I want you to stay right here."

"I won't be far away," he said. "Just continue to hold your hand up, and I'll be back soon…I promise."

With that given assurance, Mike stood to his feet and began making his way down the cavern by keeping one hand on the wall. He stumbled on a rock and almost fell, but he didn't want to strike one of his remaining matches until he absolutely needed it. Slowly he continued to inch his way along the wall until his right foot struck the metal can. He crouched down and recognized the shape as the fuel container.

Standing up, he placed the match box into his pants pocket and removed his shirt. He next removed his undershirt and put his outer shirt back on. Unscrewing the cap from the spout of the canister, he leaned his nose close to it and inhaled, smelling the unmistakable odor of coal oil. It was the most wonderful thing he had smelled in his life.

Using his knife, Mike cut his undershirt in half and twisted one half as tightly as he could. Though it was a tight fit, he fed the makeshift wick down into the spout of the container until just a small portion remained. He tilted the can until he could feel wetness on the material. Mike wiped his hands on his pants to remove any fuel on them then cautiously lit his next-to-the-last match. It crackled to life with a blue smoke, and, when the wooden stick was properly burning, he lowered the match to the undershirt wick; it popped and sputtered to life.

The canister torch smoked heavily but supplied ample light as Mike carefully lifted it with the wire handle. The light illuminated the cavern as Mike made his way back to Pam, accompanied by his much-appreciated shadow.

Pam was doing her best to hold her hand above her heart when Mike rounded the corner of the tunnel. As the flickering light fell fully on her, he could see that her face was white as cream. Mike knew he would have to get her out as soon as possible.

"Pretty smart for a farm boy." Pam mustered a smile through her pain.

Mike placed the torch onto the floor far enough away so that the smoke would not cause Pam to cough. He examined her hand and could see that the finger was turning darker. He pulled the other half of his undershirt from his hip pocket and made a sling. He placed it over Pam's head and tied it short enough so that her hand was as close as possible to her chin.

"Pam, there's not much else I can do for you, so I'm going to see if I can get us out of here. I'm going to take the torch with me. Will you be alright?"

Pam didn't want Mike to leave her again because his presence comforted her in a way that even she could not explain; however, she knew it would do no good to try cajoling him into staying.

"I'll be here when you return." She tried to act as if there were no pain.

"We'll get out of this…trust me."

And she did.

Mike picked up the torch and walked down the corridor to the place where the exit should have been. They hadn't walked far into the cavern and had been on their way back when the blast had occurred, so he knew they weren't far from the entrance. As he got closer to the mouth of the cavern, he had to struggle around several large rocks blocking his way.

Finally, he recognized the entrance but saw that it was blocked with large boulders. His heart sank when he realized that, without tools, he would not be able to move the rocks enough for them to get out. Never having been in a mine before, he was also afraid that removing some of the smaller debris could cause larger stones to dislodge and tumble down on him. With boulders behind him, he feared he wouldn't be able to get out of the way.

The air around him was becoming thick with coal oil smoke, so he made his way back to Pam. He decided that they could at least move closer to the entrance, believing help would surely come soon. He only hoped it was very soon because of Pam's condition.

It was a struggle, but he managed to get Pam to her feet and to a comfortable spot closer to the entrance yet far enough away from the rock slide to be safe. After first explaining to Pam that they needed to reduce the smoke around them and conserve the fuel oil, Mike used a rock to snuff the flame, engulfing them in darkness once again. Mike had one match left and decided to hold on to it until it was absolutely necessary to light his torch one last time.

The pair sat in the darkness, shoulder to shoulder. Mike held Pam's right hand to do his best to comfort her. There were no words between them for some time as they sat with their own thoughts about their situation. Mike felt restless and helpless to do more toward their rescue, but Pam found refuge in his presence.

Mike finally broke the silence. "You're pa's gonna kill me."

"He'll kill me first," Pam said. "You can run faster."

Though it was dark Mike could tell she was smiling with her words.

Chapter 26

Doug Sprouse was finishing a late day in his shop, and Charley was busy counting nails, when several horses and wagons sped by. Doug removed his leather apron and walked to the doorway to see what the commotion was all about. As he stood there, a man with a coil of rope around his shoulder and an iron pry bar rushed toward him.

"What's goin' on?" Doug addressed the man as he neared.

"Two people are trapped in the Red Rose Mine down by the river."

Instantly, Doug knew that one had to be his friend Mike, although he couldn't figure out who the other person might be.

"Come on, Charley, we need to go help out our friend."

"Nuts; you made me lose count."

"You can count them later."

Charley dropped the rusty can and joined his brother, who had already grabbed a large iron bar and some gloves. Doug handed Charley a lantern and a can of kerosene, and the two of them followed the parade of lights leading out of town and toward the Red Rose.

***

Jay Finch was enjoying a stupor on his rickety wooden porch when Jeeter rode up on his horse.

"Looks like you're drinkin' all your profits, Finch." Jeeter gazed at Jay.

Jay's words were slurred. "What do you care?"

"Wanna go see what all the excitement is about?" Jeeter hoped to coax Jay into following him.

Jay took another long sip from his fruit jar. "Doesn't interest me in the least."

"Now, where's that community spirit in you?" Jeeter taunted, "Looks like the whole town is turning out. Wouldn't want to miss the party would ya?"

"I said I didn't care." Jay leaned back onto his elbows.

There was a pause as Jeeter decided whether to ride off or continue to try and entice Finch into joining him. "I hear there's a couple of people trapped in a collapsed mine down by the river. Might be interesting to see if they get them out in one piece or not."

At that news a chill coursed its way over Jay's body. "People trapped?"

"Now see...you are interested in your community. I'll wait for you to get your horse.

Jay struggled to his feet and set his jar onto the porch. He set it too close to the edge and it toppled over and onto the ground, spilling its contents. Realizing that was his last jar of alcohol, Jay swore.

"Forget it...let's go," Jeeter said, leaving. "There's more where that came from. I hope you can stay on your horse tryin' to keep up with me."

"Don't worry about me." Jay had some difficulty placing his foot into the stirrup.

Seconds before he caught up with Jeeter, he leaned over and emptied the contents of his stomach. It temporarily made the nausea go away, but the world around him continued to swirl. He hoped he could, indeed, remain in the saddle. As he joined the growing number of riders heading toward the river, he winced at the thought that one of the people in the mine could be Pamela. He had seen May Bess, and they often traveled together. Hoping that his fear was unfounded, he continued to ride.

***

The first group of men to arrive at the mine entrance were amazed at the complete collapse of the tunnel. One of the men was William Gilbert.

"Michael, can you hear me?" William leaned into the rubble. "Michael!" There was no reply, so he began pulling rocks from the debris.

Jim Smith placed his hand onto William's shoulder. "Hold on, Mr. Gilbert. I know you want your son out, but we gotta figure out the best way to remove these rocks. We don't want to cause another collapse."

"I have to get him out!"

"I know." Jim spoke tenderly. "We all want them out."

With that, William reluctantly moved aside, realizing his zeal was no stronger than that of those around him. For now, he would relent and allow those familiar with this sort of thing to take charge. He watched as Jim and several others surveyed the damage.

William's patience finally gave way. "Are you gonna stare at the rocks all night or are we gonna start digging?"

After discussing the situation for a few minutes longer, several of the men went to work on the tumble of rocks. William stood among them in a type of fire-bucket line, only, instead of passing buckets of water for a fire, they passed rocks from man to man until the last one tossed them into the river. From time to time they had to move quickly out of the way of falling debris.

Progress was slow, and it wasn't long until it seemed as if every man in town was hovering around the mine awaiting his turn at the pile of rocks. Women served water to those needing drinks and were prepared to feed them if the need arose. Doc Lipscomb stood by with his medical kit, ready to tend to the injured pair and anyone hurt during the excavation.

Jay and Jeeter were among the last to arrive, stopping at the outskirts of the scene. Jeeter remained on his horse as Jay slid off and onto the ground. Though the world around him was still spinning, he weaved his way toward the crowd.

"Careful, Finch...yer a little loony tonight." Jeeter chuckled at his inebriated friend.

Jay noticed Larkin Riley lurking just outside the bright lamplight.

"Do you know who's trapped in the mine?" Jay caught Larkin off guard.

Riley spun around to see who was addressing him. He had to steady himself against a tree because he'd also had too much to drink that evening.

"Is this your handiwork, Finch?" Larkin exclaimed a little too loud for Jay's liking.

"Lower your voice," Jay snapped.

"I should have known better than to give you those explosives. Do you realize how much trouble you will be in if this gets out?" Larkin sounded threatening.

"Do you realize how much trouble we'll both be in if this gets out?" Riley studied Jay's face and realized that the information he possessed would have to remain a secret. The fear of losing his job overpowered his desire to spill the beans about Jay's involvement.

"Who's in the mine?" Jay asked again.

Larkin hesitated. "It's that Gilbert kid."

Jay pressed. "There's two…who's the other one?"

"Boss's daughter is in there, too."

Jay stepped away from Riley, realizing fully the severity of what he had done. He didn't give a dime for the plowboy, but the thought of causing harm to Pam, even though she was out of his reach, troubled him deeply.

Jay raised a finger and pointed it at Larkin. "You keep this quiet, you hear?"

Riley didn't answer.

Backing toward his horse, Jay repeated his threat. "You keep this to yerself."

Jay struggled to mount his horse; Jeeter watched. "Find out what all the commotion was about? Who's in the mine?"

Without a word, Jay took hold of the reins, turned his horse around, and headed back toward town.

"Hey, what's got you so all worked up?" Jeeter called out. Turning his attention back to the event, he mumbled to himself. "That boy needs his head examined."

* * *

Mike and Pam continued to sit in the damp quietness of the tunnel. Despite the pain in her hand, Pam had drifted off to sleep a few moments earlier. Thinking that sleep would be good for her until help arrived, Mike didn't try to keep her awake. He listened to her breathe and felt her head against his shoulder. It gave him a feeling he had never experienced.

As he held her hand, Mike thought he heard a faint noise in the stillness. He stopped breathing for a moment and strained to listen into the silence. There it was again. Faint, but it was there. The sound seemed to come from the direction of the tunnel entrance.

Mike gently nudged Pam into consciousness.

She winced with pain. "What is it?"

"I think I hear something."

"What?"

"It's faint, but it's coming from the rock tumble."

He let go of her hand and re-lit his makeshift oil lamp with the last remaining match. He carried the smoking fuel can to the rock pile and listened. "They're coming!" I can hear them working outside."

Momentarily forgetting about the pain in her hand, Pam awakened fully. "Thank you, God." She spoke out loud, believing that her silent prayer had been answered.

Returning, Mike said, "We need to move back from the rock pile."

He carefully helped Pam to her feet and away from the wall of rocks. After she was settled at a safe distance, Mike made his way back to the tumble, picked up a rock, and began hitting it against one of the larger boulders in the pile. He didn't know if they could hear him, but it was worth a try to let them know that they were alive.

With all the noise outside, the workers couldn't hear Mike's attempt at communication. They methodically

285

continued removing one rock after another. Some of the men had tired and had been replaced, but William refused to quit until his son was safe.

"It's not worth hurting yourself." Jim continued handing rocks down the line to William. "We'll get them out."

"My son's in there, and I'm not quitting until he is out."

Jim had two daughters and understood a father's loyalty to his family. "Then come over here and help me get my block and tackle ready. They've come to a big rock, and they're going to try and drag it out of the way."

William realized that he did need to catch his breath after all, and at least he would be useful preparing the ropes.

The workers stopped their rock removal so that the ropes could be placed around the large boulder blocking their progress. As Jim leaned in to secure the ropes, he thought he could hear a tapping noise.

"Quiet, everyone! Everyone be quiet!"

The crowd grew quiet as Jim placed his head close to the rubble. A smile formed on his face and his gaze was directed toward William.

"They're alive! I can hear them inside, tapping on the rocks; they're alive!"

Cheers went up all around, and the crew began working fervently on the large boulder. With one end of the rope tied securely on the stone and the other end tied to the trunk of a large oak tree, several men pulled on the rope. The tension caused the pulley to squeak with each tug. While some tugged on the rope, others used iron pry bars to help remove the rock. The process was tedious, and there wasn't much room for the work, but, ever so slowly, the dark gray obstruction inched its way further from its resting place. Within thirty minutes the rock had been sufficiently pulled away from the entrance, such that work could resume.

From inside, Mike and Pamela could both now hear the noise of metal against rock as pry bars carefully dislodged boulders. Knowing they were about to be rescued caused Mike to realize that, even though they would soon be freed, he would certainly have to face the music with Pamela's father. Unknown to him, Pam was thinking the same thing.

William worked his way to the front of the work line and began handing the newly dislodged rocks back to the others. The man prying rocks in front of him was a sturdy man and seemed to be about Mike's age. He recalled seeing him at that position from the very beginning.

As a rock tumbled to the ground, William spoke to the worker. "My son is in there."

"My best friend is in there," the man replied, surprised at the remark.

Gilbert passed a rock to the man behind him and introduced himself to the one in front. "I'm William Gilbert."

"I'm Douglas Sprouse."

With no other words they continued moving rocks, working their way further into the entrance.

"Hold on, everyone," Jim announced.

The work came to a halt as Jim surveyed the ceiling of the mine entrance. He poked and prodded with an iron bar, making sure there was no loose debris that could fall on the workers. While he was making his careful inspection, he could now hear the tapping louder, and it sounded like it was just a few feet from where they were. Content that the walls and ceiling were safe, Jim directed them to continue, but stressed caution, knowing they were close to the tunnel's occupants.

"Mike, can you hear me?" Doug yelled.

"I can hear you." Mike's reply was muffled.

Several of the workers cheered.

"Are you okay?"

"We're both alive, but Pam is hurt. She needs help."

"Step back from the wall; we're almost through," Jim commanded.

287

They waited a few moments and began again. Doug pried a rock at the top of the pile, and, as it tumbled down, they all could see that they had finally broken through. Immediately, William rushed up the pile and, before he could be stopped, thrust his arm through the hole. The hole was large enough that he could see past his arm into the glowing room and could see the face of his son.

"Michael."

"Pa?" Mike replied in disbelief.

Mike scrambled up on the rocks to take hold of his father's hand.

"We'll have you out in a few minutes, Son."

Doug and Jim placed their hands onto William's shoulders, strongly encouraging him to back away so that they could remove enough rock to clear the opening.

"We'll have you out soon." William, exhausted from hours of work, repeated his encouragement as he backed away from the hole. Slowly he sat down onto a small pile of rock debris. He watched with anticipation as the opening grew larger and, finally, large enough to walk through. Within moments, he saw Jim Smith exit, carrying Pamela away from the site to find the doctor.

William stood to see his son Michael climb over the rubble and into the lantern light. He began receiving pats on the back for his survival; but Mike's gaze immediately fell onto his father, and, without hesitation, he made his way to his awaiting arms. Dust flew from their backs as the two embraced.

"I was afraid I had lost you," William said with a quiver in his voice.

Mike was speechless as all the workers gathered around the pair, exhausted but relieved that Mike and Pamela had been freed from their rocky tomb.

Chapter 27

"It was no accident." May Bess proclaimed this again as she sat in the living room with her hands clasped in her lap.

Jacob Harrison was red faced as he paced in front of her. "Well, she shouldn't have been there in the first place. You know how I feel about her and the boys around here, especially that one. I should have been able to trust you of all people, my own sister while I was away."

"It was simply a harmless gathering of two friends, besides, I was there."

Jacob quickly interrupted, directing all of his anger at her. "A lot of good that did!"

There was a long pause as Jacob stopped pacing and stood staring out through the front window and into the mid-morning daylight. May Bess didn't dare move from her position, knowing that her brother was not finished with his rant and would dismiss her only when he was good and ready.

She finally broke the silence. "What did the doctor say?"

Jacob's jaw muscles tensed at the news he had received from Doctor Lipscomb. He turned to face his sister, whom he knew was truly concerned.

"He said that most of her index finger would probably have to be removed."

May Bess lowered her head and stared at her hands, which began trembling in her lap.

"I'm sorry.

"Sorry isn't going to change things," Jacob snapped. "None of this would be happening if her mother were here where she is supposed to be, rather than doing her best to stay away as much as possible. Always making excuses as to why her supposedly sick relatives need her more than we do."

"Don't blame Lillian; she's never wanted to be here. You promised her it would only be for a short while, and now it's been over ten years."

Jacob snapped again at Mae Bess: "You don't need to defend my wife!"

"I'm not defending her…I'm just saying that things happen, and we have to deal with them the best we can and move on."

"Things just happen?" Jacob gestured with his arms out to his sides. "Tell that to my daughter who is about to lose one of her fingers because of your negligence."

Having heard enough of his accusations regarding her lack of proper responsibility, May Bess now stood to face her brother .

"You can't keep your daughter guarded in a nice, neat little package all the time. She is practically a woman, Jacob. You can't guide and direct her every move now and most certainly will not be able to when she goes away to finishing school."

Jacob became angrier at her defiance and took a step toward her.

May Bess held her ground. Her resolve was steady as her brother's body language seemed threatening.

"Michael is a responsible young man and…"

"That farm boy is not responsible or my daughter would not be lying injured in the doctor's office."

"That farm boy may have saved her life. And as I'll repeat for the last time…it was no accident. Michael was proudly showing her his mine; I definitely heard an explosion before the mine collapsed. I saw someone on horseback ride away through the trees just before it happened."

"Who would want to hurt my daughter?"

"I don't think anyone wanted to hurt Pamela. I think someone was trying to hurt Michael."

Harrison stood emotionless for a few moments. He actually didn't care if the boy from Kingston left town with his tail tucked between his legs.

"Even if I believed your story, who would want to hurt him?"

"Jacob, there are quite a few people in this town who would have dearly loved to get their hands on that mine. Any number of people would do almost whatever it took to have it…including you."

"You're not suggesting…"

"I'm not suggesting anything. Just know that Pamela's injury is not due to Michael's neglect, or Lillian not being here, nor my irresponsibility. Someone dynamited that mine."

Jacob was silent again for a moment, digesting her words.

"Regardless of how or why it happened, under no circumstances is that boy ever to be allowed around my daughter again. Is that understood?"

May Bess remained stoic without voicing solidarity on the matter.

"I'm going back to Doc Lipscomb's." Jacob put on his hat. He walked out the door and slammed it behind him. May Bess flinched at the sound then slowly returned to her chair, where she leaned her head back and closed her eyes.

***

From Doug's blacksmith shop, Mike and his father walked back out into the hot sunlight.

"You've made a good friend in Douglas," William said.

"Yes, I have." The pair walked toward William's horse, tied in the shade in front of Rosie's store and stood awkwardly, not knowing how to say goodbye.

"Pa, why do you have to leave so soon?"

"I came to give you your money from the bank and set things straight between us. I have to get back to the farm. I'm sure your brothers have had sufficient time to let things fall apart by now."

291

They both smiled, knowing that Mike's brothers were very capable of keeping the farm in good shape.

The leather saddle creaked as William mounted his horse.

"I'm glad you came, Pa." Mike took a step away from the horse. "Sorry you didn't get any sleep last night."

"Don't worry about me. I'm glad we had some time to talk."

"Tell Ma that I love her."

William smiled. "I'll tell her."

He leaned over and held out his hand to his son, whom he saw as a man now. Rosie was right.

Mike looked at his father's outstretched hand and took it into his.

"I'm proud of you, Son."

Mike couldn't contain a broad smile. "Thank you, Pa."

With that, William tugged on the reins and directed his horse, with mule in tow, back down the road leading away from town. Mike stood there watching as they rounded the curve and out of his sight.

As William rode out of town, he contemplated the events he had witnessed and replayed the conversation he'd had with his son pretty much all of the previous night over coffee in Mike's room. Though he still wanted things to be like they had been on the farm, with Mike back home, William realized that nothing ever stays the same for very long. He knew Mike would never return to the farm, but he was satisfied knowing Mike could make his own way, and he was very proud of him.

Riding along, William surveyed the tangle of wild grape vines hanging from the towering trees along the side of the road. Some of them touched the ground, but some hung like a swing, reminding him of when the boys were little and he had tied a rope to the limb of a walnut tree for them in the front yard of the farm.

The green underbrush in the woods was no different than the way it grew back home. He watched squirrels jump from limb to limb only to sit at a safe distance and scold him as he rode by. He remembered squirrel hunts with Mike when he was barely big enough to hold the rifle steady.

The sounds in the hills were also the same: the familiar songs from birds serenading his travel, the same sound from the wings of grasshoppers as they flew across his path, and, of course, katydids chirping as they rested on the underneath side of the leaves. As William neared the main road, he smiled to think that his son seemed to have suddenly grown up and become a man, something he had stumbled into many years ago himself.

Just as he turned north toward Yellville, he spotted a rider coming in his direction. *Probably just another miner seeking his fortune.* But as he drew nearer, he noticed a silver-colored flash on his vest.

"Mornin'," Wes smith said, as he approached William.

"Good morning, Sheriff."

The pair stopped next to each other in the road.

"You headed into Rush?" William asked.

Wes shielded his eyes from the sun as he looked at William. "I am."

"Just got finished visitin' my boy there," William said proudly.

"Good…good. Most of my family is back in Yellville. You traveled to see your family, I'm gettin' away from mine." Wes laughed at his own joke.

William didn't quite see the humor in Wes's comment, but he chuckled to be polite.

"Word sure gets around fast in these parts, though, don't it?" William shifted in his saddle.

Wes seemed a little confused. "Whadda ya mean?"

"You know, the mine collapse last night and word of someone dynamitin' it."

293

Wes furrowed his brow at the news. "Didn't hear nothin' about that. Just goin' into town to bring someone back to Yellville for questioning."

William nudged his horse back into forward motion. "Well, I hope you find your man."

"I usually do." Wes resumed his travel also.

***

Mike waited for Harrison to leave Doc Lipscomb's place so that he could visit Pamela. He'd not been able to speak to her since the accident. Knowing he'd better stay out of Jacob's way until some water had traveled under the bridge, Mike had been on pins and needles waiting for him to leave. When he opened the door to the doctor's office, its creaking caused Doc Lipscomb to look up from his desk.

"You're not supposed to be here," Lipscomb said dryly.

Mike was startled at the doctor's abruptness. He gazed around the room and spotted a doorway which led into the two-patient room.

"You did hear me, didn't you, Gilbert?"

"Yes, Sir, I did: but I really need to see Pamela."

Doctor Lipscomb stood in a non-threatening manner and approached Mike.

"Son, I'm sorry, but I've been given strict orders to not allow you entry."

Mike was heartsick at the news. Surely Harrison wasn't that angry at him. After all, it wasn't his fault that the mine collapsed. "Are you sure I can't see her just for a quick moment?"

"I have my instructions, Son, and I'm sorry, but have to insist that you leave. Unless you have a medical need, you're not allowed back there."

Mike felt dejected because the girl he loved was on the other side of a wooden wall. He glanced at the doorway, back at the doctor, and relented.

"Sorry for your trouble, Doc." Mike placed his hat onto his head and walked out into the sunlight.

As he exited, he saw Jay Finch and his new friend ride away from the company store and in his direction. Anger welled inside him; he fully believed that Finch had been responsible for the explosion. He stepped into the shade of a tree to wait on the pair. When they were close, he stepped out into the sunlight in front of the horses to halt their travel.

"It don't feel too good gettin' run over by a horse." Morse chuckled.

"What do you want, Farm Boy?" Jay managed to mutter through a pounding headache.

"You hurt Pam last night. You're not going to get away with it."

"That's a serious accusation there, my friend." Morse leaned forward in his saddle. "Finch was with me last night."

Mike looked back and forth from Jeeter to Jay. "Then I guess that means you both are responsible."

"You better watch your mouth, Boy, or you'll get yerself hurt."

Mike took a few steps to the side of Jeeter's horse. "One way or another, I'll prove it,"

"You ain't provin' nothin'." Morse spoke in a defiant tone.

"Oh, he's just upset 'cause he couldn't take care of his purty little girl last night," Finch said in a mocking tone.

That was all it took. Mike turned to Finch's horse and, without warning, grabbed Jay and pulled him off and onto the dusty road. Before he knew what had happened, Mike felt a blow to the side of his face that sent him to the ground face first. He rolled over just in time to see Morse swing his leg toward him, and he was barely able to roll out of the way of Morse' boot.

He scrambled to his feet, facing Morse, who was wielding a knife. Jay stepped up beside Morse as the trio faced off.

"What's the matter, Farm Boy? Not too brave now, are ya?" Morse lunged at Mike with the knife, but Mike sidestepped the lunge and pushed Morse temporarily out of the way. Within a split second Mike stepped toward Jay and punched him square in the jaw, sending him back to the dusty ground and out cold.

As he turned, he was met by Jeeter making another thrust; but this time the knife blade stuck him square in the shoulder before he could dodge the blow. Mike yelled in pain as he held onto the knife clasped firmly in Jeeter's hand. In much pain, he threw a knee into Jeeter's ribs, which allowed him to remove the knife from his shoulder, while it was still in Jeeter's grasp.

Mike took a few steps backwards to put some distance between him and his knife-wielding attacker. His shoulder throbbed with an excruciating pain, and blood dripped from his fingers onto the ground. Just as Jeeter was about to attack again, a gunshot rang out not too far from them, and the pair turned to see a man with a badge sitting on a horse in the street.

Wes spoke with deadpan sincerity. "If you don't want the next round to be aimed at you, I would suggest you put the knife down, Son."

Morse hesitated then dropped the knife. He feared the sheriff was there on his account.

"How bad are you hurt, Boy?" Sheriff Smith asked as he dismounted.

Mike was able to move his shoulder but with sharp pain. Wes walked over and took a look at the wound.

"Well, looks like it missed a major blood vessel, or you would have already bled out in the street."

At the sound of the gunshot, several people had gathered around the scene, including Doug and Charley. Jay was groggy but made his way to his feet, wiggling his jaw back and forth, testing to see if it was broken. He didn't know whether his jaw hurt more or his headache. Either way, what he really wanted was to get out of the bright sunlight and swallow the headache powder he had just purchased from the company store.

"As long as this is settled now…and it better be," Wes said, looking back and forth between Mike and Jeeter, "could someone tell me where I could find a man named Michael Gilbert?"

"That's me, Sheriff. Is there a problem?

Wes walked over to Mike. "Well, seems there was an incident at the bank over at Kingston a few weeks back. Someone held it up and took several hundred dollars."

Mike was stunned at the news about the robbery but still didn't know what that had to do with him.

"I got a wire from the Madison County constable to bring you in for questioning. I hear you made quite a scene at the bank there the day before it was robbed by a man in a mask."

Jeeter beamed with delight at the news, hoping Mike would be implicated for his handiwork so he would be free to roam once again and get out of this pitiful excuse for a town.

Morse piped in. "That boy's been spreadin' money like water all over town."

Smith glared at Morse. "No one told you to speak, did they?"

"I didn't rob the bank in Kingston," Mike protested.

"Well, that's what we aim to find out," Wes said. "Now, do I need to cuff you, or will you come peacefully?

Mike looked around at so many of the people he had known for almost three weeks now. They all displayed stunned sadness on their faces.

"Sheriff, I did cause a scene at the bank and, for that, I'm sorry; but I didn't rob the bank."

"Well…come on, Son. We'll take care of that shoulder, and then I have to take you back to the jail in Yellville so that you can be questioned by the Madison County constable. He will expect you to be there on Friday."

Charley fidgeted as he watched the display. Mike was innocent of the bank robbery but Charley was afraid to tell what he had overheard Morse and Finch speak of the past Saturday night. He didn't want his friends to be hurt, but as

Smith decided to put the cuffs onto Mike and head first to the doc's office, Charley could contain himself no longer.

"Check his leg," Charley blurted out.

Everyone turned to see who had spoken.

Charley caught a glare from Morse, but it was too late; he had already begun.

"What reason would I have to check his leg?"

"The robber got shot in the leg as he rode away from the bank." Charley spoke timidly.

Wes stood there for a moment then remembered that he had read in the Yellville paper that the robber had indeed been wounded in the leg. He had completely forgotten that detail.

"Well, Son, I hate to ask you to drop your pants here in the middle of the street, but let me check your leg."

Mike was embarrassed to expose his underwear, but he complied and allowed Wes to thoroughly examine him.

"Well, I'll be." Wes rubbed his chin. "I think bringin' you all the way back to Yellville is gonna be a wasted trip since you don't have a bullet hole in ya. But I gotta do what I was asked to just the same. Looks like I rode all the way down here for nothin'."

Charley realized his task was not over. He had to fully tell what he knew. He walked toward the sheriff and stopped a few steps from him.

"Check his leg." Charley raised his right arm and pointed it at Jeeter Morse.

"Why would he want to check my leg, you retard?" Morse became nervous.

"Son, is there somethin you want to tell me?" Smith looked at Charley.

"Check his leg. I heard him talkin'."

Wes continued looking at Charley, trying to decide what to do next.

"Well, we don't need to have a pants-pullin'-down party right here in the middle of the hot street." Several people began to chuckle. Wes looked at Jeeter. "But, young man, if you'll follow me over to the shade, I'll just take a look at your legs and put this matter to rest."

Jeeter hesitated.

"Well, come on." Wes motioned for Jeeter to follow him.

Suddenly, to the gasps of the onlookers, Morse made a dash for his horse. He had only taken a few steps before he was tackled by Smith, who, with a couple of quick punches, had Morse on the ground with his hands held firmly behind his back and his face down in the dust.

Wes continued to put pressure on one of Jeeter's arms, using his other hand to run up and down Jeeter's legs. Within moments he felt what seemed to be a bandage on Jeeter's left thigh.

"Does this hurt?" Wes pressed into the wound with his thumb.

Jeeter let out a howl of pain that was the answer to Wes's question.

Wes held securely to Jeeter's arm and forced him to his feet. He pulled his gun for added insurance that Jeeter wouldn't try to run again and checked Jeeter for a firearm. Wes found Jeeter's pistol in the front of his pants, placed it into his own belt, and then ushered him back to his horse, where Jeeter was wrist shackled. With help from Doug, Wes placed Jeeter onto his own horse and grabbed the reins. "Looks like I didn't make the trip all the way down here for nothin' after all."

Wes looked around at the crowd. When his gaze found Mike, Wes gave him an apologetic wink. "Sorry about pullin' yer pants down in the street."

"Least my drawers were clean," Mike said. Laughter erupted from the onlookers.

Wes mounted his own horse, holding tightly to the reins of Jeeter's horse, and the pair began riding out of town. Everyone crowded around Mike, grateful that the ordeal was over; they also congratulated Charley for speaking up with what he knew.

"We better get you to the doc," someone in the crowd said. They assisted Mike across the street and into the doctor's office.

"I didn't expect you to resort to anything like this." Lipscomb offered a slight grin as he noticed Mike's blood-soaked shirtsleeve.

Mike was left in the care of the doctor, who moved Mike to his patient room. The room was divided into two areas by a heavy curtain suspended from the ceiling.

"I heard commotion in the street," Lipscomb said, "but by the time I looked out, it was all over."

When the doctor cleaned his wound with alcohol, Mike winced. . "You didn't miss much." Mike gritted his teeth, feeling as if he were going to pass out from the sharp pain of the alcohol hitting the exposed nerves in his shoulder.

"You're lucky," Doc said. "One inch over and you would have lost most of your blood."

"I don't believe in luck."

Lipscomb just looked at Mike as he dressed the wound with bandages.

"Is Pamela on the other side of the curtain?" "She is…but I gave her a sedative a while ago. She's been asleep ever since her father left."

Mike's heart sank at the news because he wanted to talk to her, though he hadn't planned on it this way.

"You need to lie back and rest for a while. Pam's not going anywhere." He grinned at Mike and left the room.

Mike appreciated the doc allowing him to stay for a while. Though he was restless, he desperately wanted to talk to Pamela, so he decided to lie still and allow the medicine to ease the pain in his shoulder. In the quietness of the room, he could hear her breathe from the other side of the curtain. He was satisfied to wait for her to awaken.

***

"I'm sure glad there's people like you in the world," Wes said to Morse as the two traveled toward Yellville.

Morse remained silent because he knew that, if he asked why, it would give his captor the satisfaction of completing his statement with something he didn't care to hear.

"Because if it weren't for people like you, I wouldn't have a job," Wes finished anyway with a chuckle aimed at irritating Jeeter.

"I'm hungry." Jeeter slouched in the saddle.

"You'll get to eat when I do, in Yellville," Wes said as he rode behind Jeeter's horse.

The pair continued making their way along the shaded, narrow road north, with dense forest on either side of them. Jeeter knew that he would certainly face other charges from the past if he were jailed. Robbing the Kingston bank was his biggest offense that anyone knew of. The thought of sitting in a jail cell awaiting trial and time in a prison didn't interest him in the least. He didn't know how trigger happy Sheriff Smith was, but the thought of making a dash for freedom, though he was cuffed, was an idea blossoming in his brain.

The forest was dense, but it occurred to him that the thickness might give him an advantage to elude the short sheriff. Even if he had to leave his horse during the escape, he knew he could always acquire another. At this point he didn't figure he had much to lose.

"If you're thinkin' of makin' a break for the woods, you might want to forget about it. I don't think twice about shootin' a prisoner in the back if he's tryin' to run away from me."

Jeeter didn't care about Wes' comment. He was still looking for his chance to flee. He would take his chances with a shot from the sheriff, and if he took a bullet…well then, he figured it was better than prison time.

Yellville was still an hour away as they plodded along. Suddenly, the moment Jeeter was waiting for occurred, and it was even better than he had hoped. A covey of quail was spooked as they passed, and the small birds flew across the road almost on top of them, causing Wes's horse to whinny and rear. Jeeter took that opportunity to jab his horse in the ribs with his heels.

Instantly, Jeeter was at the edge of the trees. Wes quickly regained his composure and drew his gun. He aimed between Jeeter's shoulder blades but couldn't pull the trigger. *Just can't do it in the back.* He kicked his own horse into action.

The pair crashed through the forest with limbs and vines directing their path. Jeeter's hands were shackled, but he was able to hold on to the saddle horn. He couldn't direct the horse and hoped it would take a relatively clear route through the trees. He had a decent head start on the sheriff, and, with some luck, he could add some distance. He planned to slide off his horse at an opportune moment and let the sheriff continue following his galloping ride. He could hear Wes behind him but couldn't see him through the thick undergrowth.

Wes followed as fast as he could through the brush. Birds flew in every direction as he chased Jeeter through the trees. Every once in a while he would catch a glimpse of Jeeter through the shadowy vale.

Jeeter grinned because he could tell that the sheriff was falling further behind. It wouldn't be long before he said goodbye to his horse and disappeared on foot. As his horse galloped through the thickness of the trees, he turned to look one last time behind him. Convinced that the time was right, he turned, again facing forward, but was instantly met by the forked branch of a heavy tree limb.

He didn't see it coming, and he hadn't felt a thing. Within a split second, Jeeter was removed from the saddle by his neck, which was shattered, and held him firmly in the crotch of the forked tree limb; his feet dangling above the leaf-carpeted forest floor.

Spotting the scene in front of him, Wes pulled his horse to an abrupt stop. He saw Jeeter dangling from the tree limb with his head hanging limp to one side. He listened for the sound of Jeeter's horse and figured it had continued on.

He stared at Jeeter's lifeless body for a couple of minutes, allowing his horse to settle down from the dash through the woods. Slowly Wes slipped out of the saddle and walked up to Morse with his horse in tow.

"Guess you shoulda ducked." He looked up at Jeeter as if Jeeter could hear him.

Wes gazed at Jeeter for another moment then rubbed his hand over his own face, as if wiping off the disbelief.

"Well, girl," Wes said, patting his horse on the neck, "looks like we're gonna have some dead weight along with us on the trip back home." He reached for a coil of rope tied to his saddle and used it to pull Jeeter down. After placing Jeeter behind the saddle, Sheriff Smith resumed his travel in the direction of Yellville.

Chapter 28

Lying on the bed in the doctor's office, Mike drifted in and out of consciousness. The pain medication had made him drowsier than anticipated. His thoughts continually swung from strange dreams to coherent thoughts of his past couple of days and the remembrance of Pam asleep on the other side of the partitioning curtain.

He sat up and forced himself to come fully awake; the pain in his shoulder reminded him of the earlier events of the day. Re-positioning himself on the pillows, Mike let out a soft moan.

"Hello." A soft voice came from the other side of the curtain.

"Pam, you're awake," Mike whispered.

Doc. Lipscomb heard the whispering but just grinned to himself, continuing paperwork at his desk in the adjacent room.

"Are you decent?"

"I'm covered, if that's what you're asking."

Mike swung his legs over the edge of the creaky bed and placed his feet onto the wooden floor. As he stood, his left arm in a sling, he became a little dizzy; but, within a few seconds, the dizziness left. He pulled back the edge of the curtain and saw Pam lying on her bed with her left hand in thick bandages.

Mike looked at her hand and was at a loss for words. Immediately, he felt the responsibility of his sweetheart's injury. He stepped to her bedside and slowly made eye contact with her.

"What happened to you?" Pam raised her eyebrows at seeing his injury.

"I got too close to the end of a knife blade out in the street with that friend of Jay's."

Pam looked puzzled and was about to inquire further when Mike continued. "How is your hand?"

"The hand will make it," Pam said, "but the finger is not so good."

"How bad is it?"

Pam hesitated for a moment then responded. "Doc's going to have to remove part of it."

Immediately, Mike's eyes watered at the news. He lifted his head and looked out over the room, trying to keep the tears from flowing down his cheeks.

"We're really a pair aren't we?" Pam tried to make eye contact again.

"What do you mean?"

"All bandaged and banged up." Mike didn't respond. He bit his lower lip, still trying to hold back his tears at seeing Pam's condition.

"It's not your fault, you know."

"Sure it is."

Pam rolled her eyes and looked off into the room at his reply. After a moment of silence she spoke. "You can put all the blame on yourself if you want to and have a good ol'-fashioned pity party, but I'm not attending."

"I shouldn't have had you in there in the first place."

"Mike, I know you feel responsible, but you know there was an explosion before the collapse."

"Don't matter," he replied softly, "I shouldn't have had you in there."

The pair remained silent for a few moments, each seeing the incident from different viewpoints.

"That was a nice kiss." Pam whispered softly, knowing that Doc was probably eavesdropping and hoping to be quiet enough to avert being heard.

Through watery eyes Mike smiled at the memory in the mine before the explosion. "Probably the last one I'll get if your pa has anything to do with it."

Though she was in pain, Pam smiled. It warmed Mike's heart, and he gently touched her on her shoulder.

At that moment Doc Lipscomb entered to check on his patients. "Well, I see you're up and around." He directed his words to Mike.

Mike took a few steps back to allow Doc to turn his attention to Pam.

"How are you feeling, young lady?" He placed his hand onto her forehead.

"My finger is throbbing."

Doc began to inspect her hand, speaking to Mike as he did so. "Mike, I left some medication on the corner of my desk for you. Take the tablets when you need them and let me look at your shoulder again in a couple of days."

Mike understood it was the doctor's polite way of saying he needed to leave now. He looked at Pam one last time, and waved slightly to her with his right hand as Lipscomb began removing her bandages.

Mike picked up the pills from the doctor's desk and left the building, entering into the bright, hot sunlight.

***

"So much has happened in the last few days that my dang head's still spinnin'." Mike sat on the edge of a wooden barrel in the blacksmith shop, talking with Doug.

"This is the most excitement that has happened around here for a long time." Doug adjusted the straps on his leather apron. "Maybe things will settle down now and get back to normal."

Sitting down to his bucket of nails, Charley chimed in. "Things been pretty dull around here till you came along." .

"Charley, that wasn't very nice."

Charley looked confused by his brother's chide. "Things is always dull round here...I'm glad they ain't as much anymore."

Mike looked at Charley with a grin. "I think I understand what he means."

At the sound of the bellows being pumped, Mike turned back around to Doug. With added air, the coals sprang to life and radiated their heat into the already sweltering afternoon. Mike moved his barrel away from the coal pit to put a little more distance between him and the unwelcome warmth.

"Harrison's not lettin' me see Pamela." Mike broached the topic as he watched the embers turn white hot.

Doug released the bellows and searched for the proper set of tongs he needed for the work he was about to begin. "Doesn't surprise me at all."

"I feel so bad that I let that happen to her."

"Don't go feelin' sorry for yerself," Doug said. "I'm sure she doesn't blame you one bit."

Mike looked down at the dusty floor. "I wish I felt as certain as you do."

Mike watched Doug return to his work. Still on his perch, he thought about how much his life had changed since he had been in Rush and about the events of the last few days. The world seemed to be speeding toward him like a steam locomotive. Life wasn't simple like it was back on the farm.

He caught himself missing the regimented tasks which the farm had demanded. It hadn't ever been very exciting, but at least he pretty much knew what to expect day in and day out. His life now seemed to be out of control, and the only thing he had been able to do was just hang on for the ride and deal with things as they happened.

Though a part of him missed his life in Kingston, he still knew that he had made the right decision. Every day seemed to bring a new surprise, and the feeling of adventure suited him just fine; but mostly it felt good knowing that his father was proud of him. If any single thing made his trip to Rush a success…it was that.

Mike was startled from his thoughts by the sharp report of Doug's hammer pounding iron. Mike watched his friend shape a hinge needed for a door at the mill. When Doug had placed the hot metal into the water to cool, Mike took the opportunity to ask him a favor. "I need to go back to the mine this evening. I left my new lantern inside, and I was hoping you'd have time to go with me."

"I'd be glad to. It's been a while since I've been inside that place." Doug reheated the coals.

"Well, I really don't want to hang around in there; I just want to retrieve my lantern then figure out what I want to do with the mine now."

"What do you mean 'figure out what to do with the mine now'?"

"All that rock is going to be difficult to move out of the way before I can even think about minin'."

"I've only known you for a short while, but you've never seemed to be the kind that would give up or back away from something tough," Doug said, trying to be encouraging.

"It's just going to take so long and be so difficult that…"

Doug interrupted. "No one said it would be easy, did they?"

Mike sighed. "Suppose they didn't."

"I can't help you move all that debris, but I know you can do it. Hire someone to help you. If you need to, go to Yellville and talk to a banker about loanin' some money against the mine. That mine has a great potential. It will just take the right person to make it work. I have a feeling that person will be you."

Mike felt the way he usually did after receiving a talk from his father. He knew he wasn't a quitter, but the task seemed so daunting at the moment. .Mike stood from the barrel. "I'll be back at six. See you later, Charley."

Charley continued counting his bucket of one hundred nails without acknowledging Mike.

***

Mike's shoulder was beginning to feel a little better as he and Doug rode toward the Red Rose Mine. There was still a lot of pain when he tried to move his arm, but at least the throbbing had ceased. As they rode, Mike's mind was continually on Pam and their future…if there were such a thing now. He caught himself lamenting the sudden turn of events that seemed more dismal than bright—as they had only a couple of days earlier.

"You know, my grandfather used to have a saying that was pretty much always right."

"What was that?" Mike looked over at his friend.

"He used to say, 'Son, no matter how many problems yer going through, just remember that the darkest part of the night is just before the sunrise.'"

"What does that mean?" Mike furrowed his brow.

"I had to think about it for a spell myself, because he would never explain it to me, and then one day it dawned on me what he was trying to say."

"Explain it to me because I'm not thinkin' too good right now."

Doug chuckled at his friend. "Well, best I can tell, he was sayin' that, no matter how bad things were, no matter how dark and dreary your life seemed, or how bad the storms were raging around you, the sun would sooner or later come up and things would be bright and fair again."

Mike remained silent at his friend's words, trying to make sense of them.

"What I'm tryin' to say is that things will get better and won't always be this bad. You'll get through this. My grandfather used to remind me to give my troubles over to the Almighty and let Him handle them for me."

Mike knew that Doug was right, but at the moment he wanted to feel sorry for himself.

"Besides," Doug continued, "you've got good friends here."

Mike looked over at his companion, who was sporting a big grin. He finally allowed himself to smile and realize that he wasn't alone. He knew things were bad, but, with friends and God at his side, the situations would eventually get better with time. *They can't get much worse.*

Finally they reached the river and dismounted. Mike hesitated at his horse as he gazed in the direction of his mine.

"It's going to get dark soon." Doug's remark broke Mike out of his trance.

He caught up with Doug as they walked along the riverbank and up the slight grade until they reached the rubble-strewn entrance to the mine.

Mike hesitated again at the opening. "Think it's safe?"

Doug looked around at the boulders and at the ceiling of the enlarged opening. "Looks safe to me, but if you would rather, you can wait here and I'll go retrieve your lamp."

"No, I'll go in too."

Doug lit his lantern and, after he adjusted the flame, the pair made their way through the entrance and deeper into the shaft. The lantern illuminated the debris on the floor and the faint haze of dust still lingering in the air.

"I think it's just around the corner." Mike tried to remember where he had left his lantern.

As they rounded the slight bend in the tunnel, Mike spotted his lantern on the floor just as he had left it. Bending over to pick up what he had come for, and inspecting his possession, he noticed that the glass globe was cracked and the silk mantle inside had fallen apart.

"I'm sure it can be fixed." Doug tried to be positive.

Mike spotted a dent in the bottom fuel canister. "I dunno about that."

Doug took time to check out his surroundings in the cavern as Mike continued gazing at his lantern. "I sure see a lot of Amber Jack in here." Doug raised his lamp for a better look at the rock walls. "The stuff is running in veins everywhere."

Mike was only halfway listening to his friend. He replayed the first moments in the tunnel after he had awakened from the blast and felt a little pain in his shoulder. "There's the boulder over there that pinned Pam's hand to the wall."

Doug gazed at the boulder and, even at their distance from it, he could tell there was something different about it. He walked closer to it, holding the lantern in front of him.

"Well," Mike began, "I got what I came for. I really appreciate you…"

Doug interrupted. "Mike, you need to see this."

"See what?" Mike turned to his friend.

"Just come over here," Doug insisted.

Mike took the few steps over to the dark boulder and stood next to Doug.

"What am I looking at?"

Doug lowered the lantern next to the boulder to give Mike a better look, and he remained silent.

"I'm not sure what you want me to see." Mike continued to look at the rock.

Doug leaned close to the boulder and inspected it as much as possible in the dim lantern light. He couldn't believe what he was looking at.

"I'll swan, Doug, tell me what you see."

Doug stood again then looked at Mike. "I'm not completely positive." Doug slightly grinned. "But I think that boulder is solid Amber Jack, and—if it is—it's gonna change your life."

Chapter 29

"Finch," Larkin Riley barked as Jay walked into the Morning Star on Friday morning, "we need to talk."

Jay followed Riley into Harrison's office and closed the door behind him. He remained silent, waiting for Riley to begin.

"No sense in beatin' around the bush here," Larkin said. "I know you was the one who collapsed the Red Rose Mine a couple of nights ago."

"I thought we already settled that matter.

"Oh, it's far from settled. You almost killed the boss's daughter."

"Not my fault that she was in there with that farm boy. I was just tryin' to scare him out of town is all.

"I should have known better than to give you that dynamite."

"Well, like I said, if you remember, if you want to keep your job, you'll keep yer mouth shut," Jay said with a sneer. "I'm sure you didn't think much about it when you were pourin' that liquor down your throat."

It was all Riley could do to keep his cool. He couldn't believe Jay was addressing him in that manner. He walked from around the desk to stand in front of Jay—in a menacing stance. "You know the sheriff will do some checkin' on it."

"Well, if he does, I have an alibi. I was here with you the other night; we were havin' ourselves a friendly little visit after I brought that paper back from Yellville."

"And what if I don't go along with it?" Riley used a tone that grated on Jay.

"Oh, you'll go along with it. I have no doubt. Harrison finds out you had a hand in it, you probly won't see the outside of a jail cell for the rest of your life."

The office door suddenly opened and one of the workers entered. "Hope I'm not interruptin' anything important, but did you hear about that feller that left with the sheriff yesterday?"

Jay and Larkin looked at each other then back at the other man, indicating they had not heard the news.

"Seems the feller shot off through the woods and hung his self on a tree limb."

At first, Jay was shocked at the news, but then he developed a smile on his face as the worker left the room. "Looks like we both have an alibi, Riley."

"What's that?"

"Seems someone broke into your supply shack a couple of nights ago and, if we remember correctly, sometime later we saw Jeeter ride back from the direction of the Red Rose just before all the excitement began."

Riley didn't like the idea of digging a deeper hole, but he realized that laying blame on a dead man could keep him out of trouble. He walked past Jay and opened the door to the office, indicating his desire to have Jay leave.

"Just bring me that other jar you promised me," he said. Jay walked past him and into the mill. He closed the door and contemplated his decision.

***

Mike dressed slowly, peeking under the bandage on his shoulder. It was red and bruised around the puncture, but there seemed to be no sign of infection. He replaced the cloth protection and, after buttoning his shirt, set aside the sling. He didn't want to walk around town like a cripple. He would have to be careful with his arm for a few days, though.

Sitting on the edge of his bed, Mike longed for another visit with Pam. Knowing he couldn't see her caused him a pain in his heart far greater than any knife could ever inflict in his shoulder. He contemplated confronting Harrison again but knew that plan would fail. Then suddenly an idea formed in his head that he hoped would work.

Quickly, he made his way to Rosie's store to ask her if she would look in on Pam and give him a report. As soon as he walked through her door, he spotted Doug at a counter with Rosie. When they saw him walking up to them, they stopped their conversation and smiled. "Did I miss something?"

"You got no idea what's in that mine of yours, do you, kid?" Rosie chuckled.

Mike was caught off guard by her sudden comment. "Appears I've got zinc that I need to get out somehow, soon as my shoulder heals."

"Oh, you got more than zinc in there." She was about to explode with excitement. "If Doug here is right, you've got something in that hole of yours that will put the Red Rose Mine on the map."

Mike looked at Doug then back at Rosie.

"I don't know what you mean, but what I came in here to find out is if you would check on Pam for me from time to time and let me know how she's doin'. Harrison won't let me get near her."

"Oh, honey. Doc had to remove part of her finger last night; but she's doin' just fine. That ol' quack said she'd be up and around in no time."

Mike closed his eyes at the news.

"Don't worry, kid. She's a tough gal. I knew you couldn't see her, so I've already checked up on her for ya. She wanted me to tell you she is just fine and for you not to fret."

"Yeah, and I'll get Sandy to check on her this afternoon," Doug said.

Mike scratched his head in disbelief that his friends were looking out for him. "Oh, I 'preciate it," was all Mike could say.

Rosie walked toward the back of the room and aimed herself at the chairs around the checker table. "I gotta get off my feet for a spell."

Mike and Doug followed her and stood as she plopped into one of the rockers.

"Now, may I finish tellin' you about what's in that mine of yours?" Rosie picked up a paper fan with a picture of Jesus on it and tried to create a cool breeze across her face.

Mike waited for her to speak.

"Zinc don't usually come in big chunks like the one Doug said he believes he saw in your mine. Seems whoever lit that dynamite did you a big favor."

"I don't understand." Mike looked at Doug then back to Rosie.

"A chunk of Amber Jack that size is worth more money in one piece than if it was ground up and sent to the smelter. In fact, I'd be willing to bet that it's probably close to a record in size."

Mike still couldn't quite understand what she was trying to tell him.

"What Rosie is saying," Doug interrupted, "is that your chunk of zinc is probably a collection piece, and there's no tellin what someone is willing to pay to have it."

Rosie exclaimed: "We're talking about a museum piece, Mike—for goodness sake!"

"Museum piece?"

Doug took a seat across the checker table from Rosie. "Mike, that big boulder of zinc will bring a lot of money for you and also notoriety for your mine. Put that big chunk on the market and you will have investors clamoring to invest in your mine and help you remove all the zinc that's in it."

Mike stood silent for a moment then grinned at Doug. "Looks like the sun's beginning to rise a little."

Rosie shot a puzzled look at Doug, and Mike answered her question before she had time to ask it.

"It means I'm ready to clear some debris and get that zinc boulder out of our mine!"

"Whatever you say, kid." Rosie continued to fan herself with Jesus.

**

Mike followed Doug to the blacksmith shop and sat on his favorite barrel as he watched his friend get back to

315

work. His shoulder was beginning to hurt and figured it was because he had opted not to wear the sling; but he was determined to continue without it.

Mike finally spoke up. "How am I supposed to get a chunk of rock that size out of the mine?"

"Well, it's not gonna be easy." Doug's hammer threw sparks into the air.

"That goes without saying."

Doug stopped pounding and wiped his forehead with the back of his sweaty arm. "You're gonna need a lot of help getting that rock outside in one piece. Then you're gonna have to transport it to Buffalo City where it can be put on the train."

"Then what?"

"Well, I'd worry about the *then what* after you get it out into the sunlight."

"Who am I going to get to help?"

Looking at his friend, Doug couldn't help but understand his dilemma and his defeated tone. Mike was a farm boy who knew nothing about mining, let alone how to deal with an opportunity of this magnitude.

"I have a thought, if you don't mind me sayin'." Doug grinned.

"I'm all ears. I need all the suggestions I can get."

Doug stood, placed his hammer onto the anvil, and walked over to Mike. "There's probably only one person in town who can help you get that rock into the right hands."

Mike sat, waiting for his friend to finish; then he realized whom Doug meant. He shook his head in reluctance. "You're talking about Harrison, aren't you?"

"Now listen to what I have to say."

"Harrison would just as soon spit as to see me right now."

"Mike," Doug began, "what do you want more than anything at the moment?"

Mike said nothing because he knew Doug didn't really intend for him to answer.

316

"That's right. You want to be with Pam, but Daddy won't let you near her, will he? Do ya think he might change his tune when you come to him with an offer he can't refuse?"

Though Mike wasn't dense, he didn't like the direction Doug seemed to be going with this conversation. "What you're sayin is…"

"What I'm sayin is that, if you offer Harrison a piece of the glory and money with that nugget, he might just help you get it into the right hands. And that just might get you in good enough with him that he might let you be around his daughter again."

Mike stood for a moment, untangling everything Doug had poured into his head, and then he blurted out, "Are you out of your cotton pickin' mind?"

***

Jacob Harrison was in his dusty office when he heard a knock at his closed door.

"What is it? I'm busy."

The door opened slowly, and Mike stepped into Harrison's office. Jacob expected the intruder to be Riley or one of the other department managers and didn't bother to look up.

"Mr. Harrison, I'd like a moment of your time, if you have one to spare." Mike addressed him in a respectful tone.

Harrison immediately recognized the voice and stood at the same time he looked up. "Get out of my office, Boy."

"Mr. Harrison, if you'll just give me a minute and hear me out…"

"I don't want to hear anything you have to say!" Harrison walked around his desk toward Mike. "Nothing you have to say will change my mind about you and my daughter."

"I'm not here to talk about your daughter. I'm here to make you a business proposition."

Harrison was surprised at Mike's words, but he was still so angry that he didn't intend to listen to what Mike had to say. "I said I want you to leave my office." Harrison gestured toward the door.

Mike stood his ground. "Mr. Harrison, I think you'll want to hear what I have to say. I'm sure you wouldn't want to pass up a deal like this one and let someone else have it."

Mike's comment captured Harrison's interest, and he indicated he'd hear what Mike had to say before throwing him out into the street. "Get to it. I'm a busy man."

Mike sat down in front of Harrison's desk. Harrison followed suit and sat back into his own chair.

"First of all, I want to apologize for..."

"I don't want to hear your apologies boy; just get to your point."

Mike leaned forward in his chair, reluctant to back down from Harrison's tone. "I've come across a situation in my mine that I need your help with."

Harrison interrupted. "I already told you I would take your zinc."

"It's much more that that," Mike continued.

Harrison now became a little more intrigued at Mike's words and leaned back into his chair. "Go on, I don't have all day."

"I've discovered a very large boulder of solid Amber Jack in the mine."

"How large?" Harrison leaned forward in his chair as he got right to the point.

"Well, it's so large that I'll need a lot of help removing it."

"And you want me to have my men and equipment get it out for you. Is that what I'm hearing?"

Mike took a deep breath before he continued. "I'm saying I need your help to get it out in one piece and get it to someone who can tell me its value."

"Let's see if I have this right," Harrison began. "You go against my wishes to see my daughter and almost get her killed in your mine, and then you come to me and ask me to help you remove a chunk of zinc for you. What kind of fool do you think I am?" Harrison slammed his hand down onto his desk, causing a few papers to flutter down onto the floor.

"Mr. Harrison, I don't think you understand what I'm saying."

"I understand what you're saying, and you can dig your own rocks out and bring them here just like everyone else does."

"Mr. Harrison, this chunk is really big. I think it is worth a lot of money, not to mention the attention brought to anyone who brings it to the right person."

Harrison stood once again and walked toward Mike. Mike stood, prepared to leave the office. Harrison stopped in front of Mike with a glare that could almost certainly spark a fire. He stood there for a few seconds, as if contemplating how to have Mike ejected from his presence, and then he cocked his head to one side and partially closed one eye. "Just how big is this rock?"

***

Jacob Harrison was filled with mixed emotions as he walked toward the mine that had slipped through his grasp. Walking toward it with this inexperienced newcomer, he was further filled with resentment. He couldn't believe he had actually followed Mike, but the thought of being a part of something with great potential had caused him to set aside his anger for a short spell.

Mike and Harrison lit their lanterns at the opening of the mine. Harrison was amazed at the damage and realized that only a blast could have caused this much rubble. *I guess May Bess could have been right after all.*

Stepping over the stones on the cavern floor, the pair entered cautiously and made their way back to the zinc boulder. Mike was leading the way and, as he arrived at the spot, he raised his lantern above the large boulder to allow Harrison to have a better look. Then, Harrison crouched next to the rock for closer inspection. It didn't take long for him to realize what he was looking at. His eyes widened.

"I told you it was big!" Mike drew himself up to his full height, proudly displaying the rock.

Surveying the brown specimen for a few minutes longer, Harrison continued to kneel in awe. Mike's arm tired of holding up the light; he was about to lower it to his side when Harrison stood and spoke. "I've seen some large chunks of ore come out of these mines, but... *never in my wildest dreams did I ever think I'd see anything like this again.*"

"Mr. Harrison, I'd like to make a deal with you to help me get this out of the mine and to the right people. For doing so, I'm willing to give you twenty percent of any money it generates.

Harrison heard Mike's words but was still too stunned to fully comprehend it. "Say that again."

"I can't get this out myself, and you know the people I need to show this to. If you help me get this out in one piece and get it to the right people, I'll give you 20 percent of the money it sells for."

Lantern light cast shadows on the walls of the damp mine as Harrison, thinking about the proposal, continued to look at the large brown boulder resting on the cavern floor between them. Though anger against Mike still roiled in his heart, he put it aside; he knew a good business deal when he heard one.

Harrison looked up from the rock and at Mike's illuminated face. Slowly he reached his right hand up and toward Mike. Mike saw the gesture and, within seconds, had placed his lantern on the cavern floor, clasped the offered hand, and sealed the deal.

"This doesn't change anything with my daughter," Harrison said in a serious tone.

"This is strictly business, Mr. Harrison.

As the pair ended their handshake, Harrison took one last look around at the mine he had dreamed of acquiring. "We best be getting back into town. We have plans to make."

"Yes, we do." In spite of Harrison's remarks to the contrary, Mike hoped this would be the beginning of his chances with Pam once again.

Chapter 30

Through the kitchen window Rachel saw her husband riding slowly down the lane toward the farmhouse in the late Saturday evening light. From a distance she could tell he was tired from sitting in a saddle all week. She wiped her hands on a towel and, within seconds, had removed her apron and was out the door to await him on the front porch.

She was impatient for William to reach the porch. "How is Michael?"

"I'm just fine dear, but my backside is a bit sore from the long ride." Teasing in his dry manner, William dismounted and hugged his wife. "He's just fine dear. Our boy has grown up."

Rachel smiled with relief and silently thanked God that He had protected their son.

"Let me take care of my horse; then I'll be in directly. I'm sure you have a question or two." William kissed her on the forehead.

"William Gilbert, I'm about to explode." Rachel couldn't wait, so she followed her husband into the barn and watched as he removed the saddle from his horse. "William, you're being a pest. Spill the beans...I want to know everything."

"Well," he said as he began brushing his horse, "Rush is not what I expected."

"Is it a large town?"

"Seems to be a lot of people there, but it's way out in the middle of nowhere."

"Is Michael eating proper?"

"Appears so."

"Are you going to make me drag everything out of you?" She knew William was playfully, causing her grief.

William hung the brush back onto its nail and sat next to Rachel.

"Your son is feeding himself well, living in a little place behind a general store. He has already made a lot of friends, too."

Rachel smiled at the news. "What's he doing for work?"

"Well, this is the part you won't believe."

"What?"

"Seems our son is the owner of a zinc-ore mine."

"Zinc ore?"

"I don't know the particulars, but he was offered a deal by a lady there whose husband had died and left a zinc mine behind. She wasn't workin' it and offered it to Mike."

A concerned look crossed Rachel's face. "Mike doesn't know how to work a mine. Isn't that a bit dangerous?"

"Well, he's already had a run in with it, and he came out just fine. I'm sure he'll learn quick. I'll tell you all about it after I wash up. I'm pretty tired and dirty." William took Rachel's hand into his.

"Oh, and I almost forgot to mention one last thing,"

"What's that?" Rachel asked, looking into William's eyes.

"Mike has got a girl."

Rachel's heart leapt inside her.

"And she's pretty too."

"I want to know everything, William." They stood to go into the house.

"Make me a bath and give me an aspirin powder and a tall glass of tea. I'll tell you everything I can remember."

Rachel reached up and placed her arm in his as they left the barn. "And don't leave anything out."

***

"I can tell you right now that it's not gonna work." Doug was warming the water for the weekly laundry.

"We've hauled loads that heavy back on the farm with a team of four," Mike said.

"Yeah, but I can guarantee it was along level ground…am I right?"

Mike, his arms crossed in front of his chest, didn't answer, because his friend was indeed right.

"You've never been over the road that takes you to the ferry on the White River. It's steep in places and rough all along the way. I don't think you realize how heavy that specimen is. Ore is heavier than just plain ol' rock. It's much heavier than it looks." Doug lifted the water pot from his woodstove.

The two took the water outside and poured it into the galvanized tub of warm water already there. Doug placed his hand into the water and swirled it around, testing the temperature.

He stood back up to face Mike. "Looks like we're ready."

"Charley, bring me your overalls and underwear. Don't forget your Sunday clothes either."

It took a few minutes, but Charley eventually exited the back door of their place with his hands full of practically all the clothes he owned. "Ya think Sandy will do the clothes when we get hitched?" Charley plopped his clothes into the wash tub. "I hate washin' clothes."

Smiling, Mike and Doug glanced sideways at each other.

"When we get hitched?" Doug faced Charley, who was taking off the overalls he was wearing to add to the tub.

"We're all gonna be together, ain't we?"

"Yes, Charley, we're all gonna be together; but I'm the one gettin' hitched."

Charley stood in his underwear. "Is she gonna do the laundry?"

"I'm sure she will, Charley." Doug stirred the clothes in the tub with a wooden pole. "But I reckon you'll probably still help."

"Shoot." Charley pouted. "I hate washin' clothes."

"Charley, yer gonna have to help," Mike piped in. "No one would want to touch your clothes."

Doug snickered and looked at Charley, who got the joke and made a face at Mike.

"I'm goin' over to the creek."

"Yer not goin' over to the creek in your underwear." Doug scolded him. "You do this almost every week, and you know you can't run around town dressed like that."

Charley protested. "Mike showed his underpants in the middle of the street."

Mike grinned, remembering that episode earlier in the week.

"It's not the same thing, Charley." Doug added more Borax to the water. "Just sit over there and be ready to start runnin' these things through the wringer when they're ready."

"I hate washin' clothes." Continuing to grumble, Charley slumped into a weather-worn chair.

After a few minutes, Mike continued the conversation about the transport of the Amber Jack boulder. "So, if we can't cart the ore nugget by wagon, how are we going to get it where it needs to go?

"What did Harrison say?" Doug continued to stir the clothing.

"He's still thinking about it. He is trying to figure out a way by wagon…"

"Which isn't gonna work.

"So then, what's your bright idea, Mr. Smarty Britches?"

"Well, if it was my rock, I'd put it on a raft and float it down the Buffalo River. I think that would be the quickest and easiest way to get it to the train at Buffalo City."

"Float it down the Buffalo River on what? There's hardly enough water to float a dry leaf right now, much less a raft with a huge rock on it."

Doug grinned because his friend didn't have much foresight.

"Do you remember the story of Noah?" Doug scrubbed the clothes on the washboard.

"Sure I do."

"It rained for a long time, and then Noah was swallowed by a whale." Charley joined in the conversation.

"Charley, you're getting' your Bible stories mixed up again," Doug said.

"We will build a raft, secure the nugget to it and, when the river comes up, we'll hop on and pole it down the river," Doug said, as if it were a simple solution.

"But that could take months." Mike readied his own clothes for the tub.

"The loggers upriver have to wait for high water...I suppose you can, too. It's the only way, Mike. I'm sure Mr. Harrison will come to that conclusion also. I know you want to do it now, but several teams couldn't pull it over the hills." Doug took the clothes out of the tub and put them into the rinse water.

Mike dropped his clothes into the soapy water and began half-heartedly stirring them. His clothes-washing enthusiasm wasn't much higher than Charley's at this point. "Harrison's gonna help with the finances to transport it and get it where it needs to go, but I have to get it to Buffalo City. I'm not sure an ordinary raft of logs will float it."

"Charley, it's time to start wringin' the clothes now." After Doug directed Charley, he responded to Mike's statement. "An ordinary log raft probably would float it, but a ferry could do the job better."

Mike sounded confused. "There's not a ferry that goes down river."

"No," Doug said, "but about a mile upriver there's an old ferry lodged in some trees above the waterline. Three years ago the river flooded really high, and it broke loose and washed down the river from just above the town of Gilbert."

"Why didn't they come get it and take it back upriver?"

326

"A ferry is built to go across the river, not up it.

Mike thought for a moment to make sure he understood what Doug was saying.

"So, if we rescue what's left of the old ferry and repair it, we can use it to transport the rock. And, since the ferry is so bulky and heavy, we'll have to leave it downriver after we use it."

"By golly, I think he figured it out, don't you think, Charley?"

"I don't know...alls I know is that I hate washin' clothes." Charley continued to run the rinsed clothes through the wringer.

After scrubbing his clothes for a few minutes, Mike said, "I'm gonna need some help to get at that ferry."

Doug completed hanging all of his clothes on the rope clothesline. "You may have to pay for some help to get it down here, and it won't be easy; but I'll be glad to help you repair it."

"Guess I'll go talk to Mr. Harrison tomorrow and see what he thinks about the plan." Mike rinsed his own clothes. "And if this is what we're gonna do, I want you to be on that raft with me."

Doug smiled. "I would be hurt if you hadn't asked."

Mike rolled his clothes through the wringer, and Doug sat nearby with Charley, who was now watching a ladybug perched on the tip of his index finger.

"I wanted excitement in my life, and I certainly got it, didn't I?" Mike said. Doug chuckled. "You always have to be careful what you pray for."

As Mike rolled his last shirt through the wringer, a button fell to the ground. He reached down and picked it up then, holding it up, he turned toward Doug.

"Know how to sew on a button?"

"Didn't your momma teach you anything?" Doug shook his head.

***

Satisfied that infection was not setting in to Pam's finger, Doc Lipscomb allowed her to go home under the care

327

of May Bess. It was Sunday afternoon, and the short ride home was hot and humid. Although the bouncing of the carriage caused her finger to hurt, the ride stopped in front of her house within a few minutes of leaving the doctor's office. Harrison helped his daughter down from the carriage and into their home.

May Bess had Pam's bed ready for her and had made her favorite: potato soup with ham. As Jacob ushered his daughter to her room, Pam resisted.

"I've been lying down all week, Daddy. Can't I sit with you in the parlor while you read?"

Jacob glanced at May Bess, hoping she would encourage his daughter to go lie down. But, to his slight frustration, she did not. "I think it would be just fine if she sits up for a spell, providing she keeps her hand elevated."

"Alright," he said, "but only for a short while. You have to heal proper."

Pam slowly sat down in the padded rocking chair. "Doc said I was out of the woods. I'm just tired of being still."

"Well, you'll do what the doctor said."

May Bess had earlier heated water on the stove and now brought a cup of tea to her brother. She turned to Pam. "Would you like a cup?"

"No, thanks; I just want to sit here and think."

"By the way, Jacob," May Bess said, "I meant to ask you what you were doing down by the river a couple of days ago."

Harrison lowered his paper into his lap and turned to look at his sister. "It was business." He glanced at Pam then back at May Bess. "How did you know I was down by the river?" He resumed reading his paper, or at least tried to give that appearance.

"Well, you know I always take clean linens to the Morning Star Hotel on Friday evening, and, as I stood on the porch talking to Samson, I saw you ride down the road and turn the corner to go home."

"I told you it was just business." He turned a page.

May Bess walked back into the kitchen and, after a few moments, finished her thought. "I noticed you weren't alone either."

Harrison's jaw muscles tightened, and he stood quickly, holding his paper in one hand and picking up his cup of tea with the other. "I think I'll go sit on the front porch and read."

May Bess returned to the kitchen's entrance. She leaned against the door frame with her arms folded, watching her brother close the front door behind him.

Pam had a puzzled look on her face as she turned to her aunt.

"It won't be long before he'll be back inside." May Bess grinned. "It's hot as blazes out there. Guess he didn't feel much like talkin'."

"Who was with Daddy, Aunt May?" Pam was puzzled at what had just taken place.

"Well, I was shocked beyond measure after what had happened this week, but, as I live and breathe, I saw Michael ridin' along with him. They split company at the old rock smelter. Michael didn't notice me standin' on the hotel porch as he rode by. I would almost have sworn on a stack of Bibles that your daddy would never be caught dead around that boy without wringin' his neck. But there they were, just as plain as day, ridin' along beside each other."

Knowing how upset her father had been at Mike, Pam smiled. She remembered how her father had vowed to do bodily harm to Mike if he ever set eyes on him again. At that moment her world seemed a little brighter. It seemed that her finger wasn't the only hurt that was healing.

Pam stood. "I think I'll go lie down now."

May Bess followed her niece down the hallway and made sure she was comfortable in her bed. She brushed her hand across Pam's forehead to both push aside some of her hair and also to check for any sign of a fever. "I'll bring some soup in a while."

"Thank you, Aunt May." Pam closed her eyes and hoped she would dream of a certain boy who now was always on her mind.

***

Mike carried his wet clothes back to his place so that he could hang them on a makeshift clothesline he had strung up. He had attached one end of a rope to the roof support column on the corner of his porch and the other end to a sassafras tree not too far away. As he approached, he spotted Rosie sitting on the front porch of her store, so he decided to jabber with her a little. Walking up the steps with the bundle of his wet clothes in a cloth sack slung over his shoulder, he noticed she was fanning herself again with her paper Jesus fan. Her fat cat, Earl, was stretched out on the porch beside her, no doubt dreaming of catching birds.

"Hi, Rose." Mike slumped into a chair beside her.

"Laundry day, huh?"

"Every Sunday afternoon," he said, "but I'm gonna get my own bucket and roller and start doin' mine on Saturday. I don't like doin' my laundry on Sunday."

"I don't like doin' mine on any day of the week." Fanning herself, Rosie closed her eyes and continued to rock.

Mike rocked alongside her in an attempt to create a little breeze in the oppressive afternoon heat.

"What are you gonna do with your twenty percent of that zinc nugget?"

"Yer already countin' yer chickens, aren't ya?" Rosie continued to rock with her eyes closed.

"Yup, and all the eggs they're layin' too." Mike smiled.

"I still can't believe you got Harrison to help you get it to a collector. Last I heard he was ready to pinch your head off and tell God you had died."

Mike laughed at her expression. "I'm learning that, in some people, the desire for money can outweigh most other desires. I hoped the prospect of making some money and

330

being part of such a find would be the start of some fence mending between me and Mr. Harrison."

Rosie stopped rocking and looked over at her companion. A broad smile lit up her face. "Kid, yer not as dumb as you look."

With that, she let out a laugh that could probably be heard as far away as the next county. Mike joined her. *I love you too, Rosie.*

Chapter 31

Jim Smith was busy managing the wood pile at the Morning Star Mill when he spotted Mike approaching. He drove his axe into a piece of wood then arched his back for a stretch.

"Mornin', Jim."

Jim extended a hand. "Mornin', my young friend. Didn't know if I'd see much of you anymore. After last week, I figured you would probably go back home."

"Can't get rid of me that easy." Mike noticed all the other wood splitters watching him

"What's on your mind? Wouldn't want Harrison seein' me standin' out here lollygaggin' fer too long."

Mike got directly to the point. "Jim, would you like to make some extra money? I sure could use your help."

Jim looked at the other workers then back at Mike. "What exactly do you have in mind?"

"There's an old ferry stuck in the trees upriver a ways and I need to get it down here as soon as possible."

Jim tilted his head and scratched behind his ear.. "I've heard that ol' wreck is pretty much torn up and would take forever to get out of the trees. What do you want it for?"

Mike proceeded to tell Jim about the zinc boulder he discovered in his mine and the need to float it down the river to Buffalo City rather than haul it by wagon.

"Well, I see what yer after, but I'm not sure that old ferry is worth fixin' up."

"You just leave the fixin' up part to me. Of course the work will be in the evenings after you get off here and any other time you have."

"You're gonna need more help than me," Jim said. "Besides, I don't know if Harrison would like me workin' on the side, 'specially for you...no offense."

Mike just smiled. "Mr. Harrison won't mind. He's helping me get the specimen into the right hands once I get it downriver. I've just come from his office."

Jim was surprised at Mike's words and shook his head. "Well, I thought I'd heard everything."

"So, whadda ya say? I'll give you twenty-five cents an hour. You think you and three other men can get it out of the trees and down the river?"

"Well," Jim said, scratching his head again, "we can get it out of the trees; but we're gonna need some equipment, and there ain't no guarantee it will float once we do."

"I'll take care of the equipment you'll need, and right now nothin's gonna float in the river. You'll have to take a team along the gravel bars and drag it here for the most part."

Jim furrowed his brow. "It's not gonna be easy."

"But you think you can do it right?"

Jim thought for a moment, as if engineering the project in his head before answering. After a minute Jim shook his head. "Where there's a will, there's a way."

Mike smiled and the pair shook hands again.

"Just give me a day to round up some fellas and figure out what equipment we need, and I'll get back to you." Jim placed his gloves onto his hands.

"I'll be around," Mike said.

The pair parted and Mike headed back in the direction of the blacksmith shop.

***

Mike sat on his favorite barrel in Doug's shop. "I'll have the ferry movin' down the river in a few days. Now I have to figure out how to get that big rock out of the mine and ready to load."

Doug pounded with his hammer. "You're lucky you've got some large sycamore trees along the river bank in front of the mine entrance. You can probably use block and tackle to drag it out."

"Ya think the iron tracks along the mine floor will get in the way?"

333

As he placed his piece of work back into the glowing coals, Doug replied. "Actually, they might help."

Mike watched Doug work in silence, expecting him to finish his thought.

"You're gonna have to protect that rock to keep it in one piece when we move it. You don't want it to break. Maybe we can make some sort of slider to roll it onto and use the metal tracks to more easily scoot it outside. Getting it over the edge and onto the ferry will be another matter, but first things first."

"I don't know what I'd do without you." Mike complimented Doug.

"Well, let's just see if it works before you start pattin' me on the back."

Mike leaned to the rear of his oak barrel and watched his friend for a while. The familiar fragrance of the glowing cinders was comforting to him. He felt a little ashamed of himself for being so pessimistic and frustrated over the past few days. He knew himself better than that and had never been a quitter. He had always worked hard and had completed every task he'd set his mind to. He was glad he had a friend like Doug who was such an encouragement to him. Though it would be difficult, he knew he could get the zinc nugget downriver and, eventually, could establish a profitable, working mine.

"How's your shoulder feeling?" Doug finally broke the silence.

"It still hurts when I move it too much. Doc wants me to come by this afternoon for a look, but it seems to be healing just fine."

"That's good. You've got a lot of hard work ahead of you."

"I'll be ready for it." Mike moved his injured shoulder.

"By the way, when are you and Sandy going to tie the knot? I completely forgot yesterday to ask you about your plans."

"Well, she wants to wait until it cools down this fall, but I'd like to go ahead and have the ceremony next month and get it over with. All this planning is drivin' me crazy."

"How much planning is there to a weddin'?"

"Well, it's not gonna be fancy; but all the relatives have to have time to get here, and then you have to arrange for accommodations for everyone, and then there's the dinnerware, and the cake, and…"

"I get the picture." Mike held his hands up to his head, acting as if all of that information was causing his head to spin.

"You think Pam will want a big fancy wedding?"

Doug looked over at his friend. "I'm sure that when Pam is asked to marry, her mother will suddenly reappear and plan the biggest wedding of the year."

"That's certainly something to look forward to," Mike replied.

Doug slowly shook his head. "You're just itchin' to get yourself into trouble, aren't you?"

***

In the early afternoon, Charley walked from the livery stable toward his brother's forge. In his left hand he held a long stick, rattling it along the picket fence as he walked. In his other hand he held a box turtle, whose head and feet were tucked up inside its shell, with only its eyes peeking out through a narrow opening in its armor.

He rounded the corner and, passing the company store, stepped to the side of the dirt road to make way for a wagon coming up behind him. Rather than pass him the wagon pulled alongside Charley and slowed to match his pace.

"I swear, Charley, you always seem to have some sort of critter in your hand." .

Although he heard the familiar voice of Jay Finch, Charley didn't look at him but continued to walk.

"I'm talkin' to you, stupid."

Charley walked faster. "Leave me alone."

Jay pulled the wagon past Charley and turned his horses, blocking Charley's path. "You don't have to be in such a hurry."

Charley stopped and looked up at him, rubbing his big toes over each other in the dusty street, as Jay stepped down from the wagon and stood behind Charley to prevent his retreat.

"Look at me, Charley," Jay said. "Turn around and look at me."

Slowly, Charley turned to face Jay, afraid that something bad was about to happen to him.

"Charley, did you know that you did me a big favor last week?"

"I...I did?"

"Sure. Because of you, Jeeter is not a problem for me anymore, and I appreciate it."

Charley halfway grinned. "Okay, can I go now?"

"Not quite." Jay stepped up to Charley and began talking in a hushed tone. "I just wanted to make sure you didn't open your mouth again. You still know some things that could make trouble for me. You wouldn't say anything else, now would you Charley?"

"Like what?"

"Don't act so stupid, Charley. You know what I mean. Just keep your mouth shut and everything will be fine. Do you understand what I'm sayin? Even a retarded boy like you can understand what I'm tellin' ya."

Jay looked past Charley down the street and could see Doug standing in the doorway of his shop watching the pair. He quickly turned his attention back to Charley. "Just keep yer mouth shut and there won't be any trouble." Jay glanced at Doug again then climbed back into his wagon.

Charley watched as the wagon pulled away and down the road, causing a cloud of dust to be pushed around by the dry breeze. He dropped his stick and continued on his route, with the turtle still in his hand when he entered the blacksmith shop. Doug was drinking from his mason jar when Charley walked in. "What'cha got in your hand, Charley Boy?"

Charley walked over to his regular perch by the nail can and sat.

"Just a stupid ol' turtle."

"Turtles aren't stupid."

"Yes, they are," Charley said. "Alls they do is just walk around all day then hide in their shell when they're scared. And I'm stupid, too. Wish I had a shell."

Doug figured Charley's dismay was due to words he had probably just had with Jay.

"Charley, you're not stupid."

Charley sat quietly, not believing what Doug had said.

"Actually, turtles are quite smart," Doug began.

"How can turtles be smart?"

"Well, when you found that turtle which way was he walkin'?"

Charley seemed confused by the question.

"Was he walkin' uphill or downhill?"

Charley thought for a moment about where he'd found the turtle and what he'd been doing.

"He was beside the road walkin' up the side of the hill."

"See, that turtle was trying to tell us something."

"Turtles can't talk."

"No, but by their actions they tell us things, and that means they're not stupid."

Charley still didn't understand what his brother was trying to say.

"Charley, when turtles walk down the hill, they're looking for water, and it usually means there's going to be a dry spell. When you see them walking uphill, they know that rain is probably coming, and they want to get to high ground."

"Yer just makin' that up." Charley set his turtle down onto the dirt floor.

"No, I'm not. And by your actions, everyone in town can see that you're not stupid. You help people, you make people laugh, and you're nice to everyone. Now, how can someone like you be stupid?"

Charley looked at his turtle, which was beginning to poke its head out of the front of its shell to see if the coast was clear.

"Don't pay any attention to Jay," Doug continued. "He isn't nice to anyone, and his actions tell everyone that he loves only himself and is selfish. If anyone is stupid, it is Jay."

Charley had never heard his brother say much bad about anyone, so it surprised him to hear Doug call someone stupid.

"There's always going to be a bully around wherever you go. You just have to ignore what they say and go on with your life. Everyone loves you, Charley, and it's not worth making yourself upset over a few words from a bully."

Charley was comforted by his brother's words but thought about what he knew of Finch. It almost made him sick to his stomach knowing that Jay had been a part of killing someone up the river.

"I'm gonna let my turtle go now. If he's tryin' to get out of the rain that's comin', then I'll put him up on the hill behind the mill."

"You do that, Charley, but put your shoes on before you go walkin' around behind the mill."

Charley heard his brother but ignored the warning. He didn't like wearing shoes, and the only time he did was when it was cold or he attended church.

Doug sighed as he watched his brother exit into the sunlight. He thought about how difficult it was going to be after he married Sandy. He had a feeling there would be trouble down the road, though he hoped his feeling was wrong. He picked up his hammer and continued his work.

***

Early Tuesday morning Jay Finch harnessed the horse teams to the wagons for another day of hauling ore over the rough and dusty roads to the ferry at the White River. He could already hear the steam hissing from the boilers as they were readied to turn the gears and belts for yet another day of rock crushing and sorting. Although he could do the work with his eyes closed, he was having difficulty with the leather straps and cinches because he was distracted by the news of Mike's fortunate turn of events at the Red Rose Mine.

The anger and hatred inside him had swollen to that of a mighty river at flood stage. He didn't even understand it himself, but his mind was constantly focused on the interloper from Kingston and how he was going to get rid of him. Though he knew he would never have Pamela, he still had the burning desire to get rid of Mike. With the news of Mike and Harrison teaming to move the zinc rock down the river to Buffalo City, Jay had decided to stay on at the mill for a little while longer. He thought an opportunity to take care of the farm boy might present itself.

As he attached the horses to the wagons, his mind wandered back to his childhood. He recalled the day he had left home, years earlier, and the tears that his mother shed; he had promised to write often and come back for Christmas. Although his parents thought he was leaving for school in Chicago, Jay had other plans. Living under the strict discipline of his father, who was a minister, Jay had looked forward to the day he could leave and live his life the way he wanted to. Leaving for school was his excuse to shed the Christian values that his father had forced upon him. He didn't allow himself, however, to entertain the prospect that he had not managed his life like he had hoped.

"Haven't you finished that yet?"

Jay looked over his shoulder to see Larkin Riley clutching papers in his hands.

"Shut up, Riley," Jay snapped as he returned to his task, "I'm about done."

Riley thought about a harsh reply but realized that the days of truly managing Jay were over.

"Harrison wants to see you as soon as you are finished. He assumed you would be done by now, so I'm sure he expects you right away." Riley turned and walked away.

Jay didn't reply but continued his task. He didn't know what Harrison had in mind, and he loathed the thought of being Harrison's errand boy. Hopefully he would soon hear news from Raif about the still in Gilbert being completely taken out so that he could expand his territory and make all of his income from runnin' shine. If he didn't have a chance to get rid of Mike while he worked at the mill, he would figure something else out later...but it would certainly happen.

***

It was late Tuesday afternoon when Mike made his way up the Buffalo River to locate the old ferry. He wanted to see for himself the condition of the flat-topped boat. Because the forest was too dense in most places, he traveled the gravel bars along the riverbed.

At this point along the river's course, the riverbanks were further apart than they were in Kingston. He could see where the current usually flowed in the widened channel when the water was at its normal level. Now, because of the lack of spring rain, the Buffalo River had been reduced to nothing more than a shallow stream, with the exception of a few pools along the gravel riverbed.

As his horse splashed through the shoals, Mike noticed debris lodged high up in some of the towering sycamore trees growing along the river's edge. The clusters of sticks, leaves, and limbs told the story of how high the water had been during the last flood. Some of the older trees leaned precariously over the water, the dirt support at their roots having been washed away during the last few years of heavy rains and water flow. Most of the root structure under the tilted trees could be seen protruding from the riverbank,

340

displaying a tangled part of the tree never seen above ground.

Mike continually peered into the growth along the bank, looking for the old ferry. His friend Doug had told him that the boat was lodged between some trees next to a small, rock bluff. He hoped he hadn't missed seeing it because of the density of the undergrowth.

He came to a pool of water that was too deep for his horse, so he directed him up onto a gravel bar next to the water. He didn't think he had come far enough, so he stopped Rusty and peered deeply into the forest. While Mike didn't see the ferry, he took a moment to listen to the sounds around him. As the breeze waxed and waned through the leaves along the Buffalo, it played a familiar tune. Birds sang and called for each other, and Mike was comforted by the riffles of water tumbling over the rocks in the river beside him. He noticed vultures further up the river circling in an updraft of hot air, probably above something dead in the woods or along the riverbank. Mike closed his eyes and allowed the sounds to conjure the memories of his youth.

Suddenly, he was aware of someone coming up the river from behind him. The loud crunching of the gravel announced Jim Smith and a couple of his friends riding in his direction. Mike smiled and waved as the trio clambered to the top of the gravel bar alongside him.

"You lost?" Jim said jokingly.

"Just soaking up the sights."

Jim introduced his friends to Mike and they all shook hands.

"Well, we have only a few hours of daylight left, so I expect we should get movin'." Jim wasn't wasting any time.

Mike looked up the river. "How much further is it?"

"Almost there," Jim said. He and his fellow workers began moving again.

Mike was pleased with their eagerness, and he joined the group.

They had only traveled another hundred yards before Jim left the riverbed and tied his horse to a willow next to the tree line. As Mike followed, peering into the shaded tangle of trees and vines, he finally saw the old ferry—cracked in places and securely wedged. He stopped his horse along with the others and made the trek uphill to the flat-topped, wooden boat.

"You sure you want this down the river?" Jim and his group looked on.

Mike stared at the wreck and didn't see how it could be repaired to float the river again, much less carry the weight of his zinc boulder and four people. Mike scratched his head and looked at the other fellows. "Well, Doug said he thought it was still useful."

"Oh, it's useful alright," one of the other men said." I could use the wood from it to cook my meals on for the next few months."

They all chuckled, but Jim quickly brought them back to the task at hand.

"First we're gonna have to cut away all of the trees around it and those blockin' our way down to the river." Jim walked slowly around the ferry. "I expect we can use the logs as rollers to get it to the gravel."

Mike folded his arms across his chest and watched Jim peer under and around the wreck.

"Think it will come out in one piece?"

"Well, actually," Jim began, "it looks like it's already in two pieces. There's a crack across the middle, and the beams underneath are cracked also."

"Them metal supports and straps are mighty rusted, too," one of the other men piped in. "Looks like it was about ready for the scrap heap anyway. No wonder they didn't come lookin' fer it."

Mike looked dejected after that comment and continued to watch Jim, desperate for some sign of hope.

While Mike remained silent, Jim and the others continued to inspect the old ferry.

Looking up and seeing the disappointment on Mike's face, Jim finally spoke. "If you still want it back to Rush, I think we can get it there. I hope you and Doug can get it to work fer ya."

Jim grabbed a heavy limb that had lodged on top of the ferry's deck. He couldn't drag it off like he had intended, so he let the limb clunk back onto the wooden surface. "Before we move it, we'll strap the two halves together to keep it in one piece."

Mike let out the breath he was holding, hearing at least some encouragement from Jim.

"Do you hear that?" One of the men sounded serious.

"Hear what?" Mike asked.

Suddenly, one of them let out a holler and slapped at his arm. In an instant the group was surrounded by hornets, which had been agitated by the disturbance of the tree limb and were angry at the intrusion.

"Head to the river!" Jim scrambled down the riverbank and toward the water.

Mike was already on his way, swatting at the flying black insects with his hat. He stumbled over a root, and, at the same instant, felt a searing pain as he was stung between his shoulder blades. One of the other men had also stumbled and rolled past him down the incline. The vines and small trees had no effect on his tumble. The group reached the gravel bar battered, bruised, and stung. They continued to flap their hats in the air and run until the hornets gave up their chase and returned to their nest.

While the men stood in the shallow water, the excitement finally over, they all caught their breaths and examined themselves .Jim still panted. "Didn't expect that."

"I got hit twice." Mike rubbed his right thigh and felt the burn in the middle of his back.

Jim looked over at one of his friends and saw that the side of his face was beginning to swell from a sting on the neck.

"Looks like I better get Levi back to town. Side of his face is swellin' up like a watermelon."

They all looked at Levi, who was splashing cool water on the side of his neck. Though there was pain, the

343

group had a good chuckle at themselves as they walked cautiously back to their horses on the gravel bar. They were glad no one else had seen them as they ran, flailing their arms in the air like a bunch of crazy people.

"Guess we'll get started tomorrow." Jim mounted his horse. "I'll bring some coal oil to douse that nest with. Hopefully no one else will get bit."

"I'll bring the can of fuel to you tomorrow afternoon at the wood pile," Mike said. "Remember, I'm payin' for this. I'll also get whatever tools you need."

"You're the boss." Jim smiled and the group turned their horses, heading back down the river toward Rush.

***

Mike tied Rusty to the railing outside Pam's house. He couldn't believe he was standing at the foot of the steps, knowing how Harrison felt about him. Even though he knew he would probably be turned away, he had to try.

Slowly, he walked up the wooden steps and stood in front of the doorway. He swallowed hard and, once again, asked himself if he should be standing there or if he should turn and go home. After wrestling with his choices for a few seconds more, he raised his hand and knocked on the door. He didn't hear any footsteps from inside, so he knocked again with more force.

This time, he finally heard someone coming to answer the knock. He cleared his throat and removed his hat from his head. He heard the turning of the brass doorknob, and the door slowly opened, revealing the silhouette of a woman rather than Jacob Harrison.

"Evening, May Bess." Mike greeted her as she now stood in full view.

"Well, Mike Gilbert, I'm surprised to see you at my door. What brings you here tonight?" *As if I didn't know.*

Mike glanced past her, not to catch a glimpse of Pam, but to see if Mr. Harrison was already on his way to escort Mike off his front porch.

"I just thought I'd stop by to see how Pamela is doin'." Mike fidgeted with his hat in his hands.

"Oh, she's doing just fine, Michael. Would you like to come inside?"

Mike panicked at the invitation. "I'm not sure Mr. Harrison would…"

"My brother isn't here right now," May Bess interrupted. "I'd be glad to go get Pamela for you."

May Bess knew that inviting Mike inside would invoke the wrath of her brother, but, since he was in Buffalo City until the next day, she decided to tempt fate.

Mike didn't move toward the door but stood in the fading evening light.

"I'd surely like to see her, May Bess, but I don't think I should come inside with Mr. Harrison gone."May Bess was impressed with Mike's manners but knew he desired with all his heart to see Pam.

"I can have Pam come sit on the porch with you, if you like," May Bess said.

"Ma'am, I'd probably best be going. I just stopped to see how Pam is. I don't want to cause anyone problems."

May Bess smiled at Mike as he placed his hat back onto his head and headed back toward Rusty.

"I'll tell Pamela you stopped by, Michael."

"You won't find a boy like that in the big city," May Bess smiled and mumbled as she closed the front door.

Mike headed to the corral behind Doug's place and put Rusty up for the night. The late evening air was still and heavy with dampness. The crickets and tree frogs began their night songs as Mike finished a good brushing of his horse and supplied him with a bucket of oats.

Just as he had completed his task, he heard what sounded like the distant rumble of thunder. He stopped in his tracks to listen again. Standing quietly, he heard the sound again and realized that it was, indeed, thunder, and it was coming from the west. He grew excited at the prospect of rain and the hope that the unusual dry spell was finally going to be over.

Chapter 32

It took Jim and his crew three evenings and all day Saturday to remove the old ferry from the riverbank and drag it through the shoals downriver with a team of mules. Although it was cracked and buckled in the middle, Jim was pleased to get it shuttled in one piece. There had been some rain during the week, but not enough to help with the move. Nonetheless, the crippled ferry was finally tied to an old maple tree by the water's edge where Rush Creek emptied into the Buffalo River.

Mike had worked along with Jim as much as possible, but mostly ran errands for supplies needed with the move. His money supply was dwindling, and he hoped soon to have his zinc boulder downriver and into the hands of a collector. He also knew he would need to start working his mine soon to create income, but that would have to wait.

***

It was almost dark on Saturday evening when Jacob Harrison emerged from Dr. Lipscomb's office in time to see Mike and his hired hands lumber into town. He had just picked up what he hoped was the last of the medication his daughter would need since losing part of her finger. Though he still harbored anger over the incident and over losing the Red Rose, he couldn't help but be impressed with Mike for his tenacity. He certainly wouldn't express his hidden feelings to anyone, but, to himself, he acknowledged that he saw some of himself in Mike.

He watched as Mike and the others separated to retreat to their homes but noticed Mike directing his horse up the lane toward him. As Mike drew nearer, Harrison caught his attention and waved him over. The old dry wood creaked when Harrison sat down on the top step of the porch. He pulled his pipe from his shirt pocket and began cleaning it, readying it for a new fill of tobacco.

Mike stopped in front of Harrison and remained on his horse.

"Evenin', Mr. Harrison." Mike reached for the canteen hanging on his saddle.

"How's the move comin'?" Harrison poked shredded tobacco into the bowl of his pipe.

"Ferry's tied up down by the creek. Now I've just got to get her fixed up good enough for one more trip."

The evening air was heavy with tension between the two as Harrison struck a match and placed it into his pipe. The puffs of blue-gray smoke hung in the air as he lit it then removed it from his lips.

Harrison stood. "How long do you think it will take to have it ready?"

Mike paused for a moment before he answered, because he really had no idea; but he knew he needed to give a man like Harrison a deadline.

"Shouldn't be more than a week...or so," Mike said with confidence.

"Just get it done, Gilbert." Harrison walked up to Mike. "The sooner the better. I've already contacted people who are anxious for it."

"I'll start work on it Monday," Mike said. "Doug will work with me as much as he can. I know I'll need some metal work for bracing."

Harrison nodded his head in agreement and, without saying goodbye, turned from Mike and walked away toward his house, puffing on his pipe. His smoke hung in the evening air like that belching from the stack of a train.

As Harrison walked into the darkness, Mike nudged his horse and continued to Doug's house.

***

Monday morning Mike stood beside the crippled old ferry along the river bank. It was his now, and he had no time to waste in getting it repaired. Although he had no experience with boats, according to Jim, after proper repairs,

347

it should float just fine. The trick would be getting it to hold together for the twenty-five-mile trip downriver.

He unfolded his wooden ruler and stretched it out across the flat wooden hull and took measurements. Mike worked all morning measuring and making sketches of the damage. He hoped Doug could understand his drawings enough to make the necessary parts, and he also prayed that the repairs would go quickly. He knew Harrison was anxious to get the zinc boulder to his contacts.

After his drawings and measurements were complete, he walked along the river's edge to his mine. He knew this would be another challenge. Repairing the old ferry was one thing; getting it to float and remain stable with the incredible weight of his rock was another.

At the entrance to his mine, standing among all the rubble of the cave-in, Mike lit his lantern. With the flame burning steadily, he peered into the abyss in front of him, took a deep breath, and walked into the cavern.

***

Rosie was taking inventory of her overalls supply when the front door of her store opened. She had been interrupted several times already since the morning had begun and needed to get her order placed. Bracing herself for yet another intrusion of her time, she looked up from her counter with an agitated look on her face. Instantly, however, her solemn expression exploded into excitement.

"Lord have mercy, I can't believe yer finally out and about!" Rosie watched Pamela and May Bess enter her store.

"I figured it was way past time for some sun and fresh air." Pam and Rosie met in the middle of the wooden floor with a long, warm hug.

"You look fit as a fiddle, sweetie. How's that hand feelin'?" Rosie looked at Pam's hand, which was still bandaged and resting in a sling.

Pam glanced down at her hand then back up at Rosie. "Now, it only hurts when I bump it."

"Then I reckon you best not bump it." Rosie chuckled.

Rosie switched her attention to Pamela's aunt. "May Bess, I'm so glad you got this child back out into the world."

"I would have had her out sooner, but her father has been making such a fuss over her. I practically had to threaten him to finally let her out today. And I received a gentle threat from him if anything should happen."

"Oh, pish." Rosie motioned the pair to follow her into the grocery side of the store so the trio could sit at a table.

"Beth, could you squeeze a few of those lemons and make us some lemonade?"

"Oh, don't go to the bother," May Bess replied.

"No bother at all." Rosie glanced over at Beth, who was behind the counter hauling an armload of inventory into the store room.

"It's no bother at all." Agreeing, Beth disappeared through the doorway into the storage room. There was a pause, and they heard Beth drop the crate onto the wooden floor.

She re-emerged, pushing her hair back out of her face. "The only problem is that it would take a while. . I'd have to head up to Yellville for some more lemons; seems we're completely out."

Rosie registered a look of frustration. "I thought we had a basket of lemons under the counter."

"We did, but some of them were bad. I had to throw them out yesterday. Looks like the rest of them went bad overnight. This heat is causing problems with some of our food." Beth sounded frustrated herself.

"Well." Rosie turned back to Pam and May Bess. "Guess its tea, then."

"It's okay, Rosie; we can't stay long. We were just out and about, and I was hoping..." Pam paused for a moment.

Rosie grinned because she could have finished Pam's sentence. Rosie looked up at May Bess and caught a slight smile on her face also.

Rosie looked back at Pam. "Mike's down by the river. He stopped by this morning to get a measuring stick and a couple of pencils."

Pam's cheeks blushed at Rosie's words. There was another pause at the table.

"He's been awful worried about you this past week," Rosie said tenderly. That was not a tone Rosie often used.

"Her father still…" May Bess began.

"Her father is stubborn as an old mule, that's what he is!" Rosie interrupted May Bess.

Pam and May Bess laughed at their expressive friend, and it gave Pam comfort to know she had another ally in her corner.

"Pardon my language," Rosie continued, "but that ol' coot has the brains of a squash beetle. He's as blind as a bat and wouldn't know a good thing if it came up to him and bit him in the…"

At that moment, the front door opened and Rosie didn't complete her rant.

"We have to go." May Bess stood. "We have one other stop to make before we head back home."

Pam and Rosie stood along with May Bess.

"I'll let Mike know you were in." Rosie winked at Pam and turned to walk to her customer.

Pam let out a small giggle and looked at her aunt. "What would we ever do without Rosie?"

"This world would be a little less exciting without her, that's for sure," May Bess said.

The pair said their goodbyes to Beth, who was still struggling with heavy wooden crates. They left the store and paused on the top step, looking out into the midmorning activity. Pam felt the brush of something soft and furry on her legs. She looked down and saw Earl affectionately rubbing against her.

"And the world would not be the same without you either, Earl." Pam reached down and petted Earl, rewarded by his contented purring.

After a moment of kitty lovin', the pair walked down the steps and climbed into their parked buggy. With a quick flip of the reins, they began rolling down the dirt street, leaving Earl on the top step of the wooden porch longing for more attention.

***

Jacob Harrison found Jason Finch in the company work shed replacing a handle on one of the picks that the miners used. The old hickory handle had finally splintered in two after many hours of rugged use, and the tool had slightly injured the user when it had broken. Finch was hammering on the wooden wedge securing the iron head into the end of the handle when he caught Harrison out of the corner of his eye.

"Mornin', Mr. Harrison." Finch mumbled and kept his head down, continuing his work.

Harrison leaned against a nearby work table and watched for a moment before finally addressing Jay.

"You're pretty good with your hands, aren't you?"

Finch thought it strange for Harrison to begin a conversation with him in this manner. Usually Harrison barked orders at Jay, and that was about the extent of their conversations.

Jay continued pounding at the wooden wedge. "Yes, sir, I can usually figure out how to fix most things, I reckon."

Harrison took another puff of his pipe as he watched Jay complete his task.

"I need you to do something for me," Harrison said abruptly.

Wonderful. I wonder where he wants me to drive a wagon to today. Jay slowly placed the repaired tool onto the work table and looked at Harrison.

"Mike Gilbert is repairing an old ferry down on the river to float a sizable chunk of zinc down to Buffalo City. I have an interest in this project, and I'm anxious to get it downriver." Harrison crossed his arms in front of him.

Jay felt a sensation of dread flow instantly through his body. Afraid of what was coming next from Harrison, he

351

had a sick feeling in the pit of his stomach. He remained silent and solemnly looked at his boss.

Harrison removed his pipe from his lips and finished his thought. "Since you're pretty good with your hands, I need you to help Gilbert make the repairs on that old ferry. Two pairs of hands are better than one, and I need that zinc down to Buffalo City as soon as possible. I also need…"

"Mr. Harrison, don't ask me to go down there and work with that sod buster." Finch quickly interrupted.

"I'm not exactly askin' you, Finch," Harrison quickly said in a stern tone. "I'm tellin' you that I need you to get that ferry in the water within a week."

Jay looked down at the ground with disinterest.

"And to finish what I was sayin', I also want you on that ferry to keep an eye on things and help get it safely down the river."

Jay's body grew rigid with anger as his words instantly flew at Harrison. "I don't exactly like that boy. Me and him don't see eye to eye on things, and if you ask me…"

"I don't believe I asked you. I need you to get that ferry fixed and down the river. I stand to make a lot of money on this and don't want anything to happen to it."

Finch's face flamed red, and his anger was apparent to Harrison.

"Gilbert is down by the river working on the ferry. I need you to finish what you're doin' and get down there as soon as you can. I also want you to report to me daily on the progress. Am I clear?"

Finch paused for a long moment, contemplating Harrison's directive, and the words of resignation were on the tip of his tongue. But then it struck him as plainly as seeing the sun rise over the trees: this could possibly be the opportunity he had been waiting for. His mind raced ahead and realized that this might be his chance to finally get rid of Mike.

He continued to look solemn as he gazed at Jacob Harrison, who was awaiting a reply from him. "Clear as spring water."

Harrison smiled and stood to leave the building. "Good. I knew you'd see it my way."

"I'll help all I can." Finch continued acting as if the task was an imposition.

Harrison placed his pipe back between his teeth and left puffs of smoke lingering in the air as he walked back into the morning sunlight. Jay watched until Harrison was out of sight. A grin appeared on his face as he began making plans for their trip down the river. He didn't know how he would do it, but he had at least a week to hone his plan. However it happened, he would finally get rid of the farm boy from Madison County.

Chapter 33

A gray heron fished beside the Buffalo River as Mike leaned against the wooden edge of his disabled ferry. He observed the bird for a while as it solemnly stood on its long legs at the edge of the shallow, running water. As Mike watched, he remembered studying countless herons along the Kings River back home; he had learned that they get their meals by being patient, not by rushing into the water. Unlike the heron, patience was not one of Mike's virtues, and he knew it. He knew that if he were a bird, he would be more like the noisy kingfisher, which flew above the surface of the water and dove suddenly into the stream to retrieve a minnow. Sometimes the kingfisher came up without a meal, but when the heron waited until just the right moment, he would plunge his long neck quickly down into the water and find his target.

Mike smiled when the heron he was watching took a couple of minnows from the clear water then unfolded his long wings to fly downstream and find another fishing spot.

A voice spoke from behind Mike. "That boat ain't gonna get fixed as long as you're daydreamin'."

Mike was startled out of his trance and turned quickly to see Jay Finch riding up to him. Instantly, his emotions changed from placid to angry.

"I'm not daydreamin', Jay." Mike turned back to the river. "Besides, it's none of your business anyway."

Jay stopped his horse and tethered it to a bush next to the dirt road. Then he walked up to Mike.

"Well, you're wrong about that."

Mike turned his head toward Jay again and looked at him inquisitively. "What do you mean?"

Jay gazed at the old ferry, which was perched on a gravel bar next to the river bank. Without a word, Mike watched Jay crouch to his knees and inspect the boat's underside.

"Ol' man Harrison told me this morning that he wants me to help you put this broken bucket back together." Jay stood and continued looking at the dried and bleached wood.

"I don't need your help."

Jay smirked. "Harrison seems to think you do."

"I'll have this boat ready to go within a couple of weeks." Mike walked over to Jay and crowded his space.

Jay looked at the anger in Mike's eyes and realized it was time for him to put his plan into action. He took a step backwards and looked down.

"Look, Gilbert, I know you don't cotton to me…but what do ya say we put the past behind us and start all over?"

Mike narrowed his eyes at Jay—caught off guard for a moment by his words of submission.

"When I was young, I raised a possum from a baby." Mike began. "I fed it, took care of it, and thought it was quite tame. It would follow me around everywhere, and I really loved that animal. One day, though, it turned on me and bit the fool out of my hand. After it turned on me the second time, my father got rid of it."

Jay chuckled at Mike's story. "What's that got to do with anything?"

"You can't take the wild out of an animal, and you can't take the mean out of you." Mike looked into Jay's eyes.

Jay's pulse quickened, because he would have loved nothing more than to knock Mike to the ground; but he held his temper because of his plan. Jay slowly walked to the water's edge and picked up a small flat rock from the gravel at his feet. He flung the rock across the surface of the water and made it skip to the other side of the river.

"Look, Gilbert, I've said some rotten things to you, and I'm sorry." Jay turned back to Mike. "We kinda got off on the wrong foot, but let's make Harrison happy and get this boat fixed and into the water."

Mike was still completely skeptical about Jay's sudden reform, but he realized that he could use someone's help, and if Harrison requested Jay to help him, then he would probably have to at least give it a try. He had a feeling, however, that Jay's words couldn't be trusted.

"I need to talk to Harrison about this." Mike leaned back onto the boat with his arms folded across his chest.

"Talk all you want," Jay said as he walked back to his horse. "You're gonna need my help for sure though...Harrison wants this thing fixed and ready to float by the end of the week."

"End of the week?"

Jay mounted his horse. "That's what he told me. I'm sure he'll fill you in with all the details when you talk to him."

Mike stood speechless at the news.

"I'll be here at the crack of dawn." Jay turned his horse and headed back up the road.

As soon as Jay was out of sight, Mike picked up a piece of driftwood and smacked the old ferry as hard as he could a couple of times then hurled the piece of wood out into the slow-flowing water of the river. He placed his hands on his hips and glared out over the water. He couldn't believe Harrison had ordered Jay, of all people, to help him with the ferry. He grabbed his hat from his head and was about to slam it down to the ground in anger when he caught himself and realized that he needed to settle down.

He leaned back onto the boat and closed his eyes, tilted his head back, and asked God to calm him and help him figure out what do to. He didn't trust Jay, and he even questioned God about this situation. He opened his eyes and looked back out over the water. He had reined in his emotions some but knew he needed to pay Mr. Harrison a visit about this new deal. Mike picked up his measuring stick and the list of materials needed to begin repairs on his boat. He placed them into his saddle bag and took one last look out onto the Buffalo River. He then mounted his horse and rode back into town. He would first go to Rosie's and Doug's to procure materials and place an order for the iron braces then go to the mill for the needed lumber, which was stored there. After making those arrangements, he would pay a visit to Mr. Harrison. It wouldn't be a social call as he had planned. No, he had serious business to take care of with Jacob Harrison. He didn't know if he could change Harrison's mind, but he was sure going to try.

***

After Mike had loaded the lumber he needed onto a spare Morning Star wagon, he quickly made his way to the mill office. Along the way he spotted Larkin Riley.

"Is Mr. Harrison in his office?" Mike yelled over the noise of the machinery.

"He went home a little early."

Mike left the mill and walked the short distance to Harrison's house. Although he was still upset with Harrison's arrangement, he couldn't help but think about Pam and his desire to talk with her. It had been so long, and his heart ached for her presence.

With confidence, he walked up the steps but hesitated for a few moments at the front door. He took a deep breath and pulled his shoulders back to make sure he was standing straight. Finally, he raised his hand and knocked on the door. Within seconds, the door creaked open and Harrison stood on the other side of the threshold.

"Gilbert, I had a feeling I would be seeing you today."

"Could I speak with you for a moment?" Mike backed into the middle of the front porch.

Harrison stepped out onto the landing with Mike and closed the door behind him.

"Why don't we have a seat?" Harrison motioned toward the wooden chairs at one end of the porch.

The pair sat and there was a moment of silence.

"You had something you wanted to talk to me about?" Harrison finally broke the silence.

"With all due respect, Mr. Harrison, why Jay Finch?"

Harrison grinned at Mike's getting down to business so abruptly.

"Finch is the only man I can spare right now. Besides, he's good with his hands, and in business you use any tool you can to get things done quickly. You can't waste any time. Even though I don't put much stock in him, personally, I think he can help you get that boat ready to float by the end of the week."

"Surely, there's someone else...anyone else besides Finch."

"Look, son..." Harrison began.

Son? Mike didn't like being called that by someone who was probably using it in a derogatory manner.

"We made a deal to get this rock down to Buffalo City and into the hands of my collectors, didn't we?" Harrison leaned forward, resting his elbows on his knees.

"Yes," Mike agreed. "But you've made the decision to send Finch to help me, and I don't like that."

Looking down at the dusty boards under his feet, Harrison grinned. "Sometimes, to get business done, we have to do things we don't like." Jacob turned his gaze toward Mike. "You just need to trust me on this one."

Mike sat silent for a moment, breaking his gaze with Harrison and looking out across Harrison's front yard and into town.

"I trust you, Mr. Harrison, but I don't know if I can work with Finch. It's Finch I don't trust."

Harrison leaned back into his chair and there was another quiet moment. "There's something else you need to know," Harrison said.

Mike looked at Harrison with the feeling you get just before something heavy you dropped lands on your foot.

"I told Finch I wanted him to go with you on the ferry to get the rock down to the landing at Buffalo City."

Mike stood quickly. "I don't need him on that boat. I can manage just fine."

"Have you ever been down the Buffalo to the White River?"

Mike hesitated for a second. "No…but I don't reckon I'll have a problem with it."

"Finch has been down that section a few times and knows the river well. You'll need four people to pole it for the twenty-five-mile trip, and he knows where the shoals are. You run that boat onto a gravel bar and you could be stuck for a long time."

Mike knew Harrison was right but still didn't want to have Jay on board. Reluctantly, he sat back down and thought for a moment. His jaw muscles tensed as he forced himself to control his anger.

"Mike, yer a good kid and, for some reason, I'm beginning to like you; but I have a vested interest in this, and I believe that Jay needs to help you get this rock down to Buffalo City. We stand to make a lot of money on this deal; after that, you're on your own."

Mike was silent again as he chewed on Harrison's words. He realized he had lost the battle and there was no way to change Jacob's mind.

"Mr. Harrison, I'll respect your decision, but I want you to know I don't like it one bit." Mike looked into Harrison's eyes.

"I wish I had a dime for every time I had to do something I didn't like." Harrison spoke solemnly as if reviewing his life.

Mike was about to excuse himself from their discussion when a surrey rolled up to the front porch. Mike saw Pam in the seat next to May Bess. He was immediately nervous with Jacob Harrison next to him on the porch. Without thinking, he quickly walked off the porch and helped May Bess down to the ground. Then, without missing a beat, he rounded the surrey and gently held out his hand to help Pam down.

At this action, Jacob Harrison stood and, in the same instant, caught the scolding eyes of May Bess. With their business concluded, he wanted to intervene and send the boy home. Without understanding why, he allowed the glare from his sister to halt his action.

Pam smiled incredibly as she took Mike's hand and allowed him to help her down from the coach. When she was on the ground beside Mike, he released her hand and walked with her to the steps of the porch. He stopped as she continued up the steps to the landing.

"I trust you have the materials you need to repair the ferry?" Harrison looked down at Mike.

Mike took his eyes from Pam and looked at Jacob Harrison.

"Yes, sir, everything's in the wagon."

"Then you'd better get a good night's sleep. You have a busy week ahead of you." Harrison briskly turned to usher his daughter into the house.

"Goodnight then, Mr. Harrison; goodnight, May Bess." Mike removed his hat.

"Goodnight, Michael," Pam said, with a smile that would melt butter.

"Miss Pamela." Mike nodded slightly in her direction.

Jacob remained on the porch for a moment after the ladies had entered the house.

"I don't mind puttin' your horse up for you," Mike said.

"Obliged, Gilbert." Harrison turned to walk into the house.

Mike watched Harrison close the door behind him. He stood there for a moment, patting the horse on the neck until he saw lamplight spring to life from behind curtains in the house. He grabbed the reins and led the horse and buggy to the back of the dwelling. His few seconds with Pam had temporarily erased the frustration he had felt earlier. He knew he had a difficult week ahead of him, but his moments with the girl he dreamed about and the touch of her hand had reenergized his heart. Life was good.

***

360

Mike awoke early Thursday morning to the sound of raindrops landing on his roof. Light rain had fallen the last couple of days during the week, hopefully signaling the end of the drought. But as Mike lay in his bed, he prayed that if there were going to be heavy rain it would hold off until the job was finished. He needed to get the ferry repaired and the zinc boulder loaded before the river rose. He was thankful that, due to the parched earth selfishly hoarding what little moisture was falling onto it, the river level had not yet seen a change.

With the darkness of the morning still around him, he thought about how the repairs to the battered ferry were going better than he had anticipated. Even his friend Doug was surprised that the old boat seemed to be looking like it was more than barely floatable. Also, he had been astounded at how well he and Finch had been able to work together. So far, barely a cross word had flown between them during the repairs. He couldn't understand why the sudden change of heart with Jay, but there was something inside him that doubted Jay's miraculous turnaround. He was working with one eye on the job and the other on Jay at all times. Though things seemed to be going well with him, he would not completely trust Jay Finch.

He got up and had his breakfast, hoping to find Doug at his forge heating up his coals for yet another day of work. Most of the wood repairs had already been made to the ferry, and Mike hoped Doug had been able to complete the metal strapping for the needed supports. Once those were in place, the ferry could be moved to the edge of the water in front of the Red Rose Mine, and the zinc boulder could be loaded.

Mike placed his hat on his head and closed the door behind him as he finished chewing the last bite of his breakfast. He bounced down the steps and onto the pathway that led to the street. The sky was beginning to lighten a bit, even though the clouds were obscuring the rising sun, and the light rain had stopped falling. He flipped his collar up as a barricade to the cool breeze blowing down his neck. Quickly he made his way to Doug's shop and, sure enough,

361

he could hear the bellows being pumped, heating up the recently lit coals.

"You're up early," Doug said as Mike entered.

"The rain sounded so good on the roof I couldn't stay in bed any longer."

"I hope our dry spell is over. I've got to plant some of the seeds over again in my garden." Doug continued to work on his fire.

Mike sat on his favorite barrel. "I didn't know you're a gardener."

"I'm not really; I just plant the seeds. Charley's good at growing things, but, if I gave the seeds to him, who knows where things would be coming up."

Mike laughed as he pictured the thought.

"Besides giving Charley something to do, it's nice to have some homegrown vegetables in the summer. There's nothin' like pickin' a ripe tomato off the vine and popping it in yer mouth."

That prompted Mike to remember the large garden his family always grew. He thought of the many hours in the hot sun pulling weeds when he wasn't working on fencing or working with the animals. There was always something to do on the farm. Even though he hated doing the garden work, he remembered how wonderful the vegetables tasted in the middle of the winter when his mother would open a jar of beans or corn she had preserved.

"By the way," Doug interrupted Mike's memories, "I have those metal braces ready for you. They're over there in the corner next to those spikes."

"Those spikes aren't mine, are they?" Mike made his way over to his order.

"Yeah. I realized that you needed something bigger than just nails to hold those braces on. You're going to be hauling a heavy load, and you sure don't want those metal straps to come loose."

"No, I don't suppose I do." He examined the metal spikes that Doug had fashioned.

Mike dropped the spikes back onto the dirt floor beside his braces and walked back to the barrel. "I've been meaning to ask you something."

Doug looked up at Mike as if to say, "What's that?"

"You still think you want to be on that boat with me? The water will be flowing at a pretty good pace, and I don't want to get stuck on a shoal somewhere. Still wanna help?"

Doug looked at his friend and smiled. "Sure. Actually, I was wondering if you were even going to ask me again. I was planning on reminding you."

"I've just had so much on my mind this week, and I've been so busy, that I hadn't gotten around to seriously asking you."

"You said a couple...do you have anyone else in mind?"

"Well..." Mike began slowly.

"How about Charley," Doug said without hesitation.

"Charley? Are you sure he could handle something like that?"

"Charley may act like a nine-year-old, but he's strong and won't have any problem poling down the river." Doug pumped more air into the coals.

"One other thing, though."

He got that look again from Doug.

"I need four people on the ferry, one at each corner."

"So who's the fourth?"

"Well, you know that Harrison has Finch working with me to repair the ferry."

"I'm afraid I know where this is going." Doug placed his first project into the glowing coals.

"Yeah, well, Harrison insists on Finch taking the ferry down the river, too. He claims Finch knows the river channels so well that we won't get grounded on a gravel bar somewhere and lose the rock in the current."

"That might change things. You know how he is and how he treats Charley. I'd be tempted to throw him into the river, I'm sure. That boy's no good."

"Doug, I really could use your help." Mike stood from his seat.

The room was silent, with the exception of the crackling sound made by the burning coals.

"I can find someone to take Charley's place."

"Cain't nobody take my place."

Mike turned in time to see Charley bound into the room with a smile on his face.

"Hey, Charley," Mike said.

"What you guys talkin' about?" Charley walked barefooted up to the pair.

Mike and Doug looked at each other to see who would answer Charley.

"Well," Mike said, "I was just askin' your brother if he could help me pole that ferry down the river to Buffalo City whenever the river gets up high enough."

"Can I come too?"

"That's what we were just talkin' about," Doug said. He removed the hot piece of metal from the coals with a heavy pair of tongs.

Charley placed an even bigger smile on his face. "Yahoo!" Charley yelped, lifting one of his arms into the air.

"Charley," Doug continued, "I said we were talking about it; but I'm not sure you should go."

The elation suddenly melted from Charley's face. "Whadda ya mean I shouldn't go? I can push that boat around as good as anyone else."

Doug stood with the hot metal cooling in the morning air; he looked at Mike. "I know Charley, but I don't think you would like to be on that boat."

"Why not? We could pretend we was pirates lookin' for lost treasure. It would be lots of fun."

"Charley," Mike interrupted, "Jay Finch has to go with us."

At first, Charley's face lost all expression, and then it turned into a look of hesitation.

"Why does he have to go?"

364

"Harrison wants him to go because he knows the river." Doug placed the cooled metal back into the coals for a second time.

Charley looked at Doug then at Mike. Mike could tell Charley was trying to decide what to say next. Charley chewed on his lower lip for a few seconds then slowly looked back at his brother. "I think I'll go…I want to go."

"Charley, are you sure? I know how he treats you."

"I'm still goin'. I think you need me to go." Charley spoke even more confidently.

Mike and Doug exchanged glances again.

"'Sides," Charley continued, "you need my help more than I'm afraid of him."

Doug smiled, seeing the determination in his brother.

"Are you sure?" Mike asked.

"Sure as there's stink on a skunk," Charley quipped with a broad smile across his face.

Mike moved his eyes toward Doug; Doug just furrowed his brow in acceptance.

"Then it's settled." Mike held out his hand to Charley. Charley grasped his hand tightly and began skipping around in circles, twirling Mike around as he did. After a few circles Mike was able to break the grasp Charley had on him and playfully acted as if he were so dizzy he was about to fall over. Charley laughed and whooped then exited the shop into the cool, cloudy morning.

Chapter 34

It took the rest of the week, but by Saturday evening Mike and Jay had installed the metal braces onto the old ferry. Mike was glad that Doug had also fashioned the spikes to secure the braces, something he would not have thought of. He felt sure that his repaired boat would now be strong enough to make the twenty-five-mile trek down the Buffalo River, hauling the zinc nugget and four passengers to Buffalo City on the White River.

During the week of repairs, word had spread around town about Mike's endeavor, and each day more and more people came to sit in the shade and watch the pair. By the end of the week, they had seen a big part of the town come to gawk and ask questions. The questions made Mike feel proud of his task, but each query fanned the flame of Jay's hatred toward the boy from Kingston. Jay had to summon all of his control to smile and continue his work as if he liked working with his partner. For his plan to come to fruition, he had to make it look like he was enjoying his work. Mike had to feel comfortable with him...just long enough for him to carry out his deed.

Mike gathered his tools and placed them into the wagon. "Jay, I reckon that just about does it. Now I need to pay you for all your labor this week." Mike walked over to where Jay was seated on the edge of the ferry. "We agreed on twelve dollars, I believe."

Jay held out his hand and accepted the bills from Mike. He inspected the tender, folded it, and placed it into his shirt pocket.

"You're gonna need help loading that rock, ain't ya?"

Mike was surprised by Jay's continued willingness to help. . I've got Jim and some others coming down Monday evenin'. Guess I could use all the help I can get. That rock is pretty heavy."

"I'll be here. Ol' man Harrison wants me involved all the way."

"Okay, but it will be volunteer help. I'm not made out of money."

Jay smirked. "Don't worry; I'm getting paid by Harrison for the rest of it."

"Then I'll see you on Monday evenin'."

Without another word between the pair, Jay walked to his horse. Mike watched as Jay rode from view down the dirt road toward town. He still had a nagging feeling inside him that Jay could not be completely trusted. He didn't know what it was, but he felt as if Jay were up to something. He hated that feeling.

It was almost dark when Mike pulled his wagon to a halt in front of Rosie's store. He pushed the brake lever with his foot and hopped to the ground.

"I hear ya finally got that beat up old ferry put back together."

Mike looked up to see Rosie seated in one of the chairs, holding a glass of water in her hand. Mike smiled and made his way up the steps then plopped into the empty chair beside her.

"It's ready to pack. Just need to get it loaded and wait for the river to rise." Mike breathed an exhausted sigh.

Rosie chuckled. "I gotta hand it to ya kid, you don't lack gumption."

"I don't know what I got; I only know that I have to get that rock down the river soon. I'm starting to get low on money."

"Why don't you get Harrison to pay you an advance on what he thinks that rock will bring?"

Mike tilted his head and looked at Rosie. "Actually I never thought about that."

"Not that he'll do it, but it's worth a try."

At that, Rosie took a long drink from her water.

"Rosie, I brought back all your tools that I borrowed. I sure appreciate you lendin' them to me."

Rosie raised her free hand and acted as if she were swatting a fly in the air. "Don't worry about it. Those were my husband's and they've seen better days. I'm just glad they worked for ya."

"I'm still gonna have to buy some rope for…"

Rosie interrupted. "Why don't you go get the rope from the company store and tell them it's for Harrison. Far as I know he hasn't spent one lousy dime on this project."

Mike was surprised at her comment. "How do you know that?"

Rosie took another drink from her glass. "I know Jacob Harrison. Am I right?"

It was Mike's turn to chuckle as he looked out into the street. "You're right, Rosie."

"Once a skin flint, always a skin flint." Rosie placed her glass onto the dusty wooden porch and comfortably snuggled into her chair.

There was a pause in the conversation as the pair listened to the crickets and tree frogs begin their serenade for the evening. Mike was about to excuse himself to put away the tools and take care of his horse and the company wagon when Rosie spoke solemnly. "It ain't gonna be easy getting that boat down the river."

Mike hesitated at her words because he could almost hear a dire warning in her tone.

Rosie turned her gaze toward Mike, and he could see that she was serious.

"When that river gets up, the current is mighty strong. It's gonna push you all over the place. And when it does, you are gonna wish you was back on dry land. Your boat is flat, and that river's gonna have its way with you."

Mike hadn't given much thought past getting the boat loaded and ready. At her words he felt a tingle rise through his backbone and terminate at the back of his neck.

"I can't stop now, Rosie. I have to get that rock down the river to Buffalo City." Mike swallowed hard. "I'm sure with four of us we can manage just fine."

"You just need to be aware of what you're dealin' with. I'm gonna be worried about you until I see you back here with a smile on your face."

Now Mike gathered his emotions and spoke as if Rosie's concern was unnecessary. "We'll be just fine...I promise. When I get back, we'll celebrate our good fortune, then make plans to get the rest of that zinc out of the mine."

Rosie didn't smile, because she knew her friend was going to be tested to his fullness. She knew he was naïve about how difficult a task getting down a flooded river would be. She had other reasons to believe it was going to be a dangerous task.

"I'm sure you will be." She stood to walk back into the store. "I'm shuttin' down for the evening. Remember to lock that shed after you get the tools inside."

Mike watched Rosie disappear through her front door and heard the door lock. He felt a knot in the pit of his stomach, and he realized it was probably good for him to hear Rosie's words of caution. Rarely did his friend speak so seriously, and he had been raised to listen to the wise words of his elders. He decided to take her words to heart.

***

Mike spent most of the day on Monday gathering the ropes and materials he thought the crew would need to get the zinc boulder out of the mine and onto his boat. In the middle of the afternoon, he was taking one last inventory of the iron bars, ropes, and block and tackle he had placed in the wagon. He had taken Rosie's advice and was able to secure some of the material from the company store. He didn't know how Harrison would react to the news, but that was the least of his worries. All the while, he continued thinking over Rosie's words of concern about the raging river. He had installed a rudder to guide the craft and hoped that would be strong enough, along with their poling, to keep the boat drifting straight in the current.

369

Just as he decided he had everything he needed, he looked up and saw Pamela and Sandy walking toward his wagon where it was parked. Immediately, his heart began pounding harder, and the corners of his lips curled up into a smile. He walked around to the other side of the wagon to greet the pair.

"Hello Pamela, Sandy."

Sandy peered into the wagon. "Looks like someone's getting ready for some hard work."

Mike barely heard her comment because his gaze was focused on Pam. "I'm surprised your daddy is letting you out of the house."

Pam just smiled. "My daddy couldn't keep me in the house any longer. I told him he was keeping me cooped up like a caged animal, and, if I didn't get outside and back to actin' normal, I was going to explode."

"That would be a pretty sight." Sandy laughed.

Mike looked at Pam's hand, still bandaged, with her arm in a sling. He was suddenly at a loss for words, because seeing her hand brought back the painful memory of the evening in the mine and how he had allowed her to be injured.

"I'm going inside," Sandy said. "My material should be here."

Pam looked at Mike with a smile. "I'll wait right here."

"I'm going to be just fine." Pam broke the silence between Mike and her. "I've got nine more."

Mike didn't know whether to laugh or continue to feel sorry for himself. Suddenly, the words that he had only been able to think for the past several days tumbled out of his mouth.

"I've sure missed you."

Pam smiled and her cheeks turned crimson. She looked down at the ground for a moment then back up at Mike.

"I've missed you, too, Farm Boy."

Mike felt a small shiver take control of his body. It was all he could do to keep from showing his emotions.

"I hear you are about ready to head down the river."

Mike took a deep breath. "Just gotta load the rock and wait for water."

."Be careful, Michael. I want you back in one piece. That river can get angry when it's up."

"So I've already been warned. Believe me, I've seen what a flooded river can do. I've seen the King's River back home uproot trees and toss them around like match sticks."

There was another pause.

"I sure wish your daddy would let me see you."

"I think he'll come around. Believe it or not, he's been talkin' about you quite a bit lately.

"He's been talkin' about me?"

"Oh, he's still upset about you getting that mine from Rosie, but I think he sees part of what I see in you."

"And what's that?" Mike raised an eyebrow.

Just then Sandy hurried down the wooden steps and back up to the couple with the bolt of fabric in her arms.

"Come on. Ma's waitin' at her sewin' machine. We've got a lot of work to do." Sandy urged her friend to follow her.

"Glad I got to see you again." Mike fumbled with his hat in his hands.

"Me, too," Sandy said before Pam could speak.

Pam just smiled and turned with her friend. As Mike watched the pair walk back in the direction of Sandy's house, Pam turned around for one last smile at Mike. It was several moments before Mike could persuade his feet to move.

***

The low rumble of thunder could be heard in the distance as Jay rode his horse slowly through the darkened trees toward Raif's still. The darkness of this night was eerily silent and devoid of the normal night sounds. He was aware of how heavy and thick with dampness the air was and how still and lifeless the forest sat around him. He knew rain was coming.

As he rode he pondered the past few days and his scheme, which was now fully developed. He would finally get rid of the farm boy from Kingston then move on to bigger dreams. His thoughts meandered from place to place, as he continued to ride, but finally rested on what his near future held. The matured hatred inside him now mingled with his growing desire to become more than just a liquor runner for Raif. His plan was to somehow replace Raif and have the whole area, including the town of Gilbert, to himself. He didn't know how he was going to accomplish this, but somehow he would.

"Gotta have dreams." Jay spoke out loud as he patted his horse on the neck.

He heard a noise in front of him and looked up in time to see the face of Pen, one of Raif's men, keeping an eye on the path. Pen relaxed his grip on the rifle and just nodded as Jay passed.

"Evenin', Pen."

"Jay."

After the brief salutation Pen slipped back into the shadows with only the glow from his pipe visible in the darkness.

The light from Raif's campfire could now be seen through the trees as Jay approached. Raif was standing barely inside the glow of the light, and Jay could see that Raif was talking to one of his boys. Jay pulled his horse to a stop and dismounted.

Raif didn't interrupt his conversation when Jay walked toward the pair. He only turned his head slightly and motioned for Jay to sit down and wait for him to finish. Jay complied and sat in a weathered old wooden chair which had seen its better days. He hoped it would hold together if he sat still.

Jay stared into the fire, the yellow blaze crackling and popping, while Raif continued his conversation in a low tone. Jay picked up a limb from the ground and broke off small pieces, tossing each section into the fire. He was annoyed at having to wait, but he would be patient. As Jay pitched the last offering into the flames, Raif concluded his meeting and joined him.

"I know it's time for you to pick up your deliveries, but it seems you got somethin' else weighin' heavy on yer mind, Jay."

Jay didn't address Raif's comment and remained silent for a moment before he spoke. "Did you get everything worked out on that still in Gilbert?"

Raif leaned forward and placed his elbows onto his knees. He looked down at the ground and spit between his feet. "It's taken care of."

"Is the still in working shape?"

"Most of it." Raif continued to look at the ground.

There was another pause between the two. Another rumble of thunder rolled its way toward them but this time was louder than before.

"I'm ready to take on that area," Jay said.

Raif sat back in his chair and chuckled.

"Boy, I don't think yer much ready for anything else right now."

The comment from Raif made Jay angry, but he maintained his exterior calmness.

"It's wide open over there," Jay began.

Raif interrupted. "You can't handle it right now; you got too many other things distractin' you. If you want that area you have to commit to this all the time. If you get sidetracked you will mess up, and, if you mess up, you will get yerself caught. That might cause me serious distress."

"Well, I certainly wouldn't want to cause you a speck of distress." Jay's tone was sarcastic. He expected a sharp rebuke from Raif at his words, but Raif only slowly leaned forward again.

"Truth be told"—Raif paused—"we had a little trouble in Gilbert that attracted some attention. You'll notice you don't see Bud or Ned here tonight."

Jay hadn't noticed but glanced around the encampment.

"What kind of trouble?"

"Seems someone else had their eye on that still, too, and with the old man gone, we butted heads with 'em. They ain't a problem no more, but Bud and Ned didn't make it back."

"Sorry to hear that." Jay tried to sound concerned, which was as far from the truth as could be.

"We brought back all we could salvage from the still, but we're gonna have to lay low for a while. It attracted some attention from the law."

"So...we just wait until some time passes and set back up over there," Jay said.

"Everything's so simple for you, ain't it, Kid?"

Jay became agitated and stood in the flickering firelight.

"Raif, I've done you a good job. I've been careful and I've done what you wanted. You're no-good partner, Jeeter, is gone, and I want somethin' more here. I've got one last thing to settle in town and then I'm in this all the time, but I need to distribute over in Gilbert to make it worth my while."

Raif calmly rubbed his oily face with his rough hand. "Get that burr out of your hind end and sit down."

Jay spat into the fire and reluctantly sat back down, hoping he had made an impression on Raif.

"Why don't you take your bottles back into town and make your deliveries as usual. When you get finished doin' whatever you have to take care of then we'll talk some business. I ain't gonna do anythin' more with you until you are ready to do this and only this. Do you hear what I'm sayin'?"

Jay smiled because he felt he had gotten through to Raif. With Raif shorthanded, it looked to Jay like Raif would have to deal him in. Soon his business with Mike would be taken care of, and he could devote all his time to this venture with Raif.

"I hear what yer sayin'…so I guess I'll get my jars and be on my way."

"They're behind that rock over there. You got the money from your last delivery?

Jay reached into his pocket and handed a leather pouch to Raif. Raif untied the drawstring and emptied the contents into his hand. He carefully counted the bills and coins then tossed the empty pouch back to Jay.

"Just take care of your business soon," Raif said as Jay turned to his horse.

Jay placed the sack of bottles into a saddle bag and mounted.

"I'll see you in a few days." He turned his horse in the dim light and headed back into the darkness.

A streak of lightning illuminated the sky, and, for an instant, Jay saw the forest standing in unnatural hues of black and silver. The lightning was almost instantly followed by the crack of loud thunder that rolled from every direction. He urged his horse to quicken its pace, hoping he could make it back to his cabin before the sky opened up.

Chapter 35

The next morning, Mike stood on his porch watching the rain. And not just any rain, but a downpour. Temporary streams cascaded down the hillside behind Rosie's store, leaping over rock overhangs and splashing onto the ground below. These unnatural flows converged at the base of the hill, eating away at a section of the dirt road as it flowed across it toward Rush Creek nearby. He continued to watch the deluge fall so hard that he could barely see the other side of the road.

Leaning against one of the support beams of his porch, Mike took another sip of coffee. He had planned to get all of the equipment down to his mine and begin working on getting the zinc nugget loaded onto his boat. He had also hoped that the inevitable rain would wait until he was ready for the trip down the river. Once again, his timing wasn't God's timing. It was almost June now, and he knew that his window of opportunity would be closing because of the normally dry summers and low river level. If he couldn't get the zinc downriver soon, he would have to wait until the fall rains. He knew Mr. Harrison wouldn't be too happy with that schedule.

"It's rainin' hard enough to drown a toad frog." Mike turned his head and saw Rosie standing at the corner of her store with a smile on her face and awaiting a reply.

"I haven't seen it rain this hard in a long time." Mike spoke over the noise of the downpour. He walked toward her.

"Have ya et yet?"

"I made myself some flapjacks," Mike said.

"You're getting pretty darn good at takin' care of yourself, ain't ya? I bet your momma would be proud of ya."

Mike lifted his coffee cup to his lips then looked around at the rain from the front porch of the store. There was a pause as he swallowed a sip.

"You miss 'em don't ya?"

Mike cut his eyes to Rosie and grinned.

"I guess I'd be lyin' if I said I didn't."

Rosie smiled a big smile, and, at that moment, she thought about her own son and what he would be if he were still alive. She saw so much of her son in Mike. And though she hadn't really known Mike for long, at times she almost thought of him as hers.

"Care for a game of checkers while we wait out the rain?" Rosie started for the store doorway.

"Well, as soon as this lets up some, I think I'll take the wagon down to the mine and get ready to load that rock. And I probably need to make sure that old ferry is tied secure, since the river's gonna be risin'."

"Suit yerself. You wouldn't catch me out in that downpour. Besides, I'd probably beat you again anyway."

Rosie left Mike standing on the front porch and disappeared into her store. He didn't want to sit down and play a game of checkers, and he didn't really want to go out in that mess. But he knew that Harrison was going to be chompin' at the bit to get the zinc downriver, and the longer it took to do it the more agitated he would become. Mike wanted to do everything he could to please Pam's father, hoping to gain every bit of favor he could with him. He took one last sip of his coffee and tossed the remaining drops out into the rain along with the coffee grounds, which had settled to the bottom of his cup.

The downpour lessened to more of a moderate, steady rain. There was no wind, so the drops fell straight down. Mike walked back to his place to retrieve his rain gear and readied himself to trek out into the weather. He placed his hat on his head, hesitated for one last moment then bounded down the steps and into the rain. The drops weren't as cold as he'd anticipated which was welcomed.

He quickly made his way to Doug's shop, stepping through the muddy, flooded, dirt road and around the corner to where Rusty was corralled. As he readied his horse under a sheet metal overhang, he could hear his friend already at work pounding metal. He thought about stepping in and saying hello, but he decided to get the gear down to the mine and at least have it there and ready when the weather let up and he had help.

All the years growing up on the farm, chores had to be done in any weather. He remembered repairing their chicken coop once when there had come a two-foot, wet snow and the roof to the enclosure had collapsed. Though it had been frigid and the wind blowing a gale, the coop needed to be repaired.

His thoughts were snapped back from the farm by the crack of thunder. Though it wasn't cold, he dreaded driving the wagon down to the river. He thought about how he would rather work in cold weather with snow on the ground than work in a hard rain. His rain gear wouldn't keep him dry for long, and he didn't look forward to becoming soaked to the bone.

With his horse prepared to pull the wagon, Mike led him out into the rain, which seemed to be letting up even more and was now light and steady. They made their way to the mill, which operated in practically any weather. He noticed a temporary covering had been erected to the side of the mill where the men were splitting wood.

"Mornin', Jim."

Jim looked up and smiled at Mike, as if taunting him because he was working in dry conditions and Mike was getting wet.

"Boy, howdy, it's nasty out there today." Mike finally made his way to the enclosure where the wagon was parked. Dale Perkins spat a stream of tobacco juice onto the dusty floor and agreed.

Mike shook as much of the water from his rain slicker as he could and began hooking the wagon harness to his horse.

"You goin' out in this?" Dale's left cheek bulged from his tobacco wad.

"Better than sittin' at home," Mike replied.

Dale looked at the contents of Mike's wagon. "You need to have this wagon back by noon, ya hear? We need to load it up for tomorrow."

"I'll have it back. I'm just gonna take this stuff down to the mine. I'll turn right around."

"See that you do." Dale turned back to the business he was tending before Mike had interrupted him.

Mike just grinned at Dale and completed his task.

***

By mid afternoon the rain had stopped, but it had rained so much that the river had risen by six feet. In Gilbert, up the river, there was a flurry of activity in the timber yard as the loggers rolled their felled logs into the flowing river. Leon Pike knew that, as low as the river had been, they didn't have much time to get some of their timber down the river A falling river was fine, because it funneled the logs through the middle of the channel; however, he didn't want to have his wood stranded along the way if the river got too low too quickly.

"You boys ready to herd these logs down the river?" Pike addressed some of his men as they readied themselves on makeshift log rafts.

"We've been ready."

Pike turned to Carl Schultz, one of his managers. They walked toward a pile of cut logs perched on the river bank. "You keep an eye on that river level. If she stays up we need to push as many of these logs into the water as possible."

"We've got only three rafters goin' down with 'em," Carl reminded him.

Pike replied as the pair continued walking. "I know we're gonna be pushin' our luck, but if we don't get all these

379

logs downriver before July, Sam at the railhead in Buffalo City's gonna put a noose around my neck. We're way behind because of this long dry spell. We'll just push as many through as we can and hope the river don't drop too fast."

"Gonna be mighty dangerous floatin' too many logs at once." Carl spoke with concern.

Pike turned his head toward Schultz. "We don't have much of a choice, now do we? Let's just hope the rains keep coming and the river stays up."

As Carl began giving orders to roll more logs into the water, Pike looked at the men waiting to shove off into the rolling river with the logs. He hoped they could handle the extra burden. It was always a dangerous task under ideal conditions…but with extra logs churning and twisting in the water, anything could happen, and they would be at the mercy of the swollen Buffalo River.

***

As soon as the Morning Star Mill shut down for the day, Jim Smith locked up the wood-splitting tools and headed toward the Red Rose Mine. Two other men from the wood crew joined him.

"We need to stop by the livery," Jim said. "Mike has two mules waiting for us. We have to take them to the mine because we're gonna need them to get that rock out and loaded onto the ferry."

At the livery, the mule team was already yoked and ready for the trip. Jim thanked the attendant, and the three began making their way to the river. When they arrived at the mine, they found Doug, Charley, and Jay securing the block and tackle onto a sturdy Sycamore tree.

Where's Gilbert? Jim looked around

He's inside tyin' ropes around that zinc chunk." Doug walked away from his task and welcomed Jim and his crew.

"Not anymore. Just finished." Mike walked out into the daylight. "I sure do appreciate you fellas comin' down to help."

"Me and the boys are glad to do it, but if you don't mind me askin', "How are you plannin' to get this out in one piece?"

Jim followed Mike back into the mine and Mike pointed to the ground at their feet. "I'm thinkin' we can slide it out on top of these metal cart rails...shouldn't be much of a problem."

"Have you ever tried to move a six-thousand-pound rock before?"

As the pair stopped at the zinc boulder, Mike looked at Jim. "First time for everything, I reckon."

"What about once you get it out?"

"Well, I have a cargo net Mr. Harrison sent with me. I think we can roll the rock into it. That should make it easier to load and help keep it together."

"I figured Harrison would be down here in the middle of all this excitement." Jim inspected Mike's rope-tying skills on the zinc rock.

"He said he had some issues in Buffalo City to attend to but would be back tomorrow."

"That's fine by me." Jim saw that Mike had, indeed, securely tied the rock.

"Well, looks good in here. Let's go see how they're doin' outside."

Mike followed Jim out of the mine and saw that the block and tackle was in place. Two heavy ropes led from the pulley system and were tied to the team of mules.

"Are ya ready to do this?" Doug handed the other ends of the ropes to Mike.

"Ready as I'll ever be, I reckon. Jay, you stand at the mine entrance, and, Charley, you go work the team."

"Okay." Charley headed toward the mules.

Mike took the ropes and motioned for Doug and the others to grab their lanterns and come inside the mine with him. He needed all their help to roll the zinc onto the metal railing. The group made their way to the zinc, set their lanterns down, and grabbed the heavy iron bars to use as levers.

It took several attempts, but the boulder was successfully rolled onto the railing, and the ropes were attached to it. Mike reached for a bucket and began applying a heavy layer of thick grease to the metal tracks. The others watched in silence as he worked. After a few seconds Mike turned his head to see the four men watching him with curiosity.

"Can't hurt." Mike returned to his task and completely greased the cold iron railing.

At the entrance to the mine, Mike tossed the bucket aside and told Jay they were ready to begin pushing from the inside.

"I'll holler when we start pushing." Mike turned and disappeared into the cavern.

"You guys ready?"

Each of the men took a position on one side of the rock. "Yup."

"Okay, Jay…tell Charley to start pullin'."

At that prompt, Charley urged the team to move forward, the ropes pulled taut, and the team inside pushed with all their might. It took all their strength to keep the rock centered on the greased tracks. The boulder began sliding along and moved with more ease than any of them had expected.

"Didn't think much of my grease idea, did ya?" Mike grunted as he strained against the rock.

As they all continued pushing with everything they had, Jim looked at Mike and grinned.

Several times the group had to stop and catch their breath, but in thirty minutes the rock had been dragged out of the mine and was sitting in the daylight.

With the exception of Jay, cheers went up from the men at the realization that their first step was complete. After another moment of catching their breath, the group made its way to the edge of the embankment that led down to the river and the waiting ferry. The churning, muddy water of the Buffalo had risen enough to lift the ferry off the gravel bar where it had been parked. It swayed back and forth in the current, next to the river bank where it was tied.

"Well, I was hoping the ferry would still be resting on the gravel bar when we loaded it, but we don't have much of a choice," Mike remarked as the group looked on.

"We can always wait until the water goes back down in a couple of days." Doug hoped to persuade his friend to wait.

"I don't think Mr. Harrison would be too happy about that," Jay piped in. "You know he wants this down the river as soon as possible."

Everyone turned their heads toward Jay at his remark.

"I'm sure Mr. Harrison don't want anyone getting hurt over this." Jim looked at Jay from the corners of his eyes.

There was a pause while the group surveyed the situation.

"He's right," Mike finally said. "Harrison has people waiting on this rock, and he does want it downriver as soon as possible."

Jim placed his right hand onto the back of his neck. "Well, if we're gonna go ahead with this, the first thing we need to do is secure that boat better. We need to take as much of the sway out as possible and secure it tight to the bank."

Before anyone knew it, Charley had already clambered down the riverbank. Holding on to saplings and roots along the way, he made his way to the floating platform.

"Charley, get back up here!" Doug yelled at him.

"I'm fine…toss me some rope."

They looked down at Charley and noticed that the platform was stable in the current with Charley standing on it.

"Send me some rope down," Charley insisted.

Against his better judgment, Doug picked up a coil of rope and threw it down to his brother. He watched as Charley immediately went to work tying the front end and the back end more securely to the roots and trees along the riverbank. When he was finished, he bounced around on all corners and edges of the boat to make sure the craft was as stable as possible.

"Okay, Charley, you can come back up now." Doug sported a relieved smile.

It surprised everyone to see Jay grab another coil of rope and toss one end of it down to Charley. Charley looked up to see Jay holding the rope and bracing one foot against a tree. Charley hesitated for a moment then grabbed the rope to begin his climb. After a couple of steps up the muddy embankment, Jay allowed the rope to slip through his hands just enough to cause Charley to lose his footing and crash back down onto the wooden platform. He landed flat on his back and winced in pain.

"Oops...sorry, Charley." Jay did his best to look concerned. "Everything's muddy and wet up here. Someone want to give me a hand with this?"

Jim and another fellow grabbed the rope with Jay, and Doug encouraged Charley to take the rope and climb up. Cautiously, Charley took the rope in his hands and made his way back up to the group. His back was hurting, so Doug convinced him to sit on a rock off to the side for a few minutes.

Quickly Mike stepped close to Jay. "What have you got against Charley?" His voice was low but angry.

"I don't like workin' with retards." With a smirk, Jay used a voice only Mike could hear.

Immediately, Mike grabbed Jay by the collar with both hands and slammed him against the trunk of a tree. Before anything else could happen, the others separated the pair.

"Mike," Doug barked. Mike and Jay exchanged glares.

"It's okay." Jay pretended to dust himself off. "No harm done."

"Come on, boys, we're burnin' daylight." Jim's remark broke the tension.

***

It took another hour of precious daylight, but with the mules tugging and straining and even with a couple of curse words from one of Jim's friends, they were able to lower the rock down the eight-foot embankment and onto the waiting ferry. The ferry listed heavily on the side where the zinc was placed. Mike climbed quickly down the embankment and stepped to the opposite side, hoping to help equalize the weight.

"Jim and Doug, I need you down here to help me center the rock. Jay, tell Charley to keep pressure on those ropes. If you don't we might lose the zinc into the current."

Jay immediately thought about motioning for Charley to let tension off the ropes, causing the weight of the zinc to tilt the boat enough for it to break through the wooden railing and slip into the river. But there were too many around, and when the river receded it could easily be salvaged and reloaded onto the boat. No, he would stick to his original plan, a plan which he knew would be better.

Along with Charley, the mule team continued to hold pressure on the ropes while three other men climbed down to the platform. Using steel bars and all the strength they could muster, the men were able to roll the rock and center it on the boat.

"Give us some slack," Jim yelled up at Jay.

Jay motioned for Charley to slowly release the rope tension.

The boat rode low in the water but maintained its balance. Mike surveyed their work. ""That's perfect. Throw me some more rope, Jay."

Within a few minutes several ropes had been tied from the wooden railing onto the cargo net surrounding the zinc. Satisfied it was secure, Mike and the others climbed back up to the top of the riverbank. After the last man was up, they all looked down on the sight of the fragile-looking, flat-top boat with a huge boulder in the center, bobbing and swaying in the current.

"We did it." Mike said as shouts of success echoed up and down the river.

"Probably be a good idea now to untie the boat and give 'er some slack." Jim spoke as everyone was still congratulating each other. "If it don't rain anymore tonight, the river's gonna go down and ya need slack in that line so the boat can come down with it."

"Good thinkin', Jim," Mike replied. "I'll get down there and do that right now."

Without hesitation, Mike made his way back down to the boat and began untying all but one of the ropes holding it against the riverbank. As the group began gathering the tools and supplies, Mike tied an extra rope to the upriver end for added strength against the current and the weight of the rock. The two ropes had enough play in them to allow the boat to rise or fall back to the gravel bar if the river dropped overnight.

Mike was about to climb back up to the group when something slammed against the boat and knocked him down onto the deck. Charley heard the thump and looked over the edge at Mike. Immediately he saw what had hit the platform.

"Doug, you best look at this." There was a note of urgency in Charley's voice.

With the final fleeting moments of daylight left, Doug turned to look at Charley and what he was pointing to up the river. The others also turned their attention to the river and immediately stopped what they were doing. They all made their way to the edge of the riverbank and almost stopped breathing.

Mike climbed up the rope and joined the group. "I just got hit by a tree or something."

"It was a log!" Doug continued to look up the river.

With the others, Mike turned his attention to the churning water. It took him a moment to realize what he was seeing.

386

"That's certainly something I didn't count on," Doug said in a nervous tone.

There was silence for an eerie moment as they watched hundreds of logs float down the Buffalo River in their direction.

"I'll swan…this isn't going to be easy, is it?" Mike watched the flotilla of logs herding themselves through the muddy water.

"It's gonna be downright dangerous." Jim continued to stare at the river. "Downright dangerous."

Chapter 36

The rain began again during the night. Not a gully washer as the day before but a slow, steady rain. Mike had been awake most of the night, tossing and turning as he listened to the drops dance on his tin roof then splash to the ground below. But it wasn't the rain that kept him awake. Fragments of memories, concerns, and challenges mingled like oil and water, mixed together and yet separate. His mind couldn't focus on one thing because he saw all of his hurdles at the same time.

First and foremost was his challenge on the river. Earlier he hadn't stopped to think about the severity of the task, but now it loomed in front of him like a mountain he had to cross. He wrestled with the conversation he would have with Jacob Harrison concerning the logs in the water. Though Mike had never strayed from a challenge, the words of warning from his friends had caused his nerves to fray.

His mind was constantly on Pam and his desire to spend time with her, and on breaking down the barrier between her father and him. Would Harrison ever relent or would he continually be an obstacle Mike would rather not challenge? He reminisced about his life on the farm and the loving family he had left behind in search of his own way. He saw the pleasures and the challenges he had faced since in Rush, with the thorn in his side being Jason Finch.

The turmoil in his mind seemed to have no solution. It was churning and swirling like the currents of the engorged Buffalo River. He prayed that by daylight he could somehow fit the fragments together like pieces of a puzzle and begin turning his challenges into something he could handle, rather than the chaos with which he was plagued.

He also knew that these challenges were things which he could not handle alone. If there were to be peace in his life, he knew it could only come from his Heavenly Father. As he lay in the darkness, he remembered one of many scriptures he had memorized from the family Bible as a child: *I can do all things through Christ which strengtheneth me.* He meditated on that verse and others and prayed for strength and protection not only for himself but for his family and those around him. He knew that God was sovereign, and, even though he didn't understand God's ways so much of the time, he believed God always had a plan and a purpose for everything that happened. Though he possessed these struggles, he would do his best to place them at his Heavenly Father's feet.

***

For the second morning in a row, Mike found himself traversing muddy ground in the rain. This time, however, he was headed in the direction of Jacob Harrison's house. He knew the words he was going to speak to Mr. Harrison would not be well received. No one could predict how long the river would be up and full of logs, but he realized that caution should be the path to travel. Surely the loggers would get all of their logs down the river in enough time for Mike to still have water to navigate to the White River.

Secure in his resolve, he stepped up onto the front porch and stood at Harrison's front door. It was still very early, but he noticed lamplight through the curtains and knew Mr. Harrison would be up. He removed his rain gear and tapped lightly on the door. Almost immediately the door opened.

"Mike Gilbert, what brings you out so early?"

Before Mike could reply, to his surprise, instead of Harrison stepping out onto the porch with him, he invited Mike in. Mike shook his rain gear one last time and hung them on a hook just outside the door. After the door closed behind him, he removed his boots while Harrison looked on.

"You don't need to get undressed, son, the floors can be cleaned."

Mike felt uncomfortable at the comment but placed his shoes next to the front door and made his way into the parlor with Harrison.

"Have a seat, Mike. Would you like some coffee?"

"No, sir, I'm fine. I had a few cups already."

The pair sat in the dimly lit room, and, for a moment, the only sound was the ticking of the grandfather clock.

"I'm sure you have something on your mind for you to come here so early of a morning in the rain." Harrison took a sip of his coffee.

Mike took a deep breath. "Mr. Harrison, I wanted you to know that the zinc is loaded onto the boat and ready to go."

"Excellent." Harrison leaned back in his chair.

"There's something else you need to know."

"Something wrong with the boat?"

"No," Mike quickly replied. "The boat is in good shape. It seems to be handling the zinc just fine."

Harrison cocked his head a little and furrowed his brow. "Then what is it?"

Mike remained still in his chair but fidgeted with his feet. "It seems that, with the river up, the loggers in Gilbert are sendin' their logs downriver to the White River."

"Well, that's typical for this time of year."

Mike continued to fidget. "Sir, they're not just sendin' down some logs, they seem to be sendin' them all down at the same time. They're so thick on the water that you could practically walk across the river on them."

All expression left Jacob's face for a moment as he pondered Mike's words.

"I was thinking that we could wait until the loggers were finished floating their logs before I took the zinc down the river."

"Well"—Harrison clasped his hands under his chin and placed his elbows on the arms of his chair—"I'm afraid that won't be possible."

Mike stopped fidgeting and politely restated his case. "Mr. Harrison, I'm sure the logs will all get downriver soon, and, with it raining, the river should stay up for a while and…"

Harrison interrupted and leaned forward in his chair. "You don't understand, Mike. For one, the loggers have been cutting timbers for quite some time and haven't been able to get them down the river all spring. I've seen the piles in Gilbert. It will be a miracle if they get them all down before summer. I'm not surprised they're dumping them as fast as they can. For another, I got back from Buffalo City last night, where I made arrangements for a steamboat there to transport the zinc. We have three days before she has to leave, so we don't have a big window of opportunity."

Now Mike leaned forward in his chair. "Mr. Harrison, I'm afraid we'll be torn apart if we put in to the river with those logs. I only hope the boat is still there when I go check on it after I leave here."

"You'll be flowing with the logs. Loggers do it all the time on makeshift log rafts. They go along with the logs to clear the jams and direct the logs. You'll be alright. It might get a little difficult at times, but you'll get downriver."

Mike hadn't thought it would be this difficult to convince Harrison to let him wait on the transport. He thought Harrison would be angry but would relent until a safer time. He was about to begin again when Harrison spoke.

"Mike, I know you can do it…you have to do it. This rock is worth more to you than just what the collectors will give for it."

"I don't understand what you mean. This rock isn't worth getting anyone hurt over it." Mike remained calm.

Harrison leaned back in his chair again and was silent for a moment before he spoke.

"About ten years ago, we were workin' the Morning Star mine above the mill, and one of the miners located and dug out a twelve-thousand-pound zinc nugget. It was about twice the size of the one in your mine."

Mike's eyes widened; he thought his was probably a record size.

"It took a lot of time, but we got the nugget out in one piece; after making a cart that would haul the weight, we managed to get it down to the river and onto a makeshift raft much like yours."

Harrison took another sip of his coffee, which was now beginning to get cold. "I'm getting some more coffee...sure you don't want a cup?" Mike just raised his hand slightly, indicating that he was fine. As Harrison walked into the kitchen, Mike thought about Harrison's words but still didn't agree that it should be no problem floating on the flooded river choked with logs.

Harrison reentered the room and sat back down in his chair. Settling into its softness, he let out a sigh. "You haven't been here in Rush long, but whenever the river is up, you'll usually see logs floating down. That's the fastest way to get them to Buffalo City."

"Mr. Harrison," Mike interrupted, "Are you telling me that you floated that rock down the river with logs in the water, too?"

Harrison sat his cup down after taking a sip, "Well no...but the river was flowing about like it is now and it had uprooted trees and all sorts of debris in the water."

"And you didn't have any problems?"

Harrison chuckled. "I didn't say we didn't have problems, but we did get it to Buffalo City."

"What happened to the nugget?"

"Well, it ended up being shown at the world's fair. It's the largest zinc nugget ever found. It won a bunch of ribbons and prizes."

"Mine's not the largest nugget, then. Why the hurry to get it down the river?"

"Because, my dear boy, that nugget will make you a lot more money than just what it's worth."

Those words confused Mike, and he tried to think about what Harrison meant.

"Mike, we will make some money on that nugget, even though it's not the largest. Collectors will bid for it, and, when we split the proceeds, you will have a nice pocket full of money."

"But is it worth the risk?" Mike still tried to understand Harrison's push to get the zinc down the river so quickly.

"For the zinc alone…probably not."

"Then why risk it?" Mike blurted, still confused.

Harrison calmly placed his cup and saucer on the stand next to his chair and leaned forward once again.

"Because there are investors, with bank accounts full of cash, who are always looking for something to sink their wealth into. When word gets out of another large zinc find, they will climb all over each other to see who can get to you first."

Suddenly, it dawned on Mike what this was all about. All along on this project, Harrison had not cared about the money he would make on the zinc. He could have quite simply let Mike haul the zinc to the mill and get paid for what it produced. But instead, and without coming right out and saying it, Harrison was trying to help Mike get recognition for his mine so that he could become successful with it.

Harrison snuggled back into his chair and placed his reading glasses onto his nose. He then picked up his Bible and opened it to where he had placed a bookmark.

He looked at Mike over the rims of his glasses. "That's the reason you need to get that zinc down the river." Harrison turned his attention back to his Bible.

Mike sat silent for a moment then stood to make his way to the door. He quickly slipped his feet into his boots. "Mr. Harrison, I have some zinc to get down the river."

Harrison didn't look up but smiled as he continued reading, while Mike stepped back out into the early morning rain.

***

It was noon when Mike entered Doug's shop. Doug was finishing some projects for one of the local mines when he spotted his friend.

"Another rainy day...hope the ferry made it through the night." Doug's hammer blow sent sparks into the air.

"Oh, it made it fine. I just got back from the river."

"Hey, Mike, when we headin' out?" Mike turned to see Charley counting nails with a smile on his face. "I got to get the nails counted so we can leave."

Mike smiled. "That's good, Charley." Mike looked over at Doug. "I was just about to talk to you fellas about the trip."

Charley immediately began singing a song about a river, but Mike didn't recognize the tune or the words. Mike then walked to Doug and spoke in a low tone. "I spoke to Harrison this morning."

"Did he agree that it would be too dangerous?" Doug plunged a strip of iron into the red-hot coals.

"No...actually, he told me that he had floated a larger nugget down the river about ten years ago. There were logs in the water then, too."

Doug thought for a moment. "I've seen loggers float their logs down the river, but nothing like what we saw last night."

Mike watched in silence for a moment as Doug continued to work. "Doug, I can find two other people to take your place. I'm not going to ask you to do something where you can get hurt."

Doug looked at Mike while he pumped the bellows. "If you go, we're going with you. I'd leave Charley here, but I'd never hear the end of it."

"Honest, Doug, don't feel like you have to go...but it's something that I have to do. I own that mine, and I need to act like it."

Doug looked over at Charley, who was still counting his nails, then back at Mike with a smirk. "Well, someone needs to go along to keep you out of trouble. Might as well be me."

Mike smiled; he had found in Doug a close friend.

He then turned to Charley. "Charley, we leave first thing in the morning."

"Yahoo!" Charley jumped up, spilling his nails all over the place. "I'll pick them up later. I gotta go get ready." Without another word, he skipped past Mike and out the door.

"Well, you made his day." Doug inspected his piece of iron.

"Doug, I appreciate that it's you comin' along. I hope, with you there, we won't have any trouble out of Jay."

"Between the three of us, I'm sure we can keep him in line…unless he wants to swim home."

Mike and Doug laughed together as Doug pounded on the white-hot piece of metal once more.

"I have some things to get ready also." Mike made his way to the door. "I guess I'll see you down by the river at first light."

"We'll be there," Doug said, without looking up from his work.

***

Later in the afternoon Mike walked up the steps and into Rosie's store. Rosie was seated alone at the checkerboard and seemed to be taking a nap. Her arms were folded in front of her and her chin was resting on her chest.

"Hey, Rosie." Mike plopped into the chair across from her.

Instantly, Rosie flinched awake, and her glasses fell off her nose and onto the floor.

"Lordy, kid, you just about made me jump out of my skin!" She leaned over to retrieve her spectacles.

Mike smiled as she wiped off her glasses and placed them on the table.

"Must have dozed off, I reckon." Rosie looked a little embarrassed.

"Well, I wanted to let you know that I leave for Buffalo City in the morning."

"I heard," she replied. "You forget that word travels fast in this little town."

"Yeah, I do keep forgetting that." Mike made a move with a checker.

"So…you want to take me on finally." Rosie made a countermove and awaited his reply.

"There's lots of logs floatin' down the river…got any suggestions?" Mike moved another piece across the board.

Rosie sighed. "I knew there would be logs in the water…just didn't want to tell you the other day."

"I didn't realize how difficult this is gonna be." Mike awaited a move from Rosie.

"Life's difficult Mike…you know that by now. It's just difficult in different ways, dependin' on what yer doin' and where you are at the time."

Rosie finally made another move and challenged one of Mike's pieces.

"But this is downright dangerous."

"Kid, how many trees did you fell as you were growin' up?"

"Quite a few…why?"

"Isn't that dangerous?"

Mike thought for a moment while he contemplated his next move.

"I reckon, at first, but you get used to it."

He made his move on the board and left Rosie open for a jump.

"You've never done anything like this. It's dangerous and always would be; but, if you hang around here for long, I'm sure you'll do it again, and you'll get used to it."

Rosie looked at the board and knew she had a jump, but it would leave her open for a double jump. She had no choice…it was the rule of the game. She made her move, and then Mike moved and took two of her pieces.

"I'm not sayin' it will be easy. In fact, I'm worried for ya. Sometimes we have to take chances."

"Think I'm ready?" Mike watched Rosie make another move and challenge him once again.

"If anybody can do it, you can. You do need a little more practice at this game, though."

Mike watched as she took three of his checkers and set him up for another bold attack.

"I never have been very good at this game." Mike was forced into a jump.

About that time, the front door opened, and Samson walked through the doorway. He stopped in the middle of the floor, looking uncomfortable.

"What can I do ya for, big fella?" Rosie loudly exclaimed from the table.

Samson lumbered up to the table and towered over them. "Sidney sent me over here to get some Epsom salts."

Rosie grinned as she looked at Mike then back at Samson. "Seems one of our customers has delicate skin and needs some salts in his bath water."

Rosie and Mike both broke out in laughter and Samson soon followed.

"Them city folk and their delicate skin," Rosie said as the trio continued to chuckle.

"Darlin', you just grab you a box from that bottom shelf over there. I'll add it to the tab."

Samson retrieved the cardboard container. "Thanks kindly, Rosie."

"Tell Sidney hello for me, will ya?"

"I'll do it." Samson exited the store.

Rosie turned back to the board. "Now where were we?"

"Well, I think we were already at the point where I have no chance of winning.

"You're gonna do okay, kid." Rosie leaned back in her chair. "Just be very careful. Don't fight the current and the logs, be part of the river and flow along with 'em. Take

397

the inside of the bends in the river. The logs will flow to the outside. If you fight 'em they'll plow into you harder."

Mike contemplated her advice and appreciated what she said.

"Guess I better get some grub to take along with me tomorrow. It's gonna be a long day."

"Beth's behind the counter on the other side; she can help you."

Mike stood and placed his hat on his head. "Thanks Rosie...you always make me feel better."

Rosie grinned and crossed her arms in front of her once again. "Be careful, kid. I want you back in one piece," she said as Mike made his way to the groceries.

***

With his supplies in hand, Mike left the store and was about to turn the corner on the porch to go to his place when he glanced across the road and spotted May Bess and Pamela exiting the doctor's office. He placed his groceries onto the wooden porch and quickly made his way to the pair as they were climbing into the buggy.

"Hello, May Bess. Hi, Pamela."

"Hello, Michael. I hear you have a big day planned ahead of you tomorrow," May Bess said from her seat.

"Seems everyone knows."

Mike looked at Pam, who was seated quietly next to her aunt but sported a smile. May Bess noticed the couple with their eyes locked.

"Mike, I need to run a quick errand before heading home. It's not very far, and the evening has turned out nice. Why don't you walk Pamela home? I'll be there directly."

The smile grew bigger on Pam's face. "If I have to," Pam teased.

Mike raised his arm and helped Pam down from the carriage. As soon as she was on the ground, May Bess flipped the reins and left the pair standing in the street.

"Was the doc taking one last look at your hand?" Mike asked as the pair began to walk the long way around to Pam's home.

"He said I was in fine shape and could get back to doin' whatever I wanted."

"I'm glad you're finally okay."

The pair walked in silence for a couple of minutes as each contemplated what they wanted to say. They walked to the corner of the picket fence next to the Morning Star Hotel when Pam finally spoke.

"I'm already beginning to worry about you and your trip tomorrow."

Mike replied in a way he felt he should as a man. "Oh, we're gonna be just fine. We'll make it down the river in no time and be back before you know it."

"You don't have to act like such a tough guy."

Mike blushed, knowing she already had him figured out. They continued to walk in silence until they rounded the next corner and neared the old rock smelter standing in the middle of the pathway. As they neared it, they both remembered the night of the dance and how their hearts had felt as they were interrupted from their first kiss.

Mike stopped as they reached the monument. "There's somethin' I need to tell you." His voice began to quiver. "I've been thinkin' about this for a while now."

Pam stood in front of Mike and looked into his timid eyes. Mike hesitated for a moment, contemplating how to say what he wanted to.

"Go ahead," Pam said tenderly. "You can tell me."

Mike raised his gaze from the ground and looked into Pam's eyes.

"Well, here goes," he said.

"I know I haven't known you for long, but…" He hesitated again, feeling awkward with the way he had begun. "Um, it's just that…I have these feelings for you and…"

He continued to stammer, which was endearing to Pam. She saw his struggle but knew what he was trying to say. Rather than allow him to stumble through his words any further, Pam decided to help the poor boy out.

"Mike, just so you know...I have the same feelings for you."

Mike suddenly felt his heart beating even more fiercely in his chest than it had only moments earlier.

"In fact," she continued, "I would have to say that I've fallen in love with you. I meant what I said in the mine a couple of weeks ago."

Mike was glad he was leaning against the rock smelter, or else he would have fallen to the ground at that moment. His cheeks flushed, and he smiled the goofiest grin he had ever sported.

"I sure hoped you felt the same way I do," he replied.

"Mike, you were easy to fall in love with. I didn't have to be around you for long to know that there was something different about you. I began admiring you and couldn't stop thinking about you."

Mike broke into a cold sweat and felt a shiver run through his body. He had never been in love before and didn't realize how weak it could make a fella.

"Your pa is definitely not gonna like this." Mike tried to lighten the moment.

"We'll worry about that later. Right now we have to get you back safely tomorrow. I don't want the man I love hurting himself."

Mike was filled with emotion at those words. He couldn't believe that someone like Pamela loved him and cared about him.

"Well, I reckon I have someone to be careful for now, don't I?"

Pam smiled. "I reckon you do at that."

Though it was in broad daylight for all to see, she took his arm and allowed him to walk her home, neither of them needing to say a word.

Chapter 37

The air was warm and thick as Mike stepped from his porch and into the street. The darkness of the morning smothered him like a heavy blanket. No stars were visible when he looked up into the sky. He stood for a moment and noticed lantern light from windows of the few early risers in town.

In his hand he clutched a bag containing a small amount of food and his rain overcoat. The crickets and tree frogs were still serenading as he closed his eyes and took another deep breath. *Here I go*. He turned and made his way toward the Buffalo River on foot. He had decided to walk rather than take his horse and make arrangements to have someone bring him back home.

As Mike passed the front porch of Rosie's store, he could barely see Rosie rocking gently back and forth in the darkness. "You need to learn to be quieter when you make your breakfast of a mornin'."

"I didn't make that much noise, did I?" Mike stopped in the street.

Rosie stood and walked down the creaky wooden steps to where Mike was standing. Though she wasn't cold, she pulled her shawl more tightly around her shoulders.

"I've been up for a spell." She stood in front of him.

"So have I."

Standing in the darkness of the morning, the pair was silent for a few seconds.

"When you get back tomorrow, I'll fix you the biggest steak dinner you've probably ever had." Rosie looked into Mike's eyes.

"How did you know steak is my favorite?"

There was an awkward silence again.

"You take care of yourself now, Mike…ya hear?"

Mike grinned at his friend whom he loved. "I will."

Rosie smiled a small, worried smile and reached out her arms. Even if Mike had wanted to, he couldn't have escaped her clasp. The pair hugged then parted.

"Well…I better not hold ya up any longer."

"See ya tomorrow, Rosie." Mike smiled and turned to head down the road. "By the way, what time is supper?"

"Just as soon as you get yer bony bottom back here." Rosie watched him disappear into the darkness. She listened to the crunch of gravel under his feet until it, too, disappeared. "God, take care of that boy." She whispered her request into the morning air then turned to walk back up the steps and into her store.

***

Mike passed the Morning Star Hotel and noticed a faint light glowing through the curtains. *Guess Sidney gets up early every morning.* It caused him to remember his early mornings on the farm, most of the time in the dark.

For some reason he had forgotten to light his new Coleman lantern, so he crouched in the road and soon brought the wick to life with a match. As he stood he heard a horse and wagon come from behind him. He stepped aside, and the wagon slowed to a stop.

"Thought you might need a lift."

"I'll swan, Jim. I'm surprised to see you up so early."

"Get on up here and I'll take you down to the river. I was headed in that direction anyway." He winked.

"Much obliged, Jim." Mike hopped into the seat next to him.

Jim flipped the reins and the pair began moving.

"You sure you don't need anyone else to go downriver with you?" Jim asked as they bounced along the rain-rutted road.

"I'd rather you go than Jay, but Harrison wants Jay to be on the boat for some reason."

"Well, Jay knows that part of the river better than me, so I reckon that's the reason. Sure don't want to get stuck on a gravel bar."

"Just the same, I'd rather you be there.,"

His words had barely left his mouth when their lantern light shone on two figures in the road ahead of them.

"Jim's stage service at your disposal, gentlemen." Mike playfully announced their presence as Jim stopped his wagon beside Doug and Charley.

"Mornin' fellas…what brings you out so early?" Doug handed Mike his lantern.

"We're out for a moonlight ride, but the moon's not cooperatin' so far."

Doug and Charley seated themselves on the back of the wagon, and the foursome moved toward the river once again.

Fifteen minutes later, the wagon crested the hill and descended to the bank of the river. As soon as Jim pulled his horse to a stop, they heard the snort of another horse off to the side. Jay walked into their lantern light. "Thought you boys would never get here."

Mike stepped from the wagon. "Well, we're here now."

"Jim, you wouldn't mind takin' my horse back to the livery for me, would ya?"

"I don't mind takin' your horse anywhere." Jim replied.

"Thanks for the ride, Jim." Mike walked to Jim's side of the wagon.

There was enough daylight beginning to shine through the thick morning clouds now, so that they could just make out the water in the river.

"You boys be careful out there today. Looks like the water has dropped a little overnight." Jim spoke with concern.

"Well, I guess that just means we'll get to Buffalo City a little slower." Mike raised his hand to shake Jim's.

"Thanks again for the ride," Mike repeated. "We'll see you tomorrow."

Jay signaled with a raised hand that he had finished tying his horse to the back of the wagon. Jim slowly turned the wagon around and headed back up the road.

"Well," Doug said, "I guess we best be getting out on the river. Maybe we can outrun the logs that I imagine are being tossed in the water up at Gilbert right about now."

"Charley...you ready for this?"

Charley grinned from ear to ear. "Aye, aye, captain."

Mike placed his hand on Charley's head and mussed his hair. "Then let's do this. I have a steak dinner waitin' on me tomorrow night."

The four took the path along the river and, within moments, were at the raft. Peering over the edge of the riverbank, they could see that the raft was still there and waiting for them. Mike noticed that Jim was right. The raft was floating almost a foot lower than when they had tied it.

Charley was the first to descend onto the boat. The others passed down their items to Charley and descended also. Mike was the last to board, so, before lowering himself, he extinguished the two lanterns and placed them into the mouth of the mine.

With everyone in their place and their long poles in their hands, Mike began untying the ropes holding them against the bank. In the dim light he finally got the ropes loosened and they were adrift. They knew that, from now on, they were at the mercy of the churning Buffalo River.

Jay's station was at the back, so he managed the rudder and guided them out into the faster flowing water. They were all amazed as the current grabbed them and pushed them faster than they had expected.

"It's like we're pirates out on the sea." Charley remembered a book his brother had read to him about pirate battles and buried treasure.

Jay looked annoyed at Charley's words but bit his tongue so the words flying through his head wouldn't tumble out.

"I'll steer as best as I can," Jay said, "but we'll have to do most of the work with the poles."

"I'm sure glad there aren't any logs in the river this morning." Mike kept an eye out for shallow water.

"You can be sure they're comin' up behind us," Doug said, looking back upriver.

"Well, if we keep moving maybe we can stay ahead of 'em." Mike tried to sound encouraging.

"I hope you're right."

***

For the next thirty minutes they floated with the current churning around them and were able to keep the heavy-laden boat in the middle of the river. Daylight was fully upon them now but was tainted by the thick, heavy clouds hanging over them. They passed numerous temporary streams of water cascading down the hillsides and splashing into the river. Small creeks, now flowing heavily along the way, emptied into the river and added to the swell, bringing along more murk and debris. And every so often they would see a waterfall cascading down from high up on a bluff, its solid flow turning into small droplets as it fell then turning into a white spray as it crashed into the trees next to the water.

Mike was amazed at how beautiful the river was. It gave him the desire to someday put a boat in at the upper end and float the entire length. The beauty of the river was striking at the upper end and became even grander where he was now, with its high bluffs looming over the river as sentinels.

"There's a rock up ahead," Charley warned, "right in the middle."

Mike was quickly pulled back into their task at hand.

"Push to the outside," Jay exclaimed as he turned the rudder.

Doug and Charley placed their poles into the water and pushed as hard as they could. The boat responded slowly and navigated safely around the rock. The action, however, caused them to float under a large sycamore tree which had been undermined by the flowing water and was precariously leaning low over the river. They all had to duck to miss being swept overboard by the large branches.

They looked back. "Won't take long for that tree to go down," Doug said.

"We're gonna go around a tight bend to the right in a few minutes, and the current is gonna want to sling us to the outside," Jay remarked.

"We want to stay to the inside of the bend, if we can," Mike interrupted.

In his mind, Jay shoved Mike overboard, but he kept his lips sealed. His time to take care of Mike was coming. Until then he would keep tending to his business.

"That's right." Jay agreed. "Doug and Charley, you two push us to the inside of the current; me and Mike will keep us off the gravel bar."

Seeing the bend of the river looming in front of them, Doug and Charley didn't say a word.

"If we hit the outside of the riverbank in this current, it could roll us around somethin' fierce, and then we'll lose control," Jay said.

The river channel narrowed before the bend, causing the current to become swifter. The six-thousand-pound cargo tied to the middle of the raft made pushing the craft sideways especially difficult in the current. In anticipation, Doug and Charley began plunging their long poles down into the river bottom to push. The action was made difficult by the pressure of the current on the poles, so it took every ounce of strength they possessed. Doug removed his pole from the water and was about to make another plunge when he spotted a downed tree wedged between rocks to the inside of the bend. Mike spotted it at the same time, but, before any of them could react, they were upon it.

"Hold on," Doug said. They all grabbed the side railing.

Instantly, the boat slammed into the downed tree and came to a halt in the current, on top of it. Charley lost his grip on the railing and came close to tumbling over. In the action, his pole slid off the deck and into the river.

"My pole!"

"Nice goin', idiot." Jay immediately chided him.

"Shut up, Jay, or you'll be goin' in after it," Doug shot back.

"It's okay," Mike said. "That's why I brought that extra pole with us."

Doug and Jay exchanged defiant glares while Mike tried to calm the situation.

"We need to get off this tree," Mike said, looking at their situation.

"How we gonna do that?" Charley wanted to know.

"I don't know...we're stuck pretty sound," Mike said.

During the repair of the boat, Mike had built a storage box onto one side. He had filled it with various tools the day before their trip. They had also placed their bags of food and supplies into the enclosure before they had departed. Mike unlatched the lid to the box and rifled through the clutter to retrieve a saw. He examined it in the daylight as he walked back to his original position. "Looks like I need to get into the water and cut that tree. It's not very big around, so this saw ought to do the trick."

"That current's a lot stronger than you think. It could take you under, and, if it pins you against those tree limbs, you won't be able to get free," Doug warned.

"I can straddle the tree, and, when I saw through it enough, the current—along with the weight of the boat— should cause it to break.

"But when it breaks, we'll go flyin' down the river without you," Doug replied.

"And you'll fall into the river," Charley added.

Mike studied the situation for a moment longer.

"Anybody have a better idea?" He looked around and got no reply. "We can't sit here all day. The longer we're here the closer those logs get behind us."

"Maybe we can push us off with these poles," Charley said.

"We're wedged too tight." Jay looked at Mike. "He's probably gonna have to cut it."

Even though it didn't fit into Jay's scheme, he dared to think that Mike would cut the tree and be swept down the river, never to be seen again. If so, it would actually be easier than what he had planned.

For the next fifteen minutes, they tried to move the ferry over the downed tree with their poles. They were able to get themselves to inch forward, but that only seemed to hold them tighter.

"Well," Mike finally said, trying to catch his breath from the strain of pushing the heavy poles, "looks like I have to cut it."

Doug and Charley looked at each other, knowing the danger involved.

"Let me get down there and cut it," Doug said.

"Sorry, Doug, but I'll do it. I told you I didn't want to put you in any more danger than necessary. Besides, it'll be okay. As soon as I hear it start crackin', I'll get back on the boat. We should be able to bounce the boat 'til the tree gives way."

"That ain't gonna work," Jay piped in. "Once it starts crackin', you won't have time to get back on the boat."

"Well, since the current's not real heavy where we are, hopefully I'd be able to grab the side and you could pull me in."

"It's worth a try, Farm Boy." Jay encouraged Mike to get into the water with the tree.

Mike allowed the *farm boy* comment to go unchallenged as he slung one of his legs over the railing. He swung the other leg over and sat on the outside edge looking down at the tree on which they were lodged. Although the current was not as strong as it was to the outside of the river bend, there was enough to cause him to hesitate.

"Just be careful, Mike," Doug pleaded.

408

Mike turned his attention to his friend. "Doug, tie a loop on the end of a piece of rope for me. Give me enough slack so I can slip my hand through it. I'll cut the tree and, when it gives, the rope around my wrist will keep me from washing away. Jay can pull me in."

"Don't know if that's such a good idea," Jay interjected. "The rope could get caught in the tree limbs."

"If the loop's big enough I can slip out of it if I get into trouble."

Doug quickly tied a loop at the end of a rope and handed it to Mike. Mike slipped his hand through it then cautiously made his way into the river and straddled the tree. The water was cooler than he had anticipated, and the current pushed hard against his body. He found a suitable spot to cut—about five feet away from the boat.

"Here goes nothin'." He steadied himself with his left hand and began to saw through the tree resting at the water's surface.

The green wood and the water rushing over the tree made the sawing difficult. As the tree bobbed in the current, occasionally the blade would become pinched in the saw cut, causing Mike to labor to remove it without breaking the blade. The balancing act on the tree, combined with the current against his legs, added difficulty to his endeavor.

The others looked on as Mike continued to saw, slowly inching his way through the wood. Suddenly, without warning, the tree popped and broke in two. Mike was instantly plunged into the cold water with his left hand gripping the rope and his right hand hanging on to the saw. What seemed like minutes was only seconds as his head bobbed to the surface of the churning water.

"Pull him in, Jay!" Charley shouted at him.

Against his desires, Jay began pulling the rope and, in no time, had Mike back onto the boat, dripping wet but successful.

Relieved, Doug and Charley poled the moving ferry to keep it in the calmer water while Mike removed the rope from his wrist.

"Thanks Jay," Mike said. "Not bad for a farm boy, eh?"

Jay simply smiled at Mike's comment, knowing what was to come as they were once again moving.

Chapter 38

Jacob Harrison sat in his office sorting through purchase orders and listening to the intense rain. The task was certainly something he could have someone else do, but he was trying to distract himself. The rain was accompanied by lightning, and he knew that, since the ground was saturated, it wouldn't take long for the river to resume its rise. He also knew that being on a raft in the middle of a river during a lightning storm was not a place to be.

As much as he tried to busy himself, he could not keep his mind on task. Out of frustration he finally gathered the papers into a pile and leaned back in his chair. He placed his pipe between his teeth and tried bringing the tobacco back to life with a few puffs, but the embers had died and would have to be relit. Rather than strike a match, he placed his pipe onto the table and crossed his arms on his chest.

There was a knock on his door. "Mr. Harrison." Billy Yates slowly opened the door and poked his head in.

"Whadda ya want, Billy…can't you see I'm busy?"

"Sir, the boys was wantin' to know if you was headin' to Buffalo City today."

There was a sharp crack of thunder within a split second after a lightning flash. "In this mess?"

"Then we'll put your horse and buggy away for you."

There was a pause. "Thanks, Billy."

"Yer welcome, Mr. Harrison."

The door closed and, once again, Jacob was alone. He continued to think about the boat with those four boys swirling down the river in the storm. He knew that the river could rise suddenly and cause more havoc. Now he began to have regrets and wished he had not pushed the trip to Buffalo City at this time.

Suddenly, he stood and walked quickly through his door and into the noisy mill.

411

"Billy!" He looked for the man who had just been in his office. Not seeing him, Harrison headed to the horse stalls.

"Billy!" Harrison called again as soon as he exited into the wagon shed.

"Over here, Mr. Harrison."

"I've changed my mind," Harrison said. "Don't unhook the horse.

Billy looked puzzled at Harrison's words.

"I'll be needin' it after all."

***

The rain was relentless as the heavy-laden ferry dipped and bobbed in the current. The strain of keeping the boat in the middle of the river was already taking a toll on the four young men. They were soaked and hungry, but none of them dared to take their eyes off the river.

Jay managed a pole and tended the rudder but was becoming anxious. He knew that just a few more miles down the river was where he would execute his plan. A small river called *Big Creek* flowed into the Buffalo. At that point there was a bend in the river, and there was always turbulence where the waters merged. Now, with the rivers gushing, he knew it would be more than turbulent and difficult to safely navigate. He knew that if he was going to make his move it would be there. He placed his right hand onto the leather scabbard attached to his belt, making sure his hunting knife was secure.

***

Jacob Harrison pulled his buggy to a stop as close to the front steps of his house as possible. He ran quickly through the downpour, leapt up the steps, and burst through the front door. May Bess was in the kitchen preparing the mid-day meal.

"Land sakes!" She jumped at the sound of the front door being flung open. "You came through that door like a bear was chasing you."

412

Jacob ignored his sister and quickly gathered rain gear and dry clothing.

Feeling suddenly uneasy at her brother's intensity, May Bess called out. "Jacob!" She left the kitchen when he didn't reply, and, drying her hands on her apron, she walked down the hallway and called again. "Jacob!"

"May Bess, I need that trunk you took on your travel last year. I need to put into it some clothing and blankets that I want to keep dry."

May Bess stood in the doorway of her brother's bedroom, watching him rifle through dresser drawers and the cedar chest. "Jacob, what's the matter?"

Jacob didn't answer for a moment as he continued his search. "Those boys are out in this storm, and, with this rain, the river is apt to come up and come up fast."

"But they're on the river, what can you do about it?"

Harrison looked up from his task. "May Bess, I don't have time to discuss it…I need that trunk, please."

Without hesitation, May Bess turned and retrieved the trunk from her bedroom. Jacob took the trunk and began stuffing the items he had gathered into it.

"Father, what's wrong?"

Jacob looked toward the doorway of his bedroom as he slammed the lid closed and latched it shut. He saw Pamela standing there with May Bess. "Those boys are on the river and it's about to get ugly with all this rain."

He picked up the small trunk and hurriedly walked into the parlor. He dropped the trunk onto the floor by the front door and grabbed his rain gear off the coat rack. Pamela and May Bess followed him into the room.

"Father, what are you going to do?"

Harrison already had his slicker on and was reaching for his hat.

"I'm going to take the trails to where Big Creek runs into the Buffalo and hopefully beat them there. I need to get them off the river."

"In this storm?" May Bess said in a worried tone.

413

"With the ground already wet and it rainin' this hard, that river will come up quick, and if it comes up very much those boys don't have a chance."

"Daddy," Pam said in a tone which captured Jacob's attention, "I want to go with you."

Jacob's first reaction was to say no and haul the trunk out the door and leave; however, something stopped him. He glanced at May Bess who had a worried look on her face then back at his daughter.

"Go get your rain gear…and do it quick."

Within moments Pam was dressed for the wet weather, and, with the objections from May Bess following them through the door, the pair climbed into the surrey and headed down the muddy roads toward their destination.

***

"It won't take much more rain like this for the river to start rising," Doug said through the noise of the rain.

It was something he didn't have to say because the others were already aware of their situation. Mostly he had made the comment because it had been an hour since they had rescued themselves from the tree and no one had been talking. Jay was glad it was raining because, if it weren't, he was sure the others would notice his perspiration. He was getting nervous because of what he was about to do.

"We're almost to a big bend in the river. It will curve to the left. Big Creek empties into the Buffalo there."

"It's bound to be flowin' pretty hard." Mike kept his eyes on the river in front of them.

"All we have to do is keep the boat in the middle of the river," Jay said. "Remember to just go with the current and don't fight it."

A bolt of lightning struck a nearby tree, causing the four to duck out of instinct. At the same moment the immediate boom of thunder caused their insides to jiggle.

"That was too close," Mike said. "This is not a safe place to be right now."

"We don't have much of a choice, though, do we?" Jay spoke in a loud voice to be heard over the still-rumbling thunder.

They noticed more debris floating in the water around them, swirling and churning in the muddy flow. Temporary waterfalls crashed down the towering bluffs along the river and over the edges of the mud embankments, adding to the murk. Mike admitted to himself that he had never in his life been as nervous, and possibly even as scared, as he was at that moment.

"I see the bend in the river comin' up!" Charley pointed. Even through the pouring rain, they could indeed see the curve looming ahead of them.

Doug glanced at Mike, who was already looking at him. "Think we can do this?"

"We don't have a choice," Doug replied.

"We can do it...we can do it; I know we can." Charley didn't seem apprehensive at all.

As they rapidly approached the bend in the river, they were able to see the outflow from Big Creek pushing hard into the Buffalo. They gripped their poles and prepared themselves for a sudden push when they hit the new current. They noticed that the river didn't look quite right as the channel made its bend. The water from Big Creek was splashing against something in the river. Mike assumed it to be a boulder near the edge of the shore or even the high water hitting the edge of a bluff. Through the rain it was difficult to see clearly.

Suddenly, they all saw the hazard at the same time but were too stunned for words. They were silent for a few seconds, not believing what they were seeing. Doug finally exclaimed, "Oh, Good Lord in Heaven, it's a log jam."

Jay was horrified at the sight, just like the others, but soon realized that this could actually help him with his plan. As they continued toward the danger of the log jam, Jay reached around and placed his hand on his knife. He slowly retrieved it and held it to his side.

"What do we do?" Mike looked at Doug in panic.

415

"Over there!" Doug pointed to a thicket of river willows on the right-hand side of the river. "We can run the raft into those willows and jump onto the shore. Maybe we can tie the boat to them and keep from losing it."

Jay knew he couldn't let that happen because it would ruin his scheme. He knew that he needed to head into the heart of the churning water and into the tangled pile of logs choking the river.

"Mike, come over to our side and help us push the boat to the right," Doug ordered. "Jay, try to rudder us over to that side of the river while we push."

Mike joined Doug and Charley, and the three fought the strong current with their poles, frantically pushing with all their strength. With each push of the poles, they came closer to the confluence of Big Creek and the Buffalo. They knew that if they hit that flow it would slam them into the logs.

"Jay, turn the rudder!" Mike realized they were not nearing the river bank.

"I'm trying, but it seems to be jammed." Jay acted as if he were working as hard as he could to move the rudder.

Lightning flashed and thunder continued to roll; the craft sped closer to the turbulence ahead.

"It's not working!" Charley yelled and the rain continued to pour.

"Jay, you better get that rudder working, or we're not gonna make it." Mike looked back at Jay.

The river channel narrowed and they picked up speed. They looked ahead again and realized now that it was too late. They had missed their opportunity and were only moments away from impact, with the force of the current pushing them into the logs.

"It's no use," Doug said. "Grab onto the railing and hang on for dear life."

They were now only a few yards from the log jam. Jay realized it was time for action. He pulled his knife up and cut the ropes holding the zinc boulder into position. He quickly cut all the support ropes on the right side of the boat.

Mike turned his head to see if Jay was braced for impact, when—to his horror—he saw Jay cut through the last rope. "Jay, what do you think you're doing?"

The words had barely left Mike's mouth when the current from Big Creek caught them from the right side and immediately pushed them sideways. Before Mike could react to Jay's deed, he felt the impact against the logs.

As the current pushed them sideways into the logs, the zinc boulder began to slide, and, as it moved, it tilted the boat toward the logs, allowing the strength of the current to get under the boat and lift it up on the right side. This caused the boulder to slide more, and, before anyone could move out of its way, it crashed into the railing, pinning Doug's leg against it.

Now the boat was tilted and banging against the logs, with the current pushing from underneath, threatening to flip the boat over.

Panic gripped Mike as Doug cried out in agony. Jay held onto the railing for a moment, surveying what he had done.

"Charley, help me move this rock!" In vain Mike tried to move the boulder. Doug pushed as much as he could, but he had become weak from the pain.

Emboldened by his action, and with the storm raging around them, Jay shouted at Mike, "You lose, Farm Boy."

"Jay, help us move this boulder!" Mike shouted back with fiery anger in his voice.

Jay shouted again with laughter. "You should never have come here…you don't belong here. Go back where you came from."

Suddenly, Mike left his position and lunged at Jay. Jay was caught off guard and was pushed into the railing against his back. He moaned but quickly regained his composure. He pushed Mike off him as Charley continued to desperately tug at the rock against his brother's leg.

The boat bobbed dangerously up and down, and Mike lunged again at Jay, determined to give Jay what he deserved. Jay swiped in the air with his knife, barely missing Mike with the blade. Mike and Jay were both thrown off balance by the bouncing of the boat against the logs, but Mike steadied himself first and threw a fist, catching Jay square in the jaw. The knife fell from Jay's hand and the blow knocked him over the railing and into the raging water. The current quickly took him past the boat and into the logs.

Seeing that Jay was out of the boat, Mike turned his attention back to his friend. Somehow, they had to get Doug out from behind the rock and off the boat. The log jam was solid enough that, if they could jump onto the logs, they could make it to the shore safely; but, with the current under the tilted boat, Mike was afraid it could flip at any moment.

Mike had an idea and—in panic—reached for the saw he had earlier used on the tree.

"Doug, I'm going to cut the railing enough to move it and get you out from behind that rock."

"You'd better hurry! I'm losing feeling in my foot."

Mike placed the saw on the wooden railing next to Doug; just as he was about to cut it, they all heard a cry for help. Mike and Charley turned their heads and saw Jay in the water, holding on to a log and fighting the current. The heavy current had no place to go but under the log jam and was threatening to pull him under it. They could see that Jay had no chance and would eventually succumb to the pull of the water. Charley watched as Jay struggled against the current and continually bobbed under the water and back up, coughing and sputtering.

Charley looked at Mike. "He's gonna drown!" Panic filled his voice.

Mike began sawing into the heavy boat railing. "He tried to kill us Charley; there's nothing we can do for him. Right now we have to free your brother before this boat flips."

"But he's gonna drown." Charley continued to watch Jay fight for his life in the current.

"Charley, you just hold on to your brother and pull him as soon as I cut through this rail. The rock's gonna slide when I go through this and we will have only a split second to move Doug out of the way."

Charley barely heard Mike's words to him. Although Jay had never been kind to Charley and had even bodily harmed him, Charley kept hearing in his head the words from Pastor MB Russell: "Charley, do you want to be like Jesus? Jesus said you are like him when you forgive others, when you don't repay evil for evil, and especially when you do good to those people who hurt you."

Though the storm was raging all around them, and his brother was hurting and in danger of worse, Charley only heard the message of helping even those who hurt him. Charley looked at Mike, who was still frantically trying to cut Doug free, then at Jay, who was losing his grip—and his battle for life—on the floating log.

Suddenly, Charley leapt from the boat and onto the log jam.

"Charley, what are you doing?" Mike panicked, knowing that Charley could fall from the logs and into the dangerous water himself.

Without replying, Charley made his way to Jay, who was now holding on with only one arm as the log bobbed and bounced wildly. With the current splashing violently against the logs, Charley balanced on the edge of the logs next to Jay. Jay had been so intent on fighting the current pulling at his legs that he didn't notice Charley leaning over as far as he could, with an arm outstretched toward him.

With more fervor and as much strength as Mike possessed, he continued cutting at the board. Doug was close to unconsciousness and began to slump forward toward the boulder.

"Charley, I need your help!" Mike cried out again through the rain and thunder.

At that moment, Jay began losing his fragile grip on the log, and his head fell below the surface of the water. Charley made a lunge, almost losing his footing on the massive log pile. That action allowed him to grab Jay's shirt sleeve. Though the logs under him were moving up and down in the water with the current, he pulled with all his strength.

It took a moment, but Jay's head broke the surface, and he sputtered as his face cleared the water. Charley continued to pull until he overcame the draw of the current and had Jay on top of the logs with him.

"Charley!" Mike watched the event from the corner of his eye. He had sawn through most of the railing and needed Charley's help to pull Doug away before the boulder shifted further.

Jay opened his eyes and saw Charley standing over him. Charley reached down to help Jay get to his feet and onto more solid logs when Jay suddenly reacted.

"Get away from me you retard." Without warning Jay pushed Charley away from him.

On the floating logs, Charley lost his balance and fell backward into the water.

Mike's heart stopped beating when he saw Charley fall into the river. He didn't know whether to continue sawing to free Doug, or rush to Charley's aid to pull him out of the water.

"Jay, grab Charley! Help him!"

Charley, buffeted by the churning water, grasped a floating log, trying to get onto the log pile. He bounced wildly in the strong current. He was stronger than Jay but could not overcome the pull of the undertow. He reached his arm up for assistance. Jay solemnly sat on the logs digesting what had occurred.

"Jay, take his hand!" Mike yelled to him as he heard the beam begin to crack from behind Doug's pinned leg.

From around the bend a tangle of floating wooden fence posts and barbed wire came rushing down the river toward them. Jay got to his feet and stood in stunned silence, not knowing what he should do. Charley struggled in the current and reached his hand up toward Jay once more. He looked up at Jay but again got no immediate response. Suddenly, Jay came to his senses and realized he needed to help. He crouched as close to Charley as he dared, but Charley was just out of reach.

"Come on, Charley, grab my hand."

Charley summoned the strength that remained and made one final lunge. He grabbed Jay's hand; the turbulence almost pulled Jay in with him.

"Pull, Jay…pull!" Mike shouted.

"Help me out, Charley." Jay pulled as hard as he could on the floating, bobbing log pile.

Charley kicked in the water and Jay pulled.

"Almost got you." Jay continued to strain.

"Charley, watch out!" Mike's cry was too late.

The barbed wire and wood posts rushing down the current hit Charley from behind, instantly entangling him. The sharp barbs clawed deep into Charley, causing him to release his grasp on the log. Jay frantically pulled at Charley, but the current was too strong and pulled him down and under the log jam. The pain and pull of the water resulted in Charley's hand slipping from Jay's grasp. To their horror, Charley sank under the surface of the muddy water and out of sight.

"Charley…no!…Charley!" Doug yelled in mortal pain and Mike stopped sawing.

Jay looked up at Mike and their eyes met. Jay looked back down at the churning water and suddenly realized what Charley had done for him. His mind replayed all the times he had tormented Charley in the past, only to have Charley lose his life to save him.

Jay looked back up at Mike and stepped back, stumbling over the logs in the jam and away from the boat.

Mike watched in agony as Jay turned and struggled over the logs toward the river bank. Doug finally succumbed to the pain, losing consciousness and slumping forward onto the rock. Tears flowed from Mike's eyes and mingled with the raindrops. He heard the railing crack once again as the listing, fragile boat continued to be buffeted by the current. He watched Jay amble his way over the logs to the muddy shore line and finally disappear into the trees.

All of a sudden, the boat was struck by something Mike had heard strike it before. He looked in time to see a log bounce off the boat and slam into the pile of logs and broken trees clogging the river. He glanced up the river only to see an armada of logs rushing toward them. He quickly made another few strokes with the saw and, with a hard bounce in the current, the brace behind Doug's leg gave way and snapped.

The break pulled the saw from Mike's hand and freed Doug's leg. Without even thinking, Mike moved Doug out of harm's way just as the motion of the boat pushed the zinc boulder further to the side and slightly over the edge. Mike looked back over his shoulder and knew he had only seconds to get Doug off the boat before the full force of the oncoming logs crashed into them.

With the boat being tossed by the current, Mike pulled Doug to the edge of the boat next to the log jam. At that moment, Doug regained consciousness.

"Doug, you have to help me as much as you can. We have to jump and we have only one chance. Ready...jump."

The pair jumped and crashed in a heap onto the floating log jam. Doug screamed in pain as he landed on the jumble of logs, with Mike falling on top of him. Within seconds they heard the pounding of several logs hitting the log jam, and they watched as other logs plowed into their makeshift boat. The force of the current and the logs hitting the boat together dismantled the old ferry. Within moments, it had been reduced to tinder; the zinc boulder slid off the edge and into the deep, churning river.

The pair continued to lie on the floating log pile trying to wrap their minds around all that had happened. The rain lessened but continued to fall. Mike looked around at the log pile then at what was left of their boat.

"We have to get off this debris," Mike told Doug. "The river is rising, and—if it gets high enough—it could break this log jam free at any moment."

Mike stood and, after getting his balance, helped his wounded friend to his feet. The pair began walking unsteadily on the logs toward the shore. Doug was having difficulty standing, and Mike could tell he was about to pass out again. After a few steps Doug collapsed; his weight took Mike down with him. Completely out of breath Mike lifted his face toward heaven in the falling rain. "Lord God, please help me get Doug off these logs. I can't do it alone."

He lowered his head and looked at his friend lying next to him. He knew that he couldn't get Doug off the unstable log pile if he was unconscious. He also knew that he needed to get Doug help soon or he might lose Doug as well. He stood and tried to roust his friend one more time when he thought he heard a voice calling from the shore. He looked toward the voice and finally saw a man standing on the river bank.

Mike began waving frantically; the man made his way onto the log jam and headed their direction. Mike turned his attention back to Doug, who seemed to be conscious once again, but barely. As he encouraged Doug to stand once more, the man from the shore got to them. Mike looked up and into the face of Jacob Harrison.

"Where are the others?" Harrison placed Doug's left arm over his shoulder.

Mike took Doug's other arm. "They're gone, sir."

The pair strained to get over the jumble of logs and finally managed to drag Doug to the shore, where Harrison's surrey was waiting.

They approached the wagon. "Pamela, get into the trunk and get out some blankets." Harrison ordered. At that moment, Mike looked up and saw Pam open a trunk and pull out some blankets to wrap around Doug. Harrison and Mike placed Doug behind the seat and swaddled him in the heavy material. They then placed rain gear over him to keep the blankets as dry as possible. Mike climbed into the back with Doug and the rain slowed to a gentle pace.

"Where's Charley?" Pam looked at Mike.

Mike just lowered his eyes; that told Pam enough.

"What about Jay?" Harrison grabbed the reigns and urged his horse into motion.

Mike responded in a low, disgusted tone. "He ran away into the woods."

The horse and passengers continued as fast as possible down the muddy, rutted pathway. None of them spoke another word all the way back to Rush.

Three Years Later

Chapter 39

The summer sun had been absent for a month. Dogwood trees displayed their deep crimson color, and the once-green river willows were golden. The dark brown bark of maple trees stood in vivid contrast to their fiery orange and red leaves. Every plant and tree in the Ozark hills was adorned with its unique autumn color; only the Creator could have displayed such a splendid palette.

The morning air was cool and crisp as Mike pulled his wagon to a stop in front of Rosie's store. He set the brake and jumped to the ground. Making his way around the wagon, he checked all of the ropes, making sure they were still tight and the wagon contents were secure. After one last inspection he stopped at the passenger side. He raised his hand and carefully helped Pamela down to the ground. She held a swaddled bundle in her arms. They paused for a moment looking at the front of the store then walked up the creaky wooden steps and entered the building.

Rosie boomed from her position behind a counter: "My soul, will you look who just walked through my door." "Hello, Rosie," Pam said. Rosie came out onto the floor to greet them.

Pam handed the bundle to Mike then welcomed a warm hug from her friend.

"Look at that young'un, will you," Rosie said in a high-pitched voice. "He's shore the spittin' image of his father."

Mike blushed and Pam beamed with delight.

There was an awkward pause in the conversation when Rosie leaned over and placed her index finger into the baby's tiny grasp.

"We stopped to say goodbye, Rosie." Mike swallowed his emotion. Rosie stood and looked at the couple with sad, watery eyes.

"I really hoped you two had changed your minds about leavin'."

Mike and Pam glanced at each other; immediately tears trickled down Pam's cheek.

"It ain't easy, Rosie," Mike said, "but I really can't pass up this opportunity."

Rosie smiled through red eyes. "I know, kid. Nothin' ever stays the same, does it?"

"You never change, Rosie." Mike grinned.

Rosie looked into Mike's eyes. "I guess I need to stop callin' you *kid*, don't I?"

"Rosie, you can call me anything you want."

They all laughed, but it was forced. Saying goodbye to one of the best friends Mike had ever had was difficult.

"So…how far you figure on getting today?" Rosie motioned them over to one of the counters.

The baby grew restless, so Mike handed him back to Pamela. Immediately he quieted.

"We're going by way of Gilbert up the river. We'll spend the night with Doug and Sandy."

"I knew you couldn't leave without seein' them." Rosie leaned down behind the counter to produce a brown-paper-wrapped package. She placed it onto the countertop.

"I thought I'd get a little somethin' for the kid. Just a few things I ordered. They're a little big now, but he will grow into 'em."

"Oh, Rosie, you didn't have to do that." Pam leaned over the counter and hugged Rosie again.

"I know I didn't have to," she grinned.

There was another pause as Mike placed the package under his arm.

"I reckon your ma and pa ain't very excited to see you go," Rosie said.

"I'm sure it won't be long before my mother comes for a visit. This will give her another excuse to get away from Rush."

They all laughed.

"Of course, my father isn't too happy."

"Well, at least you won't be too far away. Kansas is only a skip and a jump away these days."

Mike took one last look around the store. The memories of the past three years flooded his mind. He remembered the first time he had entered the store as an apprehensive but excited young man, full of wonder and adventure.

"Well, Rosie, I guess we'd best be on our way. I'd rather Pam and the baby not ride in the damp evening air."

Rosie stepped from behind the counter and walked the couple to the door.

"Now, you watch out for my father." Pam teased Rosie. "Now that you and he are partners in the Red Rose, you're gonna have to keep an eye out for him."

Rosie chuckled. "Sweetie, you don't have to worry about me. I can take up for myself. I won't have any problem keeping that man in line."

Standing with the front door open, they all laughed together. Then the mood became serious.

"Goodbye, Rosie. You've been a life saver and a great friend. I'm gonna miss you," Mike said. A lump formed in his throat.

Mike and Rosie embraced one last time.

"We'll be back from time to time," Pam said. "My father made Michael promise."

"I know it's just goodbye for a spell."

Suddenly Pam felt something soft brush against her ankles. She looked down and saw Earl caressing her with his cheek. Some of the gray fur on his face had turned white with age.

Kneeling down with the baby in her arms, Pam rubbed him one last time. "I'm gonna miss you, too, Earl."

"Well, come on, Pam; it's gonna take us some time to get to Gilbert."

Pam stood and Mike helped her down the steps and into the wagon.

"By the way," Rosie said from the porch, "I put some stationery in that bundle. I expect to get a letter from you as soon as you get settled in Wichita."

"Don't worry, Rosie, I'll be sure to write." Pam nestled into her seat.

Mike climbed into the wagon next to Pam and picked up the leather reins. He visually inspected the harness on the team one last time and released the brake.

He looked at Rosie and raised a hand into the air. Then, with a flip of leather straps, the team moved away from Rush.

***

When Mike and Pam pulled into Gilbert, the sun was about to sink behind the hillside. While the air was cool and crisp, the sunlight was warm on their skin. Mike directed the wagon down the dirt street to Doug's place of business. Mike followed the familiar path, and, within a few minutes, they were stopping in front of Doug's building. They could hear the buzzing of the saw as it cut through timber.

Inside, Doug Sprouse carefully fed a white-oak plank of wood into his table saw, sending a shower of sawdust to the floor. Three years earlier he and Sandy had moved to Gilbert, where Doug had built a stave-manufacturing operation. His business had become quite successful, and he delivered the wooden barrel components to barrel makers all over the area. Since the railroad was now nearby, he was able to ship them far and wide.

Mike stepped to the ground. "Stay in the wagon, Pam. I'll go get Doug.".

Mike entered through a sliding barn door into the noisy building.

"Mike!"

Mike saw Doug already on his way over to him from across the sawdust-littered floor.

The pair shook hands and patted each other on the shoulder.

"I thought you'd never get here." Doug ushered Mike out into the sunlight.

"Hi, Pam." Doug waved. "Sandy's been on pins and needles all day long waiting for you."

Doug's house was next to his business, so Mike climbed back into the wagon and pulled to the front of the house where Sandy was already waiting on the porch. Before the wagon had even stopped, Sandy was down the steps and to Pam's side of the wagon.

"I'm so glad you're finally here." Sandy was barely able to contain her excitement.

She helped Pam down from the wagon, and they walked around to Mike and Doug.

"Who in the world do we have here?" Doug said. Pam handed her bundle to Sandy, who was reaching with anticipation.

Pam and Mike looked at each other with a grin. "We named him Charles," Pam said.

Standing next to Sandy and the baby, Doug beamed with watery eyes but didn't say a word.

Mike looked around. "You've fixed the place up some more since I was here last."

"There's always something to do around here. Let me help you with your luggage." Doug grasped the handles of a couple of bags.

Mike and Doug took the luggage into the house. Pam and Sandy followed Doug to the bedroom, where they prepared the bed for Charles.

Doug exited the room. "I'm sure the girls don't need our help. Let me show you what I've done to the place."

Mike followed Doug outside and to the shop, where the saw was still running. Doug introduced Mike to the worker he had hired since Mike's last visit.

Mike surveyed Doug's machinery. "You've really done good for yourself, Doug."

"Well you haven't done so bad yourself. I reckon you will do even better with Coleman. Those new lanterns of his outshine anything on the market. I expect you'll be rich before you know it."

"I'm already rich." Mike smiled at his friend.

***

With the supper dishes cleaned and put away, the ladies joined Mike and Doug on the front porch. Charles was sleeping soundly, so the four were finally able to sit and enjoy the evening.

Mike looked out into the evening shadows. "I'm sure gonna miss these hills."

The tree frogs were singing one of their last few songs of the season, and the stars shone in the clear, autumn sky.

"Kansas is different country, that's for sure," Doug replied.

"When have you ever been to Kansas?" Sandy teased.

"Oh, I've never been myself, but I've talked to people who have. They say it's flat as a pancake, and the treetops all lean to the northeast because the wind is always blowing."

"Sounds like a tall tale to me," Sandy replied.

"And the winters are bone chilling, the summers are long and hot, and sometimes the ground cracks wide open from the dry spells and swallows up houses."

"Now I know yer tellin' whoppers...don't pay him no mind," Sandy said.

They conversed on the porch until Mike and Pam—knowing they had several long days ahead of them—needed to retire. Sandy followed her guests into the house to help them with anything they might need before bed. She entered their room to bring a fresh bowl of water for the sideboard.

"How is Doug doing these days?" Mike asked as Sandy set the bowl onto the wooden surface.

Wiping her hands on her skirt, Sandy got a sad look in her eyes. "He has good days and bad days." There was a pause. "Most evenings he sits on the porch by himself. Much of the time he's angry at God....sometimes he seems more hurt than angry."

"I know it's been difficult on both of you." Pam looked over at Charles, who was still sleeping.

Sandy moved to the doorway. "I don't know if he'll ever get over losin' Charley."

Conversation lulled when they heard the baby make a sound as if he were going to begin crying, but then he became quiet once again.

"If you need anything else, just let me know." Sandy and Pam hugged goodnight.

The wooden door creaked as Pam closed it.

"I really worry about Doug." Mike sat on the edge of the bed and removed his boots.

"He hasn't been the same since the accident on the river," Pam replied.

"It wasn't an accident."

Mike realized he had sounded curt. "I'm sorry, Pam. I didn't mean to sound cross."

"I know…it was just so unfortunate."

"And unnecessary. Coward ran away and hasn't been seen since."

"Well, time heals wounds," Pam said with optimism.

Mike removed his shirt. "I've got a wound you can heal."

Pam looked at him in surprise.

"My shoulder is killin' me. I must have pulled a muscle loadin' our furniture into the wagon. Think you could rub some liniment on it?"

Pam smiled and rummaged through one of their bags. She pulled out a jar of ointment.

"Come here, my big baby. Let me see what I can do."

Mike smiled and awaited her soothing touch.

431

***

"Y'all be careful on the rest of your trip," Sandy said. Mike climbed into the wagon with Pam and the baby.

"Well, it looks like it's gonna be a beautiful day for travelin'." Mike took the reins into his hands.

"Say hello to your folks for us," Sandy said.

"We will," Mike replied.

"And we can hardly wait to show them their new grandson." Pam added.

Doug walked up to Mike and held up his hand.

"Goodbye, Doug." Mike placed his hand into Doug's. "A fella couldn't have a better friend."

"You probably say that to everybody." Doug smiled.

Mike grinned as Doug stepped back next to Sandy. They all waved and, with a whistle, the wagon began rolling toward Kingston. They would stay in Kingston for a few days then move on to Kansas, where Mike and Pamela would begin building a new life together.

Chapter 40

Doug pulled a wooden lever beside the saw, releasing tension on the canvas belt and allowing the saw blade to whine to a stop. He examined the planks he had created and moved the fence on his saw to cut the timber into the desired lengths for his barrel orders. As he worked, his mind struggled between thoughts of good friends and memories of his past.

Although he hadn't seen much of his best friend Mike in the last few years, he knew now that he might not ever see him again. He began feeling sorry for himself as he stacked the wood sections onto a nearby table, making them ready for their next trip through the process. He was pleased with the news that Mike and Pam had named their baby Charles, but that only caused him to think about losing Charley three years earlier.

The bitterness and anger still felt as strong as it had years ago. A part of him knew he had no right to be angry at God, but another part of him questioned a loving God allowing someone like Charley to die. That part of him eventually caused him to leave the church and even stop reading his Bible and praying, which had been an important part of his life since birth.

"We've got enough for a full load."

Doug turned to see his helper, Ned Baker.

"If I run these through, do you think we can fit them onto the wagon?" Doug spoke over the noise of the steam generator.

Ned looked at the sections Doug was ready to cut into finished lengths. "I reckon we can figure out how to get 'em loaded."

Ned turned to finish loading the staves that were already cut. When Doug had completed his task, he once again stopped the blade then carried the cut oak sections to be stacked onto the wagon.

"Soon as we get these loaded up, I'll take 'em up to the train," Ned said. He helped Doug move the wood.

"If it's all the same to you, I think I'll take this load myself." Doug wrestled with a cumbersome armload.

Ned looked surprised because he usually hauled the product up to St. Joe, just five miles north, to the train for shipment.

"You haven't taken a load for six months. Think you can remember how to get there without gettin' lost?"

Doug smiled at his friend's playfulness. "If I'm not back in a couple of days, just send out the search party."

"Well, I'll at least hitch up the team for ya." Ned carefully placed the last few boards onto the heap.

"Thank ya, Ned. That'll give me time to grab a quick bite."

Doug removed his leather gloves and walked toward his house. He noticed the position of the sun and realized he would probably be returning after dark, but under a sky loaded with bright stars and a moon that was almost full, he would have no trouble getting home. He always took lanterns with him but enjoyed being bathed in moonlight when he could.

Doug entered the house through the doorway to the kitchen, where Sandy was preparing the mid-day meal.

"Glad you're in here for a change. I was about to bring your food to you." Sandy stepped over to Doug to receive a kiss. "Now go wash up, and I'll put it on the table."

Doug returned to the kitchen and was handed a bowl of chicken and dumplings. He sat down and leaned his face over the steamy offering, closed his eyes, and inhaled the aroma from his favorite meal.

"Is there a special occasion?" Doug leaned back in his chair.

Sandy smiled and placed her filled bowl on the table. "No special occasion. I just needed to do something with that leftover chicken from last night."

There was a pause when Sandy took her place at the table and hoped for a meal prayer; but none was offered, as Doug picked up his spoon and began eating.

"By the way, I'm takin' the load up to St. Joe this afternoon."

"You haven't taken a load for six months."

Doug swallowed another mouthful. "Yeah, Ned reminded me of that, too."

"Well, getting away from the place will probably do you good. I expect it will be late when you return, though."

There was a pause as Doug continued devouring his meal. "It shouldn't be too late."

He glanced up at Sandy, who was holding her spoon but seemed disinterested in eating. "Is there something on your mind?" Doug noticed she appeared to be distracted.

Sandy smiled sweetly at her husband. "It can wait."

The couple continued to eat in silence, Sandy watching Doug. She sensed something was on his mind, not only because he wanted to take the staves to the train, but also because he was unusually quiet. Normally, around the table, she could barely get in a word.

Sandy stood to retrieve the iron pot from the stove. She placed it on the table and deposited another ladle full of dumplings into Doug's bowl, which was practically empty. "Thought you could use a refill, since you have a long afternoon." Sandy moved the pot back to the stove.

"I could eat your chicken and dumplin's until they were runnin' out my ears," Doug said.

Sandy chuckled as she sat back down to the table. "It was sure nice seeing Mike and Pamela yesterday."

Doug tilted his bowl for the last spoonful of liquid. "Yeah, it was. I hate that they are moving so far away."

Sandy watched as he finished eating and placed his spoon into the bowl. Doug caught Sandy's gaze and smiled.

"Is something troubling you, Doug?"

435

Doug could never hide anything from his wife, even when he tried hard. He lowered his eyes and looked into his empty bowl. "Does it show?"

Sandy reached across the table and placed her hand onto his. "You put up a good front, but I can see it in your eyes."

Doug remained silent, because he didn't want to discuss his thoughts just then. "I've just got some thinkin' to do."

"Is that why you're takin' the load yourself?"

"I reckon," Doug said with a slight grin as he squeezed her hand.

***

With a flip of the reins, Doug was rolling down the lane and away from Gilbert. The mule team maintained a strong and steady pace along the rutted dirt path. He waved at Roy as he passed the general store, and then it wasn't long before he met the main road. He turned the team north for the five-mile trek to St. Joe. There he would deposit his load at the train station for delivery to a man in the town of Harrison several miles north.

On the main road he was able to look out across the hills and valleys of the Ozark Mountains. He marveled at the colors in the autumn leaves. The vivid orange and yellow leaves of the maple and sycamore stood in stark contrast to the multiple shades of red and rust of the many varieties of oak trees. Sumac bushes along the road grew in thickets, displaying their bright red leaves. As far as his eyes could see in any direction, the hillsides were painted with almost every color he could imagine. Every growing thing shared in the spectacular display.

He had traveled a couple of miles when he noticed a group of wagons and horses on the side of the road. As he neared he saw several men putting the finishing touches to a newly erected, large, canvas tent. Passing, he watched two people carry a heavy wooden sign toward the road with the words *Tent Revival Tonight* in bold, black letters.

Seeing the words caused Doug to think about how he had neglected God and his church over the last few years. Something tugged at his heart as he passed, and he realized it was the guilt he felt. He knew he couldn't run forever, but his bitterness still overpowered his desire to return to his spiritual beliefs. He still had questions to which God had not replied, and—until he had those answers—he just couldn't find peace with the Lord. He continued on, and the nagging at his soul eventually subsided as he neared the train-station dock.

St. Joe was not a large town, but the train that stopped there, made it much easier to distribute his wood product. Things were changing in rural Arkansas, and the new railhead was a welcomed change as far as he was concerned.

It was late afternoon when Doug stopped his team close to one of the docks and made arrangements for the shipment. He helped two workers unload his wagon and stack the wood next to the tracks. It took almost an hour for the unloading process and to receive a receipt from the dock manager, but as soon as he had his shipping order, he climbed aboard his wagon and headed home.

The air was quickly becoming heavy and cool as the sun faded behind the hilltops. He knew he could only make it halfway home before it grew completely dark, but he didn't mind. He pulled his collar tight around his neck and whistled a tune as he rolled south.

Within an hour, only a slight tinge of an orange glow remained on the western horizon. He marveled at the stars and watched the moon brighten as it climbed the sky. Though the air was much cooler, it felt crisp and refreshing.

Far in the distance he saw a light next to the road. He realized that it must be from the tent revival he had seen being prepared earlier. He got that gnawing feeling again...tugging at his heart. He swallowed hard and tried to ignore it, but it grew stronger as he neared.

He was close enough now to hear voices singing, as the thick, damp air carried them across the hills. He could see horses and wagons around the tent and was amazed at how many were there. He had been to tent revivals before but none as crowded as this one. Finally, as he came to the tent, the urging in his soul persuaded him to pull his wagon to the side of the road.

Doug was surprised at himself for stopping. He didn't know why, but he felt compelled to see what was going on inside the crowded tent. He sat for a moment in his wagon, struggling with his decision, but eventually he stepped to the ground as the singing ended. He tethered his team to a tree and walked slowly to the tent opening.

As he walked he began to shiver, not from the cool air, but from something inside him being stirred. It was almost the same feeling he remembered having as a child when he faced his father about something he had done wrong. He slowly continued and heard a man's voice beginning to preach.

Doug finally arrived at the tent opening and hesitated for a moment. He listened to the preacher through the heavy canvas wall, standing alone in the stillness of the night air.

"I will be preaching this evening from the book of John, Chapter Eight," the preacher began.

There was a pause as those with Bibles turned to the book and chapter.

"Tonight I want to talk about unforgivable sin."

The crowd shuffled a little and quietly murmured at the thought of an unforgivable sin.

The preacher continued. "Jesus was teaching in the Temple courts one day, and a group of Pharisees came to him with a woman who had been caught in adultery."

"Teacher,' they said, 'this woman was caught in adultery and the Law of Moses commands that we stone her. What do you say?'"

"They were trying to trap Jesus" the preacher exclaimed. "They thought that, either way he answered, they would be able to find fault with him."

Doug continued listening to the animated voice of the preacher through the canvas.

"Do you know what Jesus did?" There was a pause. "He simply bent down to the ground and wrote with his finger in the dust. That's right. He just drew with his finger. When the Pharisees continued to question him, he stood and finally said, *'Whoever is free of sin can throw the first stone.'*"

The preacher raised his voice with the exclamation to dramatize his point. Doug was intrigued with the style of this preacher.

"Once again, Jesus bent down and drew in the dust. After a few moments he stood, only to find that all of the accusers had wandered away, and he was left alone with the woman."

The preacher paused as he paced across the front to allow the scene to be fully understood by the congregation.

"Jesus asked the woman, *'Where are your accusers? Has anyone condemned you?'* The woman looked at him and said, *'No one, sir.'* Then do you know what Jesus said to her?" The preacher raised his hands as if expecting an answer from the crowd. "He said, *'Neither do I condemn thee. Go, but sin no more.'*"

At that, the crowd murmured more loudly than before.

The preacher paused to allow them to continue before he interrupted with a dramatic, wavering voice." I was stained deeply with sin. Like that woman I deserved death and punishment for my sins. Like all of us—we deserve separation from God for our sins, much like that sinful woman. But my friends, I am here to tell you that no matter how sinful your life has been…no matter how dreadful of a person you have been…no matter what you have done in your life, Jesus can forgive you and cleanse you from your sins. The only unforgivable sin is the sin of rejection of the Lord."

The crowd erupted in clapping, *amen*'s, and phrases of "Thank you, Jesus," from some of the ladies.

"It doesn't matter if you have lied."

"Yes" came from some in the crowd.

"Cheated."

"Yes."

"Stolen, or even committed murder; you can be forgiven of those sins, and Almighty God will remember them no more."

At that, the congregation began clapping again, saying *amen* loudly, and shouting, "Praise the Lord!"

The preacher allowed the crowd to continue while he caught his breath. At that moment Doug stepped into the tent to see this man, because his words spoke to his heart. He was a believer, but he found himself identifying with the words of the enthusiastic tent preacher. He realized that no matter how far away he was from God, he could be forgiven for his neglect…and needed to be. When he entered, the preacher had his back to the group, but he continued his sermon in a soft and barely audible tone.

"My friends," he began as the crowd quieted, "I have lived a life that was unpleasing to God. I was about as bad as a man could be."

The preacher began turning around slowly as he spoke. Doug saw that he was a young man with a short beard and neatly cut hair. He marveled at this young preacher's zeal and delivery of the scripture. He was impressed at the sincerity of his convictions.

Now tears rolled down the cheeks of the preacher as he continued. "One horrible and fateful day, someone showed me the selfless love of Jesus. My soul burned with regrets, and I realized that I wanted what that man had."

The crowd was moved by his words, and something about the young man looked familiar to Doug.

"One day I decided to stop running, and I found myself standing before the Lord with all my sins visible to him. I fell to my knees"—the preacher said as he clinched fists to his chest—"and I asked the Lord God above to forgive me and save me from myself and from my sins. I

440

desired to be transformed into a new person. I wanted to serve God and live for him."

The congregation once again erupted in cheers and *amen*'s all around at the preacher's proclamation of his moment-of-salvation experience.

Doug looked more closely at the young man, and suddenly his eyes widened. He realized who this young man was. His emotions leapt from identifying with the preacher's sermon to instant anger, because there—in front of him and the throng of worshippers—stood none other than Jason Finch.

Chapter 41

Doug began to shake as the anger engulfed his body. The congregation around him was now standing and continued to give God the glory for saving the preacher's soul from a life of sin. They shouted, and many even walked to the front of the tent in front of Finch to ask the Lord to forgive their sins also.

Doug wanted to fight his way through the crowd and grab Finch by the collar. He wanted to proclaim that Jason Finch was a murderer who only pretended to be who he was in order to take their money. He wanted to tell them about all of his detestable deeds. He wanted to tell the crowd how Finch took his brother from him three years earlier. But he realized it was not the thing to do at that moment.

He looked around at the crowd then at Finch, who was talking with those at the front and still proclaiming loudly how God had changed him. After struggling with indecision, Doug finally stepped outside the tent to wait until the people were gone. Then he would take the opportunity to collar Finch and make him pay for taking an innocent life and ruining others.

He lowered his head to keep Finch from noticing him and stepped further from the tent opening and into the darkness. He walked to a nearby wagon, where the grief of seeing Finch fully overtook him. He placed his hands onto one of the wheels to steady himself. He lowered his head and closed his eyes. Immediately his memories of that day on the raging river replayed vividly in his head, as if the event had just happened. He tried to choke back the tears of sadness and anger, but they resisted the attempt and flowed freely. In the background he could still hear the voices of the worshippers and of Jay, which ground into his very soul like a hard leather heel against a burning ember.

Doug opened his eyes and looked up into the sky. His emotions were ripping him apart, and he tried to understand his torment. As he looked up into the heavens, he said out loud, "God, why did you lead me here? Why did you allow this man to kill my brother? It's not fair that Charley died and yet this man fools people by proclaiming to belong to you...the very man who caused my brother to die."

He hung his head again and continued to steady himself against the wagon wheel. Suddenly he felt the presence of someone behind him. Before he could turn he heard a voice.

"Douglas?"

The woman's voice sounded familiar to him, but in his anger and grief he couldn't remember who it belonged to. He tried his best to compose himself as he slowly turned around.

"Doug Sprouse, is that you?" The woman asked softly.

Doug turned and faced the woman who had spoken to him. She was silhouetted against the light of the tent and he was unable to see her face clearly.

"Doug, it is you. My soul, I can't believe it's you." She raised her hands to her mouth.

Doug wiped his cheeks and stepped closer to the woman. "Beth?"

"Hi, Doug...you do remember me."

"Beth Hart, I'm surprised to see you here." Doug sniffled. "I haven't seen you since you quit working for Rosie almost three years ago."

"It's been a long time." She stepped toward Doug and reached out her hands toward him.

Doug took her hands and blinked hard to try and remove the lingering tears of anger in his eyes.

"I noticed you walk into the tent earlier," she said as their hands dropped to their sides.

"Beth...I...I don't know what to say. I'm afraid you caught me at a bad moment." His emotions of anger had come to a screeching halt at seeing Beth so far away from his past.

"I know, Doug, and I know why you're upset."

Doug was caught off guard by her comment. How could she know why he was so hurt and angry? She turned her head back toward the tent then back at him.

"It's been three years since you've seen him, hasn't it?"

Doug was stunned at her boldness. Anger began to boil again at the mention of Finch. "If you know who he is, then why are you here listening to him and watching what he's doing to these people. The man should be behind bars or even dead. The world would be better off without evil men like him around."

"Doug, the reason I'm here is because he has truly changed. God changed his heart after that day on the river, and he is a completely different person."

"Completely different person?" Doug proclaimed almost loud enough to rival the camp meeting inside the tent. "So that man in there can say that God changed him and forgave his sins, and that makes everything alright? No...I don't believe it and I don't care. If that's true, then it's not fair...and God's not fair."

Tears trickled again as he looked at Beth, waiting for her to respond. He wanted her to know how he hurt inside. He wanted her to understand what Jay had selfishly taken from him so many years ago. He wanted her to explain how everything was somehow, all of a sudden, magically okay.

"Jay told me about everything. He told me about how he tormented Charley. He told me about collapsing Mike's zinc mine. He told me about that day on the river and what he did. Doug, he told me things about his life that you don't even know."

Doug leaned back against the wheel of the wagon behind him to steady himself, because he felt weak from emotion. "And why did he tell you all of these things, Beth?

Why did he open up to you and bare his miserable soul to you?"

Beth looked down at the ground then back up at Doug in the calm, moonlit night. "Because I'm his wife."

Doug furrowed his brow at the news, and a new wave of emotion overcame him. "You married him after knowing who he is?"

"Yes, because he is a godly man now. He still has flaws…we all do, but God is in control of his life now, and you are right. God is not fair."

Doug was surprised to hear her agree with him; he had not expected her words.

"Doug, if God were fair, we would all deserve punishment and separation from Him. But, because God is not fair, He made a way for us to be changed. If He were fair, we would all get what we deserve—eternal death. Even though we don't understand it at times, and sometimes never do, God has a perfect plan for our lives."

Doug cocked his head sideways and grew angry at Beth also. "So you're saying that Charley died as part of God's plan? And that allows Jay to get away with everything he's done in the past?"

Beth remained calm, understanding Doug's thoughts. The pair stood in silence, and the congregation inside continued to listen to Jay's preaching.

"Doug, Jay's sins were forgiven by God, and he has been changed, but that doesn't mean he gets away with everything in his past. I can't tell you how many nights he can't sleep because he grapples with his past. God has forgiven him, but he can't forgive himself."

She paused as tears showed in her eyes and trailed down her cheeks.

"Doug, I don't understand why God allowed Charley to be taken from you; but I do know that, because of what happened, an evil man was changed into a man filled with the spirit of God. That man shares the Gospel and spreads God's message to thousands of people. So many people are changed as a result of what God did in Jay's life."

"But he took Charley from me." Doug wiped his eyes with his shirt sleeve.

"I know that Jay has been struggling with that one event in his life more than any other, and I know he has plans to find you soon and talk to you. After that…" she paused and took a deep breath, "After he sees you, he intends to turn himself in to the authorities. God's been dealing with him about his past, and he knows he has to atone for it. He's been reconciled to God and he wants to be reconciled with you."

Doug looked sideways into the darkness, now not knowing how to deal with Jay. Deep down he knew so many of Beth's words were true, but he still harbored anger toward Jay.

Beth stepped up to Doug and placed a hand on his arm. "Doug, everyone loved Charley, and I know you miss him very much. I remember you laughing one time in the store as you told me how Charley told you he would become a preacher one day."

Doug smiled, remembering that conversation with Charley so many years ago.

*

"How do I know what God made me for? What special purpose do I have?"

Doug thought for a moment. "You make people happy all over town, Charley. You always have a bright smile wherever you go. That's an ability not too many people have. Everyone likes you."

"Not everyone."

"Little brother, we all have someone in our lives we have to ignore and forget at times…even me. There are a couple of guys at the mill who cause me problems, and I just have to deal with it and think about all the other people who do like me."

Charley still sat in silence.

"And besides…how would I know how many nails I have if you didn't count them every day?"

446

"That ain't very important." Charley was still trying to figure out what his brother was telling him.

Doug smiled and looked at his brother. He tenderly placed his hand on Charley's back and said, "Sometimes it's easy to know what our purpose is, and sometimes it's hard to know. Sometimes we don't know why God put us here on earth, but it's our job to ask him to show us. You may never know exactly what your special purpose is here on earth; but God has everyone here for a reason, and you are here for an important reason, too, Charley."

Charley thought for a moment, and then his face brightened.

"I think I know what my special purpose is," Charley suddenly blurted, catching Doug off guard.

"Really Charley...what is that?" Doug began to chuckle.

"I like to preach, and someday I'm gonna help a lot of people know about God."

*

Comforting warmth engulfed Doug in the cool night air. It was a sensation he had never experienced before. A strange calmness took over and coddled him like two arms wrapping completely around him. In that moment, something became clear to Doug. In a strange way, and in a way no one could have predicted, Charley had become a preacher. He was, indeed, helping many people know about God.

A new smile formed on Doug's face as he looked up at Beth. "I think I understand God's plan for Charley's life now." He choked back more emotion.

Beth was surprised at Doug's sudden change in demeanor.

"Charley told me once that his purpose was to be a preacher." He paused as he looked past Beth into the tent then back at her inquisitive gaze. "I guess, in a way, he was right."

Doug placed his hat back onto his head and took one more look into the tent. Although he still had anger toward Jay to deal with, he believed that Jay's evil heart had truly been changed and that Charley was, indeed, spreading the Gospel in ways no one would have ever imagined.

"I guess I need to head home now." Doug took a side step toward his wagon.

"I'm glad I saw you again, Douglas,"

"It was good to see you again, too, Beth."

While looking at Beth, Doug raised a hand and waved then took a few steps backwards. With a smile, she raised a hand in return. At that, Doug turned and made his way to his wagon. He knew it would take time to fully digest what he had seen and heard tonight, but, for reasons he couldn't explain, his heart felt at peace for a change. He understood why God had brought him to this place tonight, and he realized that he, too, had some fence mending to do with God.

He climbed into his wagon and headed home. He knew now that things would be better, but what he didn't know was the surprise waiting for him at home…news that he was to be a father.

Made in the USA
San Bernardino, CA
23 April 2014